By: Victoria Yost

Chapters

1.

Part of History

The summer breeze gave relief to nearly every living creature. It came like a brief surprise that was exciting and fulfilling to everyone and everything that felt it. As the breeze flowed through the trees it silenced the birds and cicadas all for just one moment as everyone and everything felt the relief that it brought from the heat. I sat leaning back on my rocking chair in the shade of my front porch. The babies were playing in the large metal tub that their father had filled with cool well water. He was off with his brother hunting so that we could have meat other than chicken and pork to eat. All the chores had been done, the house was clean, and dinner for the night had already been prepared; it was days like these that I was left alone with my thoughts.

The babies splashed and giggled as they squirted water at each other, every once in a while they would turn and look at me to make sure I was still there for them. Each time they turned to look at me, I would still be there. My older kids were down at the beach with their cousins. To them they would never have that feeling of uncertainty of their future as I had and as their aunts and uncles had. Unlike my children, I am of the generation now known as the "Last Generation". After us there would be no one who had any memories of the events that had occurred when I was a teenager.

It had become an unwritten rule that the new generation would never know of the true horrors of what had befallen their parents. They would know that their parents were the few survivors of a great and terrible plague, and they would know what caused that plague. They will only know the superficial facts and basic lessons that my generation had learned, but they will never, ever, hear the horrors of what we had witnessed and of what we had to go through. To them, the great and terrible plague will only be taught as a history lesson of what happened to a whole generation of people who lived too close together in a world that was poisonous.

I've often thought about telling my children when they get older what really happened. I've gone over the future scenario in my head thousands of times, yet I know that as of right now, they won't question what their school is teaching them. One day, though, my eldest will come home and ask how her father and I met and got married, and I will have to tell her, and then she will ask other questions as to what a CDC officer was, and I will have to answer her. Then she will ask what Baltimore was, and I will have to tell her. One question will lead to another and in the end; she will know what happened to us. It will terrify her and she will feel sick in her heart, but she will know.

The days of the plague are long behind us now. Yet, it still lingers, and it still creeps up on some poor unfortunate soul every once in a while. When it does, it only brings back those memories of what we had witnessed, what we had gone through. We cry and we sob when it takes a member of our generation, yet we wipe our tears away and explain to our children that it won't affect them, it won't ever get them sick like it does us. Even though there were terrible things that I had seen and witnessed, there were still something's I reminisce on, and as I close my eyes, I begin to play the story through my head all over again.

2.

Odd Cases

I was only three weeks away from my 18th birthday when it all started. Mom and dad came home talking about this strange string of mysterious medical cases, were leaving all of the patients dead. I now think of myself as being so foolish and stupid for being so unconcerned about it at the time. That conversation that they had had at dinner that night was something I just tuned out. I didn't like hearing gross medical stories at dinner, yet it was a usual occurrence in the Lancaster household since both my parents were doctors at John Hopkins in Baltimore. I remember finishing that nights spaghetti dinner and placing my plate in the sink while mom and dad still talked at the dinner table.

"I think I'm going to go for a walk." I said as I entered the dining room again

"Oh, would you mind walking to Whole Foods to pick up some tomatoes and feta cheese?" Mom asked as she got up to get money out of her purse.

"Sure." I said, as she handed me a twenty dollar bill and I went to put my shoes on. We lived in a beautiful, modern row home in the Baltimore neighborhood known as Fells Point which was within walking distance of Harbor East. I pulled the front door shut as I exited the house. I just remember that day being very warm for an early April day, I only had to wear a light jacket. I walked along the water until changing paths to walk up the street to make it to the local Whole Foods. As long as I could remember, mom and dad had always shopped at the organic store. I was hit with the strong delicious smell coming from the bakery as I entered the building. It took me fifteen minutes to find the two things mom had requested, and with that I left the store to head back home. Baltimore in the spring and summer months was great. The harbor looked beautiful, and more people were out. There were always all sorts of activities, festivals, and events going on, and it was all around an enjoyable time of year. I sat on a bench for a few minutes watching the sky change color as the sun set, and I waited for the lights on the Domino Sugar factory sign to light up.

When I got home I found my dad sitting on the couch watching TV. When I asked him where mom was, he just told me that she got called back down to the hospital for an emergency. Being that my mom was a surgeon, she sometimes got called into work for specialty emergency cases. I didn't give a second thought to it. It wasn't until later that night when my dad also got called in that I got concerned. My dad was a doctor in the ER, and usually there are always doctors covering the ER in shifts, but according to what my dad told me that night, there was something happening that needed more doctors on staff. Both my parents were gone the entire night, into the following day and they didn't come back until the following evening. When they arrived home they were exhausted and went straight to bed. This happened almost every other day for three weeks until I knew something was happening. Mom and dad would get called into work; they would come home exhausted, and then repeat all over again. I tried asking them what was going on at the hospital, but they were always too tired to give me a response. It wasn't until I saw a report on the national news that I knew something strange was going on.

It was a rainy Thursday night, mom and dad were down at the hospital and I was alone. I clicked on the TV to watch the Nightly News with Brian Williams, and the first story that he reported was about an "odd epidemic" of mysterious medical cases. It was reported that across the entire nation there were hundreds of cases of a mysterious deadly disease that so far has claimed 100% of its victims. What made the disease unusual was that doctors and scientists could not figure out what was causing it. There was no treatment as of yet, and all attempts to save victims were futile. Basically, if you came down with the disease, you were given an ultimate death sentence. That initial report didn't go into too much detail as to the symptoms of the disease, but it was all just enough to raise alarm to everyone in the nation.

When my parents came home, I asked them if the reason they were gone so much now was because of the disease, they responded and said that it was far worse than I could ever imagine. That was the first time I felt scared about it, but it certainly wasn't the last time I would be. With each passing day I saw less and less of my parents and

I saw more and more news reports and political meetings about what to do about the disease that had now become an epidemic. With everything that I saw on the news, I didn't really see much of a change anywhere else. I still went to Whole Foods, I went for my jogs, and I talked to my friends as if everything were normal.

Nothing really fazed me until I actually knew someone who died from it. Her name was Samantha; I had graduated high school with her, she was the star athlete on the girls' soccer team and was in college to become a lawyer. My friend Molly told me she had died and there was going to be a viewing. Molly and I went to the viewing and what I saw made me sick. The body was laid out in the funeral home and when I went up to it I could see that Samantha's skin had a yellowish tinge to it that was covered up in layers and layers of makeup, her body looked puffy and she had lost a lot of hair. At that time I was blinded by the layers of makeup, and the clothes that covered up the true extent of what the disease did to people.

Each and every day I saw and heard something new about this sickness. I heard that the disease was affecting other countries; that hospitals were now even turning away patients, and that there was talk that the government was going to step in to manage the situation. It had been while I was jogging one day that I saw someone with it. The man jogging ahead of me doubled over and vomited blood all over the sidewalk. It stopped me in my tracks and I watched as the blood kept coming out. He vomited three times before kneeling and looking around for someone, anyone to help him. I stayed my distance, but I called 911. The operator asked me to tell her what I saw, to which she told me that the new policy was to not send an ambulance to people infected with the plague. If an ambulance was sent to everyone with the plague, there would be no emergency personnel to help with other emergencies.

I went home that night and sobbed. My mother came home and comforted me, telling me that there was nothing I could have done. She then began to tell me what the symptoms of the disease were. It all starts with flu like symptoms, then mild nausea followed with vomiting, the vomiting then turns into blood filled vomit because the lining of the stomach seemed to have melted away. It was usually after someone starts vomiting blood that they go to the hospital, but after that it's already too late, everything happens quickly; kidney failure, liver failure, confusion, and blindness all set in. In the end, the patient dies a long and painful death as their body seems to melt from the inside out. There were many times I tried to visualize what it would be like, but each time it all just seemed too fake to really be happening.

One morning in June, my mom and dad went to work as usual, only to come home three hours later. They looked confused, my mom was crying, and my dad's hands were shaking. I asked them what was wrong, they only shook their heads. I would have to wait for a better moment to receive an answer. When I was finally told the answer I was shocked. The hospital had shut its doors and sent its entire staff home. The efforts to save the patients were hopeless and pointless. Mom and dad had only gone to work that morning to fill out some paper work and then go home. Although it was a terrible thought to know that people now had to die in their homes and in the streets, I was glad to have my parents back. Things had gotten so bad that something just had to be done.

Due to the loss of so many lives the government was at a loss as to how to contain the disease. They turned to the CDC as to how to address the situation. A plan was set in place to contain major cities and populated areas of the country and monitor each region differently. A food ration system was set in place as well as new laws and regulations that we all had to abide by. The government called for a draft of healthy young men between the ages of 18 and 23 to enlist in what the CDC defined as a group of elite officers whose goal was to serve, protect, provide, and keep peace in the regions in which they served. Not only were families losing loved ones in death because of the plague, they were now being forced to hand over their surviving sons to the government.

The day the officers came was a somewhat exciting day. The few friends I still had were especially excited because they all thought that the arrival of officers meant handsome young men they could flirt with. To this day I laugh when I think about how excited they were, during those early months of the outbreak we still lived on our little clouds of innocence. I won't lie or pretend that I wasn't excited, because I was. Molly and I all walked down to Eastern Avenue to welcome the arrival of the officers. I was surprised to see as many people as I did that day. Despite the loss of life, there were still a lot of people out in the world; the plague at that point had only scratched the surface. We waved and cheered as the trucks of officers poured into the city from Interstate 95. I am sure many in the crowd thought that the arrival of officers meant that the plague would no longer be an issue. I'm sure they never thought that their arrival would bring more troubles.

The officers all wore well fitted black uniforms, along with black boots, cargo pants, a fitted black compression sports shirt, and a black bullet proof vest. The job of the CDC officers was to secure the city, distribute rations, and monitor the condition of the public. I do have to admit, all the officers were very handsome and physically fit. Yet that night when they all arrived, we were all ordered to go back to our homes and stay there until we received further instruction.

I don't remember exactly how many days we had to stay in our homes, I think it was maybe two or three, but I do remember officers coming to our door and collecting information from us such as our names, dates of birth, social security numbers, and the our former places of employment. When the all clear came for us to be able to leave our homes, we found that the outside world was a much different place. Tall fences had been erected on the corners of major streets, with check points and off limit zones. What they had done was section off the city into small, manageable regions based on population density. My family and I now found ourselves living in Region 12. The tall fence and checkpoints went from Central Avenue between Eastern Avenue and Aliceanna Street, the entire way down Eastern Avenue to Haven Street, down Haven Street to Boston Street. Region 12 covered all of Harbor East, Fells Point, and Canton, the officers nicked named our region the frying pan region because on a map it looked like a frying pan.

With the regions set in place, and people rarely, if ever, allowed to leave their region without a probable reason, the plague seemed to reach some sort of plateau. It was still out there, lingering, waiting, but for a short time, I didn't hear about it. Looking back now, it was all because I had been blinded to what was really happening on the other side of the fences.

3.

Connor Wilde

Summer went on semi normally. People still milled around the streets as they had before, only they were friendlier since everyone was confined to one space. More and more people introduced themselves to each other, made new friendships with their neighbors, whom they had previously no intention of ever befriending. Going to the Distribution Center every week became the new normal for everyone. Every week we received our weekly supplies of toilet paper and food. We had been encouraged to start home gardens which had been something my parents had already been doing for years. After the fences went up my family never ventured beyond it. We stuck together making up for lost time. We went for walks, watched old movies, sang to our favorite music, and just spent each and every minute together. It wasn't that bad; it was like a paradise inside of Region 12.

It was a July afternoon when Molly called me and asked me to go with her to the distribution center. Molly and I were the only ones left for each other, our other friends were either dead or they lived outside of our region and we couldn't see them. I walked to her house and together we went to the distribution center and both carried the large crate of rations back to her house. I basically had grown up with Molly, we went to elementary, middle, and high school together. Molly had always been so very pretty with her auburn colored hair, tanned and freckled skin, and her bright hazel eyes. All the boys in school were crazy about her, and all the girls were jealous of her.

After bringing her rations back to her house she suggested that we go for a walk and take a roll of toilet paper to try and barter with. There was a park down by the water, Canton Waterfront Park it used to be called. Since the fences went up, people brought all sorts of boxes of goods to trade rations for. It wasn't illegal, but it sure was frowned upon by the officers. The only time I ever heard of someone getting in trouble for trading was when a man was trading bags of powdered plaster and trying to pass it off as powdered milk.

Together we walked along the path in the park admiring all the junk and odd things people were willing to trade for something as simple as toilet paper. We were admiring this woman's impressive collection of costume jewelry when Molly caught the eye of a rather very handsome looking officer. That was the thing about Molly, she knew she was pretty, and she knew that boys liked to look at her. When she saw this officer staring and smiling at her, she looked up, batted her long eye lashes, and gave a shy wave.

"Moll, what are you doing?" I said with a chuckle.

"Oh it's been ages since we've had some fun." Molly said.

"I don't know Moll, an officer?"

"Oh Mona, stop being such a little pansy, have some fun, who knows, he might have a friend for you." By the time Molly had finished her little explanation the officer had already made his way over to us. He was extremely handsome with thick brownish-blond colored hair, deep brown eyes, and soft masculine features.

"Hi there." He said to Molly.

"Hi." Molly said back.

"I just thought I'd come over and make sure you weren't trading things that would break protocol." He said.

"Oh no, not us, just toilet paper for fake jewelry, that's all." Molly said flirtatiously, as usual the officer hadn't even noticed I was standing there; he was all eyes for Molly. They continued to make small talk while I just looked through all the different pieces of jewelry. At now 18 I had basically grown into the way I would look for the rest of my life, blue eyes, chestnut colored hair, high cheek bones, and a pointy chin. I took after my mother in anatomical appearances, but in outwardly traits, I looked like my dad, same eye color, and same hair color. I had been completely immersed in looking at the jewelry when I heard my name being said.

"Wouldn't that sound cool, Mona?" Molly said

"Oh, what?" I said looking up at them

"Collin just invited the both of us to go get ice cream in Region 14 tonight." She said

"Oh! That sounds cool, but, how would we get there?" I asked

"Were you listening at all? Collin said that so long as we are escorted by uniformed officers, we can cross the fences."

"Oh, sorry, I must have missed that part."

"Ok, cool, well let me go talk to my buddy and you all can meet us in front of the old Pazo restaurant at 6:30?" Collin said

"Sweet. Sounds like a plan." Molly said. Collin smiled and nodded before turning to go back to whatever he was supposed to be doing before. Molly went on and on about how insanely gorgeous and sociable he was. I just nodded and kept smiling. We both agreed that we would walk back to my house since I lived closest to Pazo. We had three hours to kill at that point, so we spent it the best way we knew how, by primping, doing our makeup, and picking out things to wear. Eventually we were ready and we walked up to Pazo and waited for Collin and his friend. As the time got closer for them to show up, I became more and more nervous.

"Moll, I think this is a bad idea." I said.

"How is it a bad idea? We're going to go get ice cream." She said.

"I don't know, I feel uncomfortable hopping over two regions to get to Region 14. I feel like we might get in trouble."

"We won't get in trouble, Mona, you're such a worrywart, and we are being escorted by officers. There's nothing wrong with that."

"I just think of all the people who don't get to leave their regions, that's all." I said honestly. I was feeling a little guilty, there were thousands of families who couldn't see each other because of the fences and here we were, ready to hop through two regions just to get ice cream because we could.

"Mona, it's all well and good that you're thinking about other families, but unfortunately, and it's terrible to say, we are more fortunate than other families." Molly said as a black CDC official truck pulled up beside us. All the CDC trucks look huge and intimidating. All they were black GMC SUVs with black rims and darkly tinted windows. The driver's side window rolled down and Collin was sitting there smiling.

"Come on, get in!" he said. I looked at Molly as she grabbed my wrist and we got into the back seat of the truck. Collin turned around and officially greeted us. He was talking to Molly at first while I put my seatbelt on. I only looked up when I heard my name.

"Mona, this is my good friend Connor." Collin said, I looked up to see another officer sitting in the front passenger seat. He turned around and gave me a crooked smile. For a moment I was kind of taken aback. He was very cute.

"Hi." He said

"Hi." I said back. Suddenly I didn't feel so bad about going through the regions to go get ice cream. He was very cute; blond hair, a strong square jaw, and a wide but proportioned nose. Molly was the one who was the leader of the conversation. She went on to ask the boys what exactly their jobs were all about, if they were both assigned to Region 12, and how long they had been here. It was an odd feeling to have the fence gates just swing open when the truck arrived. Within a matter of seconds we were though the fences and in Region 13.

"Wow, I haven't been down here in months." Molly said looking out the window as we passed the Inner Harbor and the once famous sites and attractions it held. There wasn't much in Region 13, before the fences went up it was all just big businesses, hotels, and touristy areas. We made our way around the harbor, finally into Region 14. From there I had absolutely no idea where we were headed. I was only familiar with places near my house, not to mention I couldn't think of any places that still had their facilities up and running. All restaurants and stores had shut down because of the fences and because of the amount of people that had died.

"Where exactly are we getting ice cream?" I asked.

"Oh, I guess its Region 14's distribution center." Collin said.

"You guess? You're an officer, shouldn't you know these things?" Molly giggled.

"Yeah, I guess we should know that stuff, but we only know what they tell us." Connor said.

"Conner, they tell us everything that concerns us." Collin firmly said. Connor seemed to roll his eyes at Collin's defense of the CDC. We soon pulled up to what once was Cross Street Market, but it had since been remade into a typical distribution center with secure doors and windows to keep all the rations and supplies safe. I had been here before, during summers when we were craving sushi, and the best place to get it was right there at the counter where they served it up fresh. Things had changed significantly since the last time I paid the market a visit. It was now just a big open warehouse crawling with officers and a few civilians.

"And this is where they kidnap us." I whispered to Molly once we were inside

"Will you hush, you're spoiling everything!" she whispered back. The boys led us to an area of the building that was still pretty much the same and untouched from all the changes. There was a man behind the counter, and, there was in fact ice cream. I don't remember much of the exact details about getting the ice cream, frankly that is all a blur in my memories now, I only remember holding a cup of chocolate ice cream as we walked down the street. Collin and Molly walked ahead of Connor and me.

We were quiet at first and a little awkward, but I don't remember much now. I just remember walking and smiling. Connor was sweet and polite during our first meeting; he made me laugh so much. We didn't talk about anything important; I don't remember what exactly we talked about. The majority of the time we walked together I'm sure we just spent it awkwardly avoiding each other's eye contact, and making obvious comments about things. In the end it wasn't a memorable first meeting, but it did leave me wanting to see Connor again. At the end of the day the boys dropped Molly and I back off where they had picked us up, and I was actually kind of happy about the whole outing.

It was three weeks before Molly and I saw Collin and Connor again. It was so silly of us; we were both like little middle school girls waiting in the park in hopes to see them again. We finally saw Collin again in the same spot in which we had met him. Yet there was no sign of Connor. It had gotten late in the day. Collin and Molly were talking for a very long time, so I left them in the park and headed home. As I walked home, I heard someone shout my name. I turned around to see Connor running up to meet me.

"Hey, Mona," he said.

"Hey!" I said eagerly. I was awfully excited to see him again

"How have you been?" He asked once he had caught up to meet me.

"Oh, I've been good, how about yourself?"

"Oh, I've been good too; as good as I guess anyone can be."

"I understand, so what are you up to?" I asked as we continued to walk

"Oh, I'm done with my post shift; I was just heading back to the Distribution Center." He said

"Which center are you stationed at?"

"The one that was the old trolley house right there on Thames Street."

"How is it living in there? It was abandoned for years."

"It's not too shabby, its leaky here and there, and it gets drafty, but other than that it's as good as home is ever going to be for me right now. They fixed it up pretty good."

"Well that's good I guess."

"Hey, listen, I'm free for the rest of the night, do you want to go for a walk down by the water? We can walk down Broadway and stuff."

"I would actually like that very much." I said. Upon hearing my acceptance of his invitation, he grinned ear to ear and we quickly hurried down to the water. We weren't that far from where he had suggested we take our walk, and Broadway ran right next to the trolley station that was now the Distribution Center. After quietly walking for a few moments we sat down to look over the water. Nothing much about Baltimore had changed. It was a big city with a lot of people, and although the death toll was well into the millions nationwide, it still was only in the couple thousands here. In the region in which I lived, I had yet to see any major changes. I remember the weather that day being exceptionally beautiful, the sun was out, there wasn't a cloud in the sky, and the breeze was perfect.

"So do you live near here?" Connor asked.

"A few streets up, not too far. How about you, are you from here?" I asked

"Oh no, they don't assign officers to their home towns. They take us and send us far away from where we came from."

"Why do you think that is?"

"I guess it's so we don't have any real emotional ties to the area, it makes doing our job a little easier." He said.

"So where are you from, originally?" I asked.

"It's kind of complicated." He said with a chuckle.

"How can it be complicated? Unless you're an alien."

"Well, it's complicated because no one knows where it is. I used to live in the middle of nowhere all the way up in Massachusetts in the upper left hand corner almost like where New York and

Vermont meet. I lived on a farm with my family; we lived 30 minutes from our nearest neighbors." He said.

"Wow, that really is the middle of nowhere."

"I'm a full blown hillbilly from the mountains." He said, which made me laugh

"So do you have any brothers or sisters?" I asked

"I have one brother and one sister, and my cousin and aunt and uncle lived with us too."

"Are you the oldest?"

"No, my brother is a year older than me, that's why we are both officers, we fit the age bracket. He's an officer in Jersey City."

"How long have you been an officer?" I asked

"Eight months now, officially. We always spend two months in intense training."

"Your family, do you get to talk to them much?" I asked

"Oh yeah, we get letters back and forth from our families back home, I get to telephone my brother more though, since telephoning CDC facilities is very easy."

"That's good. Is the disease a problem where you lived?" I asked.

"It took out a large town that was two hours away from us, but other than that, my family is fine and so is the village, which is the closest thing to civilization that we have anywhere near my home. How about you, do you have any siblings?" He asked.

"No, I am an only child." I said.

"And your parents?" he asked.

"I live with both of them still. They were both doctors at Hopkins before the hospital shut down."

"I couldn't really comprehend why they shut down the hospitals, it's crazy."

"It was because they ran out of everything, they ran out of morphine and other medicines, and they ran out of places to put everyone. All the nurses and doctors were over worked and some were even coming down with it." I said.

"I guess it just reached that point then." He said, we sat for a few moments of silence before I spoke again.

“Do you think things are dying down? I haven’t seen anyone with the plague and I’ve barely heard any new reports about it.” I said

“Well, I guess you can only know what you hear.”

“What do you mean?”

“Well, just because the plague isn’t that bad in Region 12, doesn’t mean its not bad anywhere else.”

“So is it bad other places?” I asked

“I really am not supposed to be giving out that sort of information, it’s against the rules.” He said.

“I see. I’m sorry for asking.” I said feeling a little embarrassed.

“Oh, don’t be sorry. It’s alright.” He said. By that time it was late in the afternoon and Connor needed to report back to the Distribution Center. We bid each other goodbye and he told me that his watch shifts at the fence always end at three in the afternoon and that he’s usually free from three until five when the CDC serves its officers dinner. I guess that was the day I agreed to go on an actual date with Connor Wilde because he asked me to meet him again in that very same spot the next day. After agreeing to meet him, and we hugged each other goodbye before I headed back home.

4.

The Stench

I met Connor every single day after that. Each day he brought something new to share with me. The first few times he brought doughnuts and then he brought fruit or bottles, water, and packets of Kool Aid. Although it might sound odd for him to bring those things, in my eyes they were the best. Having to live on rations from week to week, simple things like doughnuts and Kool Aid were luxury items and were not included in our weekly ration crates. Our weekly ration crates included flour, powdered milk, rice, oranges, Tang, potatoes, canned beans, dried peas, and a week's supply of some sort of other vegetable. Sometimes it was broccoli or green beans, other times it would be asparagus or carrots. It wasn't the best food and it soon became boring to eat over and over every single week, but I couldn't complain. There were no such things as grocery stores anymore, so the usual things I liked to eat no longer existed.

I had been seeing Connor every day for over a month and my parents began questioning what I was doing every day. They didn't question my whereabouts at first because they just assumed I was a regular bored 18 year old who needed to get out. They trusted me a lot, and I would never do anything to lose their trust. I finally told them where I was going and who I was going with. They were a little annoyed at first, but after they met Connor they were accepting. Molly and Collin were the same way; Molly officially started calling Collin her boyfriend, whereas I didn't know what to call Connor.

July brought about a heat wave unlike anything I had ever remembered up until that point in my life. It was so extremely hot that people were swimming in the harbor to cool themselves down. I suffered from the heat as much as the next person, but never did I venture into getting into that water, it was dirty and stinky and who knows what else. The air was very still during that heat wave. Nothing moved, there wasn't a cloud in the sky, just the blazing and burning sunlight from above. For three weeks it was like that, and then one day it just started storming. It stormed like nothing I had ever seen before, and when the storm passed, the heat was right back over us again, only, there was something new in the air.

I first noticed it when I was walking to meet Connor. It hit me in small waves, a smell unlike anything I had ever smelled before. It was like a cross between the smell of a garbage truck and a dead mouse. I attributed it to the dirty water in the harbor. Growing up in Baltimore it wasn't uncommon for there to be an algae bloom in the water that made the air smell foul, so I just breathed through my mouth for a little while and kept walking. I remember mentioning something about the smell to Connor, but he played it off as if he didn't smell anything, and for a split moment I let myself believe my mind was playing tricks on me.

We had our usual snack by the water and talked about our days. Connor always had more exciting days than me. He always got to see new things, whereas I spent my days home or at Molly's house. I really liked Connor, and at that time I knew he really liked me, but I didn't know exactly how much. It was that day, the first day I smelled the odd smell in the air that Connor brought a flower along with our snack, and when he gave it to me he leaned down and kissed my cheek. I must have blushed because Connor then laughed at me before taking the flower from my hand and placed it in my hair.

The odd smell that day didn't go away, and with each passing day it seemed to worsen. It soon made its way into the house and into our clothes; it was awful. When I met Connor one afternoon he decided that he wasn't hungry and that he didn't want to eat our usual snack. When I asked him if he was feeling alright, he just said that he had lost his appetite. He was very solemn and melancholy in his personality and he would seem to drift away in his thoughts while he was with me. I would take his hand in mine and try and bring him back into the world but he was lost.

"Connor?" I said to him, but no response.

"Connor?" I said again.

"Connor?" I said, this time taking his face in my hands and forcing him to face me.

"What's wrong? Tell me." I said.

"I cant."

"Yes you can. Something is bothering you. Please tell me, I won't tell anyone."

"I know what is causing the smell." He said softly.

"What is it?" I asked.

"Patterson Park."

"What about Patterson Park?"

"I can't even begin to describe it. It's awful, and disgusting, and outright horrific." He said.

"Region 12 butts up to the park, why don't you show me?"

"I can't, I wouldn't do that to you."

"Connor, then tell me what's bothering you, it can't be that bad."

"But it is, Mona, it's worse than anything I've ever seen before, and it frightens me."

"Please?" I said running my fingers though his hair.

"The plague; it's worse than I thought it ever was. Mona, they turned the park into a grave yard. My commanding officer instructed and informed us that there are only four regions that are still somewhat unaffected by the plague. Regions 12, 13, 14, and 22. Everyone else in the city is suffering."

"Why won't they tell us, the people? Why is everything so secretive?" I asked.

"Because they don't want to start an uproar or a riot. I guess they think that by keeping everyone separated and out of the loop of information it will help keep peace and keep the plague at bay."

"Have they made any progress in finding a cure?" I asked.

"There's talk that the CDC is coming up with some sort of plan, I really don't know what it is but I'm sure it'll take effect either late this month or early next month." He said.

"I can't even begin to comprehend what things are like outside the fences. I feel like I am living in isolation from the rest of the world."

"That's exactly what they want you to feel like." He said. It was true. The CDC was trying various methods in keeping the plague from spreading, but nothing was really working. At that time, the CDC's only effective method of keeping people alive was to keep them isolated and uninformed. We still didn't know what was causing the plague and where it was coming from. It was still 100% fatal, and it showed no discrimination as to who it infected. When Connor had told me that they turned the park in to a graveyard, I really didn't quite understand what he truly meant by it. It wasn't until I walked up there one day by myself to take a look that I saw firsthand what he saw every day.

The stench hit me like a wall as I drew closer to the park, and to the farthest and north most section of region 12 fences. The closer I got to the fence the more officers there were. I suddenly began to feel as though I shouldn't have come. I was getting weird looks from the other officers, but no one stopped me. I kept my eyes on the ground as I walked. I was only a few feet away from the fence when I finally looked up and regretted the moment that I did. The once green park had been dug up and overturned into a brown, stinking mess. On the other side of the fence were men pushing wheelbarrows that were filled with ridged dead bodies. I saw them, the bodies, how they were just thrown, one on top of the other into the shallow holes in the ground and then covered with a thin layer of dirt. My stomach churned at the sight and the smell of it all. I quickly shut my eyes and turned away only to bump right into Connor who had been standing behind me.

"What are you doing? Why are you down here?" he asked taking me by the shoulders and then leading me away from the area.

"I don't know, I don't know what I was thinking." I said with tears coming down my face.

"Go home, I'll see you later." He said in a harsh tone.

I should have never gone to the fence. I cried all the way home. When my mother saw me crying she did little to soothe me. They had seen it all, they saw what it was like for a person to die from the plague; I was an innocent. I guess I could say that was my very first time really realizing how bad things had gotten. My small little paradise inside of Region 12 was crumbling.

That night, Connor came to my house, but I was still very traumatized. He tried to soothe me, but the images of the bodies were still fresh in my mind. How could he deal with that every single moment of the day? Was he numb to it? Did death affect him at all? It did affect him, but he hid his emotions well. When he saw me crying he choked back tears as well, trying to be strong. It was his job to be strong, it was what he was trained to do as an officer. He had to be able to look at all those carcasses and not flinch.

"So now you see how bad things are." He said as he ran his fingers through my hair.

"Yes. I never realized." I said.

"The CDC is trying to keep it all quiet, they don't want people to panic."

"They need to keep us informed."

"You are told what you need to know for you to survive, nothing more and nothing less." He said. I was completely traumatized and inconsolable for the next few days afterwards. I suddenly became very suspicious of the world around me. When people smiled at me as I passed them on the streets, I didn't smile back. They were fools, all of them; it was only a matter of time, a matter of time before the plague crawled its way over the tops of our fences and into Region 12.

The wretched stench lingered in the air for weeks. It was nauseating and took its toll on the happiness of those who once smiled at me in the streets. Even Molly lived in total ignorance. When I saw her she didn't even bother to acknowledge the stench; she just scrunched her nose and occasionally took breaths through her mouth. I finally got sick of Molly lallygagging about how nice the weather was and about how great Collin had been treating her. I finally just boldly asked her what she thought was causing the stench. She paused for a moment, looked up at the sky, and then back at me.

"It's the harbor, it smells bad this time every year." She said.

"Well it's not." I said.

"What is it then?" she asked.

"Ask Collin, or better yet, go up to the fences by Patterson Park, you'll see what it is." I said. I have to admit, I was pretty snippy to her, I probably should have apologized, but I was too frustrated, disgusted, and scared. I left Molly and I didn't hear from her for a few days until she showed up at my house. She had gone to the fence, and she saw the things that I saw. She was angry at me for telling her to go there, and purely sickened by it all.

"I thought it was alright, I thought everything was alright!" she cried.

“It’s not alright, and I don’t think it’ll ever be alright.” I said. If I was ever right about one thing, it was that. From that moment on things were never alright. Nothing would ever be the same.

My only memories of those first few weeks of summer are tarnished with the memory of the stench and the extreme heat. With the passing days the stench and the heat worsened. The rotting bodies were thrown into shallower and shallower graves as the death toll rose. We were trapped inside our fences, trapped under a blanket of putrefied air and lethal heat. What was to come next made the horrid heat and stench feel like a dream.

5.

Adrenaline Vials

With my mother and father no longer working at the hospital, they were home every single day. Although I tried to busy myself by walking to and from Molly's house and seeing Connor, I was with my parents the majority of the time. They had seen more than me when they worked at the hospital during the initial outbreak. They literally watched people wither away and die. After my experience at the fences, I respect them much more for what they had to go through. I do have to admit though, it had changed them. My father was much more solemn and my mother had grown very paranoid, often cleaning and cleaning for hours, mumbling to herself. At times it would scare me, how she would be on her hands and knees just scrubbing the kitchen floor and mumbling. Dad would just come over to me and take me by the shoulders and gently guide me away.

They loved each other dearly, and they loved me more than anything. During those days, Dad worked hard to make sure we were safe. Sometimes I would go get our rations, but he was the one who almost always went. Mom would just stay home and scrape things up to keep us fed. We were well fed during those first few months. It wasn't fancy food as I had mentioned before, but I don't remember ever being hungry during that time. With the city decreasing in population week by week, night time brought an eerie silence that replaced the heat of the day. Growing up in a big city, I was unaccustomed to hearing silence at night. There was an absence of the sound of cars, trucks, busses, and people. It was uncommon and very unsettling if you pause to really try and listen. I even began to notice how there were more stars in the sky at night. Not that the stars were never there before, they were always there, they were just hidden by the bright lights of the city. Night by night, lights turned off and stars appeared more and more. It had even gotten to the point that the Domino Sugar Factory sign no longer lit up. That was when I knew for certain that the world was crumbling into a different type of place.

I was lying in the darkness of my bedroom when I heard a few thumps from the hall. I rolled over in my bed and saw the light from the bathroom flick on from the crack under my door. For a few moments there was nothing but the soft hum of the bathroom fan that crept into my room; but then I heard someone choking and heaving. I threw the blankets off of me, opened my door and went down the hall to the bathroom. My mother was standing in the hall looking into the bathroom with a blank expression on her face as she leaned against the wall. I drew closer and looked into the bathroom. My father sat kneeling over the toilet just vomiting. It didn't last long; he finished, stood up, looked into the toilet, and went to reach to flush the toilet.

"Don't!" My mother said, she wanted to see if it was blood or not, but he didn't let her. If had been blood, had my mother seen it right then and there, she would have fallen apart, and my father knew this. He stumbled back to his bedroom and crawled back into bed. This was it, it had touched us here. I went back to bed and cried. There was nothing to do, nothing. That night he would occasionally get up again to vomit, but then he would drag himself to bed. By morning we knew for certain that we had the plague in our house. My mother's mentality changed and she was now in doctor mode. Her years of experience as a doctor allowed for us to get prepared for the next phases of the plague. What we needed was medicine, and that was extremely hard to come by. My mother gave me strict instructions to go to the very eastern edge of Region 12 to a warehouse where it was rumored that they traded goods for medicines. It happened to be very humid and the sky was cloudy. Despite the clouds, the heat was still heavy in the air, and the humidity made the stench worse.

The warehouse was a very good distance away, and when I arrived I really had no clue what to do. There were people walking around inside the big empty space, some had tents and little living areas set up around the boxes that were left over. I just wandered about trying to figure out what to do. It wasn't until I overheard another woman bartering with a man over Tylenol that I found who I was supposed to talk to. He traded me a good amount of morphine for six potatoes. That was all I needed. It was pointless to try and treat the plague, nothing ever worked. We just needed dad to be comfortable. I had taken too long getting the morphine and missed meeting up with Connor. When I got back home, he was sitting on the front steps of the house.

"Is everything alright?" he said getting up.

"Wait here." I said sternly. I left Connor outside and went upstairs to where my mother was tending to my father. He had reached the second stage of the plague, he was in agonizing abdomen pain and a high fever had set in. I waited and watched as my mother administered the morphine, and within a matter of moments, my father was calm. I turned away from the scene and went back outside to Connor. He stood on the sidewalk with such a worried look on his face. I just stood there on the top step and started crying.

"Hey, hey, what's happening?" He said coming over to me and pulling me into an embrace.

"My dad has it." I said. We stood there only holding each other for a few moments before Connor pulled away a little and kissed my forehead.

"It'll be alright." Was all he could say.

"He's dying, and there's nothing we can do." I said.

"I know, it's not fair, I know." Connor coaxed me to sit down on the front steps with him. Despite the heat and humidity, I sat there letting him hold me and run his fingers through my hair. My tears had stopped and I was calm again. I took Connor's hand in mine and just ran my little fingers through the spaces of his.

"When did it all start?" he asked

"Last night. I went this morning and got morphine from some warehouse out of the eastern edge."

"That's like black market stuff over there. You can get in trouble for that." He said.

"We needed morphine; it's the only thing that'll work." I said.

"I know, I know, just don't go over there again, don't go often." He said.

"I don't plan to." It had gotten close to the time Connor had to go back to his headquarters, but before he did that he checked on my mom and saw my dad. I walked him down to Broadway Street. For the first time in our relationship I really was upset that Connor had to leave me at that very moment. He knew how distressed I was, he cupped my face in his hands and leaned down and gently kissed me. It didn't really make an impact on me at first, I was too upset over everything, but it relieved me a little bit.

Each day melted into the next. My mother hardly slept, she just sat by my father's side, and I looked on as he progressively got worse and worse. He had nothing left in him to vomit anymore, but his skin turned yellowish, a sign on jaundice. We knew that by now his liver and kidneys were failing; it was only a matter of time. My mother and I both knew that the last and final stage of the plague was coming, and it was coming quickly. Neither of us would survive seeing dad pass that way. After four days, he was unconscious, blind, and just wasn't there anymore; he was a breathing vegetable. In a fit of anger and hysterics, mom got up from her chair at dad's side and left the house. I didn't bother to follow her, at that moment it didn't matter to me where she went. I just took her place in her seat and put my hand on top of dad's swollen and yellowed hand.

"Dad, I know you're not there anymore, but in case you are, I love you very, very much" It was such a stupid thing to say and do, I had so much more I would have rather said, but it just wouldn't come out. In the silence of the house, all I could hear was the crackled and liquid breathing that my father produced. After hours mom finally came back from wherever she had gone. She placed her hand on my shoulder and I got up from her seat. She carried with her a small black box. She placed it on her lap and opened it. Inside were a syringe, needle, and a vial of medicine.

"What is that?" I asked.

"Adrenaline, Mona…." She was about to speak, but she paused and closed her eyes to collect herself, "I am going to inject this whole vial into daddy's vein, it'll stop his heart."

"But…" I said before stopping myself, what would I stop her for? Was this murder or a kindness? I'll never know. I just looked at mom and nodded my head. I turned away while she did it. It all took about five minutes, and after that short time there was this sudden release of tension in the room. I turned around to see mom slumped over in her chair and my father lying just as he had been moments before. I could hear mom's soft sobs. I slumped to the floor and just cried. I crawled to her and we cried together.

The plague had touched us. It had gotten into our house and destroyed our family. When Connor came later that night, I was just so brokenhearted. Connor put on a very brave face and he and two other officers kindly removed daddy's body and brought us hot coffee from the headquarters. That night Connor was given special permission by his leading officer to stay with us for the night. Mommy slept on daddy's Lazy Boy while Connor and I lay out on the couch. He twirled my hair until I fell asleep.

6.

Infirmaries

Funerals had become a thing of the past, we had no ceremony, no place to visit, nothing. All we could know was that somewhere, in one of the parks of Baltimore, Dad had been buried, along with countless other victims. With the loss of a family member, it meant that our ration supplies had been cut. Our ration supplies had been cut in the past due to dwindling supplies, but now it was barely livable. We barely had enough to get us from week to week. The temper of Region 12 shifted as the plague moved in. The bodies of the plague's victims began to be carelessly thrown onto the street corners with little more than a sheet to cover them; there they lay until they were collected to be buried.

Come August, things shifted. No matter how blue the skies were or how beautiful of a day it was, everything was gray. That's the only way I can describe it. Gray. Gray because that was the color of the rotting corpses after the yellow had faded and decay set in, gray because that was the skin tone of all those who mourned their loved ones, and gray because that was the uniforms of the new CDC Scout Officers that moved into the city. These new officers were unlike the officers that Connor and Collin were apart of and who we had grown so familiar with. These new officers were heartless and relentless towards us people. The Scouts, as we all started calling them, were tasked with counting the population of the city, making sure rations were not being abused, and shifting the fences of the regions. The scouts were responsible for mom and me losing our healthy supply of rations. When they came to take our information they deemed us, and I quote: "Capable, petite, females with the need of government aid at the urgency requirement of: MINOR." This review of us made absolutely no sense. Sure we were capable, but the extent that they cut our ration supplies was astronomically cruel.

I asked around to see if other families got this sort of rating, and it seemed like almost everyone I talked to was deemed "minor". Even families with very small children had their rations cut back significantly. And there was talk about officers being switched out and moved to other regions or states. I was terrified; I didn't really know what to believe. After hearing this little rumor, I asked Connor about it. He too had heard the rumor.

"They wouldn't move us anywhere, it wouldn't make sense." He said.

"Why wouldn't it make sense?"

"There are problems in other cities. Cities like Detroit, Los Angles, Las Vegas, and New Orleans."

"What sort of problems?"

"Riots; in those cities, the people have just about revolted against the officers and the CDC, it's pretty bad. It would make no sense to move us to a different city since those cities have just about been abandoned by the CDC."

"So are all cities under control of the CDC?"

"Not all, major ones are. Boston, New York, Philadelphia, Washington, Houston, and Phoenix, just to name a few. With major cities like Los Angeles and Vegas revolting and failing, the CDC is reevaluating their initiative that they put into place."

"Is there talk as to what they might have in store?"

"I heard rumors that came from our commanding officers who heard them from the Scouts. It seems like the CDC is trying to get all their ducks in a row, as it were."

"What do you mean?"

"The Scouts were sent here to count the population, and to tell whether or not this city is worth saving. They are also here to find people to draft into their new initiative."

"By draft you mean whomever they pick wouldn't have a choice?"

"Exactly. Right now they are counting the population of doctors, lawyers, scientists, and medical personnel." He said. I immediately thought about my mother. It had not been too long ago that she listed her profession to the Scouts that came to interview us.

"What would they be drafted into?"

"They are calling them infirmaries. Compound and prison like institutions where the work of all those people would be nonstop, 24/7, to find a cure for the Plague."

"And that work would be mandatory, I'm assuming. There would be no way to get out of it?"

"It's all just rumors right now, Mona, I really don't know."

"We have no idea what to believe anymore, all we can really do is assume that there is a little truth in everything we hear."

"You're right. If I knew anything, I would tell you right away. Keeping you safe now, is one of my top priorities. I have duties as an officer that unfortunately has to come first because of this whole mess, but everything I do as an officer is in the endeavor to keep you and your mother safe from now on."

"Connor, I don't deserve that kind of devotion, if that's what you want to call it." I said. He didn't give me any sort of verbal answer, he just leaned down and kissed the top of my forehead. We had been standing not too far away from Connor's Head Quarters at the old trolley house. I took a step closer to Connor and took his hand in both of mine. I was attempting to stand on my toes so I could be tall enough to kiss him but that tiny moment was crushed with the sound of a commanding voice.

"You there, officer!" I took a step back to see a daunting looking Scout coming over to us. Connor's whole demeanor changed and he stood to attention like a soldier.

"Yes sir." Connor said.

"Shouldn't you be at a post?" the Scout said in a terrifying tone.

"My shift for the day is over sir, I have an hour of recreation between my official shift and dinner, sir."

"Well I suggest you better take your leave and report back to your commanding officer at HQ, now." He commanded.

"Yes sir." Connor said with a bit of an annoyed tone.

"And you miss, you better go back where you came from, a curfew is soon to be enforced here, you better start practicing." He said to me. The Scout walked away and I just turned and looked at Connor.

"Will you get into trouble?"

"Nah, he's just being a jerk wielding his authority, but you better get home anyway." He said. Connor and I parted ways and I returned home. A few days after the confrontation with the scout a curfew was indeed imposed on our region. The curfew stated that we were to be in our homes before 7:30 in the evening, and were not to emerge until 7:30 the next morning. The penalty for disobeying and breaking the curfew meant that you could be arrested and sent to a holding facility.

During the days of the Scout's occupation in the city and the lingering stench that loomed in the air, I hardly saw Molly. There were days when I would walk all the way down to her house and bang on her door, but no one would answer. I began to become fearful that she too had become another one of the Plague's victims, but that was not the case. Her parents both had succumbed to the plague, and in a panic, Molly left her house and was trying the best she could with what Collin could get her from HQ. I found all this out when I saw Collin leaving HQ one morning. I rushed up to him and asked about Molly.

"I got a room for her down in a shelter home that was set up on Fagley Street where that old German restaurant used to be. I'm doing as much as I can for her, but as long as those damn Scouts are here, my hands are tied." Collin said.

"Thank you Collin, I just need to know that she's ok."

"You should go see her, I think she would like that." He said before turning away from me as a Scout passed. I spent the rest of the day walking all the way up to Fagley Street, which was right at the edge of the region. The building that had been turned into a CDC shelter for young adults who had found themselves on their own, was once a really old German restaurant called Eichenkranz. The building itself looked scary and dilapidated from the outside, but inside was relatively nice.

I pulled open the front door and saw that the restaurant area had been completely changed into a large room with beds all in a row up the walls. There were a few people sitting on the edges of their beds, but none of them were Molly. An officer came up to me and asked me if I was looking for someone, I asked for Molly and he told me she was up on the second floor. I found Molly sitting all alone in a very small room with a very small bed.

"Molly?" I said as I stood in the doorway. She turned and looked at me, her once shining and bright eyes faded with grief.

"Oh, Mona." She said. I just entered the room and sat with her. Everything that had happened to her made no sense. After her parents died, the CDC deemed her an unclaimed minor and was told she could no longer reside in her house. I sometimes forgot that Molly was younger than me, not by much, she was only a few weeks away from being 18.

"You should come live with me and my mom." I said.

"No, they won't let me, I'm stuck here, and I can't even see Collin that often." She said.

"Things are all screwed up now that these Scouts are here, Connor said they won't be here forever."

"It's getting worse Mona, I know it, and we won't make it out of this city alive. You have no idea what's coming. What's coming is far worse than what the Plague has already done." Molly said.

"What's coming?" I asked.

"I heard rumors. Rumors from the Scouts that guard here at night. I heard that they are setting up these facilities outside of the cities, these places where the Plague can be studied and tested on. These facilities need people to work and study on the plague, where do you think they are going to get these people?" she said.

"Molly, I don't understand."

"You don't understand now, but you will. It's getting late, you better head home, or else you'll be caught out after curfew, and you'll be the first to find out about the facilities." She said grimly. I left Molly there that night and just went home. Things were not making sense to me anymore. I wanted so badly to know what was going on. There were things happening right in front of my eyes, plans being set in motion right before me, yet we were all too blind to see it. When we finally knew what was happening, it was too late.

There was a loud knock at our front door, and before either I or my mother could answer, the door was swung open and Scouts entered our house. The Scouts were armed and the looked like they were in our house to do major damage.

"We are looking for Dr. Christine Lancaster." Said one of the Scouts.

"I am Dr. Lancaster." My mother said.

"Dr. Lancaster; by order of the United States Government and the CDC, you are hereby required to accompany us to your new housing location and work facility at a CDC operated research facility. Whether it be by force or by peacefully surrendering yourself, it is mandated that you vacate these premises immediately."

"Wait. I do not understand!" My mother said.

"Dr. Lancaster, you must come with us immediately."

"What about my daughter?" She said looking at me.

"Our records show that your daughter is 18, legally able to care for herself."

"I... No... I won't! I've lost almost everything!" she screamed, one of the Scouts stepped forward and grasped my mother's wrist

"No!" I cried out taking hold of my mother's other arm.

"Please! Give me a chance to say goodbye!" My mother screamed. The Scout let go and my mother latched on to me around my neck.

"Mona, please, whatever happens; just survive." She said

"I promise." I said hugging her. With a sigh, my mother let go of me and walked over to the Scouts. I watched helplessly as they took her away. I was all alone, forced to try and survive and make it through.

I knew not exactly where they took her at first. All I knew was that they were called Infirmaries. These Infirmaries were fortified facilities behind tall fences and walls. They were where the CDC took every surviving doctor and scientist in the country. It was both an effort to preserve the human race, as well as to study everything about the plague. Of course test subjects were needed, and if you were arrested for any reason, you were taken to an Infirmary where you were tested and often times died in the efforts of finding a cure.

The city had grown quieter once the Scouts left, mostly because they took thousands of doctors and scientists with them. It didn't matter what kind of doctor or scientist you were, you had to go. With the Scouts gone, I was free to spend some time with Connor again. He was all I had left in the world.

7.

Silence

The CDC left everyone in the dark as to where our loved ones had been taken. I knew my mother was at an Infirmary, but I had no idea where. Rumor had it that there were three dozen infirmaries located across the country, meaning there were three dozen possibilities as to where my mother had been sent. With the fences guarded, and no news from the outside world, it seemed as though time began to stand still. The possibility of there ever being an outside world beyond the fences of Region 12 seemed like a fantasy.

The heat of summer began to fade, the stench was blown off of the streets, and the leaves began to lose their green luster. It would only be a matter of weeks before things began to change and the cold would set in. During the hours that Collin and Connor worked, Molly and I tried to stick together. As soon as she turned 18 she was kicked out of the shelter on Fagley Street and told to move back into her house. So many restrictions were set in place since the Scouts came and left. Most of the restrictions were set in place to make sure rations were distributed properly. It seemed easier and safer for Molly and I to just continue living in our own homes, since any violation, however small, could result in being arrested and sent away.

Being only one person in the house meant that my ration supplies were cut yet again, and I soon found myself debating if I should eat the moment I got hungry, or wait until I couldn't take it anymore. Whenever I saw Connor, I would put on a happy face; I didn't really want him to know how miserable I was becoming. He got three hot meals a day whereas I had to choose between eating lunch or dinner every day.

One afternoon it began storming very badly. The rain came down like a wave of flooding waters, and the thunder shook the house. I heard a banging on the front door, when I went to see what it was; I saw that it was Connor standing out in the pouring rain. He was drenched. I let him and got him a towel.

"What are you doing?" I asked. It was still early in the afternoon, and he should have still been at his post at the fence.

"When the storm rolled in, we all just left, it's too bad to be standing out there. They told us to take shelter."

"Here, come sit down." Connor took off his boots and tried his best to dry his clothes with the towel before sitting down on the couch. Connor finally gave up in trying to get dry, so I went and did the only thing that seemed logical. For the first time in months, I went up and opened my father's dresser drawer. I brought Connor a clean t-shirt and a pair of sweat pants. While Connor changed his clothes, I put his wet uniform in the dryer. In the pocket of his pants I found a thick envelope addressed to him from a CDC post in Jersey City. The envelope was still sealed, so when Connor came out of the bathroom, I brought it to him.

"They handed it to me before I left HQ this morning, I haven't had a chance to read it." Together we sat down on the couch and he opened it and began to read it. Once he read it all the way through himself, he then read it out loud to me.

"It's from my brother. It says:

'Dear Connor, This letter is going to have to be brief, and I apologize for it. I got word from mom and dad a few weeks ago, they are alright. So far they haven't had any cases of the plague in the town, and the farm is doing well to support the family. That's all the news I have from them. As for news here, there is so much that has happened, so much that is happening, but so little I can actually tell you. I hope that your post is not keeping you in the dark as so many posts out there are. What I will tell you is this, and it will serve as a warning to both you and those in your region and district. There are rumblings in the west. Nomadic rebel gangs have formed and they march from city to city, liberating those under the CDC's protection. These gangs may feel like they are trying to help, but they are militaristic and they use deadly force. Already Seattle, Detroit, and Atlanta have fallen to these gangs. It looks like they are trying to move east. Their crusade is against the CDC and everything it stands for. Although I do not agree with the CDC's decision to remove doctors and scientists from their families, I feel that the CDC has done more good than harm so far. Every day new reports come in describing how deadly and dangerous these gangs are. In the event that a gang should march on Baltimore, please little brother, remember what we often spoke about before we parted ways. Remember the plan.

With love, your brother, William.'"

"What plan was he talking about?" I asked Connor after he finished reading the letter.

"We talked about what we would do if we had to flee. The plan would be to somehow meet up and try and make it back to the family on the farm. Once we found out where we were being sent, it was decided that if the need ever arose, I would go to William and he and I would go back home together."

"And these gangs, did you know about them?"

"I knew that there were cities where there had been trouble with revolting, and I knew that the CDC was no longer supporting Seattle, but I didn't know the real reason."

"I guess with all things that have happened so far, we will just have to wait and see."

"My brother is so quick to still be supportive of the CDC, he never likes to think ill of anybody or anything. I wish I could be like that. I hate the CDC with every ounce of my being." He said

"Why?"

"You don't know what goes on, Mona, I don't even know what goes on half the time either. They took us from our families, and they took your mother away from you! Now winter is coming, and I know exactly what's going to happen."

"What is going to happen?"

"The rations are going to stop Mona; people won't be dying from the plague, but from starvation."

"I can already see that happening. My rations got cut once mom was taken away. Even now I'm hungry."

"Mona, as soon as the first opportunity arises, I promise I will get us out of here. I'll get us to where it is safe, and you won't have to worry about the plague, or gangs, or the CDC."

"I know you mean that too." I said. Connor couldn't stay long. He stayed long enough for his clothes to dry and the rain to slow down a bit before he went back to HQ. When the rain subsided late in the afternoon the next day, I took the opportunity to walk up to Molly's house. Her situation being alone was no different than mine. Her rations where low, and she was terribly lonely. Unlike Connor, Collin had not gone to visit her during the storm. Life was beginning to get very, very boring, and a silence was beginning to fill the streets of the city.

There were only certain times out of the year when I saw the city at a standstill. One of those times was when the Ravens were playing in the Super bowl, the city was so still, someone could have robbed a bank and gotten half way to West Virginia before police showed up. The second time being on Christmas morning, when everyone is where they ought to be for the day. This new silence was very different. It was a silence that came due to the lack of life in the city. Connor had begun to tell me that a lot of the regions on the other side of the city had been shut down since there were no survivors left. Seventy five percent of the city was gone; buried down in shallow graves in a city park. Sitting on the front steps of my house I closed my eyes and just let the silence sink in. There were no sirens, no machines, no air planes, no trains, and no ships. It was a total lack of sound, a vortex of nothingness that scared me and made the inner thoughts of my mind seem so much louder.

Why was I still alive when so many had already perished? Why was I still here when clearly I had been exposed to the plague on many occasions? I knew that there were people involved with the CDC, and officers that were succumbing to the plague. Connor had told me this. It was all a mystery to me at the time, a big mystery that would not be made clear until years later.

The silence was just beginning to drive me mad. It was beginning to fill every aspect of my life. I soon began to fear making noise myself. I tiptoed my way to Molly's house, and I drew close to Connor and whispered to him when we spoke. Apparently somebody else out in the city was finding the silence hard to cope with, because they broke into the old news and radio stations up on TV hill, and booted up a radio station. They called it ALIVE on 106.5, it was just a radio station dedicated to playing all sorts of music from every genre and every time period. In the mornings they played pop, in the early afternoon they played rock and roll, in the evenings they played a mix of Indi and folk, and through the night, they played a mix of soothing classical and soothing Irish traditional music. The radio station was a welcomed change to the dead silence and loneliness. Within a week, the one person controlling the radio station grew to a team of four people. Together they worked to play messages from one side of the city to the other, and air reports that seemed relevant to the whole city. The saddest things that they aired on the station were the names of the dead, listed in alphabetical order, region by region. It soon became obvious that even the CDC officers of Baltimore were being cooperative with the station, working to get news from one area to the next.

Hearing the music and the voices of other people through my radio definitely helped lift my spirits. I never turned the radio off, I kept it on at all hours of the day, and I never missed a thing. Connor would come every evening and we would listen to the weather report, the latest headlines from each region, and then we would just lie together on the couch and listen to music until it was time for him to go back to HQ. With something as simple as a radio station now available to us, the world was just so much more bearable. Someone wrote into the station and suggested that the station start airing recordings of books on the radio. It was soon decided that the first book to be read on the station would be The Hobbit. The first day it was to air, I had Molly come over to listen with me. They read for an hour and then remind listeners about the curfew. When the reminder came on the radio, Molly left, and I continued listening until I had heard the entire story.

8.

Propaganda

The radio had brought me such joy, yet it was soon to bring me much pain. I remember sitting on my front steps with a small bowl of white rice sitting on my lap as I listened to the reading of The Great Gatsby. The air had a chill to it and the leaves on the trees were just slowly starting to brown and flicker to the ground. I began to observe the rest of the houses on my street. I estimated that I was the only one left still inhabiting a house on my side of the street, with maybe two or three other people living on the other side. I had my eyes on some leaves that were being twirled about on the cobble stones of the street when my radio began to crackle and the station began to get fuzzy. It had never gotten static before, it was a digital radio so there wasn't a knob I could turn to get the station clear.

I turned my head and looked into the house toward where the radio was. I could faintly hear the words that F. Scott. Fitzgerald penned through the static, but then the station cut off, and there wasn't anything to be heard. I finished eating my bowl of rice, and got up to go see if there in fact was something wrong with the radio. As I entered the house, the radio clicked back on, only it wasn't the familiar voice or tune of ALIVE 106.5. The music was dark and sinister, and the voice was an unfamiliar voice I had not heard before.

"Are you tired of the CDC cutting your rations? Are you separated from your family by tall fences and burdensome restrictions? Do not worry city of Baltimore, your liberation is on its way." Said the voice, the music played for a few moments longer and then there was static again before the reading of The Great Gatsby came back on. I stood there just trying to process what I had just heard before I heard hurried footsteps from outside my door. I turned around and saw Connor jogging up to the house.

"Did you hear that?" he said all out of breath.

"What was it?"

"A gang. They are currently trying to liberate Washington, Baltimore is next." He said.

"What does that mean?"

"It means we have to get out." He said.

"When did they get to Washington, how bad is it?"

“We were briefed last night after I left here. The gang is nearly 1,500 strong. They have trucks, cars, weapons, and tactics that out surpass us. With each city and town they liberate, they get stronger, their numbers grow, and they learn fast. They showed us pictures of what happened in Atlanta just last week. It’s bad, Mona, really, really bad. I’ve seen some bad things so far, but what they are doing is horrific.” I could hear that Connor was choking up in his voice.

“What are they doing?”

“They weed through survivors like livestock, picking out those who are healthy and disposing of the very young and the very weak. They give us officers a choice to either become a part of their fighting force, or to be executed. More people are dying at the hands of these gangs than the plague now. 900 people were executed in Atlanta, hundreds more left to die with no means of surviving come winter. They ransack and pillage everything they can, leaving nothing. The gang that liberated Detroit just lit everything on fire, right now that whole city is burning.”

“What are we going to do?” I asked frantically.

“Washington is the most guarded and secure city that the CDC has under its control right now. It’ll take the gang a very long time to make it crumble; but we have to get out, and we have to get out as soon as we can. We have to beat winter, and we have to do it while there is still food to be eaten.”

“What do you mean, ‘while there is still food to be eaten’?”

“The first thing the gangs are going to do is stop the supply of rations. Our rations come out of Washington; we won’t be getting any more food.”

A small part of me panicked inside, no food? I barely had food at that moment. My supply of food had dwindled, and it was barely supporting me. Over the past couple of weeks I had noticed a change in myself. My pants weren’t fitting anymore, and my shirts were hanging off of me. I had lost 10 pounds off of my normal 112 pound body, and it showed. I stood in front of Connor with myself hidden under sweatpants and a sweater.

“I’m already used to having to go hungry sometimes.” I said pulling the sweater I wore off over my head, where the scoop neck of the shirt I wore underneath showed my protruding collar bone

Connor took a step forward and laid his hand near my neck on my shoulder, gently tracing the outline of my collarbone with his thumb.

"I'll bring you food." He said.

"You'll get in trouble, if things are getting serious, then we need to be careful. We don't want bad things to happen if everyone else is acting out of desperation." I said.

"But I don't want you to starve." He said.

"I won't starve. You tell me what to do and we can get out of here." I said.

"Tonight, pack what you can in a backpack; wear clothes easy to move in, I'll come for you in the morning. Don't go anywhere until I come for you." he said. I nodded and he leaned down and kissed the top of my head before he left. Once he was gone, I began doing exactly as he said. Taking a backpack and packing what I believed would help us; two blankets, a couple changes of clothes, nothing fancy, just Under Armour leggings and sweaters, they were easy to move in, like Connor said. I took matches, a knife, a couple bottles of water, and my parent's wedding picture. That was it, out of everything in the entire house; those were the only things I needed in order to leave. I placed the backpack by the door and I sat on the couch to sleep and wait.

The radio announcement from the gang was played every hour, interrupting anything that the station was playing. For the first time in the weeks that I had been faithfully listening to the radio, I got up and turned it off. I knew exactly what they were trying to do. They were trying to paint themselves as the good guys, the ones that would save the city, but I knew the truth.

When morning came, Connor did not. I waited all morning until finally he came at his usual time. With a heaviness in his voice and sorrow in his eyes, he explained to me that it was impossible for us to leave now. The commanding officers at HQ had caught on to the fact that they might lose a number of their officers by them deserting. If an officer was found leaving or planning to leave, he could risk being arrested and sent off to an Infirmary. The perimeter of the region had been reinforced and in a matter of hours, it had become nearly impossible for anyone to leave.

"They won't even let the citizens out?" I asked.

"No, we are to continue obeying CDC order and stay inside the regions. The CDC knows that we are going to lose rations, and they know that the gang is going to take weeks, if not months, to make Washington crumble."

"So they have given us a death sentence, a sentence of starvation."

"There's hope that rations can get here from New York." Connor said.

"Connor, when will those rations come? I have maybe a cup of rice left, and that's it, I have nothing else!" I said.

"I'll find you something, I promise. I promise that we won't stay here much longer."

"These promises are beginning to sound nearly impossible to keep."

"If nothing else, I promise that I will not leave you. You're my girl." he said.

"That I know I can trust." I said with a smile.

"I have to get back to HQ, technically I'm not even supposed to be here."

"Do what you have to. If anything, I'll go and find you, don't risk being arrested just to come see me." I said; with a kiss and an embrace, Connor left me. The darkest of days were beginning to set in upon us, and a small acceptance of impending death had grown in my heart.

***

The trees were barren, their leaves blowing and tossed on the ground. With grey skies looming overhead I made my way down to HQ. There was a chill in the air as I worked my way down the street. For the first time in three weeks, since our last good ration delivery, we were finally getting rations. Connor had been smuggling little items of food here and there to me, but it had taken its toll, my eyes were now beginning to pop from their sockets and my cheek bones were pointing out; once squishy parts of my body were beginning to get pointy. I had given in two days prior and eaten my last cup of rice. For two days I survived on what Connor brought me.

When I neared HQ I saw that there were quite a few people gathered to get their rations. They all looked just as malnourished and deprived as I was. A line had begun to form by the main door of HQ, I got right in there, not nearly towards the front, but close enough. The more people arrived, the more I felt compressed and uneasy. I was surrounded by a lot of people now, far too many than I had been used to in the past couple of months. They had all come, from every corner and alley of the region, all to get their food. Officers had begun to gather, with rifles slung around their shoulders, I knew their intent was to make sure things went peacefully, but there was just so much tension in the air.

I caught sight of Connor, he was standing in a line of officers keeping a watch on all of us citizens. I looked at him, and for a brief moment we made eye contact, but by the look on his face, now was the time that he wanted me to pretend that I was not his girlfriend. I looked straight ahead as the line began to move. People at the end of the line were beginning to grow impatient and I felt myself being hurried and pushed forward.

"Ow!" I said as the man behind me jabbed me with his elbow. I finally reached the front door and I braced myself against the doorframe as the remainder of the line grumbled in frustration. Once inside I was handed my small box of rations that consisted of one five pound bag of rice, some powdered milk, powdered juice drink, and canned meat. I could hear the officer that was controlling the line begin to speak as I made my way away from HQ. I felt a firm hand grasp around my arm as I walked, I turned to see that Connor was guiding me quickly away from HQ and down a side street.

"What's the matter?"

"There wasn't enough rations for everyone," he said, I could hear some shouts coming from the area of HQ, the shouts intensified.

"Come on, let's get you home before chaos breaks loose." He said. We had made it far enough away that I felt safe and out of harm's way. Yet I could still hear what was happening. I heard all the people who had not gotten rations yelling and protesting, and then I heard four gun shots. I looked up at Connor who looked down at me, and we quickened our pace.

"Stay inside, don't come out, lock the doors and the windows. I'll come to you." he said when we reached my house. He stayed long enough to see me put a pot of water on the stove so I could have my first real meal in days.

"I really don't want to leave you all alone." Connor said.

"I'll be fine. I won't leave the house; I'll just be here on the couch." I said .

"I'll try and come tomorrow." He said before leaving. I watched him leave from the front window before I pulled the blinds shut and went to eating my rice. That night the propaganda announcements from the gang that was liberating Washington changed. They talked about how the CDC was purposely starving us, and how all the big fancy CEOs of important companies got to flee the country and that all the senators and congressmen got to leave as well. I knew that it all had to be lies, if not half-truths. I would have turned off the radio, but I couldn't stand the silence. The propaganda announcements only lasted a minute or two, and then the normal station was back on again. I could bare it.

With each broadcasting of a gang related announcement, I was reminded how close we were to danger. Only 45 minutes away there was a city under siege, and we were being starved out because of it. It would only be three days after that that Washington would fall and the gangs sweep through the capital of the United States, and on the fourth day, they were now marching for Baltimore.

9.
Smoke

The small brawl that broke out by HQ due to the fact that there were no more rations led to the deaths of three citizens and the injury of one officer. Since that fatal moment, the temper of the city and the region felt black. A storm was coming in the form of the gang that now made its trek north towards Baltimore. The only sounds I heard from the streets were the movement of all the officers who were now working tirelessly to reinforce the fences and make sure the city could survive the best that it could. Sure, the officers might survive; they have enough food in reserve to last for months, but not the citizens.

When Connor came to visit me, he kept me updated on what was going on outside. I had been very obedient in listening to him, from the day of the brawl at HQ; I had not left the house. With each of Connor's visits, the news he brought was getting worse and worse. The CDC had decided to shrink the circumference of the fences that went around the city, leaving so many people on the outside, unprotected. The presence of officers increased since the changing of the radius of the boarder fences. Connor even told me that when the gang liberated Washington, they executed CDC officials. If the fences are breached here and the city liberated, anyone working for the CDC could see the same fate. There was a plan though, a plan for people to get out and be moved to another city, most likely Jersey City. The plan was kept very low key and very secret. Only a few officers knew about it. Connor only knew about it because somehow he got a letter from his brother when supplies for protecting the city came in. The CDC could send weapons and supplies, but they couldn't send food.

Connor was very adamant about me going to Jersey City if the opportunity arose, but I didn't know how to feel about it. I still had all my things packed from when Connor and I first thought about leaving, and it all seemed logical to do so, but if it came down to it, would I really be able to make myself go? Within a matter of days things were beginning to come together and a small caravan of four trucks would take a select few to Jersey City. How these select few would be selected was a complete mystery to me, but Connor urged me to report to the eastern border. Connor escorted me there myself, and when we arrived there were four large trucks loading up children and teenagers. There were parents loading their children into the trucks and saying good bye to them for what would be the very last time.

"Come on, Mona, there's room for you too." Connor said pushing me towards the truck.

"What about you, you have to come too." I said.

"Mona, I can't, they might transfer me. You have to go, my brother knows you're coming." He said.

"No. I won't go."

"Mona, please, they're getting ready to leave." Tt was true, they were taking last minute calls for people to step forward to be selected to go, but I didn't move, I just looked at Connor.

"I have someone right here!" Connor said raising his hand and grabbing my arm.

"What? Connor, no!" I said as he dragged me along.

"Alright, one last one, what's you're name, miss?" Said the officer Connor took me to.

"I'm not going." I said.

"She's going." Connor said.

"Shouldn't we let the young lady decide?" said the officer to Connor.

"Mona, please, you'll get to live, you'll be safer in Jersey City." Connor pleaded with me.

"I'm not going if you can't go. You're all I have left in the world now, I won't make it all alone," I said, in the few moments that I looked away from the officer loading the trucks, he had taken another child from the crowd and placed her on the truck in my place. The engines of the trucks started and they pulled away.

"That was it. That was our chance!" Connor said as the caravan drove away.

"Ours? You were sending me away!" I said.

"You would have lived. William would have gotten you to my family's house." He said.

"No. Where you go, I go. We have come this far together; it would be foolish if I had gone. I shouldn't even have come here to the border." I said. Connor just rolled his eyes and took a few steps away from me. I just stood there in the chilly air and waited for him to say something. He turned back to me and opened his mouth to say something, but then he turned away again. After a few moments he stepped forward to speak.

"Fine. It's over and done with now. We'll figure things out." He said.

"It'll be ok." I said, knowing full well that things were not going to be ok. It had been a blessing that I didn't get into one of those trucks. Connor came to the house the next morning, wrapped me in his arms and cried into my hair. He then told me that while traveling to Jersey City another gang that was moving from Philadelphia stopped the caravan, ransacking it, and taking prisoners. It was horrific, all those young ones, those children, they were either taken by the gang or killed. Learning this made me both sick, and so grateful that I had not gone. With the news of the caravan being lost, we now knew that there were now two gangs working their way towards Baltimore; one coming from the south and one coming from the north. We didn't know if they were two divisions of one major gang, or two separate groups. If they were all from one gang, then we can be certain that we would be overrun quickly. If they were two separate gangs, then they would meet here in Baltimore only to fight over territory. Time would only tell what would happen.

We got first word that the gang from the south had arrived on a rainy Wednesday. The rain pitter pattered on the roof of the house, causing everything to seem cold, and the dead leaves in the street to stick together in brown and black wads. Through the chill and the rain, Connor banged on my door. He was wet and his nose and cheeks were red with the cold.

"What's the matter? Get inside before you get sick." I said pulling him into the house and shutting the door.

"They're here; they started setting up camp in and around M&T Bank Stadium. It won't be long now."

"What about that other gang?" I said.

"Give it a day or two and they'll be here." he said.

"How many are there?"

"At least a thousand; it's a lot. They are well armed, well fed, and some of them are well trained. They came with machine guns, one tank, and riot gear."

"Where did they get all that stuff?" I asked.

"From liberating cities." He said.

"They aren't really liberating are they? Liberating is a positive word, they are killing people."

"They believe in equality. They save those who they consider to be the average American citizen, and they punish those who they deem as privileged or a contributing factor to the suffering."

"What are we going to do?"

"The fences will fall, that I know for certain, from that moment on, we have a very slim chance to get far enough out of the city that we won't be questioned by anyone. We just need to be ready at every moment of the day." Connor said.

"I haven't stopped being ready. If it were possible to climb those fences now, I would." I said.

"We have to wait though, the opportune time will come." He said.

We had started a waiting game. The first part of that game started when the first gang arrived. With their camp well established now, they stared blaring their propaganda on the radio 24/7 now. Trying to poison the minds of the people inside the fences, urging them to revolt from the inside and join the gang. I feared for those who would act out of desperation and be all too quick to join the gang. Everyone was desperate. The city was now dead, and the residents were scrambling trying to survive themselves. There was no food now that the gang had arrived. Ration transports could not reach the city.

When the second gang arrived, it quickly became clear that they were two separate, rival gangs. The gang that had liberated Philadelphia was larger, stronger, better equipped. Their origins began in Vermont, they grew in number as they went through Maine, down to liberate Boston, and then through the more rural areas of Connecticut, upstate New York, and Pennsylvania. War broke out between the two gangs, a brawl that lasted a week before the northern gang squashed the smaller southern gang. They called themselves the Northern Liberators; they flew a flag with a symbol of an arrow diagonal through a circle on a burnt orange background.

They commandeered the radio transmitting devices of the fallen gang and began playing their own propaganda, which was far darker and more gruesome than what had been played before. They didn't make an attack on the fences for three days, instead they urged willing citizens to climb the fences, join the gang and receive high privileges. They even made a call for CDC officers to join them. The call was heard and some answered that call. Molly and Collin answered the call. They climbed the fence in the middle of the night, desperate to try and survive. Molly didn't even look back, she didn't bother to think about what would happen to her once she made it to the gang, and Collin carried with him a list, a list of all the names and pictures of all the CDC officers that remained in the city loyal to keeping the fences standing. My heart ached for them; they had deserted the city, Molly succumbing to her desperation, and Collin to his need to always be on the winning side.

The siege began first by the gang lighting the buildings that bordered the fences on fire. Baltimore burned, the streets flooded with smoke, ash and embers falling from the sky like snow, and the sun hazed over with soot. As each day passed, I sat in the house praying, pacing, and wondering what was about to become of us. Connor had been called away day and night to man the fences. The officers and loyal volunteers struggled to make sure that the fires didn't touch any of the buildings on the inside of the fences. Nature was on our side though, for after three weeks of raging fires burning through the majority of the city, rain came, a rain that smothered the fires and reduced them to smolder. There was a small window of quiet and peace before the next attack came. Connor came to the house as soon as he was able. His clothes reeked of smoke, his face was black with soot, and his hair matted with ash. In the hour that he was able to be with me in the days that I had not seen him, he bathed and I washed his clothes. I was grateful to see that so far he was safe and unharmed. He too was very happy to see that I was alright, I was frail, but alright.

He took note to how my long dark chestnut colored hair had thinned, how my eyes bugged out of my head, and how my shoulders seemed pointier. I kept the true extent of my suffering hidden under sweaters and sweatpants. The truth was, I could count my ribs and vertebrae in my spine, and my legs looked like little straws. Each day I found myself moving less and sleeping longer, I knew that that couldn't be a good sign, but I couldn't tell Connor. I was not dying; not yet, I would live to see myself out of the city in good time.

10.
Breach

I could feel darkness in the air, an evil that spoiled and soured the city. The gang was encamped around the fences, ready to make their next move. I neither saw nor heard from Connor for days at a time. All attention was required at the fences in order to secure them. There was no leaving the city now. Nothing was allowed to enter, and nothing was allowed to leave. How long until the next part of the gang's attack? In my mind I expected a full on war and battle between the two sides, but I was very much wrong.

The gang expected to starve us until they could walk right into the city. Yet with each passing day, and with winter encroaching, the gang grew restless. They stationed their guns and pointed them at the city, ready to aim and fire; but the officers were ready as well. Time had allowed them to move guns and weapons into position. Yet day and night they waited, each with weapons and men aimed at each other. In the dark cold of the night a shot was fired and soared across the fence, neither side knew who shot the first bullet, for the bullet had gone astray and was lost, so no one saw what it hit or where it had gone. Both sides took it as the other side starting the fight, and so the fight ensued.

With bullets, fire, and man power, both sides struggled; behind brick walls and in thick buildings officers hid as guns went off and Molotov cocktails were thrown. Men were moved around to keep the officers well rotated. Connor had been rotated from the front lines back towards HQ. He would have three days of rest before having to rotate back to the front. It was during this rotation that I saw him. His uniform had been scorched in some areas and cut in others. Even though I washed and dried it, it was hopeless. His uniform wasn't the only thing that had been harmed during the siege. He was covered with cuts and bruises; he had scabs covering his knuckles, a swollen cheek, and a split lip. He looked like he had gone to war.

"It's like something you see in the movies. There are things flying overhead, men screaming, bullets firing inches away from where you stand. They don't even have a chance to remove the bodies of those that were killed, they just lay there where they fell, some look like they are only sleeping, others are mutilated beyond recognition.

It's pure madness." Connor said as we huddled close together on the couch under the sounds of distant gunshots and small explosions.

"How far away is the front from here?" I asked.

"It is west from here, on the other side of the harbor. The fences that are getting attacked the most are bordering Charles Street and Fort Ave. It's far enough from here so that I am not too worried about you from where it is all happening."

"Worry about yourself, I am fine." I said.

"You're smaller every time I see you. I'm afraid the next time I see you, I'll find you as a pile of dust on the floor." He said squeezing me tight against his chest.

"How long do you think the fences will hold?" I asked.

"I would give it a day or two more. The other officers are exhausted, the fences are badly damaged, and it's just a losing battle. We are out manned, out gunned, and it seems like no one in the city wants us to protect them anymore." Connor said.

"What happens when the fences are breached?"

"The gang will flood the city, looting it and taking everything they can. This reminds me, when it happens, and you'll know when it happens, you'll have to hide, take what you can and hide." He said.

"Why?"

"They'll take everyone who they think is useful. They take the young to be soldiers, and the women are given to the higher ranking gang members as trophies. You don't want that. Is there anywhere you can hide?"

"There's a cubby upstairs, my parents just used it for storage." I said.

"Show me." He said, as we got up and I brought him upstairs to where there was a little three foot tall door that opened up into the wall where we had boxes of old stuff stored away. Connor pulled the boxes aside and looked behind the space. It was small and dark, but he nodded, it would do. He pulled some of the insulation down from the inside of the wall and made a very small section of space.

"Bring up that back pack, a blanket or two, and a few pillows." He said. Despite his weariness he worked hard to make a hidden section for me in the crawl space behind the boxes. While he did that, I took the time to shower and put on new clothes. I put on a pair of Under Armour leggings and a thick pair of sweatpants; I also wore a baggy t shirt under a thick sweater. With my hair still wet, Connor had me climb in the hidden area, which he had set up nicely with the blankets and pillows.

"Here is my radio." He said handing me his black walkie talkie that he wore clipped to his belt. "When the fences are breached they'll announce it on this. You'll be the first to know, don't move from this spot until I come for you myself." He said.

"You'll be at the front when the fences are breached, what if you don't make it here in time?" I asked.

"I'll make it, I promise. I might not be at the front when it happens, I might still be here on rotation." Connor kissed me goodbye before sealing me into the crawl space. The only thing left to do was wait, and although I only waited a day, it felt like an eternity. I heard everything happen over the radio Connor left with me. I heard the officers yelling for help, asking for assistance; I heard them yell that the fences had fallen and that the gang was making its way over the fences. As the hours melted together, I heard the pleas for help on the radio grow more and more desperate. I feared hearing Connor's voice over the radio, but not once did I hear him. When morning came, there were no more pleas over the radio; instead I heard calmer voices, voices that spoke of different things. They were gang members; they had started using the radios to communicate with each other. I knew not what happened to all the officers that once had possession of those radios; I feared that they had all been killed.

Hours passed, and Connor did not come. I grew tired and scared, I had no idea what was going on outside, and the voices on the radio led me to believe that the looting and ransacking of the city had already started. My mind wondered, I began to imagine Connor injured in the street somewhere. I imagined him hiding in an alley trying to come for me. I even imagined that he was dead, it was that vision in my mind that drove me mad. Where was he? He promised he would come, he promised that he would make it here.

I cried in the darkness, praying and whispering his name, hoping that at any moment I would hear his footsteps coming up the stairs towards the small door. My head shot up when I did hear steps. I heard heavy steps echoing through the house. They were slow and they moved all over. I heard voices too, unfamiliar voices. My body stiffened as those steps climbed the stairs. I quickly turned the volume down on the walkie talkie.

"There ain't nothin' here!" said one of the voices.

"There's always something, you just gotta look." Said the other.

"We came looking for food, that's our job, food and weapons. All I seen so far is a bunch of empty houses, some with dead people in them!" The voices were getting closer and closer to me, I could hear them breathing through the walls. I stiffened myself against the wall, and tried my best not to breathe. Somewhere in the house I heard something fall and shatter. The footsteps grew closer again, and the cubby door was pulled open.

"Hey, look there's boxes in here!"

"Well pull one out, see what's in there." I heard a box being dragged out of the crawl space only three feet from where I sat.

"It's just empty picture frames."

"There's nothing here."

"Let's go, we have to finish this street." I heard the cubby door slam closed and the men leave, I continued to wait, but Connor did not come. Another day passed, and he still had not arrived. My worst fears had come true, by now Connor was either captured or dead, I kicked aside the insulation and left the crawl space. My eyes stung as they adjusted to the light. At that moment I would have left the city had I only known where to go. Instead I lingered in the house, silently, trying not to make a noise.

The radio in the house played, it played the announcements from the gang. The city had now been liberated, food was being distributed at certain areas of the city, and a city wide rally was going to be held in the inner harbor. I pulled my hair up into a black cap and made myself look as impossibly useless as possible. For the first time in weeks, I exited the house and stood in a street that I would have never recognized as my own. Ash and snow dusted the street and sidewalks, the fronts of the houses were blackened from the soot of the fires, and the trees looked brittle and dead. I walked slowly down the street towards where the radio had announced there would be food.

The gang had taken over what once was HQ, and they had broken into the CDC's supply of food and was handing it out. I was given a large potato, it felt so heavy in my hand and I walked back to the house. I sat, huddled in the corner of the living room, eating the potato as if it were an apple. I ate the whole thing until there was absolutely nothing left. With my stomach and body finally satisfied after days and days of having nothing, I moved myself again. I needed information; I needed to know what to do next. I was alone now, and the only way I could get information was if I went to the rally.

I hobbled down the street, slowly and steadily I made my way to the harbor where many had gathered in droves to hear the leaders of the gang speak. I could distinguish gang member from city citizen based solely on the fact that the gang members were well fed, and we citizens were not. Hostility was in the air as gang members and citizens gathered. I scanned the crowd, hopeful that I would see Connor's face; instead I caught the eye of someone else. Their hazel eyes looked me up and down, confirming my identity, and then with large strides, dressed in little more than a slinky tank top and rags, they made their way swiftly towards me.

11.

Spilled

The air was cold. I could see the vapors of my breath in the air, yet Molly stood before me, barely covered in proper clothing. She placed both her hands on my shoulders and looked at me, trying to make sense of things, as I was also trying to make sense of things.

"Mona. Mona is it really you?" she asked.

"Yes, Molly, it is me." I said.

"I am so happy to see you, so very happy. I am glad you are safe and you are still living," Molly's manner of speaking had changed since that last time we spoke. She spoke with nervousness in her voice and a twinkle of fear in her eyes. I examined her once again. She was better fed than I was at the moment, her hair had what looked like either a few dreadlocks or a few matts. She had a patch of soot on her forearm, which led me to notice the patch of burnt skin that rested right above it; it wasn't just any patch of burnt skin. It was a branding, a branding in the shape of the letter "J".

"Will you join the gang, Mona? You will have food to eat, safe beds to sleep in, and people who care about the same things."

"I do not know what I shall do at this moment, Molly. I'm trying to make sense of things." I said.

"Since leaving the city and joining the gang, I can tell you it has been the only reason I am still alive. I was dying before, Mona, as you are dying now. Come with us, you won't go hungry ever again."

"Molly, where is Collin?" I asked. Molly dropped her arms to her side and looked down at the ground.

"As with all changes in life, things don't always stay exactly how you want them to, and there are names we are not allowed to say." She said softly.

"Molly, please tell me what is going to happen, what is going on?"

"Come with me." She said taking my hand. We walked through the crowd, around a platform the gang had set up for the rally and towards a large group of gang members.

"Do you see the man with the dark hair, in the brown leather jacket?" she said pointing him out of the crowd. I still vividly remember what he looked like. He was tall, with broad shoulders and a muscular frame. He was beastly in appearance, yet very nice to look at. He had a thick head of black hair which was slicked back, and his face was sharp, with a well sculpted chin and high cheekbones. Although very attractive, his demeanor and way of walking and talking frightened me.

"Yes, I see him." I told Molly.

"That is Joe, he is our leader, our protector, and our liberator. It is because of him that cities have been freed and thousands saved from the corrupted hands of the CDC. He was one of the first people I met when I crossed the fences. He liked me, so he took me in, made me part of his family, I am well protected and cared for. If I introduced you to him, he might like you too and we could be in his family together, or he will put you with one of his assistants." She said, I was trying to comprehend her meaning of the word family, she said it in a very unusual way. As I thought and I looked around, I saw other girls and women, dressed similarly to Molly, all with a branding on their arms of initials. Molly had the letter "J", "J" for what? "J" for Joe? At that moment I had a hard time grasping what I had just realized. I had uncovered the truth as to what had become of Molly when she crossed the fences. Connor had described it to me once before, telling me that the gang members take girls as their trophies, Molly was nothing more than a trophy, a prize, a living, and expendable doll.

I took two steps away from Molly, giving her a look of disbelief. She just stared at me, trying to make sense as to why I was so frightened and disgusted.

"Mona, what's wrong?" She asked.

"Molly, when you say 'family' what does that mean?" I asked, looking for her to deny and prove false what I was just beginning to believe.

"Well not like a family with a mother and father and brothers and sisters. There are three other girls, he takes care of us, and we take care of him. It's safe."

"I don't want to be part of that kind of family, Molly, that's not me, and that's not you and you know it, and how can you live with yourself?" I said drawing closer to her.

"We all have to live with ourselves eventually. We all have to do what we can to survive, and you're right, it isn't me, but it's what life has become," She whispered to me, "I can only be grateful that Joe isn't cruel like some other men."

"This is not what life has become. I can see it in your eyes, Molly, you hate it."

"I do hate it. I lost everything, nothing has been spared for us. Nothing will be spared for you either. You can either join us and survive, or stay here and starve to death."

"Molly, there are other ways, not this. Moll.... Where's Collin?"

"We made a mistake, Mona," She said with tears flowing down her face, "We believed we would be spared, we were so wrong. I was spared, but Collin was not. When we crossed the fences, they treated us like heroes, we feasted, and we were promised things. When we were presented to Joe, Collin... Collin handed over that list of all the officers in the city. Joe looked at the list and smiled. They took Collin away, and I was left alone. Joe told me that if I forgot Collin, I could join his family and be safe." She said

"But what happened to Collin?"

"I do not know." She said. Just as she uttered those words an announcement was made for all the citizens to gather around the platform. The rally was to begin. There was a lot of talk about nonsense. Talk about how the CDC was protecting the wealthy and privileged, how the plague was deliberate, and how the CDC was purposely starving us. There was all this talk about the CDC this and the CDC that. It was all nonsense to me, nonsense that now I know to be untrue, but at the time it made me doubt for a few moments. After the first speaker finished speaking he announced that Joe was going to speak. Joe got up on the platform and spoke with such force and fury that it made me pause a few times and think about what he had to say. Promises were made that I knew for sure were going to be broken. Promises of wealth and prosperity, promises of freedom and peace. How could those promises be true with a gang marching from city to city killing innocent people?

He paused. He lingered and looked into the crowd. I stood beside Molly still, she leaned close to me. I began to notice that we were standing very close to the front of the crowd, close enough for Joe to look down and see Molly. He saw her and he looked at her and smiled, she looked up and smiled back. He did not see me, he did not notice me. I was grateful for that.

"So how should the CDC be punished?" Joe began

"Should we march on their headquarters? No, they moved their key officials out of the country! So how can we send them the message that we have had enough? I'll tell you how! The CDC created soldiers, selected men trained and groomed to be elite and powerful, men who would guard cities like this, holding the people hostage and starving them while these men got to eat three meals a day! These men are the CDC officers! The CDC values their officers above everything else, so let's hit the CDC where it'll hurt them the most." With the nod of his head, five injured and battered CDC officers were dragged up onto the platform, their hands and feet bound, and their heads held low.

"These five officers will be the first five examples we will send to the CDC, and there will be thousands more! I have a list," He said lifting a thick packet of paper into the air, "A list of every name and picture of every officer in this city. Every officer will be hunted down like the dogs they are. They will be hunted down, captured, and executed!" One of the officers that was being held on the stage lifted their head, it was Collin. He scanned the crowd, looking and seeking, until he found the face of Molly.

"No." Molly said softly, I grabbed Molly's wrist to keep her from lunging forward.

"These five officers will be the first to die today. Anyone who is proven to be sympathetic or loyal in any way, shape, or part, towards the CDC shall also receive their same fate!" Joe declared. Five men with rifles got up on the platform, each one standing behind one of the poor officers.

"No! No! Collin!" Shouted Molly, it was too late, I couldn't stop her. I reached to grab her, but she had already gone forward. I backed up and blended into the crowd, trying to disappear, blending myself into everyone else. My eyes squeezed shut and my hands covering my face. I began humming, tuning everything out, I could hear her voice over my humming, the shrill of her pleading, the scuffle of footsteps, the firing of five shots, and then after a pause, the firing of a sixth. I dropped my hands, no one in the crowd had moved or flinch. I saw as Joe let go of Molly, and she fell into the crowd.

“Let that be the first example of how we will not tolerate any loyalty to the CDC.” He said. The crowd and gang members began to disperse; once Joe and the men with the guns were gone I made my way over to Molly where she lay looking up at the sky. She was lying in a pool of her own spilled blood, her hand covering the wound to her abdomen. I lifted her head up onto my lap and pressed my hand against hers.

“I’m so sorry, I’m so, so, sorry.” I cried.

“Not as sorry as I am.” She muttered.

“It’ll be ok.” I said, but I knew that it wouldn’t be.

“We are best friends you and I. Things always went right when I stuck to you.” She said.

“Things aren’t like they used to be.” For a few moments Molly just focused on her breathing. Her skin was growing pale, and as I held her, I could feel her growing cold.

“Mona, I saw Connor this morning, he’s trying to find you, I know it. They’ll find him first.” She managed to say before her final breaths escaped her. I stood up, my hands wet and red with blood, I just turned and ran. I ran from the harbor and back to home. I ran to hide in the only place I knew would be safe.

12.

Flight

I must have ran all the way home. I ran through the front door, slammed it shut and locked it and climbed all the way up the stairs and back into the crawl space. I huddled under the blankets and just cried. Was what Molly said true? Was Connor out there? I just continued to believe that it was the end for me. Darkness enveloped me; night had come, bringing with it coldness and a wave of hunger in my stomach. If death had taken me that night, I wouldn't have minded, but it did not. When morning came, I was awake, starving again, and terrified. There was nothing at that moment that I could think of to do. I could only wait.

I emerged only once from the crawl space, I went out into the house to shower and change my clothes. Removing Molly's blood that had covered me. I stared at myself in the mirror, I looked horrid. My hair had gotten long and scraggly, my eyes looked scary blue against the paleness of my skin as they hovered over my sunken in cheeks. As I braided my hair I heard the slow creek of the front door downstairs opening. A part of me doubted the fact that I had actually heard something; I walked out into the hall as I tied off my braid, and I heard the distinct footsteps of someone wandering on the first floor.

My heart began to pound in my chest as I tiptoed my way back into the crawlspace and into my hidden spot. Although my heart raced, I was not panicked or frightened. If it was another looter, they would find that there wasn't anything here, if it was Connor, he would soon be up with me in the crawl space. I sat huddled under the blanket with my legs drawn up and my arms wrapped around my knees. I heard the footsteps come up the stairs and move slowly towards the opening. My heart began to flutter as the door was opened and a little stream of light came through into my space. The insulation was pushed back and Connor came crawling into the space.

"Oh thank God." He said crawling towards me and pulling me towards him.

"I thought you were dead." I said.

"No, no, I'm here, I'm here." he said running his hands through my hair. For a few moments we just stayed huddled together in the corner, grateful to have each other back again.

“Where did you go? Why did you leave me?” I asked.

“When the fences were breached they rounded all the officers up, I was ready though, I left the fence before it was really breached, I made it a few blocks, but when they rounded up all the officers and I realized they had the list of all of our information, I knew it was going to be hard to get to you unnoticed. All I had on was my uniform; I broke into the basement of some house and stayed there until night. I had to move so slowly, the streets were crawling with gang members. I didn’t want to risk anything, I made it here the day before last but you were gone, and I panicked, I took some clothes and got rid of my uniform and told myself that you went to get food.” He said. I looked at Connor, noticing that he was in fact wearing the same black sweatshirt and grey sweatpants that once belonged to my father.

“Connor,” I began, “Molly is dead, so is Collin, I saw them, I was there.” I said.

“You were there?” he said with shock and anger in his voice.

“I went to see what things were all about, I wanted the food, but I saw Molly, she tried to get me to join, but I saw her, I saw what she had become, and then they killed her, like she was a sick little animal.” I said feeling a ball well up in my throat.

“I know a way out of the city. The fence is gone on Eastern Avenue and Kane Street, people are leaving every day. If we can get there and make it all the way to Martins Airport, there are trucks that leave every day, taking people north. It’s all very top secret, but I think we can do it.” he said.

“I know we can do it.” I said.

“Rest now, we will leave at midnight.” He said. I rested my head on his chest and was finally able to fall asleep.

***

When Connor woke me, he and I worked together to gather the things that we could carry. That included the back pack I had already packed to go, and one that he packed himself. We would have to barter our way north with a driver once we got as far as the airport, I didn’t have much to work with. Jewelry and money was all worthless now, I had no food, and clothes were useless unless I knew what size the driver was, all I had was a small half-filled five gallon plastic container of gasoline in the basement. It was good enough.

With the moon high in the sky, and the stars the only things looking down on us, we left the house and made our way to the broken portion of the fence.

I didn't bother to look back at my house, there was nothing left that I wished to reminisce, I would never have the life that I had before the breakout, and I knew for sure that I would never be back in the city again. We began the walk, at first we were very optimistic to the fact that we might make it out of the city unnoticed and unseen, but the closer we got to the fence, the more we felt like we were being watched.

Gang members patrolled the area, seeking out officers and anyone they deemed fit enough for their gang. We slipped by cautiously. Connor in his baggy sweatshirt and sweatpants, and me bone skinny in an oversized sweatshirt and tight leggings, they didn't pay us any attention. Yet when we got to the fence, it was clear that we would be seen, Connor and I hid behind empty trashcans in an alley while we gazed at the fence opening. The large opening was heavily guarded as innocent citizens tried to leave, a line had formed, each person questioned as to why they were leaving the city. Occasionally two or three were pulled from the line and pushed into another group that was led back into the city, undoubtedly to be forced into the gang.

"We won't make it," Connor said.

"You don't know that." I said.

"They are looking for officers; they'll check the list when they see me." He said.

"They won't be able to tell you apart from another citizen." I said.

"Even if they don't realize I was an officer, they'll see me fit to be a gang member." He said.

"What do you suppose we do?" I asked, Connor cautiously stood up and looked around,

"You'll go through the fence, they won't stop you, get through and go to the Home Depot, wait for me on the far side, nearest the highway overpass." He said pointing it all out to me.

"Are you crazy!? What are you going to do?" I asked .

“I’ll walk down a bit, I’ll climb over it, there are a few weak spots, I’ll make it to you, I promise.” He said.

“We are supposed to be doing this together.” I said.

“You can do this Mona, you don’t need me, be brave, you’re a lot tougher than you look.” He said.

It was a done deal, before we parted ways one more time, I kissed him goodbye and made my way towards the opening. I waited in line with my back pack while gang members circled the line looking at each and every person as if they were an item for sale. I hunched my back a little and pretended to shiver. It took a good fifteen minutes before I got up to the front to be questioned, by that time I knew what sort of answers I was going to give when they asked me. The ones who had be honest in why they wanted to leave the city were either let go, or laughed at and sent back into the city, I didn’t want to take the chance of being sent back, so I knew I had to give them what they wanted to hear.

“So, who are you?” asked a tall, muscular, beast of a gang member. He was shining a flash light down onto my face so I couldn’t really make out what he looked like, only his silhouette.

“I’m Mona,” I said.

“Well Mona, are you traveling with anyone?” he asked.

“No, my father is dead and the CDC took my mother from me I’m all alone.”

“So why do you want to leave the city?” he asked.

“I have family in Dundalk, in the East Point area. I haven’t seen them since before the CDC put these horrid fences up to lock us in.” I lied.

“A lot of people have died, what if that family of yours is dead?”

“Then I’ll come back, blood is what I’m loyal to, if they’re dead, I’ll come back.”

“How do I know you’re not lying?” He prodded.

“Look at all these people; most of them are the ones that are lying. They’re all scared, and weak. If my family is dead, I’ll come back because you all mean life, you can provide for me, but my loyalty to my family is greater. I hope you can understand that.” said.

"I can understand that. Alright, you may go through." He said allowing me to pass, I showed no emotion as I walked by, and I just looked straight ahead and tried my best to keep a decent pace towards the entrance of the Home Depot. Connor was right, I did it, and I didn't miss a beat. I squatted down in by the farthest corner of the abandoned home improvement store and waited. If morning came and Connor wasn't here, I would leave, I would go myself and I would do it all myself. Connor did come; he came not too long after I had sat down on the ground to wait. He was out of breath and dripping with sweat. He had run the whole way, managing to climb a weak point in the fence and make it here. We had done it, we had made it out of the city, but there was still miles and miles of plague ridden land separating us and the airport.

***

It would take us maybe two or three hours to walk all that way. Hours of passing carcasses of what once were thriving establishments and happy neighborhoods. As we walked, we passed other travelers, each one probably traveling with their own stories and reasons for leaving the city. It was an extremely long and cold walk to the airport. I was under the impression that there would be large trucks waiting to load dozens and dozens of people up and take them away. I was wrong. Scattered here and there in the gray mist of the early morning, were random cars and pickup trucks, some were nice and some looked like if the wind blew the wrong way, they would fall apart. We went to each truck and car telling the driver where we wanted to go; they all said basically the same thing. None were willing to go near another city, especially a city that hasn't been liberated by a gang yet, no one would get anywhere near Jersey City or New York.

As the hours passed and early morning turned into late morning, it was clear that we were not making it out of Maryland any time soon. Other refugees weren't as picky as we were, it didn't matter where other people went so long as they got away. So we sat on the cold ground leaning on each other watching as one by one the cars and trucks left. Afternoon drew on and when the sun began to set Connor and I began to wonder if we had made the right decision. We had spent an entire day waiting. After the sun had set, a few more cars and trucks showed up, Connor went to nearly every driver and once again we were turned away. As Connor came back to me, a man pulled up in a shaky blue pickup truck and leaned out his window.

"They tell me you two want to go to Jersey City." He said.

"Yes, sir, are you heading there?" Connor asked.

"Darn right I am, my son is a CDC officer up there, and I intend to bring him home before a gang goes there. Why do you folks want to go there?" Connor looked down at me as if asking permission to tell the man why we were leaving; I gave him an assuring nod.

"I was an officer in the city, my brother is an officer in Jersey City, and we want to meet up with him and go home, back to our families." Connor said.

"Well, if I can reunite with my son, you can reunite with your family, hop on in." he said. Connor helped me up and we got into the cab of the truck. The man was older; maybe in his late 50s or early 60s, he looked like your typical tough old guy with a raspy voice.

"I hear the road is dangerous, there are highway men, can you believe it, highway men, like in the old western days of cowboys and robbers. Not to mention smaller, rouge gangs. It's a five hour drive, so I hope you are prepared." He said as we buckled up. Connor pulled out the little container of gasoline and handed it to the man; he looked at it, took off the cap and took a whiff. He nodded his head and got out of the truck to pour it into the gas tank. With it empty he threw it out the window and we began to head north.

13.

William Wilde

We arrived in Jersey City early the next morning. The kind old man drove us the whole way, we had no problems or run in's with any danger. It would be the easiest part of our journey. The city was surrounded by well-fortified fences and cement walls, it was much more of a secure place. We entered through a gate and were questioned by CDC officers, Connor rummaged through his things and found his old ID badge, once he flashed that he was ordered to report to a facility where he had to be debriefed about what happened in Baltimore. The old man had already disappeared, I saw him hours later, reunited with his son. They were sitting on a bench embracing one another.

Alone again, I just lingered outside the facility where Connor was being debriefed. He had been in there for at least four hours since we arrived. I hadn't had anything to eat, and I was growing exhausted. I found a comfortable spot on a bench that sat near a door that opened and closed often, allowing me to be hit occasionally by a gust of warm air. Outside the city there was no threat coming our way, but it was inside the city that held the most danger. With the influx of survivors and other officers from other cities, the city had grown densely populated, and with so many officers, many of the newer officers had found that they had more time on their hands than they were used to. As I sat on the bench and waited, I felt a squeeze on my shoulder. I looked up to see an officer looking down at me with a sly look on his face.

"It ain't wise to travel alone anymore, bad things happen to all sorts of people." He said.

"I'm waiting for someone." I said scooting away from him.

"Really? We are all waiting for someone, but in these days and times, those people are less likely to show up now." He said taking a step closer to me, I stood up from the bench and began to walk away, but he grabbed my arm.

"Hey, where are you going? I'm just trying to be friendly." He said pulling me close to him, with my other hand I slapped him across the face, my nails scratching his face, drawing blood.

"Leave me alone." I said.

"So you're going to be like that? I see how it is." With one fluid movement he grabbed both of my arms and began dragging me away, I was crying out and struggling, but everyone kept moving about at their own leisure, ignoring me. Officers abusing their power had become a common place in the city, and the citizens learned to just ignore it and let it happen.

There was a loud thud and my attacker let me go, I fell to the ground and looked up to see a second officer with his rifle in his hand. The second officer had struck my attacker with the butt of his gun.

"Don't you have a post to be at?" said the second officer.

"Yes… Yes sir." Said my attacker before he got up and ran off. I lingered on the ground before the second officer turned and offered me a hand. After what had just happened, I didn't know if I should be scared or if I should trust him. As he helped me up my eyes glanced over his name badge that was sewn into his black shirt, on it was written "W. WILDE" It was then easy to put two and two together. I looked up half expecting to see someone who looked a lot like Connor, but instead I saw someone who was completely different. Sure, the eyes, and the mouth were the same, but there were major differences.

"William?" I asked

"Only if you're Mona Lancaster." He said, it was indeed William; up until that point I pictured Connor's older brother to have the same dirty blond hair, brown eyes, and square jaw. Instead I faced someone totally different. William was much, much taller, he was taller and he had a stronger muscular build than Connor, his hair was black and thick, he had a two day old beard look to him. Connor and William shared a brotherly resemblance, but yet at the same time looked like two different individuals.

"Where is Connor?" I asked.

"He has about an hour more of debriefing, I ran into him and he told me to come looking for you. Man, I love my brother, but he's never been that great with describing, I must have stopped 20 other girls asking them if they were you."

"You and Connor are so different," I couldn't help but saying. "I mean, you guys look the same kind of, but at the same time you don't." I said.

"Yeah, people back home say that Connor is the brains and I'm the brawn, we make up for each other what we both lack." He said.

"I guess that's a good thing."

"Come on, let's get you cleaned up and fed before pretty boy gets done with his debriefing." He said putting a protective hand on my shoulder and leading me away.

***

William was the boss. There was no questioning any decision he made. At the public cafeteria they served all sorts of good food, but because I was so malnourished and starved, he only let me eat potato soup. All it was, was potatoes and carrots boiled and served in chicken broth. The soup wouldn't have been my first choice, especially since it was being served next to heaping piles of sweet potato fries and mac and cheese, but I obeyed William's command and I slowly ate the soup. It was delicious, but it stung my stomach, and after 10 minutes, I couldn't help but throw it all up again. William comforted me and got me something simpler to eat, grits. Grits were like cream of wheat, a hot cereal that was gentle enough to fill me and not upset my stomach. After eating William took me to a building where they supplied clothes, it was clear that Under Armour leggings and a baggy sweatshirt were unsuitable for the new part of our travel. I was given sturdy boots in my size, thick socks, thermal underwear, jeans, a thermal shirt, a thick wool sweater, a coat and a knitted cap. I looked like a very skinny, bland, lumberjack, but it was what William ordered them to give me.

There were plans at work already, plans to leave Jersey City. William and Connor already knew what they were doing, and I just had to go along with it all. I felt so helpless and useless, like a parasite trying to survive. I had to keep reminding myself that I was not useless, given the opportunity I could fight for myself, but at that moment in time, I was just too weak to do so.

After receiving new clothes we went back to the building where Connor was being debriefed, just in time to see him coming out. With the little stamina I had left after a day of constant movement, I ran to him and embraced him. In his hand he held a small packet of papers.

"Discharge papers, I'm no longer an officer." He said proudly.

"What about William?" I asked turning to look at Connor's older brother.

"I made a deal with my commanding officers weeks ago, I told them that if my brother showed up alive they could discharge us both, if not, I would serve the CDC till death." William said.

"Are you serious?" I asked, not believing him at all.

"Yep, they didn't believe for a second that anyone could make it out, so they held me to my deal of staying on till death, and I held them to theirs of letting me go if Connor showed up. I knew it would work." William said with a big grin on his face as he smacked Connor's back.

"So now what?" Connor asked.

"Well, now that we are both free, I know where we can steal a truck and start heading north." William said.

"Let's do it." Connor said.

Connor was a changed person now that he was reunited with his brother. He was happier and more energetic, yet at the same time still very ultra-keen to me and what I was doing. I was exhausted, yet there would be no rest for me. We walked a great distance once again, all with a heavy backpack on my back. William was still in his uniform and everywhere we went he received nods from other officers. We reached a lot that was filled with trucks that were owned and operated for CDC use.

"We have to work quickly, soon the documents will be let out that I was discharged and they won't give me access to any of these things." William said as we walked right onto the lot. We walked up and down aisles of trucks, until William finally picked one. I had imagined that we would have to hot wire a truck and have people chasing us, I didn't expect it to be as easy as walking onto a lot and William pulling out the keys of his CDC assigned vehicle. I climbed into the back seat and the boys stayed in the front. We drove casually through the city towards a gate that would easily let us out, yet we had to be questioned again by the other officers that were there. William flashed his ID badge and the officer at the gate nodded.

"Just transporting civilians to their family homestead outside the fences." He said to the officer, the officer nodded and then looked down at the tablet he was carrying to authenticate William's information. I could see him tapping on the screen a few times.

"Oh, there's been trouble with the connection as of late, had the same trouble this morning." William said, fully knowing that the reason the officer couldn't access his file was because it had been locked and was getting ready for deletion.

"Carry on then." And with that we were through the gate and on our way north. It was a huge relief to the three of us, at the moment it seemed like we were home free, and that by morning we would be safe. Yet it was not to be the case, with Jersey City far behind us there were two things that were of concern.

"Will, you couldn't have picked a truck with a full tank of gas?" Connor said pointing to the dashboard where the gas gauge read that the truck had a little less than a half a tank of gas left.

"We'll be fine," William assured, the second thing that concerned us was the fact that unless we went completely out of our way, we would have to drive through New York City, which by that time, the truck we were in would be reported as stolen and William will be looked for. While the boys debated as to what they should do, I tried to remember the way my family had driven through New York. Three summers before, my mother and father had decided to take a family vacation to Cape Cod, and they decided to drive. To avoid traffic, my father took a rout outside the city, it wasn't too far out of the way, but it would most defiantly be outside New York City Fences.

"I think I know a way around, but I cannot remember the name of the bridge." I said.

"What are you saying?" Connor turned around to ask.

"My family drove through New York once, only we didn't have to drive through the city, we went around, and it didn't take us too long. We went over a bridge, it sounded like trapeze or chimpanzee or something like that." I said.

"Oh! The Tappan Zee Bridge, I know what you're talking about!" William exclaimed.

"Will it be around the fences?" asked Connor.

"Yes, it's miles outside the fences; we'll get there in about an hour." William said. With that matter settled, I laid back in my seat and just allowed the outside world to pass by through the windows.

14.

Fever

I do not remember if it was the lack of motion that woke me up or the fact that Connor and William were grumbling loudly, but I had managed to sleep for most of the journey, and when I awoke we were stopped on a road surrounded by thick forest. It took me a moment to come out of the fog that was left by deep sleep, but when I did, I realized that the reason we were stranded was due mainly to the fact that we had indeed run out of gas.

"How far away are we?" I asked.

"Well, if we still had gas we would be another two hours, but now that we have to walk, it's kind of iffy." William said.

"It's alright, we can walk until its dark, make camp somewhere, then walk again in the morning, we'll be alright." Connor assured his brother.

When we got out of the dead truck, I looked up at the sky to see that it was a dark shade of grey. If there was one scent I was familiar with, it was the scent of oncoming snow, it was a crisp scent, a scent that smelled moist yet slightly metallic at the same time. From looking up at the sky, I looked ahead to see that Connor and William were already a few yards away from me, I moved quickly to catch up with them, but that quick burst of movement for only a few short yards left me breathless and my heart pounding. Connor stayed close to me while we walked down the road. We walked in silence with only the steam of our breaths and the sound of our footsteps echoing off the frozen pavement and sleeping trees.

After an hour of walking, I needed rest. I was having a hard time keeping up with the two boys, Connor urged me to eat some food he managed to pack and to drink some water, but the funny thing was, I was neither hungry nor thirsty. I just wanted rest. We sat for a half hour or so, with William nervously pacing up and down the road, eager to move on. I pushed myself up, also eager to move, and we went on again. We walked and walked and walked, everything looked the same to me; we were on a road with only the yellow lines in the pavement leading us on, with nothing but trees on either side of us. Gradually our path started to lead us up an incline. I found this to start to have a tremendous toll on my body; I could feel my legs slowly turning to rubber. I thought for sure the incline would plateau out and we would be walking flat again, but it didn't. Connor noticed me struggling, and he slowed his pace, but William kept trekking onwards, up and up.

"It's because we're going up the mountain." Connor said as we walked.

"My legs are starting to hurt." I said.

"It's getting late, we'll make camp soon." He said, when we looked up we saw that William was high up ahead of us, only a little black speck in the haze. Soon couldn't come quick enough for me, we walked on for another hour and that was when it had begun to snow. It came down lightly at first, but then quickly picked up into a more moderate downfall that was starting to stick to the ground and trees. My lungs were burning from the cold, and the addition to moisture on my face and in my hair wasn't helping me to keep warm. It soon became evident that Connor's slowest pace wasn't even slow enough for me. William even stopped ahead of us noticing that we were very far behind.

"We have to stop." Connor said to William once we finally reached him.

"We have an hour or so of day light left." William said.

"We need that day light to make camp, and Mona needs warmth and rest." Connor said putting his arms around me and squeezing me to him.

"Fine." William said walking off into the woods.

"He isn't this heartless, I promise." Connor said giving me a kiss on the forehead. We went off into the woods and found a wide enough area to make a small camp. We had tarps and rope with us, enough to make a well suited tent to shield us from the snow and the wind. While the boys made up the camp and the fire, I sat on a broken stump shivering in the cold. Once everything was made, I felt as though my body was frozen, my shivers had become more like convulsions and I had this throbbing going up and down my back and legs.

"Mona, come on, everything is ready." Connor said waving me over to the tent, but I couldn't move, I was just in pain and it was so, so very cold.

"It's.... so cold." I shivered. Connor gave a very concerned look and came over and scooped me up and brought me to the tent. They had built the fire right outside the opening of the tent so it would be warm, and on the inside they had laid out the blankets. I just curled up on one of the blankets and tried to stay warm, but no matter what I did, I just wasn't getting warm enough, and the ache was growing stronger in my back.

"Mona, don't you want to take off your shoes?" Connor asked, putting his hand on my forehead, only when he did, he quickly pulled it back.

"You feel so warm." He said.

"I don't feel warm." I said as I shivered. William too came over and placed a hand on my forehead.

"It's a fever, get that damp sweater and coat off of her and get her wrapped up." William commanded his brother. Connor was very gentle, but moved very quickly to get my shoes, coat and sweater off of me. He wrapped me tightly in two blankets and held me close, as he held me William placed a blanket over the two of us. They didn't say anything, and if they did I didn't care or notice. I was so very cold, yet at the same time so very sweaty, and I hurt so badly. I drifted in and out of consciousness, occasionally seeing Connor's face or William's in the glow of the fire. When morning came, there was no hurry to go anywhere, the snow had not let up. Through the haze and the confusion of my fevered mind, I heard Connor reassure me that everything was going to be alright. For a few moments I woke up and was alert, although I was still freezing and in agony, I was terribly hungry. Connor and William got me a few crumbs to eat before I curled back up on Connor's chest.

"She's not getting any better, she's getting worse." Connor whispered to his brother.

"I'll go out and see how far we are, I have a feeling we can make it." William said. I heard the rustling of the tent and then I drifted off again into a fever stupor. The next thing I remember was feeling movement and sensation on my arms and feet. My eyes opened to see Connor tying my boots onto my feet.

"We're only a couple miles away, we'll make it, Mona, can you try?" Connor asked me.

"We can make it." I croaked out. Connor leaned towards me and undid the cocoon of blankets he had wrapped around me; the shock of cold air was enough to make me cringe and cry as Connor worked quickly to redress me in the sweater and coat. As he did so his hands lingered on my wrists, as if he was weighing my frailty. With my sweater and coat on, he rewrapped me in two blankets and urged me to try and move. Every fiber of my body forbade me from moving, but somehow I overcame and stood and left the tent. It was not without agony though. The cold air stung my lungs and my walk was between a limp and a drag of my limbs. We moved slowly through the forest and back up to the road.

"Five miles, that's all we need, Mona, five miles. Can you do it?" William said once we rejoined him.

"Yes." I managed to say. It was night time as we moved down the road. There was a layer of snow on the ground, and every once in a while my head would fall back and I would look up and see the black sky densely filled with stars. I had never seen the sky filled with so many stars before. They dotted the blackness of space covering the abyss like fine gauze, and they shimmered like the gleam of a Humming Bird's feathers. They were so beautiful. As we walked I was led by the hand by Connor, allowing me to just tilt my head back and stare up. As I stared up, it made my mind numb, and I was happy. My body could go no farther, without warning I collapsed down on to the pavement. Connor quickly crouched down and scooped me into his arms. It hurt to breathe, hurt to move, and it hurt to think. My vision was warped, my breathing came with pauses, little moments of me holding my breath. Connor squeezed me close, I couldn't go any farther.

"Mona, we are so close." Connor said, I could hear him choking up and fighting back tears. I couldn't even bring myself to give him an answer of reassurance. My head just flopped against his chest and I squeezed my eyes closed. I remember nothing.

15.

Light

I had visions of kind faces, long hair, and soft whisperings; and I had remembrances of soft hands, and the color of red hair. When my eyes opened I was greeted with the scent of pumpkin and the faintest hint of lavender. I was laying on something soft, a bed, a bed with soft white sheets, and a warm comforter. I leaned forward, fully aware that I had a stiffness to my back and neck, and an emptiness in my stomach. I was in a baby blue room with dark hardwood floors, white wainscoting, and a fireplace with a roaring fire at the foot of my bed. The room was decorated softly with a mirror on the wall above my bed and an oil painting hanging above the fire place. The room was filled with light that streamed through a curtain-less window. I ran my fingers through my hair; it was soft, tangle free, and smelled of lavender, even my skin felt smooth and refreshed. I turned in my bed and faced an open door, as I looked out a girl, about my age, dressed in a long grey dress passed by, stopped and smiled at me before continuing down the hallway. I heard some whisperings before she returned and sat on the edge of my bed.

"You're awake! I'm so glad." She said. She had very long dark, black hair and bright green eyes that were framed by a thick set of eyelashes; she had a familiar look to her that I couldn't quite put my finger on at that moment.

"I am too, I guess." I didn't really know what to say to the stranger who was now sitting on my bed.

"My name is Amelia, I am Connor and William's sister." She said, I couldn't help but smile, we had made it to the farm and we were alive.

"I am so glad." I said leaning forward to hug her; the hug took her by surprise because she gently nudged me back.

"Be careful, you're not in the best of conditions you know, when you came here, we didn't know if we were going to lose you or not."

"I don't remember anything, I just remember falling and seeing Connor."

"You were out cold, for two solid days, Gran said she'd never seen anyone with a fever as high as yours, Connor and William took turns carrying you in the snow. We half expected bandits or something when they showed up banging on the front door. It was quite a surprise to see my brothers standing there in the darkness holding this tiny little bundle. I thought Connor was carrying a rolled up blanket, but inside it was you! I couldn't have been more surprised to see a human in that little roll."

"I was asleep for two days?" I asked.

"Well not entirely, you were awake or asleep, but for the most part you were very out of it, not quite normal. It looks like you're doing a lot better now though."

"I feel semi normal, for the most part. My neck is all stiff." I said rubbing the back of my neck.

"I can go get you something for that."

"Oh, no I think…"

"No, hold on, stay right here." Amelia said before getting up and leaving the room. I could hear her light footsteps hitting the wooden floorboards as she went through the house and then down a flight of stairs. I shifted my weight in my bed and sat up in an attempt to get out of bed and walk towards the window. Standing straight up I felt as though my legs had been asleep for a very long time and were just now beginning to wake up again. I took the five easy steps toward the window and leaned on the wide windowsill for extra support. Outside, the land was covered in white crisp snow. The sun was just above the tree tops of the dense forest that surrounded the large open field that I could only guess the farm house sat on. Thick forest surrounded this vast open area of cleared space, as I looked out I observed that there was an incline of a hill that led up to the edge of the forest and above that was where the sun sat in the blue sky. At that moment as I tried to observe the outside of the house, I couldn't quite grasp how big the farm really was, I was only seeing a very small part of it through a very small window.

I heard the wood of the floor creak a little and I turned around to see a woman standing the in the doorway. She had this dirty blond hair and a soft smile, her eyes were green and she had this very elegant look about her, to me she seemed to be much, much older than I, in fact she was, she had this motherly air to her, a way about her that reminded me of my own mother. She moved softly and gracefully towards me, not taking her eyes off of me, yet not saying a word either.

"You shouldn't be up moving about, we need to get you all better." She said carefully placing a hand on my elbow and another on my opposite shoulder. She carefully guided me back into bed, although it really was the last place I wanted to be. I wanted to stretch my legs a bit and have a look around.

"Here, have some water." She said getting up for a moment and going to a pitcher that sat on one of the nightstands in the room and taking the glass that sat next to it, pouring water into it and handing it to me. When I sipped the water, I paused and looked into the glass; it had a mineral taste to it, something I was very unfamiliar with.

"Its well water, it tastes a bit different than regular tap water." She said.

"Oh, I like it, kind of." I said.

"My name is Charlotte, by the way. I'm Connor's mom." She said as she looked down and smoothed the blankets on my bed until they were wrinkle free.

"It's very nice to meet you, I'm Mona."

"Oh, I know all about you, Connor has said a lot." She said.

I couldn't help but blush when she said this, for some reason to me it was all very embarrassing. Before either of us could say anything more, another person entered the doorway. She was a tall yet older woman, with very long red hair that had light streaks of greying hair which was braided down her back. She wore a long dress, like all the other women I have seen so far, and she had this stern look on her face, as if she meant business, yet at the same time there was a kindness about her. Her eyes looked me up and down and she put her hands on her hips and sighed.

"Well, it's nice of you to finally join us back here in the world of the living. Let's get you all cleaned up and find something for you to eat." She said with this loud and commanding voice just as Amelia came back into the room. I just shook my head, as Charlotte stood up from the edge of my bed and left the room with Amelia. As the two left, I couldn't help but notice that Charlotte had her hand on Amelia's shoulder as they left the room together. Once the two were gone, yet another woman entered the room, this fourth person to make their presence known to me resembled a younger version of the older woman with the red hair. After a few moments of conversation between the two, I realized that the younger woman with the sharp features, glowing smile, and tall elegance, was named Cora. Cora kept referring to the older woman as "Ma" so I assumed that they were mother and daughter.

At the moment I really didn't know what they were doing, Cora and her mother were rummaging through a chest of drawers, taking out clothing, unfolding it, looking at it, and then folding it up again. After they finally gathered a few items of cloth into their hands, they turned to me.

"Alright Miss Mona, oh, my name is Elizabeth by the way, this is my daughter Cora, you already met Amelia and Charlotte. Now, let's get you into a nice warm bath to make you feel even better and then we'll move you on downstairs for some dinner." Said the older woman.

After only meeting these people for what felt like the very first time to me, I was given a bath by two women whose names I had just learned and dressed in clothes that were not mine. I stood in front of a full length mirror as Cora tied a ribbon around my waist to keep the long navy blue dress I was wearing from falling off of my frail body. I was dressed in an entirely new kind of clothing, a clothing that had been handmade, the dress was handmade, the camisole I wore underneath was handmade, even the little cute bloomers I wore were handmade. As they dressed me, and combed the knots from my hair they explained that the entire farm was self-sufficient; they knew how to make everything. Since the outbreak they even resorted to making their own clothes, which was what I had found myself standing in. I had to admit, despite my skeleton like appearance, I looked a bit better. I had color to my face and for once my hair looked decent.

Before I could go downstairs and eat anything, Ms. Elizabeth had me stand on a scale first. I looked down briefly to see that the little needle sat somewhere between 80 and 85 pounds. My heart sung deep down into my stomach. I guess they could read the look on my face because both Cora and Ms. Elizabeth assured me that I would be back to my normal self in no time. With that, they helped me down the stairs and into a small living room that had a nice fire going in the fireplace. I was given a seat in a soft, plush wing chair closest to the fire, and was wrapped in a blanket to keep from getting a chill. They both assured me that they would be back with something for me to eat. While they were gone I took the opportunity to look around from my seat and examine the small living room. There were three floor to ceiling windows to let in the light, a mirror above the fireplace, and bookshelves on the farthest wall away from the entrance to the room. Like all living rooms there was a couch and chairs, a rug covering the wood floor, and pictures sitting on the mantle. It was all very simple yet elegant. Nothing was modern furniture yet at the same time nothing screamed of the usual antique flamboyancy. The colors were muted and soft, there were a lot of whites, creams, and powder blues, and like before the air smelled of pumpkin and lavender.

As I looked around, I noticed that I was not alone; on the couch next to me was a friendly little black cat that had a cute, mustache like white patch on his nose above his lip. He perked up when he saw that I had noticed him, and with one leap, landed on my lap and made himself comfortable.

"Oh, that's Sam, he's my baby." I looked up to see that Amelia had spoken, and she was coming into the room carrying a tray that had a bowl on it. After having to shoo my new friend, Sam, away I welcomed a bowl of hot cereal onto my lap and began to carefully and slowly eating it. After a few spoonful's, it occurred to me that I should ask Amelia where Connor was. I had been wondering about him, but with all the introductions of new people I thought it might be rude if I just up and asked for Connor right away. With the hot cereal half way devoured, Amelia told me that William, Connor, and their cousin Peter had gone out hunting for the day, their goal was to get a turkey and have it ready in time for dinner.

"We hunt a lot here. I'm not a fan of it, before the outbreak, I would always give my dad, uncle, and brothers a hard time whenever they went out, and I wouldn't eat anything they killed. I've kind of accepted it now though, since hunting is what keeps us alive and fed. When William and Connor had to leave my dad started taking me hunting, I cried for three hours after I saw dad shoot a deer. I didn't like it at first, and I still don't like it, but it has to be done, especially in the winter when nothing grows that we can eat." Amelia explained to me.

"When do you think they'll be back?" I asked.

"Oh, before two, otherwise they'll never have a turkey ready in time for Gran." She said with a small chuckle.

"What time is it now?" I asked.

"A little passed twelve. Are you all done with that? I can take it back to the kitchen." She said pointing to my now empty bowl of hot cereal. I nodded and handed it to her, she stood and left the room while little Sam the cat hopped back up onto my lap. The house was quiet, except for the occasional sound of someone walking about. I really wanted to see more of the house and what it was like, but I was confined to the chair in the living room. As soon as I felt like I could stand up and maybe take a look around myself, Amelia came back into the room and sat back down on the couch.

"You look bored." She said.

"I am a little, but I shouldn't complain, I've just been used to constant movement and activity as of late, I guess I'm just not used to relaxing anymore." I said looking down at the cat on my lap. Amelia said something funny that made me laugh before Charlotte appeared in the doorway.

"Why don't you girls come in the kitchen, I'm sure Mona can help us peel a few potatoes for tonight's dinner." she said. Amelia helped me up and through the house, from the living room we walked through the large entry way that had the tall ceilings and the very wide and open staircase. I liked the fact that one could see right upstairs onto the second floor through banisters that wrapped around three sides of the second floor. We then walked through a dining room that had a long old wooden dining room table with twelve chairs all together, a large black chandelier with half melted candles hanging from the ceiling and old fashioned oil lanterns attached to the honey colored walls. One thing that I kept noticing time and time again as we passed through the house was the amount of light that came in through the large windows; it was as if my eyes were having trouble adjusting to all the brightness.

Off of the dining room was the kitchen, and it was the largest kitchen I had ever seen, and the oldest kitchen too. The kitchen seemed endless, yet at the same time every space was managing to be used. I looked up to see a vaulted ceiling with exposed beams, I could even see the nails that held the shingles down sticking through the wood. On one side of the kitchen there was this massive fireplace, like one I once saw in a museum about colonial life, only this one was real and Ms. Elizabeth was using it. It was just all this brick, with a fire roaring inside and a large pot hanging over it, there were even holes in the brick for bread to be baked. I couldn't understand why anyone would use a fireplace to cook, I saw that there was an electric oven and stove on the complete opposite end of the kitchen, but they weren't being used. Amelia saw me looking around and I must have had a puzzled look on my face.

"We had a bad storm months ago over the summer, we haven't had electricity ever since. So we started using the old fireplace, and things have been working out well." Amelia said.

"It's defiantly dirty work, but boy does it make the food taste better and it heats up the house." Ms. Elizabeth said as she wiped her hands on the apron that she wore. I smiled and continued to look around. There was a large porcelain sink that had both a modern faucet and an old fashioned water pump. At the center of the kitchen was this big square table that was about waist high and looked to be about 200 years old. On it was a basket of potatoes and a basket of onions, a bowl of rising bread dough, and chopped up herbs. Amelia sat me down on a small stool close to the fireplace so I could stay warm and placed the basket of potatoes next to me.

"You know how to peel potatoes right?" Charlotte asked me.

"Yes, of course." I said.

"Well here," she said handing me a skin peeler, "Get to it, skins go in the bowl Amelia is bringing over and she'll help you peel them all." I looked up at Amelia and she smiled as she sat on the floor in front of me and handed me a very large potato. As we got started peeling, I smiled, happy to feel useful.

16.

Renewal

After helping to peel all the potatoes that afternoon, I was very surprised and disappointed with myself when I realized that the small amount of activity had made me tired. Ms. Elizabeth reminded me that I was still slightly sick, malnourished, and despite my two day rest, I was still very fatigued. I was moved once again back into the living room, served a cup of herbal tea, and told to nap. I didn't like being told to do something as childish as take a nap, but Ms. Elizabeth seemed to be the kind of person who knew what to do when it came to health. Although my mind complained about being told to take a nap, my body soon made a decision of its own and I was comfortable on the couch and fell fast asleep.

I was awakened by the sound of a familiar voice and the touch of a large but warm hand. When I opened my eyes I saw Connor slowly trying to make room for himself on the couch next to me, as well as William standing in front of the fireplace and a third boy who was just standing there cracking his knuckles.

"I'm so glad you're awake." Connor said leaning down and kissing my forehead.

"Amelia said you were hunting, did you get anything?" I asked.

"We got a turkey, just what Gran wanted." Connor said as he ran his hands through his hair. I just smiled and looked over at the third mystery boy that was standing in the room.

"That's Peter, our cousin." William said. Peter nodded and gave a small smile, he didn't look like Connor or William; in fact he didn't look related at all. With his round face, red hair, peachy colored skin and freckles, he wasn't as tall as Connor or William, and he wasn't as muscular either. Peter just finished rubbing his hands together and then slinked out of the room.

"He's shy." Connor whispered to me. After Peter's awkward introduction, I met two final members of the family, Connor's father Jonathan and Peter's father Luke. That first day for me went by very slowly , mostly because I did nothing, but when the sun set and dinner was eaten, it was as if I was in a world vastly different from the one I had left behind in Baltimore. That night at dinner I had mashed potatoes and gravy, turkey, and stuffing. It was the first real meal I had had in months, and the heaviness of the food in my stomach made me feel ten pounds heavier. I slept soundly and comfortably without fear, and when I woke up the following morning, I was greeted with the scent of bacon, eggs, and fresh bread.

For the first few weeks of living at the farm I was confined to the house. Ms. Elizabeth set certain goals for me to meet, most of the goals revolved around my weight. For the first two weeks, Ms. Elizabeth wanted me to gain five pounds, and then the two weeks after another five pounds and so on. I was constantly fed every few hours during the day, they weren't full meals, just snacks. I would start my day with hot cereal, fresh bread, bacon, and eggs. Between breakfast and lunch I was given tea, corn bread, and milk. For lunch I had a thick sandwich of ham, turkey, and cheese, with another cup of milk. Between lunch and dinner I was given a small sliver of pumpkin pie and apple juice, and as always, Dinner was always the feast of the day. At first I was never able to finish the food that was set before me, and I felt guilty seeing the food whisked away to the kitchen. Yet after a few weeks of what Ms. Elizabeth called "body retraining" I was able to eat more and more.

This period of rehab that Ms. Elizabeth and Cora put me through was actually beginning to show its results. With the few pounds I had put back on, my cheeks plumped up and color came back to my skin, my hair was shiny and silky, and my stamina and strength increased day by day.

"Would you be mad if I told you, you were getting pretty?" Connor said one day while we were standing in the kitchen and I was rinsing off some fresh eggs that came in from the chicken coup.

"What do you mean getting pretty? You thought I was ugly before?" I said with my voice getting a little high pitched.

"Well, you looked like a Halloween decoration; you know the little ghost figures they used to hang from trees and stuff?" He said with a chuckle.

"Yeah, yeah, I know. I was hideous." I said.

"Not hideous, just not yourself." He said taking a strand of my hair in his fingers and twirling it around.

"Leave me alone, you think I'm hideous." I giggled as I jokingly swatted him away.

"Yeah, you're a big fat ugly beast." He joked as he took a carrot from out of the basket on the counter and going back outside to finish whatever chores he was doing. The days flowed on, and each day I learned something new. Charlotte sat and taught me embroidery one day, and I sat with her for a couple of hours until I mastered making little flowers on white fabric. I was then shown how to knit, and after spending a whole day with Amelia showing me, I made a scarf, which I draped around Connor the very next morning before he went hunting with William and Peter.

After a month and a half in the house, I no longer felt like a guest, but rather a member of the family. Amelia and William teased me, Ms. Elizabeth ordered me around just like she did with Charlotte, Cora, and Amelia; Charlotte liked to have both me and Amelia sit in front of her by the fire place and braid both of our hair. Cora would pinch me and tell me to hold my shoulders back. There was never a dull moment in the house, and there was always laughter.

I was finally allowed to go outside for the very first time when I, at last, weighted 100 pounds. The morning I stepped on the scale and the little needle finally hit that number, Ms. Elizabeth let out a little joyful cry and pulled me into the biggest bear hug ever.

"100 pounds means I feel safe with you going outside!"

"Really? I can finally go out?" I rejoiced. It seems very stupid for me to be so excited to go out in the cold and in the snow, but after weeks and weeks of being in the same place; I was in the mood for some change of scenery. Yet even though I itched to go outside, I had no reason to go outside. I sat looking out the window at the white landscape outside, trying to think of an excuse to go out. Amelia saw me and told me that the boys were out today chopping down a tree for firewood.

"We should go see them." I said.

"Why? It's boring. they're just hacking away at an old dead tree." She said sitting down next to me.

"I don't know what the farm looks like outside, and Ms. Elizabeth said I could go out."

"Well, you have been sitting here looking like a sad puppy." She said.

"I'm actually bored today." I said.

"Alright, if you really want to go out that badly." She said.

I just smiled and together we went to the entry way of the house where there was a coat rack and small chest of drawers that stood almost invisibly behind the front door. Next to the drawers were a little row of boots, she threw me a pair of familiar looking boots, they had been the ones I came here with. Next, she threw me a very thick and heavy knitted....thing. Mine was red and hers was navy blue, I watched her put hers on, it basically was a thick knitted sweater dress that was lined with fabric on the inside and knitted on the outside. It was made to go right over the dresses we were already wearing. When I put it on I already felt toasty warm. She also handed me a scarf and gloves, and when we both were properly dressed, she opened the door and a rush of cold air came in.

I felt the crunch of the ice and snow under my boots and the crispness of the air on my face. It felt wonderful. The world was completely different from the outside. I could see that the farm house was painted white with gray shutters. The farm house sat atop of a hill that looked down the driveway, which in turn disappeared into thick woods. The entire farm was surrounded by thick woods. There was about a mile and a half radius, with the house the center of just plain open land with no trees, and the rest was all woods. We went down the front path, on to the main driveway and around the house to where the kitchen would be. We saw Charlotte in the kitchen window by the sink and she waved to us as we walked by. When we made one more turn, we faced the large, big, red barn that sat about 100 yards from the back kitchen door. I had seen the barn from a few windows in the house, but I never really appreciated its height until I now stood in front of it. We walked up and through the barn. Once we were out of the back of the barn there was a partially frozen pond in the distance with ducks quacking and waddling about. The pond was very large, at least the size of a community swimming pool.

"Do you have fish in there?" I asked.

"Nah, it's too shallow and the creek that feeds the water in there is very small, just the ducks use it." She said as we walked up and around the pond, past a small orchard of 20 or so apple trees and directly into the woods. There wasn't a distinct path that Amelia was taking, I was just following her lead as we walked through what to me looked like just thick forest, yet to Amelia, who was so familiar with the land and the forest, she knew exactly where she was going and how far away from the house she was. After about fifteen minutes of walking, we started to hear the boy's voices and the sound of them hacking away at a tree. We had been really close to them, but because of all the trees and the glare of sun light off of the snow, I was surprised when we came upon them so quickly.

"Hey!" Amelia said as we met up with them.

"Hey, what are you doing?" William said.

"Mona wanted out of the house." Amelia pointed at me.

"I know this sounds stupid, but guess who weighs 100 pounds!" I cheered, putting my hands on my hips.

"Really? 100 pounds you say?" Connor took three strides over to me and in one fluid moment lifted me up under one arm.

"Ahh! Put me down!" I laughed.

"You do feel like 100 pounds, that's for sure." He said plopping me down in the snow.

"That's great news, Mona; do you know what that means?" William said.

"Well after that, I'm scared to know." I said pointing to Connor.

"Does it mean we can toss her around a little without being afraid she will break?" Connor asked.

"Well you can toss her around; I was thinking more something like this..." William said as he threw a snowball at me.

"Hey!" I said. Some of the snow had also gotten on Amelia because she made a snowball and threw it right in her brother's face We had started an all-out snowball fight that lasted a few brief moments and left everyone covered in a thin layer of snow. The boys decided to finish cutting down the tree so they sent us back home.

"Your nose is all red." Connor said before I left.

"Is it?" I said lifting my hand up and pinching my nose. When I dropped my hand Connor leaned down and left a little kiss on the tip of my nose before Amelia and I went back to the house.

Once we were back, Ms. Elizabeth saw us coming from the kitchen and she stood in the kitchen door, her hands on her hips, and a mean look on her face. When we approached her it was clear she was not happy with us.

"I said you could go outside, I didn't say you could go start rolling around in the snow and catch pneumonia! Get in the house and take off that coat and go sit by the fire! Both of you!" She hollered at us. Amelia and I could do nothing but laugh as we walked by.

17.

Poppy Holland

Large and menacing clouds could be seen starting to brew in the sky from the north. Jonathan suspected it to be a snow storm or a rain storm. Either way we needed to be prepared. I learned a great deal during the hours before the clouds hung over our heads. Even with the security that I felt at the farm, nothing was certain or truly reliable. Although the threats of starvation and an attack of a gang was still a possibility, even here on the farm, our biggest threat came from Nature itself. We relied on the land and the weather to provide, and if a storm came, it meant we had to protect everything we had.

During those hours all rules were out of the window. Although I was back to my normal weight and I was perfectly healthy again, Ms. Elizabeth insisted that she keep a close watch on me at least until spring. Yet with the threat of a possibly severe storm, I had to work just as hard as the others, and boy was it rewarding. Lugging logs of wood up to the house and making sure there was a good stack in every room that had a fire place. Herding all the animals into their little shelters that were built and locking them in so they would be safe and pulling together to make sure that here was enough food and supplies in the house. It took only a few hours to close up the house and make sure all the animals were safe and accounted for, but during those few hours I worked up a sweat and felt the muscles in my legs and arms ache, a sensation that I missed from the days of going for a jog or going with Molly to the gym. Those days were long gone, and the feeling of true hard work felt very gratifying and pleasing.

Just as the first few snowflakes began to fall and the wind began to pick up, the entire family, myself included, gathered in the living room by the fire. I remember nothing much happening for the remainder of that day, we all just lounged around the fire. Ms. Elizabeth had prepared soup for dinner, and it just sat in the kitchen bubbling all day. Charlotte sewed, Cora mended the boy's clothes, Amelia knitted, Ms. Elizabeth crocheted, Jonathan and Luke were reading, William was sharpening the tips of all the arrows the family owned, Peter was out in the entryway playing with the three house cats, and trying to get the two outside cats that we had brought inside to be friendly.

Connor and I sat in a little nest of blankets in the corner of the room by a window and bookcase. For some odd reason Connor picked the first book off the shelf he saw, Sense and Sensibility. For the remainder of the day we took turns reading it back and forth to each other, we thought we were the only ones who were listening, that is until Cora told me to speak up because she was listening too. After hours and hours of straight reading, Connor finished the last chapter of the book just as it was time to eat dinner. The rest of the family had enjoyed hearing us read so much that they insisted that we pick something else to read. The next choice was still Jane Austen, but this time William picked it right out of Connor's hands and began reading the opening lines of Pride and Prejudice in a very snobbish and poor English accent:

"It is a truth universally acknowledged that a single man in possession of a good fortune, must be in want of a wife." William began, without meaning to we seemed to have made it into a game. We passed the book around from person to person reading portions in our own outrageous interpretations of the characters. Ms. Elizabeth did an amazing job playing the part of Mrs. Bennett. She would stand in front of the fireplace, and would take the book, hold it out in front of her at arm's length, stand with her head held high and her shoulders back, and with her reading glasses balanced at the very end of her nose, she would read in this hysterical, overly exaggerated English accent whenever the parts of Mrs. Bennett came her way.

"Oh Mr. Bennett, how can you abuse your own children in such a way? You take delight in vexing me. You have no compassion on my poor nerves!" Ms. Elizabeth read out loud in her hysterical voice. We all laughed and occasionally got mad at each other when the next performance wasn't as good as the last. Night had come and we had not even made it half way through the book before the yawns started. We decided that we would save the rest for another night, and we placed a marker where we left off and we all went off to bed.

The snow had not let up and although no one really took the time to look out the window, we could tell that it was a nasty storm outside. The wind whipped around the house causing howls and whistles. Even late in the night there were a few claps of snow thunder and a flash or two of lightning as the storm reached its peak.

When morning came, there was sunshine and blue skies, it was as if a storm was never in the sky, yet from the four feet of snow that laid on the ground, we knew the damage had been done. It was a full team effort to get paths cleared out of the house and to the barn and such. With those pathways cleared we just tried our best to lug our way to the snow to see if the animals were alright. For some reason that day, I went with William out to the pig pen instead of going to the chickens with Connor. When we got to the pigs we noticed that they were all out of their little shelter, all trying to plow their way in the snow.

"How did they get out?" William said as we approached the enclosure and attached little shed.

"Did the wind open the gate?" I asked.

"It must have been a gust of wind that had a hand and fingers because that latch is hard to open." He said.

As we approached I noticed off on the other side of the enclosure there was a secondary path, a path that was partially covered with snow that had fallen over the night, but seemed to me that it was made while there was snow on the ground. When we reached the enclosure I peaked my head inside the shed, everything looked alright, I scanned a few times and then saw a lump of rags laying in the corner. There was something odd about it, as I looked harder, the lump moved and out of it I saw one blue eye.

"William!" I said jumping back.

"What?" He said looking at me like I was crazy.

"There's someone in there." I said. William immediately hopped the fence and went inside. I was ready to run if I needed to but I waited. I head William move around in the shed and then I heard a small groaning sound.

"Mona, go get Gran, and tell her to get ready for a patient." William said coming out of the shed with the pile of rags swaddled in his arms. I just nodded and half way ran and stumbled all the way back to the house.

"What's wrong with you?" Ms. Elizabeth said as I fell into the kitchen.

"There was a person in the pig shed." I said.

"What?"

"A person hiding in the pig shed! William is bringing them down here now." Just as the words came out of my mouth, William was in the door way with the stranger hanging limp in his arms. Ms. Elizabeth took one look at the stranger and began to bark orders.

"Cora! Charlotte! Get in here!" She yelled, "Mona, get a pot of water on the fire, and then go get me scissors." She said as she cleared the large wooded table in the kitchen. With the table cleared, William set the stranger down on it as if it were an operating table. Ms. Elizabeth shooed William out of the kitchen and requested that only Charlotte, Cora, and I stay.

We worked to cut the mangled and dirty clothing from the poor girl's body. She was conscious and awake, but not fully mentally there, she just looked around the room in a bewildered state as we worked to clean her up. With warm towels we removed dirt and dried blood from her skin. She had been through something rough judging by the bruises that spotted her body from head to toe. Her knees were scrapped raw, as were the knuckles on both of her hands. She had what looked like claw marks on her cheek and a small bruise above her left eyebrow. Her fingers and toes seemed stiff and cold; Ms. Elizabeth explained that the poor girl had started to succumb to frost bite.

We bathed her as best as we could, scrubbing her clean with towels that were soaked in hot water and lavender leaves. For her scraped knees and battered up knuckles, Ms. Elizabeth applied her own beeswax salve to shield the damaged skin from any more harm and to help it heal. Cora went to take a comb to the poor girl's hair, but the comb got stuck and the handle snapped when she tried to set it free it. When we heard the snap of the comb we all went over to Cora and stared down at the knots and mattes of the girl's hair. I estimated that the girl's blond hair would have been about as long as mine was, but it was knotted, matted, and had chunks of leaves and dirt in it to the point that water beaded up and rolled off of it.

"Do what you can, but cut it." Ms. Elizabeth said. Cora just nodded and turned around and took the scissors from the counter. I cried for the girl, who by that time was unconscious on the table, she was so very pretty under all the bruises and scrapes, I watched as Cora took handfuls of the blond locks and snipped it away. All the hair went into the trash bin and when it was all said and done, the girl had hair up to her ears, from that Cora took the scissors again and evened it all out.

"There is no reason she shouldn't wake up with a decent haircut." Cora said as she shaped the girls hair into more of a pixi cut. It took hours to clean her up, even after all that, we could still tell that the poor girl had been through much; she was beaten, bruised, and malnourished. We dressed her in clean undergarments and a warm nightgown, and had William carry her up stairs to the room I had been in when I first arrived.

"Sorry Mona, but this is the sick room." Ms. Elizabeth said as we placed the girl in the bed and covered her in blankets.

"Someone should watch her." Charlotte said.

"I'll stay." I said pulling the chair that sat in the corner of the room to the side of the bed. The hour of the day had grown late, we had skipped dinner, and with the business of trying to get this girl back together, the others left the room. I took my spot on the chair.

***

I had woken up in the middle of the night to use the bathroom. Getting up from my spot on the chair beside the bed, I went and when I came back, in the dim light of the fire I saw that our patient had awoken and her hands were up in her hair.

"Shh… shh, it's alright, you're safe here." I said rushing back over to my spot and taking her frail and wounded hand.

"My hair." She said.

"It was in mattes, we tried to comb it, but nothing worked, it had to be cut." I whispered.

"Where am I?"

"The Wilde family farm, we found you in our pig pen," I said.

"It was so cold." She shuttered. I could see her blue eyes welling up with tears.

"Well you are safe and warm now, my name is Mona, I came here from Baltimore, and this family saved my life, as they did yours." The girl took a moment; she just looked at me with a stray tear rolling down her cheek. After what seemed like an uncomfortable amount of silence, she began to tell me her story.

***

Her name was Poppy Holland and she was 20 years old. Poppy was born and raised in a small fishing town on the northern coast of Maine, almost near the Canadian border. Poppy's father was a fisherman and her mother was a stay at home mom, for a few weeks out of the year Poppy's father would go out to sea and when he would return with the season's catch, he would have enough money to support the family for the rest of the year. One day, when Poppy was eleven, she and her mother stood on the docks and waved her father goodbye, four days later a storm developed off the coast, the storm claimed both ship and crew, and in a matter of a few fateful hours, Poppy was fatherless.

To keep them from living on the streets, Poppy's mother started waitressing at a local pub, and they moved into the small one bedroom apartment above the pub. The kids at school would make fun of Poppy, telling her that if her father had been a real fisherman, he would have worked for one of the bigger fishing companies with the fancier boats that didn't sink. They would tease her, call her names, and tell her that her mom was a floozy. Poppy could only take so much, until one day in the eighth grade, a girl was calling her names, and Poppy turned around and punched her in the face. The two got into a serious fist fight, and Poppy won. By high school, Poppy had gotten into more school yard fights than she could keep track of, and she had won every single one of them. In her heart she wasn't a violent person, but she had been attacked every single time, she wasn't violent, she was defensive.

Poppy was expelled from high school at 17 for a fight that escalated to her accidentally hitting a teacher. It was at that point that Poppy knew things had gotten out of hand. She took a waitressing job alongside her mother at the pub and they worked together to keep afloat. When the breakout of the plague initially happened, the government came in and shut down all the big fishing corporations, leaving the majority of the townsmen without jobs. The CDC came in to hold a town meeting and they invited everyone and anyone who wanted to voice their opinions about the decision to close the fishing business in the town. Poppy's mother told Poppy to stay home and that she would go to the meeting.

While Poppy's mother was at the meeting, a large number of the men did not like what the CDC had to say, they left in an outrage, they left and they walked right into a bar, fueling their anger with more talk and booze. It was there at that bar that those men decided they wanted to voice their opinion. They voiced their opinion with guns and walked right into the town meeting. When it was all said and done, Poppy's mother and 12 others were left dead, and the plague was just beginning to reach its fingers into the town.

Months passed and Poppy made due where she could, but she was struggling and the town was dying. Late one night there were the sounds of gun shots and screaming. Poppy went out into the street only to discover that the town was under attack. Before she could even think, a group of men encircled her and dragged her away. A nomadic gang had claimed her, taking her into custody. The raiders dragged her along, tied to other prisoners. When the prisoners were presented to the leader of the gang, he ordered his raiders to "dispose" of the weaker ones, but to Poppy, he said that she could stay. She was fed, and given new clothes, and for the first few days she thought that maybe she had been saved, but that was only until she was given an order, she was ordered to join the team of raiders and pillage the next town. Believing that if she was obedient she would be rewarded, she agreed. It was during that pillage, while Poppy was trying to steal food that she got into a fight with a townsperson. While she fought the other raiders looked on, and when they got back to the gang camp with the goods that had been taken, a favorable report was given to the gang leader about Poppy.

Poppy was continually used during town raids. She hurt people she didn't want to hurt, and stole things that might have helped innocent people survive. She did all this in an effort to survive herself. She told me that she never wanted to hurt anyone, but that she was given no other choice. She saw what the gang did to people who weren't obedient, and what they did to them was worse than death itself. So she did things, things she would have normally not have done.

The gang picked up camp and marched for two days before making permanent camp again. After a day or two more gangs joined them until it was a large gathering of different gangs. All the gang leaders talked amongst themselves, and they decided to take all the gangs that were there and split them in two large massive super gangs. With the division of the gangs taken care of, the two new head leaders fought over how all the supplies and provisions would be split. They then decided that they would pick their best fighters and have a tournament, winner of the tournament got to decide how the provisions would be split.

Poppy's gang leader chose his 10 best fighters, and Poppy was included among them. Poppy then found herself fighting for her life, during the fifth round, Poppy lost for the first time. When the tournament was all said and done, the winning leader divided the provisions and even claimed Poppy as among those provisions. Thrown into another gang and treated like mere property, Poppy suffered, but was determined to survive. Along the way disagreements among the gang leaders broke out, and some would leave the gang to form their own, taking with them provisions and supplies. The gang leader was growing tired of people rising up against him that he threatened that if he even suspected you to be challenging him, he would kill you, Poppy kept silent and hoped she would either meet a swift and clean death, or she would somehow be freed.

What was left of the gang broke into a fight amongst them; Poppy took it as an opportunity to run, she deserted the gang and had been on the run for days before she came across another gang, a much smaller gang of only 35 members or so. This new, smaller gang took her in with no problem, not even questioning where she had come from. With that gang she marched back north, she marched until this new gang made camp at about a 7 days walk from here on the farm. It was there that a feud between the two gang leaders broke out; Poppy saw no good coming from a feud, so during the night she fled again. She walked until a storm brewed in the sky and even then she walked until she saw a shed like structure in the darkness. When Poppy finished telling me her story, I cried with her. She had seen many horrors and was truly repentant for all the things she did in hopes of survival.

"I may have survived, but I did it the wrong way, I would have much rather have died than have to have experienced all that. Even now, I'll never be the same." She said.

“You can be a new person here; here you are with a family who will accept you.” I said.

“That’s if they’ll even have me after all I’ve done.” She scoffed.

18.
Acceptance

For the first two days of Poppy's recovery, I made no mention about her past as a gang member. I only told the family what they had to know, like her name, where she was from, and that she was an orphan. No one asked me any questions, Poppy just slept and said please and thank you when she was given things. When there was no one around I would go in and sit with Poppy and just assure her that everything was alright. Although Poppy's condition was far better than mine had been when I arrived, mentally she was not alright. She would have nightmares, and she was very jumpy. Eventually we got her to come down to the living room with us during the day.

Eventually questions did need to be answered, and the big question that loomed in the air was how Poppy made it from Maine to our little farm. We had been sitting in the Living room after dinner, finishing up our family reenactment of Pride and Prejudice, finally. With the last few lines read and the book placed back onto the shelf, Peter turned around and looked at Poppy.

"So, you're from Maine?" Peter asked.

"Yes, I am." Poppy answered from her spot on the couch.

"What brought you down here? I mean it's a long way." Peter asked, Poppy grew quiet and began to twist the blanket she had on her lap in her hands. There wasn't really anything else she should or could do other than to tell the truth about how she came to be here with us. I had told her over the past couple of days to just tell the truth, but leave out the details. I knew that if the family downloaded everything at once as I had, they would be shocked. Poppy looked around the room at all the waiting faces and let out a sigh.

"I never meant to leave Maine, but a gang attacked my town, I was taken prisoner and I remained a prisoner until I ran away. I have been on the run until you all took me in, I am very grateful." She said solemnly.

"Oh you poor thing!" Charlotte said rushing over to Poppy's side.

"Why didn't you say something sooner?" Amelia said, but Poppy gave no answer.

“Wait… If you made it here, then that means there’s a gang nearby.” Connor said, shattering the mood of peace in the room. I just looked over at Connor and gave him a very disapproving look. Although it was a good point of concern on Connor’s part, I did not believe that it was the right time to bring up a delicate topic such as that.

“No… no. I was traded from one gang to another, to a much larger and terrible gang, but I ran away from that one. I… I joined another one, it was much smaller, only 35 people. I ran away from that one too, not because I was in danger or anything, but I saw that the two leaders began to fight. I walked for days before coming to you, there’s a very small chance that there’s any other gang around here.” She spoke in defense.

“There’s still a threat, gangs are moving around the area, that area could be a four day’s walk from here, but still…” Connor said.

“Connor, please, we need not worry about all of this now.” I said walking over to him.

“Well when should we worry about it? When they knock at our door?” he stated. I just turned away from him and looked over at Poppy who looked so very, very upset by the whole topic.

“Let’s not discuss this now. The matter will be discussed privately.” Ms. Elizabeth commanded. Poppy had a few stray tears roll down her cheeks, I went back over to her and helped her up from the seat and I began to walk her up stairs so she could go to bed.

“It’ll be alright. Connor just worries about things, that’s all.” I assured her as we reached the beginning of the staircase. I heard a few footsteps behind me and Poppy and I turned to see William standing behind us.

“Don’t worry, Poppy, no one’s going to make you leave or anything. How about tomorrow we get you out of the house for a bit and show you around? Would you like that?” He asked.

“I would like that, thank you.” Poppy said to William before turning again and climbing the stairs. The next day, staying true to his word, William showed Poppy around. As much as it pained him William allowed Connor and Peter to go stack firewood. I had come to the realization that William was the kind of person who liked to be in control, although he had full faith that his brother would do the job just as well as he could, he just didn't trust Peter. From the beginning I had known Peter was different from the rest of the family, as to how different I hadn't learned until much later. Cora, Jonathan, and Peter had only just started to live on the farm. Peter had gone to a normal public high school, he had been on the football team and lacrosse team at that school, and he was very studious and was planning to attend college. His only time on the farm had been during the weekends when his parents went up to visit the rest of the family. What made Peter so different from Connor and William was the fact that he didn't see the importance in what had to be done on the farm, he just didn't seem to understand, nor care, and this annoyed William.

The morning was rather very beautiful as William guided Poppy through the premises of the farm. Most of the snow had melted away, revealing the brown muddy earth beneath, but the sky was forever blue with fluffy white clouds, the air was very still allowing for the chill to be enjoyable. I wanted to be a part of William's tour of the land, but he was so very attentive to Poppy that I felt slightly awkward, so I took a few steps back and followed from behind. I listened carefully as William joked and talked to Poppy, it was a side I had never seen of him before and it was very strange.

"And over there is the pig pen, but I'm sure you're familiar with that." William joked making Poppy laugh.

"Yeah, it was a lovely experience." She laughed. We walked down and around and up into the barn where William proudly opened up one of the large cabinets that stored all the hunting equipment.

"And this, this is all our hunting stuff, guns, traps, bows, arrows, fishing rods, hooks, nets, you name it we got it. If it walks, gallops, swims, or flies, I can catch it." William said.

"Oh stop boasting, no one likes a bragger." We all turned to see Amelia walking into the barn with two dead rabbits slung over her shoulder.

"Who said you could go hunting?" William asked in a demanding tone.

"No one, I didn't even leave the farm, your majesty, I saw these two in the field from the dining room window, got my bow and shot them myself." Amelia said as she placed her bow back to its place.

"Well it looks like you have some competition." Poppy said.

"Anyone can catch a rabbit." He huffed.

"Ha. Ha. Ha." Amelia said as she left the barn.

"My dad used to take me hunting when I was little." Poppy said picking up one of the arrows that was laying a stray.

"What did you hunt?" William asked.

"Deer and ducks mostly." She said flicking the tip of the arrow.

"What did you use?"

"I used a bow; dad didn't want me with a gun so young."

"Well let's see if your aim is still good." William said pulling a bow and a few arrows from their spots. We followed him out to the south side of the barn where there were little targets painted onto the side of one wall. William stood Poppy a few yards back and handed her the bow and arrow.

"I haven't done this since I was eleven." She said.

"Just try, we won't make fun of you." William assured, Poppy stood her ground and fumbled with the bow and arrow before taking her stance. After a few silent moments, Poppy fired the arrow and it veered completely off to the left by like five feet, missing the target completely.

"Aww, good try." William said stepping forward to take the bow from her.

"Give me another one." She said, William was a little flustered when she asked for another arrow, but he handed her one anyway. Taking her stance again, she fired the second arrow and missed the target by only about three feet.

"Another." She said, she did this about four more times before she hit the target right in the bull's-eye, and even after she hit it, she did it three more times just to be sure.

"I'll get better." She said handing the bow back to William.

"That was…. really good." He said a bit shocked.

"Maybe you can take me hunting with you next time." She giggled. We continued the tour around the farm, ending the tour where Connor and Peter were stacking the fire wood against brick of the chimney by the kitchen. Even in the cold air, Peter and Connor had managed to work up a sweat, removing their jackets to just work in their t-shirts. The stack of evenly chopped wood was almost as tall as me and nearly stretched the length of the portion of the house.

"I think we did good." Connor said to Peter.

"Yeah, yeah, I need a shower." Peter said wiping the sweat from his brow.

"Peter; do one more row of wood then you can go inside. I need Connor for a few minutes." William dictated as we began to walk away leaving Peter to do just so.

"What's up." Connor said putting his arm around me, but I swatted him away, he was all sweaty and stinky.

"What?" he said looking down at me.

"You stink." I laughed, he responded to my comment by full on grabbing me and forcing me into a hug for a good 20 seconds.

"Ahh, let me go, put me down!" I laughed.

"Connor, come on." William said.

"What?"

"Poppy knows how to hunt." William said looking down at Poppy.

"Oh really now?" Connor said a bit surprised.

"I'm no pro, I haven't gone hunting since I was eleven, but I can shoot an arrow." She said bashfully.

"Tomorrow, let's take Poppy hunting and let Peter stay and milk the cow." William said.

"Really, you want to do that?" Connor said surprised.

"Sure, why not."

"I haven't been here long, but I'm sure we have to ask Ms. Elizabeth first?" Poppy asked.

"Of course, we have to ask her everything." William laughed.

The four of us walked back into the house through the kitchen where Ms. Elizabeth started to tell us to take off our shoes, wash our hands, and go get ready for dinner. Of course dinner wasn't for another few hours, but she just wanted to give us something to do. Poppy went off with William into the living room where Amelia was busy with some sort of sewing project. Connor and I walked slowly through the house stopping at the staircase. Before Connor went to go up the stairs, he took one last opportunity to rub his nasty body odor all over me by playfully rubbing his hands all over my face.

"Ew! Stop it!" I laughed slapping him away.

"Alright, I'm done." He said gently dropping his hands to my neck. He kissed me once before turning and going up the stairs to the bathroom while I went and joined the others in the living room. Evenings seemed to be the slowest parts of the day. With all the chores done and everyone ready to relax, the hours seemed to creep by until dinner was to be had and even after that when we all lounged around after cleaning up the dining room and kitchen from the meal. Poppy brought up the question about her going with William to go hunt, Ms. Elizabeth gave Poppy a very quizzical look and sat silently for a few moments before giving her reply.

"It won't be an all-day affair, you go for a couple of hours, and you be back at a decent time. I think it would do you some good." Ms. Elizabeth said. Poppy lit up and was excited and William was grinning ear to ear. The very next day, no one had really high expectations that the two would come back with anything, we all wished them well as they walked up the hill towards the woods with hunting gear on their back. Neither Connor nor Peter went with them instead they just stayed by the house doing odd jobs. The sewing project that Amelia had taken up was that of making new clothes for herself for the spring. She showed me the pattern that she was using and showed me how to alter it so that I could make some dresses for myself.

We spent the day in the living room; Connor and I sitting closely on the couch while I sewed and he winded fishing line onto a spool. I did have to admit that the days were beginning to get a bit boring and mundane, but I could not complain. I could focus on making the perfect little stitches that Cora had shown me for hours and if I had no interruptions I could make dress after dress after dress but Connor had finished making spools of fishing thread, and was poking at me asking me to go with him down to check on the sheep. I put down my sewing and went with Connor down to see the sheep.

I could tell that spring was coming soon just by the way the air outside felt on my skin and how it smelled. Together, Connor and I walked along the path all the way up and around to where the pasture was for the sheep. Like little white puff balls against the muddy ground they had to trod on, the sheep bahhed and moved around their enclosure. Connor pointed out one sheep to me that seemed slightly bigger than the rest.

"That one is going to have the first baby of the year." He said.

"When do you think it'll be born?" I asked.

"It's hard to tell, I would say next month, but who knows." He said taking my hand in his.

"Why did you want to come down here?" I asked.

"Oh, just to get out of the house for a while, it can get a little boring." He chuckled, dropping my hand and exchanging it for a strand of my hair. I was occupied by the sheep, so much so that Connor grabbed my chin and forced me to look at him.

"What?" I chuckled.

"Look at me!" he laughed.

"I'm watching the sheep." I said.

"I can see that." He said taking a step closer to me and pulling me close.

"You're squeezing me too tight." I said.

"I'm cold." He lied.

"No you're not." I laughed. Connor and I were having a moment, a wonderfully romantic moment standing by the pasture with no one around, that was until Poppy's shrill voice could be heard coming down the hill from the forest. Connor and I turned, not breaking away from the embrace and saw Poppy and William coming down from the hill, dragging with them a large buck.

"No way!" Connor shouted once he saw that they had killed something.

"Let's go see." I pulled Connor along with me and we went to meet Poppy and William. They were both grinning from ear to ear as they worked to drag the large Buck down to the farm.

"Who killed it?" Connor asked.

"Poppy did." William said proudly.

"I really don't know how I managed to, we were so far away and there were so many trees in the way." Poppy said.

"You're just a natural that's all." William laughed and Poppy blushed.

"Well let's hurry and get this thing bled and skinned so we can start cutting it up before it goes bad." Connor said taking the rope that held the back two legs of the buck from Poppy. The boys went off, dragging the buck down to the barn while Poppy and I walked behind.

"You really killed it all by yourself?" I asked.

"I did, I can't believe it." She laughed.

"Maybe you'll have to replace Connor when hunting." I joked.

"I don't know, William said the same thing." When we got back to the house and showed Ms. Elizabeth the Buck that they had brought back, Ms. Elizabeth did a little hop of joy and clapped her hands. She pulled Poppy into a suffocating hug and told her that she could go hunting as often as she wanted, so long as she always brought back something good and both Poppy and William seemed to agree to that idea.

19.

Spring

Spring came just as cabin fever was beginning to set in on all of us. Each day brought a warmer breeze from the south, and the stirrings of the coming change in the season could be felt in the land and in the trees. The grass began to grow and turn green, buds appeared on the branches of the trees, and this freshness aroused the feeling of bliss and serenity in all of us. With the coming change, there was work that had to be done; the house had to be stripped of all linens and curtains and rugs and carpets, all of which had to be hung on a long rope that stretched from the house to the barn so that all those items could air out. The floors were scrubbed using vinegar and warm water, and the windows were opened to allow the winter dust and dull air to be filtered from the house. The soil in the garden was turned and fertilized with a mixture of egg shells and cow manure. The work that had to be done for the coming spring was hard and tiresome, but it was fulfilling.

When the soil in the garden had been turned and fertilized, Ms. Elizabeth announced to us that it was time to journey back into town to get supplies we had run out of over the winter. I was rather shocked to hear that there was a town nearby, for the entirety of winter we had been self-sufficient, I had no idea there was a town anywhere near us. With the strictest of instruction, we were told to take a couple of chickens, one pig, and four glass bottles of milk up to town to trade for much needed items such as soap, seeds for the garden, cloth, bullets, oil, and certain herbs that Ms. Elizabeth wrote down. Because we had to drag with us a pig and some chickens, we were forced to walk all the way to the town. It would be my very first time stepping onto that road again since I had arrived at the farm. We walked for about an hour and half up and down the hills and around the curve of the road until we came to a stretch of land that seemed to have been burnt down to ash.

"What happened here?" Poppy asked looking around at the wide open space that no longer held living trees, but blackened carcasses of once mighty oaks and maples, and scattered here and there were the skeletons of houses or the footprints of building foundations. Connor and William made no answer for the sight was even new to them; instead they looked to Amelia and Peter for answers.

"The plague did reach the town. With the threat of the gangs and the amount of abandoned and empty houses, the survivors of the town built a wall around the surviving parts of down town, and as for the rest it was all burned." Amelia said.

"The town is now only about two or three miles big." Peter added.

"Wow…" William said, we continued walking until we saw a wall ahead of us, it was a rather strange wall that wasn't all even and varied in height and thickness in some areas. As we got closer we could see that the wall was made out of various materials such as bricks, cement, rocks, metal, fencing, and even furniture, I could see the metal frames of beds, the legs of chairs, couches, and even some mattresses. The whole wall was approximately ten feet high and it seemed to encircle the town. Spanning across the road seemed to be a gate or large door of some sort, roughly made out of wood and metal. This door or gate was closed and when we got near someone called out from behind it.

"Who goes there?!"

"The Wilde's." William shouted back, the gate was pulled open from the inside and a tall man appeared in the opening.

"My God, I thought for sure we lost you folk after the third snow storm, and to see you and Connor here, nothing can kill you all, you're invincible." The man bellowed as he came close to us.

"Made it out of the cities away from the CDC and the gangs by the skin of our teeth, but we are here." William said.

"And who are these two unfamiliar faces?" the man asked.

"This is Mona, my girlfriend; I met her while I was an officer in Baltimore." Connor answered.

"My name is Poppy, I too escaped…" she said trailing off at the end of her sentence. I looked at her and gave her a nod of approval, the man need not know any more as to where Poppy came from. The scruffy man just nodded and smiled without turning away from Connor and William, we were welcomed into the other side of the wall where it was a dramatically different world. On the inside of the wall was a completely normal functioning town. Peter went on to explain to us that the majority of the historical part of the town had been saved, and that included the library, country store, a few historic houses, the post office, the school, the town green, and a large plot of land for growing food. There were approximately 200 people left either living in the town, or just outside the walls; where we lived on the farm was the farthest anyone lived away from the town and the safety of the walls.

There were children laughing and playing in the town green, it had been the first time in a very, very long time that I saw small children. There were men and women all gathered on the front porches of the houses or sitting in chairs watching the children play. There was no sadness amongst the faces of the people of the town, rather the feeling of joy seemed to permeate through everyone. We walked along, following Peter who, for the first time, seemed to be taking the lead since he was the one who had often gone to town while Connor and William were away. We followed him up to the front steps of the country store where he told us to wait.

"So much has changed." William said.

"Well, I'm just happy to see so many familiar faces." Connor said looking around.

"It's so lovely here, there are so many children." Poppy smiled as she watched little toddlers wrestle in the grass.

"Hey, the store will take the chickens and the milk in exchange for all the seeds, cloth, and bullets we need. We can take the pig down to the Wilson farm and they'll give us the oil and the soap, and Mrs. Miller will give us the herbs just for seeing our faces." Peter said as he came out of the store. We all shrugged and shifted our weight from one leg to another, Connor handed me one of the wooden crates that one of the chickens were held in and I followed him and William up into the store while Peter, Amelia, and Poppy stayed with the pig.

The inside of the country store felt like walking through a time portal and being sent back about a hundred years or so. There were old wooden counters and shelves that displayed various items and goods. The store smelled of old wood, berries, and apples. The dim lighting also added to the coziness of it all that I felt as I walked up and down the narrow aisles of goods while Connor and William made their request for seeds and bullets to the woman at the counter. I was surprised to see just how much was for sale. There were fresh cheeses, deli meats, beef jerky, breads, cakes, homemade jarred foods and soups, and odd ends and trinkets. There were items of clothing thrown into the mix as well as handmade jewelry. There was nothing about the amount of goods in the store that would make it clear to me that there had been a plague going on. There was an overabundance of things that held me to the thought that what I had experienced in Baltimore had not really happened.

"Mona, why don't you pick some fabric since Gran wanted to make new dresses and stuff." Connor said coming over to me and pointing to where all the large amounts of fabric were stacked against the wall. I went over and took six yards of red, white, lavender, navy blue, and rose pink colored fabric. It would be more than enough to make new dresses and odd items around the house. While we were still in the store I encouraged Connor to look at the men's jeans that they had stacked up too, since his jeans were beginning to wear at the knees. He just shrugged and promised he would get a new pair next time we were in town. We left with a wooden crate full of all the things we needed and rejoined the rest of the group outside.

It was a very odd feeling to be seeing other people, I had gone so long either being alone or it just being the family at the farm, that to see new faces felt foreign to me. We walked farther through the town, leading the pig along with us until we came to a very small little white house that sat at the end of a narrow side street that jutted off of the main road. A little white haired old woman came out of the front door, dragging along with her a wooden cane.

"Can it really be? Is that Connor and William Wilde? Oh my stars! I thought we had lost you two boys!" She said with tears welling up in her eyes. I quickly understood that this woman was Mrs. Miller, the town's second herbalist, the first being Ms. Elizabeth. She hugged all of us, despite her having never met Poppy or I. Leaving the pig tied up on the fence post, she welcomed all six of us into her tiny home where she brewed us tea and made us eat her home made butter cookies. She wanted to know just about every single detail about all of our lives, including mine and Poppy's. Poppy was of course uneasy about all the questions, but Mrs. Miller was a nonjudgmental, yet nosey soul who pried it out of her while the rest felt the agony that Poppy must have felt.

"Well there ain't no harm done to you, you made it to quite possibly the only safe place in all of New England, and we are delighted to welcome you Miss Poppy Holland." Mrs. Miller said with a smile as she poured Poppy a second cup of tea.

"Mrs. Miller, we love staying and chatting with you, we wish we could stay all day, but the farm has had it rough over the winter. We did well and all, all the livestock is still alive, we never ran out of food or drink, but Gran's herb garden was destroyed by the cold, and when Mona and Poppy arrived, Gran's supply of dried herbs depleted. We were wondering if you could give us some snipping's Gran could use to build up her garden again." William requested.

"Oh darling, you don't even have to ask, here come on now, you all come out back and I'll show you everything." We followed Mrs. Miller through her small home to the back, where attached to her small house was a large, functioning green house where she had just about every sort of useful plant and herb known to man. She gave us snipping's of just about everything and folded them in delicate cheese cloth and placed them in the crate we had along with the seeds for the garden. As we left Mrs. Miller's to take the pig to that other farm, Connor told me all that he knew about the old woman. She was nearing her 80's and before the outbreak, she made a living making hand crafted essential oils and medicines that she could sell to various health food stores and local families. She was very wise and loving, yet at the same time very eccentric and hyper. It was Mrs. Miller who trained Ms. Elizabeth the art of natural healing when Ms. Elizabeth was a young midwife before she married and had children.

We were then taking the pig to the Wilson farm, where Mrs. Wilson knew how to make soap as well as use the byproducts of soap making to make candles and oil for lanterns and such. We just about got a year supply of oil and soap from the woman who was over joyed to have a pig. With all of our deeds done in town, we now had the task to carry all the things back to the farm. Someone in the town was kind enough to give us a little children's wagon so we could pull the things along, it helped a lot while we took the journey back to the farm. It was very refreshing to walk in the sunlight and have a change of scenery.

When we arrived back at the farm Ms. Elizabeth was thrilled with everything we got. She gave us the rest of the day off and we could skip out on our chores. It would mean that we would have double to do the next day, but we didn't care. Instead we took the opportunity to go on a small adventure. William and Connor suggested that we go down to the river, it was far in the woods and a good distance from the farm, but for some reason that day we didn't care. We took the opportunity and ran off, hiking through the still barren trees and through the soft muddy ground until we reached the rushing river. I was exhausted and out of breath by the time we arrived, we had basically run the whole way there. There was a sheer drop of rock that led down to the actual rushing river, it gave Poppy and I a moment for pause while the others seemed to know exactly how too gracefully and effortlessly climb their way down the sheer slope and rocks down to the water. I was not planning on swimming, the air was still chilly and I expected the water to still be near freezing temperatures, but Connor and William tore their shirts off and jumped right it.

Poppy and I fumbled and scrapped our elbows and knees as we tried to slowly slide down the slope, once Poppy even slipped and began a terrible fall towards the water and rocks, but it was a thick exposed tree root that saved her from the fall. She held on to it and slowly lowered herself down on to a large boulder where she could easily climb down. I still had to work my way down, but when I did, I found my way to a fallen tree that hung over the rushing water. I tiptoed my way across it and sat down straddling the trunk of the fallen tree and allowed my toes to skim lightly over the frigid water. We all managed to find something to do by the river; William and Connor waded around in the water, swimming and looking for interesting objects beneath the surface, Peter was tossing rocks and sticks across from one side of the river to the other, Poppy made for herself a nice little spot on top of a massive boulder that jutted out into the water, and Amelia was walking around in the more shallow areas of the water where it was only knee deep.

"Come swimming." Connor said grabbing hold of my ankle with his wet hand.

"No, it is freezing; you're crazy for being in that water." I said.

"It's good for you."

"Good for you, deadly for me." I said pulling my foot away.

"It won't kill you." he laughed, this time grabbing hold of my whole leg and pulling me down towards the water. The best I could to was grab hold of the tree with my arms and hang on like a little sloth as Connor tried to pry my arms and legs away to get me into the water. Soon enough though I was tickled out of holding on and I was in the icy water. I immediately wished I could just jump right out of the cold and up onto the tree again, but there was nothing for me to do but to hiss and whine as Connor laughed at me.

"I'm going to kill you!" I spat at him in anger.

"No you wont." He said pulling me close to him.

"No, this time I'm serious." I said trying to push him away, but he was stronger than I. I could hear the others laughing and I looked over to see Poppy hysterical on her little rock with William sneaking up behind her.

"What are you laughing at? You're next!" William said picking up Poppy and throwing her over his shoulder and bringing her down into the water and she kicked and screamed. Once she was in the water, Poppy had this look of absolute terror on her face, she looked down at her wet clothes and then back up at William before punching him straight in the face.

"William! It's freezing! How could you?" She said.

"Ouch! You punched me!" he responded.

"Yeah well you deserved it!" She snapped back. William retaliated by taking both of Poppy's wrists and holding them effortlessly with one hand while he poked and tickled her with the other until she fell into the water again. We were all laughing and when Poppy came up out of the water again she couldn't do anything but laugh either.

The sun was setting by the time we got back to the house. We were freezing, our clothes and hair were soaked, our feet muddy, but we didn't care, we had had too much fun. The water had been refreshing and energizing and I felt as if I were my absolute best.

However, the look on Ms. Elizabeth's face was priceless when we all walked through the back kitchen door, our clothes wet, and our noses and cheeks raw and red. She began bantering on about how we were all going to catch pneumonia and die and that we could get frost bite and hypothermia. We just laughed and went up to our respective rooms to change into warm dry clothes and meet for dinner.

20.
Fireflies

With each passing day the weather and the world around us seemed to change. We saw day by day how the earth began to awaken from its winter rest. The birds sang and fluttered about, the buds on the trees grew day by day, the grass grew thick and green, and little microscopic purple flowers began to pop up on their own. Each day felt more blissful than the last. Our garden was planted, the sun was shining, and there was this new feeling of contentment in the air.

I helped Connor deliver that little lamb that he had pointed out to me only weeks before. We named her Sheila and jokingly said that she would be our baby. I saw a new attitude in everyone now that the days were warmer and getting a little longer. Jonathan found an old record player in the attic of the house and set it up in the living room so now we had music just about all the time. We had to use the records that were there, which consisted mostly of Billie Holliday, Glen Miller, Louis Armstrong, and Frank Sinatra. The music carried on the light breezes through the open windows of the house and could be heard just about anywhere on the farm.

Each and every day we were having fun doing the chores we had to do to keep the farm running. We were all very comfortable with each other, and the boys were having fun playing practical jokes on us. I noticed a distinct change in Poppy and William in the way they behaved towards each other, I began to suspect that they might like each other, but I never thought to ask Poppy. It was however on a bright sunny day, when there wasn't a cloud in the sky, that I saw William approach Poppy while she was watering the garden and hand her a flower. He held it up to her without saying a word and Poppy looked at it and smiled before taking it. I saw her mouth the words "thank you" before she stuck it in her hair behind her ear, and then William walked away. Connor was standing next to me and we both saw what happened.

"Why don't you ever pick me flowers?" I jokingly said.

"You don't need flowers." He said.

"I don't need flowers, but they are rather nice." I said.

"Why flowers when this is just as good?" Connor said taking one step closer to me and grabbing my face, pulling me into a lovely and long kiss.

"You're right, who needs flowers." I sighed a bit out of breath once it was all over. Connor just gave this smug smile before leaving to go tend to more of his own chores. After he left, I bent back down to pick up an empty bucket that I was taking to go milk the cows with. Ms. Elizabeth had taught us all how to milk the cows, today was my turn. I had to double wash the bucket out with soap and hot water before taking it down to use to fill with milk. On my way down to the cows, Poppy caught up with me, the flower still behind her ear.

"I saw that." I said as I continued to walk.

"Saw what?" she said.

"William give you that flower."

"Oh, shut up, don't act like no one saw that kiss Connor gave you either. I'm pretty sure everyone in the house saw you." Poppy said, she and I both laughed for a few moments before making it to the stable where the cows lived and were free to walk around in a little enclosure. We had two cows, Colleen and Maggie. We alternated milking the two every couple of hours so that we would have enough milk for the whole family. I hadn't really realized how important milk was as a food staple until recently. We went through a lot of milk. Milk was just about used every day, in just about everything. Ms. Elizabeth made cheese, we used it in cooking, we used it for drinking and it was even used cosmetically for some of the concoctions Ms. Elizabeth made.

I sat down on the milking stool and placed the bucket right underneath Colleen while Poppy petted the cow nicely. Normally milking the cows was something I did alone with no one else around but today Poppy was here. She was humming a very light and airy tune as she pet the cow. I had gotten a couple dozed squirts of milk out of Colleen before I sat straight up to ask Poppy a question.

"So do you like William?" I asked.

"What?" she stammered.

"I think you heard me."

"I heard you, I don't know if I want to answer you." She said.

"Aw come on, you can't keep it to yourself forever. There are only eleven people that live here on the farm."

"Alright… I think I do." She said.

"I know you do."

"But you can't say anything!" she commanded.

"Well I won't say anything, that's all on you. If you want to know my opinion, I think William likes you back."

"How do you know?" She asked all sheepishly.

"He gave you a flower for goodness sakes!" I said pointing to the flower behind her ear. It was rather humorous as to how red and embarrassed Poppy got after I said that. She was all flustered and she stammered as she tried to think of what to say next.

"He doesn't like me." She snapped back before turning on her heels and leaving the stable. I just chuckled as she marched away in anger. Over the next couple of days, William actually was working towards telling Poppy that he liked her, but he was trying to tell her without really telling her. Connor told me that he had feelings for Poppy, but Connor and I both decided to not interfere. William would try and tell or show Poppy that he liked her by either giving her more flowers or giving her other small simple projects. He made a little sculpture out of a piece of wood he carved himself, and made her a bracelet out of strings and old buttons. Nothing seemed to work, with each act of affection Poppy drew further and further away, even purposely trying to avoid William. I knew that she liked him, but her actions were just so strange and odd. William was beginning to get disheartened and upset, cranky even. Connor didn't know what to do about his brother, and I didn't really know what to do about Poppy.

Connor and I sat in the field together just talking and having quality time together all the while trying to figure out if there was anything to be done. The recent tension between William and Poppy could be felt in the whole family, and it was very awkward.

"I think we need to talk to them." Connor said.

"But how?" I asked.

"You tell me that Poppy likes William, but that goes completely against the way she is behaving."

"William has tried everything, I do have to give him that; it's Poppy who is being the stubborn one." I sadly said.

"You should talk to her. There's something she isn't saying or is having difficulty saying. We need to find out what it is." Connor said.

"She's been hiding lately, not even doing her chores, when I find her, I'll talk to her." I said. I found Poppy after it had gotten dark and after the family ate dinner. She was hiding in the bedroom that we shared, in the space between the two beds on the floor where she couldn't be seen from the doorway. She sat with her knees drawn up close to her chest and a book balanced on top. Trying not to totally disturb her, I sat down beside her and waited for her to acknowledge me.

"What?" She said without looking up from the page she was reading.

"Nothing, you weren't at dinner, aren't you hungry? Ms. Elizabeth made chicken wrapped with bacon and seasoned with sage." I said.

"No. I'm not hungry."

"Well then you must be sick, only sick people don't want to eat."

"I'm fine, Mona, now go away."

"I can't go away, this is our room, and you're leaning against my bed." I said, Poppy looked up, rolled her eyes, slammed the book shut and scooted over to the opposite side and leaned against her bed.

"Are you happy now?" she sarcastically said.

"No, not entirely."

"Then, what?" she sassed.

"I want you to tell me what's bothering you; you've been acting funny lately."

"It's not me that's been acting funny lately, it's William."

"What is he doing?" I asked.

"He… he… I don't know." She stammered.

"What do you mean you don't know?"

"I mean… it's hard to explain."

"Well, I've got all night." I got up and closed and locked the bedroom door and went back and sat across from Poppy. Her face seemed all flushed and she was so very, very nervous.

"I think you were right, about William liking me." She began.

"How was I right?"

"The flowers.... The presents.... The touching..."

"Wait... I knew about the flowers and stuff, what about touching?"

"Last week I was going through all the arrows, looking to see which ones were good to use and which ones needed some repair. We are supposed to go hunting tomorrow. Well, I was going through them and he came over and was talking to me, I didn't pay attention and I nicked my hand on one of the arrow heads, well it really hurt and I kind of made myself jump a little and drop the arrows. I was bleeding and all but it wasn't that bad, it just startled me; well, he got all worried and he took my hand and wiped the blood off with his shirt and stuff, but he didn't let go of my hand, he just held it gently, he just looked at my hand for a while, and then leaned down and kissed my fingertips. Well... I freaked out, I pulled my hand back and... ran away." She just about whispered. In my mind, I thought the whole story was the most romantic thing I had ever heard, why could Poppy possibly be so disturbed about it?

"Do you not like William, is that why it bothers you?" I gently asked.

"No... that's not it."

"Did it make you feel uncomfortable?"

"No... I... I liked it, and I like him, but..."

"But what is it?" I said resting my hand on her knee to comfort her and to soothe her rising nerves.

"Why would he like me? Me, of all people! I should be the last person on earth he should like!" she exclaimed.

"Why do you say that?"

"I'm... I'm un lovable." She said with a tear falling from her eye.

"That's impossible. Everyone is lovable if they allow themselves to be. I love you, Poppy, everyone here on the farm loves you."

"Everyone and everything I have ever loved has been taken away from me." She said balling her fists up in anger in the skirt of her dress.

"That was then, this is now. Every day since you have arrived we have told you that no one will ever hurt you here."

"I know… I know."

"To me, you have proven to be the kindest and truest friend I have ever had. With you I feel that you could never lie or intentionally hurt a fly."

"But I have hurt things before, I hurt people, I beat people, I've probably even killed someone." She began to sob.

"What you did then… what you did when you were part of those gangs, that's not who you truly are, you had to do those things to live. We all go into survival mode and for a very long time you were stuck in survival mode, doing what you had to do to survive. The only thing you can do now is beg and pray for forgiveness. You know what happened back then was bad and terrible, but that is not who you are. If you keep dwelling on what once was, then you will continue to feel the pain of what had happened."

"What do I do?"

"Tomorrow… you go hunting with William. Be nice, don't run away anymore. You like him and he likes you. If it is meant to be, it shall be." I said leaning over and giving her a hug.

"Ok… I won't hide anymore." She laughed, someone began to knock on our door. I got up and opened it to see Connor standing there panting and all excited.

"What?" I said looking at him all confused.

"Come quick!" he said grabbing my hand and pulling me from the room. I turned back only briefly to wave Poppy on. She followed as Connor dragged me through the house and out the door towards the field. We stopped just at the edge of the field and looked out.

"What is it?" I asked Connor trying to make out what he was so excited about. The sun had just dipped below the horizon, leaving the sky a shade of deep pink that faded into blackness. William was out standing in the middle of the field, he stood still like a sculpture watching as we did. I didn't notice it immediately, it wasn't something I was looking for, but it had been surrounding me the whole time. Fireflies. They were everywhere, blinking and flying about. I had never seen so many in my entire life. I had seen scenes in movies where two characters ran through a field and fireflies flew and glittered in all directions, but I never knew for such scenes to actually be real.

"I've never seen so many before!" Amelia said running through the open field with her arms spread out as if she were flying. Peter followed after her with a butterfly net and a mason jar with the goal of catching a few. Amelia and Peter managed to capture a good amount of fire flies that they watched in the jar with bewilderment, holding it up to the sky and tapping on the sides of the glass.

We ran to where William stood, with fireflies zipping up from the knee high grass that we ran through. It was all rather exciting and so very beautiful. Connor made a game of it, running this way and that while I chased after him. When I finally caught up to him, he pulled me down into the grass and we rolled a bit, laughing the entire time. We stayed lying there for a while, watching the fireflies fly above us. A short distance away, I observed Poppy bend down and pick a small flower out of the grass, she slowly walked over to William and held it out to him. He smiled and took it from her and put it behind her ear and placed his hand on her shoulder. They stood there for a long time, softly talking to one another, while Connor and I continued to lie on the ground concealed by the grass. It would be one of the first blissful nights of that summer.

21.
Volunteers

Poppy and William went hunting on the day they had said they would, they left acting slightly awkward towards one another, and came back acting as if they had been in each other's lives forever. Within a matter of weeks they went from being slightly estranged to being completely and utterly enthralled with one another. They were perfect for one another; I couldn't have pictured any two people who were more ideal for one another. William and Poppy were always managing to find some sort of activity that they could do together, almost like a little date. Connor and I would join in on the fun with them, going down to the river, climbing trees in the woods, or just walking into town together.

There happened to be a day when we walked into town that we were greeted by more people than usual. Contrary to what we had all originally thought, there were more survivors in the area than we had anticipated. Two or three more families showed up in town, carrying items that they could trade for supplies for their continued survival. William, Poppy, Amelia, Connor, and I sat in the town green just watching the new families come and go around from place to place trying to get supplies. William and Connor knew the families, and were quite delighted to see that they had survived not only the plague, but the winter as well. While in town we were offered random items to take back with us to the farm. One man offered us an old dirt bike, which Connor and William were quick to accept. Connor and William zipped around on that dirt bike, laughing and joking around like they were toddlers. We just about tore a path through the crisp grass in the town green doing so, but it was so worth it.

An old man approached William and Connor and began talking to them, pointing back over to a house in the distance and then pointing back at Connor and William. Once he had gone, Poppy and I asked the boys what that all was about. Apparently the old man had been a bus driver for the schools before the outbreak, and now he had a fairly new school bus parked in his back yard and he wanted to know if the boys would want to do anything with it.

"What would we do with a school bus?" Poppy asked.

"I don't know, I'm sure we can think of something." He said wrapping his arm around her waist.

"Where's Amelia?" I asked looking around to see where she had gone off to. We spotted her siting on the front steps of the library talking to a boy.

"Hey! It's Brady!" cheered William.

"Brady? Brady Campbell? Are you serious?" Connor asked in disbelief.

"Look!" William said pointing over to where Amelia was. Brady looked to be about William's age, and as tall and muscular as William was, Brady proved to be even bigger. He stood a good three inches taller than William and Connor and had this deep bellowing voice. He was sure nice to look at, and no doubt Amelia felt the same.

"Look who I found!" Amelia giggled when we all came over.

"Brady!" William and Connor both said at the same time before jumping on their old friend. The three boys started talking for a while and the puzzle as to who exactly Brady Campbell was began to work itself out. The Campbell family had a single cabin off a good half hour from town, due to the fact that the cabin had been so isolated even before the outbreak, it was always self-sustaining, with a well, working fireplaces, and cast iron stoves. When electricity got knocked out, it wasn't a problem for them at all, they cooked over open fire and made due where they could. Like our family, the Campbell's could hunt and grow what they needed to eat, but the winter had been harsh, and they did take some losses, including their grandmother and a dear cousin. Brady seemed to be a genuinely nice and an outgoing guy, he could make all of us laugh, and he was a great story teller. We could have stayed talking to Brady for hours, but we all had to go home, including Brady who had to take a half hour hike back to his home.

"Dude, you'll have to round up the Campbell's and bring them down to the farm, we'll have a good old fashioned cook out and we will see if we can continue our family tradition of crushing the Campbell's at horse shoes." William joked, slapping Brady on the back.

"Yes, please do visit." Amelia chimed in.

"I'll make it a point." Brady said looking down at Amelia and smiling. On our way home, Poppy and I couldn't help but poke fun at Amelia and her obvious crush on Brady. She was like a giddy school girl, turning bright red every time we mentioned his name.

Ms. Elizabeth was furious that we brought home a dirt bike; she kept insisting that one of the boys would fall off and break their neck, but they paid her no mind, and kept zipping around the house to annoy her. Just as it was about to get dark, Connor brought the bike right up in front of me and told me to get on. I hadn't yet been on the bike, so I was a bit nervous at first, but once Connor zipped off and I had my chin practically digging into the back of his shoulder, I felt only slightly safer. Connor took the bike down the drive way and instead of making a left, which is the way we would normally go to get into town, he made a right and took me down the road a way I had yet to go since arriving.

"Where are you taking me?" I shouted over the sound of the bike and the wind that whipped by our ears.

"To the top of the world!" He said as he made the bike go even faster. I squealed a little bit just as we began to climb a steep hill that seemed to keep going up and up. After a while I could hear the motor of the bike struggling and then we seemed to start to slow down. I had had my face hidden, squished against Connor's back, but when we slowed to a stop, I lifted my head up to see that we sat on top of this vast hill that overlooked a valley. In the orange and dimming light of the sunset, it all was so beautiful. The way the sun hit the budding treetops and the deep blue of the sky that framed it all. We got off the bike and Connor parked it off to the side of the road as I just stared down into the valley. Through the trees I could see the red structure of a barn, and a field of some sorts.

"Is that another farm down there?" I asked pointing down.

"Yeah, it used to be a dairy farm, the owners of it contracted the plague, and it's abandoned now." Connor solemnly said.

"How sad." I said.

"I don't remember this view, did we see it when we came up here?"

"We did, well, William and I did. I had to carry you up the hill, you were so sick, remember?" he said taking a piece of my hair to twirl in his fingers.

"Oh, yeah, that's right."

"I love this view, but it's my favorite especially in the fall. All the trees are all shades of red and orange and it just looks amazing from up here. In the winter, these trees that kind of grow over the road here," he said motioning to the branches that canopied the road, "They get icicles on them that glitter when the moon light hits them just right." I couldn't help but smile, Connor was quite adorable when he described things he cared about. He would get all enthusiastic and would use his arms and hands to motion while he was talking. He turned back to look at me and got all serious.

"What? Why are you smiling?" He asked

"No reason." I said

"Are you making fun of me?" he asked

"No! It's just, you get so excited when you talk about something you care about, and it makes me smile." I said; the sun was just beginning to get to that point in the sky that a red hue was beginning to blanket everything, signaling the nearness of the sunset. There was a large, old tree with a wide welcoming trunk at the crest of the hill where Connor made himself comfortable and I joined him. Together we watched the colors of the sky change until there was nothing left but a pink line on the horizon.

That night, Poppy and I stayed up until very late, whispering under the blankets of our beds. The rest of the house had gone to sleep and were probably deep into their slumbers by now, but Poppy and I were restless.

"We should sneak out." Poppy whispered.

"And where would we go?" I whispered back.

"We can go to yours and Connor's little date spot you were talking about. I can only imagine how beautiful the stars would look from there."

"Ms. Elizabeth probably sleeps with one eye opened."

"Well… that's what will make it fun." She said throwing the sheets off of her head and getting up. In the darkness, I could hear her fumbling around for the box of matches we kept on the night stand.

She struck one and lit out little oil lantern and gave me a mischievous smile. She went over to the window and looked out before she opened it and leaned as far out as she could.

"The trellis, we can climb down." She said.

"Alright, let's do this." I said getting up and putting my shoes on. As silently and swiftly as we could, we climbed down the trellis and ran across the grass towards the barn. The night was so very clear and the stars were twinkling. It was the night of the new moon, so there was no orb to guide us on our way.

Together, Poppy and I stole the bike and pushed it down the drive way and down the road for a bit before starting it up. Poppy was and would always be braver than me, so she drove and I held on in the back as we whipped down the road in the darkness. The bike was well equipped with a single headlight to guide us on our way, and soon we reached the top of the hill. Poppy turned off the bike and we parked it off to the side of the road.

"Wow, this is amazing." Poppy said. Like gauze spread over infinite blackness, the stars lay thick and glittering in the sky. The denseness of their glittering was enough to light the land. The soft chirps of crickets cheeped in the silence while Poppy and I sat in the middle of the road, on the two yellow lines that ran down its center. As to how long we planned on staying out, we did not know.

"If I told you that William told me he loved me the other day, would you think it was crazy?" Poppy said.

"No, I don't know. Did he say that?" I asked.

"Yes, and I didn't know what to say." She said.

"You didn't know what to say because you don't love him yet?"

"I don't know. I mean is it possible for someone to love another after only knowing each other for a couple of months and only being their girlfriend for a couple of weeks?" she asked.

"In a different time, I would have said it was impossible, and I would have said William was crazy; but life has changed, and we have changed with it. It's very well possible for William to love you even though it has only been a short amount of time, for him there is no other person in the world who he cares about as much as you;

besides his family of course." I answered after taking a few moments to think.

"I suppose the rest of our lives will be spent here this way on the farm anyhow." Poppy said solemnly.

"They say the world was a big place, but looking back, it seemed so small. With computers and cell phones and televisions we could connect with the other side of the world in a matter of seconds. Now, I think the world has become much bigger, there are things we can rediscover and explore." I said.

"You may want to travel and discover things, but I am perfectly happy staying right here and never going any farther than this hill for the rest of my life. The world was cruel to me before the outbreak, and for a short time after. Being on the farm with William and you and Connor, and the rest of the family; I feel like I now know what true paradise feels like."

It was true, what Poppy had said. Despite all the trials and hardships each of us has gone through up to this point, life had truly become more fulfilling than it had been prior to our arrival to the farm.

Poppy and I stayed out on the road until the sky began to lighten and turn a shade of violet I had never seen before. Just as we decided it would be appropriate to get back to the farm, Poppy spotted two bright lights coming up the road. From our vantage point we could see for what I estimated to be at least three miles down into the valley. The two bright lights turned into four and then six, it was clear that a group of vehicles was making their way up the mountain, and Poppy and I were in their path. We quickly jumped up and pushed the bike into the woods and hid it behind a tree while she and I hid behind another. We sat so that we would not be seen from the road, but so that we ourselves could see what was to pass.

My heart raced in my chest as the seconds passed and the sound of the engines of the vehicles could be heard coming up the hill. Poppy grasped hold of my arm and squeezed tightly. They were three black Jeeps that came over the crest of the hill; they were going at a decent pace as they drove down the road towards town. On each of the sides of the Jeep there was the insignia of the CDC also with the label "Volunteer Research" under it. The vehicles came and went without even noticing our presence. Once the sound of their engines faded away, Poppy and I quickly got on the bike and road back to the farm. In my mind I anticipated seeing the three Jeeps circled around the house with men in black uniforms dragging William and Connor away, but that wasn't the case. There were no more signs of the Jeeps or of anyone else at all. We put the bike back where we found it. We climbed our way back up to our room and climbed back into bed as if we had never left. We agreed that we would not breathe a word about what we had seen until we knew for sure where those Jeeps had gone. Poppy and I soon fell asleep, but it only lasted a few hours before our blankets were rudely pulled from our backs and were awoken by the sound of a clanging pot.

"Rise and shine ladies!" Ms. Elizabeth sang.

"Ugh! It's so early!" Poppy snapped.

"Well if you went to bed like you were supposed to, instead of sneaking out, maybe this wouldn't have been an issue!" She said with a huge smile on her face, "Now get up and go get the eggs from the chickens, and I'll be nice and you can go back to bed." Poppy and I both groaned as we rolled out of bed, not even caring to put on our shoes, we just went out to the chicken coup and tried to work the fastest we could to gather all the eggs we could find. My body wanted me to go back to bed, my brain was hurting, and my eyes were constantly trying to shut, but we managed to get all the eggs back to Ms. Elizabeth. With the eggs safely in the kitchen, Poppy and I made the long climb back up the stairs to our room. Along the way we passed William, Connor, and Peter who all looked a bit confused as to why Poppy and I were completely out of it.

"I don't think I'll ever pull an all-nighter again." Poppy said as she flopped back on to her bed.

"Me neither, never again." I said as I pulled the covers up to my ears. I don't know exactly how long we slept, but I do know that when we were woken up again, we felt fully rested. We woke to the sounds of someone running through the house and hearing someone yelling in the distance. My first reaction was to just roll over and try to fall asleep again, but Poppy threw her blankets off of her and stood right up and ran to the window.

"There's someone here." She said leaning out the window, she rushed and grabbed a sweater which she put on over her night gown and rushed out of the room. She was gone before I could even fumble out of bed and get a sweater on myself. Everyone had gathered in the front entry way at the bottom of the staircase with Jonathan and Luke standing right outside the door, and William and Connor standing a short distance behind them.

"Good afternoon!" I heard an unfamiliar voice call.

"Afternoon." Jonathan said very bluntly.

"How are you folks doing today?" The unfamiliar voice said.

"We are doing well. What can I help you with?" Luke said.

"My name is Thomas Phillips; I am a volunteer researcher working for the CDC. My team and I arrived in your town early this morning." I tried to step closer to see if I could see what was going on. I stepped further down the stairs, past Ms. Elizabeth, Charlotte, Cora, and Amelia who was all huddled together on the bottom stair scared stiff. Poppy was right up against the window peering out through the curtain. I went to join her, but Connor and William both snapped their fingers and told us to get away from the window.

"Where's Peter?" William whispered.

"I don't know." Amelia said, as Luke and Jonathan continued to talk to the stranger. Suddenly the talking stopped and Luke called out to his son. We heard Peter's footsteps come up the front porch and then he made his way into the house and sat down on the floor farthest away from the door.

"Where the heck where you?" William snapped at his younger cousin.

"I was down by the ducks." Peter said.

"Didn't you hear us call?" William said.

"Yeah, but I didn't think anything was happening."

"You listen when we call!" William said giving Peter a slap behind his head.

"William!" Cora snapped at her nephew.

"Everything is alright, there's no danger." Jonathan said returning into the house. We all sighed a bit of relief and we all went out on to the front porch to face the stranger. He was a man dressed in kakis and a black polo shirt. As we all came out of the house one by one, I could tell by the look on his face that he was not expecting so many people to be living in one place.

"Wow… there are a lot of you. Eleven of you… that's amazing." This Thomas Phillips said.

"What's it to you?" William said defensively

"William…" Charlotte said cautioning her son.

"Well, let me give a proper introduction to all of you then. My name is Thomas Phillips, I am a volunteer researcher for the CDC. I came to this area with 9 others in my team in hopes to make an estimate as to how many survivors there are in the region, as well as to collect stories and accounts of survival, and data to help our research."

"And what is your research exactly? You must have a goal or theory in which you would need research for." I said.

"That leads me to my second point," he began, "As some of you may know, the original goal of the CDC was to contain the plague by providing protection and fencing off large metropolitan areas. Unfortunately, due to the aggressiveness of the plague and the hostility of some gangs, the CDC lost the battle to protect the cities. Officials for the CDC retreated into their well secured and well-fortified Infirmaries where they have kept and continue to keep our leaders in science, technology, and medicine in their custody. Before the outbreak I myself was a medical student, because I had not yet received my doctorate or any recognition in the field of science or medicine yet, I escaped the CDC's draft of doctors and scientists. After the draft and abandonment of the CDC, a few colleagues of mine got together and proposed a volunteer initiative. Since the CDC wasn't going out to see how the survivors were fairing, we thought we would. The CDC officials are scared silly, they won't leave their little infirmaries, so they funded us with equipment and supplies to do the research." Thomas finished.

"You still didn't answer my question, what exactly is the research and data for?" I asked again.

"We have a hypothesis, which will be covered tomorrow at our official town meeting. This is why I came here today, to invite you to that town meeting tomorrow at three o'clock. I and two others will be speaking tomorrow and every detail as to what we will be doing here in the town and area for the next three days will be covered. I do hope you will cooperate. We are not here to draft, or take anything from people who have obviously worked very hard to survive, and we are not here to make any sort of reports that might put the community in jeopardy or danger. We are here to help, and make life safer and more secure for the future."

"Thank you for coming, we will be there tomorrow." Luke said.

"Thank you for being cooperative." Thomas said before turning away and walking back down to his jeep. It was just like that, within a matter of a few minutes that we were all reminded of the horrors of the plague, the power of the CDC, and that outside the farm and the town, things were not a paradise.

22.

Town Meetings

The little library that sat near the town's center was completely jammed packed at the time of the meeting. We had seen the team of 10 CDC volunteers walking around town and conversing with some of the people here, but it was still very unclear as to why exactly they had come and what exactly they were going to do. We all gathered into the cramped library, taking seats where we could, trying to get a good view of the podium that was set up for the leaders of the volunteers to speak. When it began Thomas Phillips got up onto the podium and just introduced himself just in case no one knew who he was, and then he went on about the history of the CDC Volunteer program.

The program was still in its infancy at six months old, and so far the team has only covered western Massachusetts in their travels. They were based out of the massive Infirmary in Amherst, Massachusetts and that was where they were getting their funding and supplies. Thomas also went on to state that once they return to Amherst they will report that there is a large population of survivors and that supplies would be sent to us so that we would better be able to protect ourselves and help each other.

The second speaker to get up on the podium was Mark Downs, he was a medical student like Thomas before the outbreak, but even before that he had been in the Marines. Mark brought a lot of points and suggestions to the table when he talked to us as a town and as a community. He informed us that of all the small settlements he has seen so far, we were the largest and healthiest. However, he did inform us that a threat from a gang was a very high possibility for us. Using maps, Mark showed us where gangs made their own settlements. He explained to us that according to his resources, these gangs would remain sedentary for the spring and summer months, but come fall they would be on the move again searching for towns and areas where they could claim food and supplies for themselves. We were in no threat at that very moment, but we would be in the future. We were told that the CDC would supply us with more building supplies to help build up our walls even more, we would also receive weapons and vehicles that would aid us during an attack.

The third and final speaker to take to the podium was a woman by the name of Abigail Blake. She started off by rattling off a bunch of numbers that related to population counts and mortality rates and blah, blah, blah; but then she stopped and got really serious.

"Although all the research that has been done at the CDC infirmaries has yet to yield the cause of this terrible plague, we have pin pointed the starting point of the plague." She said, there was a soft rumbling of voices in the audience, although this wasn't a cure or an answer, it was a breakthrough.

"We've managed to pinpoint the origin of the plague to a couple of Midwest towns at the start of spring two years ago. They were very isolated cases that took out whole families and eventually whole communities. The original blame was on well water poisoning due to nearby factories, but our further tests proved that all to be false."

"Now that you know this origin, is it possible to trace it back further to see the exact source?" Someone called out in the audience.

"That is our goal. We have a team out in the Midwest now investigating those first few communities, but our goal here today is to not only to solve this mystery, but preserve the future." She said.

"Mr. Thomas mentioned to my family yesterday that there was a hypothesis that you were working on, and that that would be covered today." I shouted out.

"Yes, yes, that is true," Abigail began, "Through all the tests and trials and research that has already been done, there is a whole list of things that have already been ruled out as to what the plague could be. The plague was not caused by a bacteria, virus, fungi, cancer, parasite, or toxin; frankly we still don't know what the plague is. What we wish to do as independent researchers is look at the places the CDC didn't look at; we have a strong feeling that the cause of the plague is a matter of lifestyle on the modern human rather than any sort of other issue. We do know that the plague has affected nearly every modern country in the world, what we find unusual is that this plague is not found in any third world or underdeveloped countries. Our focus is to study how individuals were living before, during, and after the outbreak to hopefully crack the code." She said, this was all new information to us, and it was all very interesting. We were then told that the volunteers wished to interview each and every person in the town as well as take harmless samples to study. The interviewing process would start the very next day. The nearly two hour meeting ended and we were told to register with some of the other volunteers to find out what time we ought to report for our interviews and sample collections.

On our way back to the town, Amelia went off and met up with Brady who was just lingering by the country store, and William urged Connor, Poppy and I to follow him to go see that school bus the old man was talking about the other day. This school bus was just sitting in the back yard of the old man's house taking up potential garden space. When he saw William coming, he quickly got the keys of the bus and ran them out to us.

"Here, I knew you would come and take it!" The old man said to William.

"I don't know, let me look at it and I'll see." William laughed. The bus was in great condition, it had only been used for half of a school year before the outbreak and the smell of fresh paint and plastic was still strong on the inside. William walked up and down the aisle of seats on the inside of the bus, counting with his fingers and taking measurements with his arm.

"Hey, what are you doing?" Poppy asked.

"There would be a lot of room in here if we took out the seats." William said.

"Your grandmother is going to kill you if you come home with this bus, she's still fuming about the bike." Poppy said.

"I can pop a hole in the ceiling here and run a little chimney pipe and a stove can sit right here." William said.

"Are you even listening to me?" Poppy said.

"Yeah, yeah, Gran will be mad, but we aren't going to drive this thing around." He said.

"Well then what are we going to do with it?"

"I'm going to take all the seats out. Put a small wood burning stove in over there, I can run a pipe through the floor and connect it to the well and we can have a sink." William said pointing to different areas of the bus. Poppy just looked so confused, as was Connor and I.

"What the heck are you talking about?" Poppy said a bit frustrated.

"It'll be our house, a bus house." He said to her.

"This? A house? What?" she was very flustered.

"Our house." He said seriously, Poppy just sat there on one of the bus seats and started wide eyed and blankly at William.

"We could get married and stuff, and this can be our little house." William said softly, a small "aww" escaped me and I just looked back over at Poppy, who was just flabbergasted and wide eyed. She then quickly stood up and left the bus and began walking back towards the center of town. I stood up too, and saw that Connor and William were both just looking stupidly at each other.

"Was that supposed to be a proposal?" I asked William.

"Yeah." He sheepishly said.

"Give me 20 minutes, and she'll say yes." I said as I went after Poppy. She had walked and ran all the way to the gate of the wall and was a few yards down the road by the time I caught up with her.

"Pop!" I called out.

"No… no… leave me alone." She said waving me away.

"Poppy, what's wrong?" I said placing my hand on her shoulder.

"I can't… I couldn't…" She stammered.

"What can't you do?" I asked.

"I can't marry him." She said.

"Why not?"

"I'm no good… I'm broken." Poppy just had this blank look on her face, she was there, she was talking to me, but at the same time she wasn't all there. Poppy did have her moments, she had her moments when she would disappear into herself and draw this blank stare. At night she would have nightmares and would just up and leave the room to walk around the house. She was cracked but she was not broken.

"You're not broken. You are a little scratched, we are all a little scratched, and life as of now has scratched us all really bad. But it's nothing a little polishing can't fix." Poppy just covered her face with her hands and shook her head, I was beginning to lose her, she was disappearing into herself, and I was afraid that if I pushed too hard I would lose her completely.

"You said you never wanted to go farther than that hill the other night," I said pointing down the road, "You love William very much, anyone can see it, and he loves you too." I said.

"I do love William." She said dropping her hands from her face.

"He was going to propose to you."

"I figured."

"So what do you say?" Poppy took a deep breath in, ran her fingers through her chin length hair, and turned around to head back into town. She was gaining her composure and slowly becoming the normal Poppy again. We didn't even make it back to the boys before we saw them driving the bus towards us. Poppy just laughed as they stopped and allowed us to board, William beeped the horn and waved for Amelia to get on too. Amelia looked a bit frustrated to have to leave Brady, but she bid him farewell and came on the bus with us. William drove us all the way home and parked the bus behind the barn, and that was where it was going to stay.

"I'm going to like this bus. I'm sure little curtains for all the windows will be easy to sew." Poppy said once the engine of the bus was off.

"Really?" William said a bit shocked.

"Yeah, when do we get started?" Poppy said, William just stood up from the driver's seat and literally picked Poppy up off the ground and kissed her he was so happy.

"Wait… what's going on?" Amelia said.

"William and Poppy are going to get married." Connor said.

"Really? No way!" Amelia shouted.

"What the heck is this!" We heard Ms. Elizabeth shouting. The rest of the family had left and gone back to the farm as soon as the town meeting was over. With her apron on and her face all red, Ms Elizabeth was charging at the bus, all up in arms and ready to yell at us.

"No… I want it gone. William Edward Wilde, what has gotten into you?" she said as we all climbed down from the bus.

"Aw, gran, you don't like it?" he said with his arm around Poppy.

"I want it gone."

"But it's my house." William said.

"What do you mean your house?" She said with her hands on her hips. By that time the rest of the family had gathered around, with Luke and Jonathan busy checking out the tires of the bus.

"I asked Poppy to marry me, she said yes." William said confidently. Charlotte and Cora let out little sighs of happiness and Cora ran up and pulled Poppy into a hug. Ms. Elizabeth calmed down and didn't complain anymore about the bus. Instead she too hugged Poppy and William and declared she was going to bake a pie to celebrate.

It was agreed upon that work on the bus to convert it into a house would start the very next day, and that when we all went into town the next day as well, we would see if there was a way for William and Poppy to be married within two weeks. William was confident that he would have the bus completely finished by then, and Cora was determined to sew the most beautiful wedding dress there ever was for Poppy.

23.

Questions

William woke Connor and Peter up really early the next morning to get work started on the bus. Their first goal was to remove all the seats. Poppy was rather bubbly about it, it was as if overnight she turned into a blushing bride. By the afternoon, at least half of the seats were gone, and it was then time to go back into town for the interviews. Connor and I went together to get interviewed, we both assumed we could just sit together for the process, but in typical CDC fashion, everything had rules and we were separated. Before any questions were asked of me, the volunteer that was assigned to me took all the samples that were needed. He cut a few strands of hair from my head, swabbed a cotton ball inside my mouth, and drew a vial of blood. I picked at the band aid that covered the vein on the inside of my forearm as he got the paperwork ready for me to answer all the questions. I was suddenly growing very nervous and antsy. The first few questions were very basic, like my name, where I was born, where I was living prior to the outbreak, and if I had been working. All the questions that were asked were lifestyle questions, like what sort of diet I had, if I exercised, and what sort of illnesses I had ever experienced. At times I felt as though the questions were repetitive, but everything was all very thorough.

"Could you describe to your best ability your own personal account of your experience during the spread of the plague?" He asked.

"It was all very bearable at first. After the fences went up it was a little scary, but life went on. We were confined to the small area that we had in our region, but it was livable. I still had my family and a few friends, and then I met Connor. For a while I didn't see anyone who had contracted the plague, but it did eventually start to rear its ugly head. My father contracted it, he had been a doctor prior to the outbreak, and so had my mother. My mother sent me to go to this black market of sorts that was operating on the edge of our region, I had to get medicine for my dad, it was there that she also went and got a vial of adrenaline. My father didn't have to suffer anymore after that, my mother administered it to him and that was it. After that my mother was drafted and I haven't seen her or heard from her since.

The food started running out and winter was coming. I lost a lot of weight and I was very sick, but I still had Connor who faithfully looked after me and cared for me. Then the gangs came and it was all very, very bad. I saw my best friend Molly get killed, and I thought for sure I would die just like her; but Connor and I made it out and we made it north. We met up with William and just made our way here, on the way I got very sick and had to be carried, I don't remember much until I woke up at the farm." I said, the man who was interviewing me just scribbled out everything I had said onto his notepad and then looked up and smiled at me.

"Your mother, you said she is in custody?"

"Yes, she is." I said.

"What is her name?"

"Christine Lancaster." I watched as the man took out a tablet and type in my mothers name into the device. He scrolled for a while before he clicked on something and then turned the screen towards me.

"Is this her?" I stared at the screen in amazement, there she was, my mother, her picture right there on the screen in front of me. I covered my mouth with my hands and fought back tears.

"Where is she?" I choked out.

"She is at the infirmary that is located on the former Umass Amherst campus here in Massachusetts."

"Is she alive?" I watched as he scrolled some more and sighed before looking back up at me and then down to the tablet.

"The report here states that in December she volunteered herself for clinical studies on the plague. The clinical studies were inconclusive and had major side effects. She is alive but is living more so as a patient at the infirmary rather than a doctor. The official report says that: 'due to an immense amount of depression, Dr. Christine Lancaster donated herself with the hopes of dying in the process. The loss of her husband and daughter threw the doctor into a depression. Dr. Lancaster's survived clinical trials but lives in the ward as a resident. She has lost the function of her left arm, and an experimental brain surgery left her unable to speak.'" At that point I was crying. My mother thought me to be dead, and due to that she had tried to cease her own suffering. I felt this immense amount of guilt on my shoulders that I could not shake. A dagger plunged deep into my heart and turned as I thought about how my mother was suffering as an incapacitated vegetable.

"I am alive… she must be told. Is there no way for her to be released?" I begged.

"As of right now, the best I can do is update Dr. Lancaster's official file to report that her child was found alive and hopefully she will be informed."

"Please… please do that." I said.

"I shall. Mona, this concludes the whole interview today. Our next step is to send all this data back to our home base and then report to the CDC so that we can get the town supplies and protection. In the process, I will personally try and locate your mother within Amherst." He said.

"Thank you, thank you so much. What did you say your name was?" I asked

"Mark Shaw."

"Thank you Mr. Shaw." I said getting up from my seat and running out. Connor was waiting right outside for me. I just ran to him and buried my face into his chest as I cried. I told him all about how my mother was alive and what had happened to her.

"If I could, I would take you right now and we would storm that infirmary and bring her here." Connor said running his fingers through my hair.

"I know you would."

"Please do not be too sad, it hurts me when you are sad." He said wiping the tears from my eyes. I was having a bit of a hard time getting a hold of myself, the tears would not stop coming. Connor just guided me away and we left town. We just started to make our way back to the farm. The whole time he tried to make me laugh by reminding me of things or trying to tell me a joke, but I just was so unhappy.

"Everything will be alright, Mona, I promise, and I've never broken a promise. Please stop crying, please." He said just as we walked our way up the driveway to the farm. I wiped my face dry and just looked up at him, he was right, everything will be alright, Connor has never made a promise he couldn't keep. I wrapped my arms around him and buried my face into his chest again and he squeezed me back.

"I love you very much Mona, I hope you know that."

"I've always known that, but it's the first time you've said it." I said.

"With everything that's been happening with William and Poppy I didn't want you to think that you were left out when it came to all the love. Not for one moment do I want you to think that since Poppy and William are getting married that I don't want to do the same one day."

"But just not now."

"Just not now, I am extremely happy with the way things are just like this, nothing more, nothing less."

"And I am very happy just like this too."

"By the time the CDC volunteers come back, Poppy and William will be married and we will know more about your mother, let's look forward to all of that." Connor took my hand and guided me over towards the barn. We climbed the stairs up to the loft and he opened up the loft door so that we could see out and look over all the land. Together we sat, uninterrupted by the others. We watched the sky and the clouds change, Connor held me close to him and left little kisses on my cheeks and shoulders, making sure I wasn't going to cry again.

24.
Sewing

As William and the boys worked extremely hard to get the bus remodeled into an ideal home, we ladies worked tirelessly to put together a wedding. A wedding dress and bridesmaid dresses needed to be made. Word had even gotten out in the town that there would be a wedding soon. The people in the town were rather excited about it, to the point that the level of hysteria reached levels that were close to the levels reached for a royal wedding. Everything had to be brought together by the end of the two weeks. Poppy and William would be married on a Saturday by Mr. Wilson, the town's only surviving lawyer. The location of the ceremony would be inside the library. The original plan was to then come back to the farm and just enjoy a good dinner, but the people of the town had their own ideas, and insisted upon having a full out reception in the town green.

It would end up being a splendid and beautiful Spring wedding, wildflowers dotted just about every inch of the land, where they had come from was a mystery, but they made everything so beautiful. The temperature was perfect for everything, and there was this feeling of complete balance among us all. Cora and Charlotte would be the ones working on Poppy's wedding dress; they planned on keeping it a total secret until the wedding day. The rest of us, Poppy included, worked tirelessly on the bridesmaid dresses. Poppy wanted both Amelia and I in the wedding, with me as Poppy's maid of honor. I was very honored by the gesture, and I did my best to be a right and proper maid of honor given the circumstances. With the world such a changed place, bachelorette parties, bridal showers, and spa days were now a thing of the past.

While we were working on the actual wedding, William and the boys kept the bus a top secret, not allowing Poppy to go anywhere near it. I was allowed to see it one day when it was very close to being done. With all the seats removed the bus was very large and spacious inside. William had covered the metal floor of the bus with a smooth wooden floor, they had taken a very small old wood stove that was in storage under the barn and placed it at the center of the bus with the little chimney going up through the ceiling. It had not yet been decorated at all, and it was still raw in appearances, but I just knew Poppy would love it.

William proudly talked about the plans he still had to complete for the bus. He talked about needing to get a bed, which would sit at the very back of the bus, he wanted a little table and chairs where he and Poppy could eat a little breakfast together, and he wanted a small sofa. All of these things William was able to obtain through the generosity of the people in the town who were very eager to give William anything and everything he wanted.

It was all so stressful to pull everything together, but as it neared closer to the date, we began to feel more comfortable and carefree. The boys had their own version of a bachelor party by going hunting for a day. While they were gone, I insisted that we put the sewing needles down for the day and just goof around.

"I don't even want all of this." Poppy said throwing down the soft yellow fabric that would be a bridesmaid dress. "It's all Cora, Charlotte, and Ms. Elizabeth's doing. I would much rather go down to Mr. Wilson's little house, sign a paper, and be done with it." Poppy said.

"But where is the magic and romance in that?" Amelia asked, "Before the outbreak, didn't you ever dream about having a big wedding?"

"No." Poppy said.

"You didn't?"

"I used to…. until a knock came at our door from the Coast Guard saying they found the wreckage of my father's boat floating around in the ocean. After that, there was no point in dreaming about something that was pointless to have without someone to walk you down the aisle."

"Poppy." I said sadly.

"I never thought I would get married."

"Well there's no aisle in the library, you just kind of walk in…" Amelia said, obviously trying to be helpful.

"I was thinking I would just walk with you guys, ya know, all three of us can walk in together."

"Really, Poppy, is that what you want?" I said putting what I had been sewing down, and standing up.

"Yeah, why not? You guys are like my sister's now." She said with a smile on her face.

"The bride has spoken, it shall be done!" Amelia said getting up and throwing her hands in the air. We decided to spend the day going down to the river and swimming. Amelia knew about a section of the river where there was a large rock you could jump off of into a very deep part of the water. We spent a few hours climbing up the rock and then jumping back down again. When we were tired, we laid on top of the boulder and sunbathed until our clothes were dry. When the sun started to get low in the sky, we decided to make our way back to the farm.

When we arrived back, we saw that the boys too had come home. Hanging on the side of the barn, waiting to be cleaned and skinned were three rabbits, two turkeys, and one deer. The boys had had a good day. They were smelly, covered in dirt, had stains on their elbows and knees, and their hair was all a mess. Poppy and I's first reaction to the boys was to grimace and turn in the opposite direction from them. But they pulled us to them and made sure we got a good whiff of how bad they smelled.

We didn't have to endure their torment much longer, because dinner was soon ready and Ms. Elizabeth refused to let them sit at the dining room table all messy. After dinner, William allowed Poppy and the rest of us to go see the finished bus. As the sun started to set we all climbed up into the bus, led by Poppy to see how it all turned out; William managed to make a home out of a school bus, it was absolutely beautiful. He had painted the walls a light rosy color, the wood floor he installed himself was smooth and polished with wax, and he hung curtains and built a table and chairs. There was a small baby blue couch and a bed that sat on its box spring on the floor near the back of the bus.

Poppy was brought to tears when she saw the work completed. It was everything and more that she had wanted. We were all equally impressed, the wedding was now only three days away, and with little work left to be done, the family as a whole was growing excited. With nothing much left to do other than to finish sewing a few articles of clothing, we gathered in the living room to start reading another book as a family. The book that was chosen was chosen by Peter and so we began to read The Fellowship of the Ring out loud, taking turns as we had done with Pride and Prejudice. Connor and I lounged together on the couch while Peter read the first chapter of the book and the rest of the family sat listening while doing other activities.

"What does your dress look like?" Connor whispered in my ear

"My dress?"

"Your bridesmaid dress."

"Oh, it's yellow, and it kind of flows down to my feet, it's very pretty." I said

"You're terrible at describing things."

"You'll just have to see it." I playfully said; the night went on with Peter reading until it was decided that we all needed to go to bed. The day that came after that was filled with various trips back and forth to town in preparation for the wedding. Poppy was rather shocked to see that the town had been decorated with white and yellow flowers. The library too had been decorated inside and out, and much to Poppy's despair, the bookshelves had been rearranged so that there was a small aisle leading down from the front door towards the fireplace in the back where a little arbor had been set up.

"I didn't want an aisle." Poppy said as she gazed at the whole set up. Cora who was standing there with us seemed shocked and a bit upset when she heard Poppy say this.

"Why not?"

"An aisle means someone walks you down it."

"Poppy," I began, "Just the other day you told Amelia and me that you wanted us to walk with you." I reminded her.

"I know, but I still don't want an aisle." She said.

"All these flowers and the arbor came from the Campbell's, Brady came down yesterday and rearranged everything." Cora said, Poppy just looked down at her feet.

"I'm sorry.... It's beautiful, I love It." she said before walking out of the library. Cora, Amelia and I were left to stand there looking back and forth at each other once Poppy had gone.

"I don't understand." Cora said.

"Seeing an aisle reminds her that she doesn't have a father to walk her down, that's why she's upset." Amelia said before leaving to follow Poppy.

"I should have them put it back to the way it was." Cora said looking back down towards the whole set up.

"No, no don't do that. Poppy may change her mind, we will talk to her." I said as I too went after Poppy and Amelia. I found Poppy and Amelia standing in the town green watching as tables and chairs were being set up. Poppy was holding her shoulders slightly slumped and relaxed, she looked as if she had just been defeated.

"Poppy, we can have them move the bookcases back." I said.

"No… no… everyone has gone through so much work. I can't do that." She softly said.

"Poppy, it's your wedding." Amelia reminded her.

"Everyone has gone through so much work, work that I never asked for; I can't dislike something someone did out of the goodness of their own heart." She said.

"But we don't want you to be unhappy." I said.

"Look, Brady is coming over." Amelia pointed out as Brady jogged towards us.

"Poppy, I'm sorry, do you want me to change the bookcases; it's no trouble at all." Brady said as he slowed to a stop in front of us.

"No… no. It's fine. Everyone has just done such a good job; I don't want to make anyone change all their hard work."

"It's no big deal. I can…"

"It's fine." Poppy said cutting off Brady, Brady just nodded and began to turn away, as Brady left; Amelia caught up with him and left with him. I could tell that Poppy was genuinely pleased with all the hard work everyone had done, but she didn't look like a blushing bride, more like a prisoner on her way to death row.

"Come on." I said grabbing her arm and taking her away from the town green. I took her to the only place I knew how to get to by memory, Mrs. Miller's teeny tiny little house. The elderly woman saw us coming and was already at her front gate waiting for us as we entered her little yard. She took us into her humble home and served us iced tea. She wanted to know about details of the wedding, but Poppy was being very general in her descriptions. Mrs. Miller sat back in her seat, put her shoulders back and analyzed Poppy as she sat in that chair.

"I have a diagnosis to what you are feeling." She said after a few moments of silence.

"A diagnosis?" she said.

"Yes... yes.... you're not smiling, you're pale, and you're eyes are dull, and you talk as softly as a mouse. You are ill child."

"Oh no...." Poppy said gravely.

"I have something that will make you feel better." Mrs. Miller said getting up and going into the kitchen. We could hear her opening and closing cabinet doors and the clinking of glasses.

"I can't be getting sick." Poppy said grabbing my arm.

"You look healthy to me." I said.

"But she's a professional.... She heals people for a living." Poppy whispered to me. Mrs. Miller came back into the room carrying a small glass with a small amount of brown liquid in it.

"Drink this... and drink it fast. It's meant to be swallowed all at once." She said handing it to the nervous Poppy. Poppy held it at arm's length, examined it in the light and then brought it up to her lips and knocked it back all in one gulp.

"Ow! Sheesh! What was that? It burns!" Poppy said.

"It's whisky." Mrs. Miller said with a laugh, I too couldn't help but laugh after hearing Mrs. Miller say that. Here I was and here Poppy was, we were both thinking that it was probably some sort of dense herbal tea meant to cure Poppy of some sort of ailment, but it was just very, very strong whisky.

"Whisky!?" Poppy said once the sensation of the liquor dissipated from her chest.

"Whisky... yes, it's the sure cure for the common wedding ailment of cold feet." Mrs. Miller said with a few chuckles.

"Stop laughing at me!" Poppy said to me, but I couldn't control myself.

"You are nervous, Poppy Holland, and you are right to be. Do not let yourself succumb to this anxiety, for in two days it will no longer be a worry." Mrs. Miller said; Poppy just sat there looking blankly at the kind woman. Was Poppy nervous, did she have cold feet?

"I guess I am nervous, and I guess that whisky did help, i only have to make it through one more day… just one more." Poppy said looking at Mrs. Miller then at me and then back at Mrs. Miller.

"Here… I'll get you another shot of whisky." Mrs. Miller got up from her seat and went back into the kitchen and returned with another glass. After Poppy's second shot of whisky, Mrs. Miller sat with us for a bit and gave Poppy grandmotherly advice, she wrote down simply recipes and gave her useful trinkets Poppy would be able to use in her own little home. When we left Mrs. Miller's house to head back to the farm, Poppy was just a tad bit clumsy as we walked home, but she wasn't as nervous or skittish as she had been previously. Despite her physical strength, Poppy was a bit of a light weight, she giggled at anything I said and thought the most mundane things were hilarious. I urged her to get it in check by the time we reached the farm, but it was no use, when we got to the farm, she jumped on William and clung to him like a Koala would to a eucalyptus tree and began telling him that his hair looked nice.

"Poppy…. Are you drunk? Mona did you get my fiancé drunk?" William looked at me with anger in his eyes.

"No… tipsy… she's tipsy… Mrs. Miller did it." I said after face palming myself.

"She said I had cold feet, and I was nervous, and that whisky fixes it." Poppy explained.

"Well…. Mom and gran decided that until the wedding Connor, Peter, and I are going to stay in town, that way you won't be so nervous anymore."

"What?" Poppy said letting go of William and flopping to the ground.

"You're leaving us?" I said sadly as well to Connor.

"Only for a day and a half, then I will see you at the wedding." Connor said before leaving a kiss on the tip of my nose and then slinging a back pack over his shoulder and walking down the driveway.

"No… don't leave." Poppy said to William as he too went to leave.

"It's an old Wilde family tradition, you'll see me in a day and a half, and then I'm all yours." William said with a wink to Poppy that made me want to gag. William and Connor left and a few moments afterwards, Peter went running down the driveway still stuffing a pair of pants into his backpack. We were left with nothing else to do other than to sew the remaining buttons on our bridesmaid dresses, and wait for Saturday to come.

25.
Exchanges

The sun rise of that Saturday morning was seen by every individual who had stayed in the house the night before, with the exception of Poppy. While we worked hard to finish up last minute details of the wedding, we allowed Poppy to sleep a few minutes more. She had paced the hallway and gone for a walk up to the duck pond in the dead of night due to some last minute nerves that kicked in. We all took turns taking baths, and getting all clean before getting into our dresses. I would be the second to last person to get into the bathroom, mostly because the buttons on my dress hadn't come out exactly how I wanted and I spent the time redoing them while Ms. Elizabeth, Charlotte, Cora, and Amelia all bathed and rubbed themselves down with freshly made lavender lotion Mrs. Elizabeth had made the day before.

The rest of the men of the house had left the day before to join William, Connor, and Peter down in the town, with the lack of men in the house, there was an occasional scantily dressed female running from one end of the house to the other looking for some sort of item of clothing or another. After I finished sewing the final button to the back of my dress, I hung it on the hanger that balanced on one of the bookcases in the living room. Someone had put another old record on so that there would be music playing in the house, I couldn't tell what was playing or who exactly was singing, but I could tell that it was French of some sort, and it was very light and bubbly. When I began to climb the stairs, I felt a warm breeze tickle my ankles from the open windows in the living room, when I reached the top I saw poor Amelia standing in the hallway, wrapped in nothing but a towel with her hair dripping wet, she was knocking on her mother's bedroom door, and Cora was just not opening up. Once she did, she disappeared inside, and I took the opportunity to sneak into the bathroom so that I could finally take a bath.

The air in the bathroom was moist and steamy, and it faintly smelled of Lavender. I opened the window wide to let all the humidity out and began to undress and fill up the tub. Once the tub was filled, I looked around the room for the bottle of bath soak that Mrs. Elizabeth had made, all I found was an empty glass bottle that had nothing left in it. I soon found myself taking one of those naked, towel wrapped trips to Mrs. Elizabeth's room in search of something. Mrs. Elizabeth only had one thing left for me; sitting on her dresser she had one bottle of jasmine bath soak and a matching bar of soap and lotion. She also had a milk bath and a sugar scrub, which was intended for Poppy's use only. I just took the jasmine stuff and went back to the bathroom.

It had been a while since I got a really good bath, sure I took a bath every other day, but that was just with plain water and plain scentless soap, it was a rare occasion to have the lovely smells and aromas, which took Mrs. Elizabeth a good amount of time to make. I scrubbed from head to toe, and double shampooed my hair. As the water in the bathtub drained I dried myself and applied the lotion, I was actually glad we had run out of the lavender soap and lotion, the jasmine smelled much better. I put on my undies and dressed in a robe, when I opened the bathroom door, I had Poppy standing there, still half asleep and ready for her bath.

"You're awake! Today's the big day!" I said.

"Mm mm." She just groaned.

"Who woke you up?" I asked.

"Amelia." She said before pushing me aside and going into the bathroom and shutting the door.

"Poppy wait, Gran has a few things for you!" Amelia said running down the hallway carrying the milk bath and body scrub. Poppy just leaned against the doorframe as Amelia put them in the bathroom.

"She's a crabby pants." Amelia said after Poppy closed the door.

"She only got like four hours of sleep last night." I laughed as I went downstairs to get dressed. I first asked Cora, Charlotte, and Mrs. Elizabeth a few questions to make sure it was safe to put on my dress. I didn't want to have to do anymore chores or tasks in my dress. I got dressed in the living room. It was the first time I put the dress on with it 100% complete. It was a light sunny yellow, we had found yards and yards of plain white chiffon from someone in town, and they gave it to us to not only make Poppy's dress, but to make ours as well. We dyed it, measured it, and hand stitched everything. The top part of the dress was tightly fitted with a sweetheart neckline and it stayed well fitted until right about to the middle of my ribcage and then the rest of the chiffon flowed out here and there with loose pleats, and it pooled lightly around my feet. The dress was neither bulky nor over abundant, and it was very Grecian in appearance. I had sewn clear glass beads around the neckline and up the shoulder straps that were about the width of three of my fingers, and in the back of the dress I had 12 pearl buttons that buttoned me in to it. Once I was into my dress, I had to have Cora button me in.

None of us had yet to see Poppy's wedding dress, it had been kept extra secret and it was worked on these past two weeks in the cellar of the house where no one cared to go. When poppy came out of the bathroom, Charlotte quickly grabbed her and took her into Mrs. Elizabeth's room where the door was closed and I suspected we wouldn't see Poppy again until she was ready to go. When Cora finished buttoning me into my dress she had me go up to her room so she could do my hair while it was still wet. Amelia had already gotten her hair done, and it looked very beautiful. Cora needed my hair to still be a little wet for her to braid it the way she wanted. She put a few drops of lavender oil in her hands and rubbed it through my hair before combing. I sat for nearly a half an hour while she tediously braided all of my hair up and onto my head. It was a gorgeous up-do made up of just a single braid that started at the front of my head and wrapped its way around my head delicately. Once she was finished she added white flowers so that it looked like I had little delicate white flowers intertwined in my hair. Amelia and I had been completed; now all we had to do was wait for Poppy. Cora and Charlotte and Ms. Elizabeth were already dressed in the dresses they had made. Cora wore a navy blue gown with green glass beads on the bodice, and she had taken the time to curl her blond hair with a curling iron she had to heat in the fire in the kitchen. Charlotte had on a rose colored, one shouldered dress that had a bow on the one shoulder, and she had slicked her hair back into a chignon with a rose at the base of it. I saw a brief glimpse of Mrs. Elizabeth; she had on a mint green dress with her long red hair curled and half of it braided up with little flowers in it. Amelia's dress and mine were the exact same color, but Amelia opted to make her dress have a V neckline and her shoulder straps crisscross in the back. It gave her much more of a womanly like appearance, and she looked very sultry, but she was beautiful nonetheless.

We waited for a tad bit longer before finally Poppy was ready. When we saw her from the bottom of the stairs, it was as if she was a completely changed person. She was all smiles and she posed for us in her dress. When Poppy came down the stairs we could more easily see how radiantly beautiful she and the dress was. Cora, Charlotte, and Elizabeth had painstakingly taken pieces of lace from their own wedding dresses and seamlessly stitched them together. The only tell tail differences were the variations of yellowing of the lace that gave it away. The top of Poppy's gown had a scooped scalloped neckline of lace that went down to quarter length sleeves, under the lace was a sweetheart lining that just showed a little teeny tiny bit of Poppy's cleavage, but it was semi concealed by the lace. The rest of the bodice was tailored closely to Poppy's torso until it reached her hips and then it flared and flowed out. She had a modest yet elegant train, and the back of her dress had little yellow buttons that matched mine and Amelia's dress.

The dress was perfect for Poppy, and it complimented every aspect of her, and she just looked over abundantly happy in it. Her short blond hair had been curled and she had little crystal hair pins keeping her hair out of her face. While we giggled and laughed and complimented each other in our dressed, Cora came downstairs carrying Poppy's veil, Cora neatly and carefully helped Poppy put it on, it was a Spanish style veil with scalloped edges, and to hold it down to Poppy's head, Cora placed a little wreath of yellow flowers.

"I think the people in the town picked just about every single white and yellow flower for today." Cora said once everything was secure.

"I think so too." Poppy laughed.

"Is it time yet?" Amelia asked.

"As soon as Mr. Greene gets here with the van, it will be time." Ms. Elizabeth said looking out of the front window. Mr. Greene was a very kind man in the town who offered to start up his old van and use the remaining amount of gasoline to shuttle us back and forth from the farm. I felt like I wasn't being humble and that I was bragging, but we all looked so good. When Mr. Greene arrived, he was dressed in what we could tell to be his best suit, upon getting out of the van and seeing all of us, he choked up a bit and said that we were the prettiest ladies he had seen all year. We all piled into the van and at noon sharp we were heading to town, we had seen the town only a few days before, but so many more things had been added, more flowers, more decorations, and a dance floor had been built in the town green. Poppy was speechless, and shocked to see how much more the town had transformed. It looked like a fairytale. Everyone in the town had gathered outside the library, with the exception of Jonathan, Luke, Peter, Connor, and William, who were all inside the library already.

"Are you ready?" I whispered to Poppy as we got out of the van and I arranged her dress so that all the wrinkles from her sitting dissipated.

"Yes." Poppy said confidently. Amelia and I lingered with Poppy outside the library while Charlotte, Cora, and Ms. Elizabeth went inside. Everyone from the town who was watching was ooing and ahhing, and shouting their well wishes. Mrs. Miller leaned out through the crowd with bouquets of flowers.

"What's a wedding without bouquets of flowers!" she said. They were very simple bouquets, we gave the largest one to Poppy and Amelia and I held the other two in our hands. Poppy opted to link arms with both of us as we walked up the stairs and then into the library. The inside of the library had remained unchanged from the day Poppy had first seen it, only this time it was filled with our family as well as the addition of Mr. Wilson's wife. I was very surprised to see that all the boys managed to find suits to wear. I couldn't help but smile to see Connor all dressed up, I had never seen him looking so clean cut and gentlemanly before, the suit he wore might have been a bit tight on him, but I think I kind of liked it like that. I had to quickly remind myself to turn my attention from Connor and look at William who was utterly shocked to see Poppy all dressed up and looking so radiant. When we reached the top of the aisle, Amelia and I hadn't planned on doing any sort of special thing to "give" Poppy away, instead I just let go of Poppy's arm and pushed her forward, and Amelia said, "Here ya' go!" to William, before I went to stand next to

Connor and Amelia stood next to Peter. Our little "display" made everyone laugh, including Poppy.

The ceremony was extremely simple, only about a half hour in length, Mr. Wilson, not having any marriage certificates, and since there was no longer an official state government, or any government for that matter, was at a loss for how to make a marriage official, so he drew up a contract and a little ritual of his own which included him reading the contract out loud and having Poppy and William read certain portions out loud. The contract had just basic things in it that everyone knew; it had important bible verses, promises, and little tidbits about William's history and Poppy's. Of course one thing that did not change were the vows. At the very end Mr. Wilson had Poppy and William answer the question that nearly everyone knew by heart.

"William Edward Wilde, do you take Poppy Therese Holland to be your lawfully wedded wife?" Mr. Wilson asked.

"I do." William said.

"And do you, Poppy Therese Holland take William Edward Wilde to be your lawfully wedded husband?"

"I do." Poppy said with no hesitation.

"Ladies and gentlemen, I now have the pleasure of presenting to you, Mr. and Mrs. William and Poppy Wilde. William, you may kiss you bride." William kissed Poppy and we all applauded. After the kiss, Poppy and William had to sign the contract, which Mr. Wilson also signed, since I was the maid of honor and Connor was the best man we also had to sign, and then Mrs. Wilson put the contract into a lovely gold picture frame and gave it to William and Poppy. When we all left the library, everyone outside had gathered and cheered and threw flower pedals in the air for William and Poppy. It was really and truly a surreal sight to see every single person in town dressed to their best. With the actual ceremony over, someone in the town brought their camera, and offered to take pictures. We all posed and played around while the pictures were taken. The nice man who took the pictures promised Poppy and William that they will have a few nice pictures printed out for them by the end of the week. After that, everyone was ready for food and celebration; it was destined to be a night full of merriment.

26.

Potatoes

There were tables set up all around the town green, all arranged in such a way that everyone was in view of the dance floor and stage that was set up. A group from the town who had formed their own band got together and began playing, it was more of a folk band more than anything, and it consisted of a guitar, banjo, violin, drums, and a bass. There was more than enough food for everyone to get two or three helpings if they wanted to, and not to mention the dessert. There were pies, cupcakes, ice cream, and not to mention the cake. I don't know which family in the town made it, but it was clear that they worked very hard on it. It was three tiers with buttercream icing and roses and flowers made out of the icing. Poppy and William lacked nothing when it came to their wedding, they got everything and then some. When the sun began to set, candles were placed in mason jars which were then hung from string in the trees here and there.

Everyone sat and watched Poppy and William dance their first dance to a song that was written by the band. I sat on Connor's lap as they danced and we just listened and watched. Connor reached down and held my hand and we rocked back and forth to the music.

"Don't tell Poppy, but I think you upstaged her in that dress." Connor said in my ear.

"What? No, I did not, are you crazy, Poppy looks beautiful." I said.

"Indeed she does, but to me you look even better." He said taking a piece of the fabric of my dress and rubbing it between his fingers. We sat for a while together just talking and observing everyone around us before Connor decided that we should dance. We danced to some of the fast songs, and to all of the slow songs, I even ditched Connor a few times to dance with Poppy or Amelia. We had so much fun, everyone did. William soon decided that it was time for him and Poppy to leave. Connor had me come with him to go around behind the library where Connor had parked the dirt bike and decorated it with streamers and flowers.

"Here, get on, we'll ride it around to them." Connor said, I laughed and gathered the skirt of my dress so that I could get on the back of the bike with him, we rode it around to where Poppy and William were, and when they saw the bike, they both laughed.

"What did you do to it? You made it all girly!" William exclaimed.

"I like it, come on, hurry up!" Poppy said as she trotted for the bike. William gave Connor a hand shake and me a hug before catching up to Poppy. With the whole town watching and waving goodbye, they zipped away.

The night was still early and everyone wanted to continue to party and have fun. So the music and the fun continued until the only people left on the dance floor were me, Connor, Amelia and Brady. Even members of the band had given up and gone home so that it was just us four left dancing to basically nothing. It was then time to go home, but I was so tired and sleepy.

"Come on, Mona, let's go home." Connor said just holding me to his side as we left the dance floor. "Amelia, come on." Connor called back to his sister, Amelia took a few minutes before she caught up to us as we began to leave the town.

"When did everyone else leave us?" I asked, noticing that it was just us three walking home.

"Everyone just about left two hours ago." Amelia said.

"Oh…" I said before yawning. We walked down the dark road. Neither the moon nor stars were out that night, an overcast of clouds had gathered and the air began to change, signaling the nearness of rain. I must have been walking slowly, because after a while, Connor stopped and had me jump on his back so he could carry me the rest of the way home. When we got back to the farm, there were no lights on, and no smoke coming from the chimney, everything was just dead quiet. We climbed the first few steps of the house and went inside. We climbed the stairs and all went our separate ways to our bedrooms. I just went into my room and began to project of undressing and unbraiding my hair. It took me forever to do in my exhausted state, but I got it all done. I threw the dress over on to the chair that sat in the corner and crawled into bed in nothing but my underwear and my hair as unbraided as I could possibly get it in the darkness without a mirror.

***

I woke up the next day to find out that during the night, Poppy and William had packed up for a week long camping trip in the woods. Connor was the only one who had known about the plan for them to leave, the rest of the family had somehow expected that they would stick around, but that was just wishful thinking. With the wedding now behind us, there was a load of chores and projects that needed to be caught up on. Weeds had started to grow in our garden, a section of fencing fell around the chicken enclosure leading to the escape of several hens, and there was a new litter of kittens that needed to be accounted for somewhere, not to mention the biggest project of all, the plowing of the field that would grow our crop that would feed us for the winter. There was still no decision as to what we would grow, but Ms. Elizabeth insisted that we plow the field. So the task was left to Connor, Peter, Jonathan, and Luke, while Amelia and I weeded our garden.

I was very proud of how our herbs, tomatoes, green beans, peas, corn, and cabbage plants were coming along. They were nowhere near being ready to be harvested but I was very impressed with how big they grew each and every day. Amelia and I made the poor choice in wearing white sun dresses while we weeded, so the hems and knees of our skirts were brown with dirt while we sat and rolled around plucking weeded from the soil. The sun beamed down on us the entire time, and I could feel beads of sweat rolling down my lower back as we worked, it was awfully hot for a spring day. I worked to the sound of Amelia humming and the distant shouts from the boys who were off in the field plowing.

The section of the field that was to be plowed was only about the size of a tennis court, but the soil was dry and packed down and it needed to be turned over, and Ms. Elizabeth insisted that manure be mixed in.

"I'm thirsty, are you thirsty?" Amelia asked.

"Yes, I am." I answered. Amelia got on her feet and took my arm and pulled me up. She and I walked down the hill to the well where we threw the bucket down and hoisted it up to take turns sipping the fresh cold water.

"I think we are almost done, and then we can go and see if the boys need help." Amelia said.

“Let’s take a break from weeding for a bit and just take them water.” I said tossing the bucket back down into the well and pulling it up again. Amelia and I both held on to the handle of the bucket and carried it up to the field where we were welcomed by the boys who were both exhausted and dripping in sweat. I wanted to say that the bucket was a five gallon bucket, but by the end of the boys going through it, it was empty.

“Good Lord!” Amelia said once she was handed back the bucket.

“Thanks, we needed it.” Peter said as he sat down in the grass.

“No lying down, we still have so much more work to do.” Luke said scolding his son.

“Ugh!” Peter said getting up again.

“What’s wrong with the garden, won’t that be just fine?” He said taking the shovel from his father’s hand and walking back out into the field. We all just nervously laughed as he walked away, I turned to Connor who raised one finger to me and walked towards a little wooden crate.

“Here I got these for you.” Connor said carrying back the crate.

“What is it?” I asked, when he drew near I saw that inside the crate were the kittens we had been looking for, four of them.

“Oh. My. God. They are adorable!” Amelia squeaked when she saw them. I dove my hand into the crate and picked up one. They were so small and so fluffy and so squishy. They mewed and squeaked as we cuddled them and stroked their little heads.

“They’ll be good little mice hunters when they’re bigger.” Connor said taking the little kitten from me.

“Aw…. what are you going to do with them now?” I asked.

“Put them over in the barn so their mommy can feed them.” He said. Connor took the kittens to the barn and Amelia and I still had a bit more of weeding to do. At that time we only thought that the unusually warm spring day was nothing more than unusual, we had no idea that it could possibly be signaling something worse to come. That fist week after the wedding we worked hard to get the land ready for our winter crop. Ms. Elizabeth eventually chose potatoes to be planted in the tennis court sized field. The boys made little tiny holes with rakes while Amelia and I placed little potato spuds into each. We waited for two days hoping for some sort of moisture to hit the ground but there was nothing, we had to lug buckets up the hill to the field to water it ourselves. It was exhausting, and every muscle in my body ached from the exertion.

When Poppy and William finally came back from their week long outing, they were surprised to see how much work we had gotten done. Through all the work it took to prepare the field, somehow it was even managed to get the front door, kitchen door, and barn doors repainted.

"You've been mighty busy bees." Poppy said as she and I walked past the newly painted barn doors down to the bus. She and I were carrying some freshly cleaned laundry that needed to be moved from the house to Poppy's and William's bus.

"It was exhausting. I still can't sit down without my muscles hurting." I said, she laughed.

"I feel bad, you all worked so hard, and William and I spent a week doing almost nothing. We hunted a bit, but with the heat there were hardly any animals."

"Yeah, what's with this?" I asked.

"I don't know, I can't remember it being so warm this early in the spring, maybe three weeks from now, but not this soon." She said as we climbed the stairs up into the bus. I stood in the entry way of the bus as Poppy walked through towards her small dresser where she began to put the laundry. It truly had become a little home inside the bus, Poppy had a small bouquet of wildflowers on their little table next to a handwritten love note that William had left her that morning before leaving with the boys to go into town for a few things.

"The bugs are starting to come out now; I told William that we needed to get a mosquito net of some sort for the bed. I hope he finds something in the town, I already have three bites on my leg." Poppy said as she took the pile of clothes that I carried from my hands

"I haven't noticed." I said.

"Well there are screens on the windows in the house, we don't have screens here."

"Oh yeah…. duh." I said with a laugh.

"Well that'll just about do it for now." Poppy said once all the laundry was away.

"When did the boys say they would be back?" I asked.

"Uhh… I think around four."

"Did Amelia go with them?"

"What do you think? Of course she did, if it meant she would get to see Brady, then yes."

"Has she said anything to you about him?" I asked.

"Me? No… has she said anything to you?"

"Nope."

"Well she better fess up soon as to if she likes him or not because William is getting suspicious." Poppy said with a laugh

"She will, in her own due time." I said as we left the bus. With all the work that had been done, everyone just about wanted to take a break, with little to do and like motivation to do anything. Poppy and I went under the large oak tree that sat off a bit from the well to just lounge until our boys came home.

27.

Return

The weeks went by and the weather took a sudden turn from delicate spring, to full blown summer. The world had skipped the whole "April showers bring May flowers" memo, and just went straight into suffocating heat and baking sun. Our tiny garden was being baked day in and day out by the sun and there was no progress of growth in our winter crop field. With no air conditioning and only shade and minimal movement our only cures to the heat, we tried our best to make ends meet with the heat wave. Our priorities became keeping the animals alive as well as avoiding heat stroke ourselves.

There was a small promise of relief during the third week of May. Dark black clouds lingered over us with loud menacing claps of thunder and lightning strikes. It was a storm that left no rain, just a lot of noise and wind, and then it was gone. Without rain or some sort of relief from the sun and heat, our winter crop was threatened. We managed to keep our garden alive by manually lugging buckets of water up from the well and pouring it into the soil, but that was all we could do. By the last week of May we were very worried. Every morning Jonathan would go out into the field to rub the dry soil in his hands and then stare at the sky. Without rain, we would have no crop, and with no crop and no other resources for winter, we would surely suffer.

Ms. Elizabeth knew the severity of our situation, if anyone had the right to be worried it was her. She was the rock of our family, the wise and all-knowing individual who had an answer to every question and a remedy to every need. But this, even this was beyond the wisdom and knowledge of Ms. Elizabeth.

"Those CDC volunteers ought to be back any time soon. They said they would." Ms. Elizabeth said one day. They had been gone well over a month and a half now, and they said they would return. When they finally did return on the very last day of May, they brought with them truckloads of supplies and even more people. We were given updates as to what was going on in other places outside the town; and we were told that the entire New England region was caught in a historic drought, a drought that didn't look like it was going to end any time soon.

We were all required to meet with CDC volunteers again, they wanted to see how we were faring, and they wanted to do another health screen to make sure we were all still healthy. I met again with Mr. Mark Shaw, the same man who met with me the first time. When I sat down at the little table that was set up inside the library he looked up from his paper work and smiled.

"You have news about my mother?" I asked.

"I do, yes, I got to meet with her myself." He said, my heart instantly fluttered and my stomach got all up in knots of excitement.

"Really!? How is she? What did she say? Can she come here?" I asked His face then got really serious and he looked back down at his paper work before looking back up at me, I took that to be a very bad sign.

"I told you last time what the report said, do you remember?"

"Yes, it said something about brain damage, and that she couldn't speak anymore, and that she couldn't use her left arm anymore."

"I'm afraid that the report was a relatively kind description as to what state your mother is in."

"Spare me no details, I must know." I said seriously as I braced myself in the chair.

"The trials and medical tests that your mother allowed herself to endure were very invasive. Some involved radiation, and others involved various surgeries, biopsies, implants, and transfusions. It was a brain surgery that left your mother paralyzed in one arm and unable to speak. Had it not been for extreme high levels of radiation and a terrible cocktail of experimental drugs, she would have lived a relatively normal life. Due to the fact that the drugs were very experimental and very new, no one could really know what side effects they could have, the drugs were very addictive, and your mother became very dependent upon them. When I met with her, she seemed to be able to comprehend why I was there, and when I told her you were alive and where you were she perked up a bit and began flapping her right hand. The doctor that was overseeing her told me that that meant she was happy. Mona, due to the fact that you are her only next of kin, and that your mother can no longer coherently express her wishes, the authority falls to you as to what can happen next to your mother."

"What do you mean?" I asked.

"You can either opt for her to continue the way she is, or you can opt to put her through another trial that would involve them trying to get her off of the experimental drugs and hopefully be able to leave the Amherst Infirmary."

"Isn't the choice obvious? I want my mother to be able to leave the infirmary."

"Mona, I don't think you quite understand the power and the effect these drugs have had, hundreds of other patients have gone through the weaning process, and the majority of them do not survive."

"These drugs, what do they exactly do, what are they doing to my mother now?"

"They cause fatigue, hallucinations, joint pain, insomnia, coughing, sensitivity to light, and much more. They result in the patient only being able to handle a small dark room."

"And what does the weaning process involve?"

"It is very simple, they just start lowering the dosage day by day until the patient no longer needs it, but usually the body starts to shut down and go into shock before it can fully work."

"Is it a painful death?"

"No." Mark answered.

"If it is not painful, and it is only going to do my mother good, then I want her weaned off. Her being on that medication is worse than death, and if she dies then it would be a relief from the suffering."

"Is that what you want?"

"Yes." I answered, Mark shuffled through his paper work and pulled out a single form for me to read and sign. It was for my mother and it meant that she would be put through this one final trial. With that part out of the way, Mark went on to tell me that I was a very healthy person and that I didn't have any health concerns. I felt very depressed as I left the library afterwards. The news about my mother did not have the effect that it had had on me the last time. Instead I now had this hope, this small minuscule amount of hope that she could come home.

Everyone in the town was milling about; with all the new volunteers that had come, much work was to be done. The CDC Volunteers had brought with them large amounts of supplies, those supplies ranged from everything from multivitamins all the way up to heavy duty weaponry which was being installed at different points in the wall to help keep the town safe from potential gang attacks. Every household also received a large stainless steel bin that was about three feet in length and six feet in width and it was a foot deep. Inside these stainless steel bins would be enough supplies to sustain the house hold for a month if used properly. These bins were very durable, waterproof, and airtight once sealed. We were instructed to take the bins and find a spot on the land in which we lived to bury it. In the event of a gang attack, these bins would be our survival source if the town were to be ransacked.

Ms. Elizabeth demanded that some of the volunteers come down to the farm to see about our drought situation. We were the largest family in town, and although a survival bin would do us much good, it would be useless during the winter months. Something had to be done about our winter crop. All the men in the town were being trained by the volunteers on self-defense skills and how to use the new guns that would be supplied to the house. The majority of the men in town were well accustomed to shooting a gun, but they only knew hunting rifles, not heavy duty equipment. The amount of guns given to a family was based on how many adults were in the house, since we had eleven people living in the house, we received five guns. Ms. Elizabeth thought it was a bit excessive to have so many weapons in the house, but her son Jonathan assured her that they would be kept in a secure place and would only be touched if an attack was imminent.

The town also received 20 ATV's and one full eighteen wheeler tanker truck that was filled with gasoline. There was so much new equipment everywhere that the town looked like it went through rehab and update. Everything was just moving at a fast pace, the town wall was being reinforced, small construction jobs were being done, and everyone was busy at work, except for me. I just stood in the middle of it all trying to figure out where I ought to go next.

I saw Poppy sitting on the front steps of the town country store, looking all sour and upset over something. When I went over to her I could see that she had been crying and that she had since stopped. She just sat there emotionless with a blank stare off into the grass.

"Poppy…. Poppy, what's wrong?" I asked.

"Nothing." She said snapping out of it and sitting up straight up.

"Don't lie to me." I said sitting down next to her, she just let out a long sigh and what sounded like a sob, and she shifted her weight and pulled out a little packet of papers that were stapled together.

"Here… read it." She said handing it to me. I looked at the top of the paper to see that it was a printed out form of her health report. I had not received one, I wonder why she did? I started to scan the pages; was Poppy ill? Was that the reason she received these papers? No… everything was good, she was very healthy. It was what was written at the bottom of the very last page that startled me. Under the section titled "Women's Health" Poppy checked out as a very healthy person, except for one thing, Poppy tested positive under the little marking that said "Pregnancy". Poppy was pregnant.

"Oh my gosh! Oh my gosh, oh my gosh, oh my gosh!" I said all excited and flapping my hands.

"Shhh! Will you calm yourself! People are going to stare!" Poppy said grabbing me.

"This is so exciting!" I said pulling her into a hug.

"No! No it's not!" She said.

"Why? You're not excited?" I said as I grew very serious.

"A part of me wants to leap for joy, but an even bigger part of me wishes that this didn't happen. We are in the middle of a drought; we might not have food for the winter, and there is still so much danger out there. How could I possibly be excited to bring a child into this world at this time?"

"Poppy… You're just scared and nervous; it's no reason to be so upset. I'm sure once you tell William you will be more excited and so will he."

"Of course he is going to be excited, he wants a big family, having children is one of his biggest dreams." She said.

"And had it ever been one of yours?" I asked.

"Not until recently, but now I'm just so scared. Why now? Why did this happen now?" she said as a few tears fell from her eyes.

"Well… you know what they say." I said.

"What do they say?" she asked

"If you play, you pay." I said jokingly, Poppy, fully comprehending that statement punched me in my arm and then slumped over and hid her face in her lap. I thought Poppy was crying, but she was just quietly laughing.

"I guess you're right." She said sitting up again. Together Poppy and I got up and went to walk back home. Back on the farm we found that Ms. Elizabeth was directing a half a dozen volunteers across the land as they tried to solve the issue as to how to save our winter crop. We decided to let them be and went into the barn where Jonathan was rearranging a stall to put all the new weapons. Not wanting to get involved with that we just kept on going until we found Amelia sitting on an old wooden crate polishing what looked to be knives.

"What are you doing?" Poppy asked Amelia as we made little spots for ourselves around her.

"Polishing my knives, I haven't done it in a long time." She replied.

"These are nice, where did you get them?" I said taking one out of the dark, shiny wooden box that they lay in.

"My grandfather got them for me for my sixteenth birthday, right before he died." Amelia said.

"Are you any good?" Poppy asked, Amelia looked up, took the knife that she already had in her hand, and with the flick of her wrist that knife whipped through the air and made for itself a new home on the barn door.

"I guess that answered your question." I laughed.

"Amelia, I've never thought to ask about your grandfather. I mean, I've wondered about him, but William never talked about anything." Poppy said.

"Yeah, come to think of it, Connor never says anything either." I said.

"That's because it was a terrible time for my family when Gampy died. I know it's hard to believe now, but at one time, my grandmother wasn't always the rock and driving force of the house and the family. It was my grandfather, he had been our driving force, he was the one who knew how to work the land, he knew it all better than the back of his own hand. Don't get me wrong, my grandmother was just as great as she is now back then, but my Gampy was more so. He knew how to do anything and everything. One day he was out in the field, and he just fell over. It had been a heart attack that took him from us. It was so shocking, so unexpected, that we couldn't handle it. After it happened, we didn't know what to do. We kept asking ourselves 'what would Gampy do?' but we could never do it as he would have done. We realized that there was no one else on earth who could do things the way he had done, so we had to do things our own way, and we had to rely on the only other person who had just as much knowledge as Gampy, and that was Gran. We don't talk about it much because it still hurts a lot. William and Connor were very close with Gampy, he would be very proud of them today." Amelia said.

Poppy and I had no idea. We were very saddened to hear about the story of Ms. Elizabeth's husband. We both lost people, but something about how Amelia described her grandfather led us to believe that he truly was an extraordinary man. We could both hear the pain in Amelia's voice as she talked about it. We decided that we would never ask about it again.

Later that day, the CDC volunteers that Ms. Elizabeth commissioned to come to the house devised a solution to our problem. With the use of hoses and siphoning from the well, water was able to easily be brought up from the well up to the field. It would save our crop, but we would have to be very careful how much water we siphoned because now we risked running the well dry. After consulting with Jonathan and Luke, Ms. Elizabeth decided that it would be best to water the field every third day and that baths would have to be once a week now in order to conserve water. I groaned at the decision about the baths, but we had no choice, in order to still have a winter crop and to have water, it was something that needed to be done.

With the threat of possibly losing the crop no longer a worry and the excitement of all the new supplies from the CDC, that night at dinner was the perfect time for Poppy to announce her news. The topic came up at dinner as to how everyone's health tests came out. We all said that we were very healthy and there was nothing to worry about, but when it was Poppy's turn, she got real serious and put her fork down on the table.

"They gave me paper work, I tested positive for something." She said seriously, the whole table got quiet and there were ten pairs of eyes that were filled with worry looking at Poppy. Poppy took out the paper work from a pocket in her dress and handed it to William who sat beside her.

"On the last page, the very last line." She said, William scanned the page and when his eyes fell on that very last line, he began to cry. He put the paper on the table and just leaned over to Poppy and was crying. Charlotte jumped up and snatched the paper. When she saw what William had seen she began to jump up and down, screaming with excitement.

"Would somebody tell me what in God's name is going on!?" Ms. Elizabeth yelled.

"Poppy is pregnant!" Charlotte giggled before running around the table and pulling both William and Poppy in to a hug. After that exclamation the whole table erupted with congratulations and laughter and just plain excitement. It just turned out to be a wonderful night.

28.
Lessons

It was only a matter of a few days afterward that Poppy began to feel the early symptoms of her pregnancy. She soon became repulsed by the thought of food, and even the previously delightful scents of flowers or of something cooking sent Poppy running to the bathroom. Ms. Elizabeth examined Poppy, and due to Ms. Elizabeth's in depth knowledge from when she served as a midwife and even now as an herbalist. It was determined that Poppy was little over two and a half months gone with her pregnancy and that she would be due approximately in December. William right away wanted to start making a crib for his baby, but Ms. Elizabeth halted any further efforts or ideas he had. Ms. Elizabeth held strong to her old fashioned belief that the first few months of pregnancy were the most dangerous and delicate, according to her, only after the fourth month of Poppy's pregnancy would the preparations begin.

Poor Poppy was put on strict new rules as to what she could and couldn't do. There would be no more hunting, no more fishing, no more heavy lifting, and no more hanging around the animal's pens. Poppy was either confined to garden work, her bus, or the house. With her down to only a few mundane tasks, it was up to Amelia and I to fill in on the chores that Poppy once could do. Back before the outbreak I never heard of such rules being evoked on a pregnant woman, but Ms. Elizabeth had her old fashioned time honored beliefs that never failed her, and due to the fact that we had no access to regular modern medicine such as prenatal vitamins and antibiotics and ultrasound, it was all just better to be safe than sorry.

As Poppy begrudgingly did little mundane tasks around the house with an ever doting William never too far from her, Connor began work to teach me how to hunt. William had made the decision that he no longer wanted to be more than a couple miles from Poppy at any given time, so I had to become Connor's new hunting partner, which I was rather excited to do. It meant more time with him.

A while back the boys decided to just start using the bows and arrows to hunt instead of guns, the reason was because bullets were scarce to come by now, and it was best to conserve what we had. I wasn't half bad at shooting the arrows; it was the aiming part that I needed major work on. Connor was a good teacher though, no matter how many times I screwed up, he would just laugh and show me again and again.

"Ok… this time, I want you to hit the target. It doesn't matter where, just hit the target." He said handing me another arrow as we practiced on the side of the barn.

"Alright, I'll try my best." I said taking the arrow from him and readying it. I held my left arm out and pulled the string back, and just before I released, I held my breath and just let it go. The arrow invisibly flew through the air and hit the barn a mere two feet from the target.

"Ugh! I'll never get it!" I said throwing the bow down into the grass.

"No… no…babe, it's ok, you're shooting perfectly, we just need to work on aiming, and that comes with time and experience. If you're going to hunt with me, I need you to at least be able to hit something, I'm not asking you to straight up make a kill with one shot, just hit it or at least graze it." he said coming over to me and pulling me in for a comforting hug.

"I'm trying." I just said.

"Here, let me try something different." He said bending down and picking up the bow and putting it back in my hands. I got another arrow and began to start to reload the bow, but just before I pulled the string back, Connor stopped me.

"Ok, now this time, I want you to stand with your legs just a tad wider apart. He said putting his foot in the space between my feet and kicking my legs out apart further from each other. After that was settled, I pulled the string back, but he stopped me again.

"Ok, now hold it right there. Just stand very still." He said coming up directly behind me. He reached around and pressed his hand flat against my stomach coaxing me to stand up a little straighter with my back pressed flat as a board against his chest.

"Now, from the moment you pull the string back you should just train your body to go right into this position and then you hold your breath, and….. release." When he said release I let go of the string and the arrow went flying and hit the target. It wasn't a direct bull's-eye, but it was good enough.

"Yes!" I said jumping up and throwing my hands into the air. I turned around and flung my arms around Connor's neck and kissed him.

"Ok, ok," he said prying me off of him, "Let's not celebrate to soon, do it again." I not only did it again, I did it three more times after that too.

"This is a good start, a very good start. Let's let that be all for today and tomorrow we will practice again" Connor said with a small hint of pride in his voice. I helped Connor collect everything that we used to practice and put it all back in the barn before going back up to the house. It was nearly the hottest part of the day and soon we would all be struggling to find relief from the heat. Connor and I held hands all the way back up to the house, once inside we found Poppy sitting on a small milk stool in the corner of the kitchen, resisting Ms. Elizabeth's requests to help chop up carrots. Poppy looked green in the face over having to sit in the kitchen with all the food, so I told Ms. Elizabeth that I would chop the carrots instead so Poppy could go do something else. Poppy flew out of the kitchen as soon as the words came out of my mouth.

The kitchen was quiet as I worked with Ms. Elizabeth to prepare a few things that would be served for dinner. It had been voted upon that we ought to not have the fire running in the stove in the kitchen, not only would it raise the temperature to twice it was already in the house, but it could also potentially cause some poor unfortunate heat stroke if they were in the kitchen too long. So we had become accustomed to having cold meals. Mainly consisting of anything that could be prepared that didn't require heat or an oven. That night's dinner would consist of a salad, and hard boiled eggs which we would boil over a fire outside the house.

The day lingered on and on and the sun seemed to beam down on us as if it were mocking us in its own demented way. When the heat reached its peak, we all took refuge inside the house to perch ourselves by a window in hopes of a stray breeze, but none came. The air was dry and still, unlike anything I ever had to memory. There was nothing I wanted more after a whole morning and early afternoon of learning how to shoot a bow and arrow than to take a bath. I was dirty, sweaty, and smelly; but with the new rules, I wasn't allowed to take a bath for a few more days. I could not bear the feeling of the grime on my skin for a moment more. I went up to my room and took for myself fresh clothes, a bar of soap, and a towel. I managed to find Amelia also sitting around doing nothing and I proposed my idea to her. We would take a walk down to the river to wash and bathe; surely there would be no harm in that.

Amelia was on full board with the idea, yet she seemed a bit antsy as we got ready to leave. We told no one of our plan, since basically everyone was taking a nap to escape the high afternoon heat. As we walked up through the field Amelia kept looking back down towards the farm until we could no longer see it anymore.

"We should have told someone." She said.

"Its fine, we won't be gone long, and it's not like we will be swimming, so there's no danger." I said as we walked through the dry bush of the forest. When we made it to the river, it didn't surprise me at all to find that river wasn't flowing as strong as it had earlier in the spring, it was still deep and it still had a current to it, but it wasn't as overflowing as it once was. Amelia and I found our own little private spots where we could wade into the water up to our waists. The water was cool and refreshing and brought the much needed relief from both the head and how dirty we felt. The soap we had brought with us foamed up and just floated away down the river. We had no worries as to if it would be harmful to the water since it was soap that had all been hand made by Charlotte and Ms. Elizabeth only a few weeks prior. I didn't quite want to get fully dressed yet after washing, so I sat on a nearby boulder and combed out my hair with my fingers and just basked in the sun. After a few moments Amelia came over too and did the same. The heat didn't feel so bad now that we were clean and cooled off from the refreshing water, in fact it felt very comfortable where we sat.

"Mona, can I ask you a question?" Amelia said after a few moments of enjoyable silence.

"Sure." I answered, I was leaning back on the boulder on my elbows with my eyes closed and my head up towards the sky, Amelia took a few moments to respond after that.

"Do you think that we will be stuck here on the farm and in the town forever, like the people that are here, are they the only people we are going to know for the rest of our lives?"

"That's a pretty loaded question, Amelia, why do you ask that?"

"I'm just wondering, we don't really know what more is out there, the CDC volunteers tell us that there are other towns, but how can we be so sure?"

"We can't be entirely sure, but when the time comes I suppose we will find out one day. Once the volunteers have gathered all the information they need, I am sure that they will tell us."

"What was the plague like? I never saw any one who had it."

"It was bad, Amelia, unlike anything I had ever seen up until that point. I don't really want to describe it to you, you're better off not knowing." I responded, for a few moments we sat in silence as the afternoon ticked away.

"How far does this river run?" I asked.

"I'm not really sure, I know that if you follow it up stream more it'll take you by the Campbell's farm." She said.

"The Campbell's, I've only met Brady, never anyone else."

"That's because he's the oldest and the strongest, they had it rough during the winter and not to mention that they did lose a few family members to the plague. I guess the others are scared to leave, or they just choose not to. Like us they are very self-sufficient on that farm."

"I wonder if they had problems with the drought like we had."

"Not too bad, they have a relatively new pumping system that pumps water up to their field from their well."

"Do you talk to Brady often?" I asked leaning over onto my side to become more comfortable.

"When I see him, yeah."

"It seems like every time we are in town he is in town as well, is it always a coincidence?" I asked.

"No, not always. He ought to be more on the farm helping his family, by the likes to make the trips into town, even if he needs to or not."

"Has he told you why?" I asked.

"Yeah, a few times."

"What are his reasons?"

"Mostly because he wants to run into me or my brothers. He told me that he likes me, but I don't know what to do."

"Well… do you like him?"

"I do, I do like him, but I'm not so sure."

"What makes you not so sure?"

"Before the outbreak, before Connor and William were told they had to become officers, the town was much bigger. There were tons of nice little neighborhoods and new houses that sat on nicely manicured pieces of land, and there was a high school. When the plague came, it destroyed all of that, killing everyone in those neighborhoods and in those nice houses. The few that survived moved into the center of the town, they built the wall out of everything they could, and then they burned the rest; the burning didn't take place until long after William and Connor left. Ever since then there hasn't been many people, I didn't know of anyone else my age besides Peter. Brady is a few years older than me, he was always William and Connor's friend, not mine. I like him, but I'm just afraid that we like each other simply because there are no other people around."

"I guess when you put it that way; I can see where you are coming from. I guess you have to trust in your own gut and your own instincts. And you aren't the only girl in town around Brady's age; there are two or three more that I've briefly met through William and Connor. I don't see them with boyfriends or with husbands or anything. Our world is much different now; time and unforeseen occurrence has brought us all together."

"It's just scary. Did you feel like this when you met Connor? Were you scared?" She asked.

"I met Connor under very unusual circumstances. I had a very outgoing friend who was always a flirt. Her name was Molly, and she met another officer named Collin. I met Connor because whenever Collin and Molly wanted to hang out, he brought Connor. I did have my bouts of nervousness, but eventually I felt very comfortable with Connor." I said.

"What happened to Molly and Collin?" Amelia asked.

"I watched them both get killed at the hands of a gang." I said as I turned away from Amelia. Images of that day flashed through my mind. I could see Molly's green eyes again, her hair all matted and tangled, and my boney tooth pick like fingers covered with blood from the wound she was then killed from. Amelia could see that the turn in the topic of conversation was upsetting me. They had been memories I wished to forget, and up until that point I had managed to never recall.

"I'm sorry. Connor doesn't like talking about it either." Amelia said.

"I'm just happy I am here with a family that truly loves each other and with friends whom I love." I said.

"We should get back to the farm. The sun is getting glow." She pointed out, I stood up and began to get dressed in a set of clean clothes. We made the walk back down to the farm. The rest of the family was just beginning to get up and start moving again since the heat of the day was just beginning to subside. As we neared the house and the barn, it was clear that we had a visitor. Parked in the middle of the driveway between the house and the barn was a rusty old dirt bike that I had not seen before, I turned to Amelia and saw that she was smiling.

"Who's bike is that?" I asked.

"It's Brady's." She responded; Brady had come to visit the farm. It had, after all been a good week since any of us had gone to town, and my guess was that Brady wished to see Amelia.

"How do you feel?" I asked Amelia as we prepared to go into the house.

"Comfortable." She said nodding her head.

"Good." I smiled.

29.

Healers

The world went on day by day, night by night. The month of May came and went and June had arrived like a roaring lion. Rain clouds did come for a few hours in the early days of the month. Giant droplets of water fell from the sky and pelted into the ground; but the ground was so dry, the little amount of water that fell, beaded up, rolled away, then evaporated with the return of the sun. It did bring a few hours of relief with it, but after that the relentless heat came once more. This time it was June and the heat intensified as the season changed over from spring to summer. We didn't realize how easy we had had it during the previous weeks, sure the temperature had been in the high-70s, but it had since then rose to the high 90s and low 100s.

Connor continued to work with me, teaching me how to hunt. We practiced every day in the early morning before the heat got too bad. I was getting good at shooting a bow and arrow, Connor was very proud of me. He often talked about taking me on a real hunting trip so we could get some real game; but until then we would just work on hunting small things, like rabbits and the occasional wild turkey. I had yet to actually kill anything for myself, but I liked to think that I was a great help to Connor.

One morning, before the sun had risen yet, and before anyone else had woken up. Connor broke Ms. Elizabeth's number one rule: he snuck into my bedroom. He snuck in to wake me up and show me that there was a whole flock of wild turkey just perched in the field behind the house. We both snuck out of the house, Connor was still in his pajamas and I was still in my night gown, and we went down to the barn to get our bows. Without shoes we moved quickly and silently though the prickly and dry grass to get a clear shot of the field. We waited and stalked the turkey before we took our picks of which ones we wanted to aim for.

"You've got this, Mona, it's practically sitting waiting for you." Connor whispered to me in the hazy morning air. Connor and I both pulled back the strings on our bows and aimed at our targets. We both let go of the strings at the same time and the arrows silently glided through the air and hit their targets. Connor's arrow hit his and it was a clean, painless kill; but not mine, the rest of the flock had flown away, leaving Connor's turkey in the grass and mine just injured trying to get away. I ran over to the turkey as it tried to hobble away. It was gobbling and chattering, clearly out of pain and fear. I was mortified. My heart sunk to my stomach and I couldn't help but cry. Connor came over to me and saw my predicament.

"It's ok, it's ok." I couldn't tell if he was talking to me or the poor little turkey. I watched Connor take a knife from his pocket of his pajama pants and I just immediately turned away. I could hear Connor still saying "it's ok", and I knew that he wasn't saying it to me, but to the turkey. When I realized this I turned back around to see that the turkey lay still in the grass and Connor was patting its back. He had killed it with his knife I knew that much. I watched him clean the knife in the grass and then put it back in his pocket. He had a sad look on his face as he stood up and walked over towards me.

"It's never easy when it's not a clean shot, but its ok now." He said putting his arms around me.

"I don't think I can be a hunter." I said.

"It's always rough the first time you shoot at something that's alive."

"Does it get easier?" I asked.

"Not for a long time, but it has to be done."

"I know, I know." I said pressing my face into his chest.

"Why don't you go inside and wait for me in the living room, let me get these two taken care of and I'll be right in." He said motioning to the turkeys. I nodded and blotted the few stray tears from my face and turned to go inside. The house was still silent when I went back inside. The white house cat, Allie, was perched on the mantle of the fireplace when I went into the living room. I sat down on the sofa and just waited for Connor. It only took a few moments before Allie the cat jumped off the mantle to join the other house cat on the floor. I watched them hop around before climbing up onto a table and then out of an open window into the yard. I sprawled out on the couch and waited. When Connor finally came in he practically just laid on top of me and crushed me. I tried to swat him off but he just chuckled and made himself more comfortable, burying his face in my hair.

"Connor, seriously, I can't breathe." I breathlessly said.

"Too bad, I'm comfortable." He grumbled, I just sighed and tried to kick and move around enough under his weight until I was no longer being crushed. We stayed like that for a long time until we heard footsteps in the house. We both shot up quickly when we heard someone clear their throat in the doorway of the living room. It was Poppy who was standing there in the doorway.

"Just remember kids… if you get knocked up, you suddenly have to pee insanely too much. I thought the peeing part didn't start happening till later but I guess not!" She said before going up the stairs to the bathroom. I just laughed and got up from the couch to go upstairs and get ready for the day; but Connor grabbed my arm and made me sit back down next him. He pulled me close to him again and buried his face in my hair again.

"Everyone is starting to get up, we should go get dressed." I said.

"No." He said, it made me jump a bit because his breath tickled my neck.

"Come on," I said trying to pull away, but he just would just squeeze me tighter to him.

"Hey!" Connor shot up and we both looked over towards the living room door to see William standing there.

"What?" Connor said.

"Who shot those turkeys?"

"We did." I said.

"Oh… good job." William said as Poppy reappeared from upstairs.

"Do we have anymore eggs, I'm hungry." Poppy asked me.

"I thought I saw like two in the basket last night." I said.

"Good enough for me," she said pushing William aside to go towards the kitchen. It was obvious that Connor and I had had enough time together and it was time to get our day started. He eased up his embrace and let me go. Other than the early start to the day, everything seemed like it was going to be a very uneventful and average day.

Poppy and I worked with Ms. Elizabeth in the garden that afternoon. As we knelt in the grass, Ms. Elizabeth went on and on about the different types of herbs that she was growing in the garden. Many of them were either for seasoning or tea, and others had therapeutic or other properties that might be of use. The sun was beaming down on us and it was getting close to being the hottest part of the day. I had my hair tied up high on my head to help elevate the heat that I felt against the back of my neck, Poppy say fanning herself with her hands as we listened to Ms. Elizabeth. The heat was baking, and when Ms. Elizabeth spoke she would often pause to breathe or massage the temples of her head. I began to get suspicions as to the way Ms. Elizabeth was acting as she gave us this impromptu lesson in the garden, her cheeks were flushed, and she began to slur her words and stagger her sentences. I stood up and went to her as she placed her hand on her head.

"Poppy, go get Cora or Charlotte, hurry." I said to Poppy; Poppy could also sense that something was wrong with Ms. Elizabeth. She went from educating us one moment to almost completely forgetting that we were before her a moment later. Poppy hurried down to the house from the garden as I knelt down next to Ms. Elizabeth. I had never seen her in such a state before. She was always the ideal picture of health and vigor; nothing could ever do her harm. She looked up at me briefly, I could tell just by looking at her eyes that something was terribly, terribly wrong.

"I feel very, very faint, Mona." Was all she could manage to say before I watched her eyes roll to the back of her head and her body fall limp. I caught her and held her on my lap.

"Cora! Charlotte! Someone!" I began to yell, "Ms. Elizabeth please wake up, please, please, please." I said gently patting her cheeks in an attempt to help her regain consciousness. From my cries for help, everyone ran from where ever they had been. Everyone had looks of horror on their faces and no one was being quick to act.

"Don't just stand there! We need to get her out of the sun!" I commanded. William was the first to act, lifting his grandmother up and carrying her into the house. Charlotte and Cora stood wide eyed and in shock as the limp, unconscious Ms. Elizabeth passed them. William stood in the kitchen awaiting further instruction as to where to lay his grandmother, Cora was then the first to say something that made sense as to how we should treat Ms. Elizabeth.

"Amelia, fill the bathtub with cold water, do it now. Poppy, soak some rags and put them in a bucket and then store the bucket in the cellar until we need them. Mona, you'll help me." Cora ordered.

William laid Ms. Elizabeth down on the large wooden island that stood at the center of the kitchen. Charlotte shooed everyone from the kitchen, telling them to go back to whatever they had been doing. With wet rags we began to blot Ms. Elizabeth with the hopes that the coolness would help her to come to. Once Amelia returned to tell us that the bathtub was ready, the four of us worked to gently carry Ms. Elizabeth up the stairs. We didn't even bother to remove her clothes, we just submerged her body into the water. Cora sat on a stool by her mother's head and held her head above the water.

"Heat stroke, it's only heat stroke." She muttered to herself.

"Mona, help me." Charlotte said as she began to remove Ms. Elizabeth's outer clothes. We placed her soaking wet baby blue dress, socks, and shoes in the sink , and left her to float in the cool well water in the thin white chemise that she wore under it all. Every few minutes we would drain some of the water and refill it with fresh cool water. This went on for a matter of twenty minutes before she opened her eyes and smiled at us.

"Oh, thank God." Cora said leaning down and kissing her mother's forehead. We had reached the point of immense worry as to the fact that she was not waking up. The room and the house had been silent, but with Ms. Elizabeth's eyes open and a faint grin on her face, we knew that although things were not quite alright just yet, we knew that we no longer had to stand in a suspended state of extreme anxiety.

"It seems I might have startled you all, I'm sorry." She faintly said.

"Yes, yes you did, Ma, but don't worry about that all now. How do you feel?" Cora asked.

"Like I took a steak knife to the brain." She said, Cora had a look of minor confusion and worry on her face.

"Charlotte, take over for me." Cora said before switching places with her sister in law. As she passed by me she grabbed my wrist and pulled me out into the hallway.

"I know heat stroke, I've seen it before, but I just need to be sure. I need you to take Amelia and go down to town and get Mrs. Miller's advice." Cora said to me, I just nodded my head and got Amelia to come with me. We took the dirt bike down to town and went directly to Mrs. Miller's. The sweet old woman was delighted to see us, but became gravely concerned when we told her what happened. She began asking us questions and wanted to know what we had done so far to care for Ms. Elizabeth. We told her everything and she just nodded and stopped to think for a while.

"Well there isn't much one can do for a heat stroke anymore, all we can do is everything you folks have already done. I would need to assess Elizabeth myself in order to know what steps to take next." Mrs. Miller said.

"We came by dirt bike, I agree that the best thing is for you to see her, but I don't think it'll be safe for you." Amelia said.

"Miss Amelia Sybil Wilde, in all my years living in this town, I have traveled by horseback, motorcycle, wagon, race car, and everything in between, if you drive steady and safely, I can get to the farm on your dirt bike." Mrs. Miller said, I couldn't help but laugh.

Amelia did not feel comfortable taking Mrs. Miller on the bike so it would be up to me. We left Amelia at Mrs. Miller's house while I took the sweet old woman down to the farm. Mrs. Miller held on to me tightly as we made our way back down to the farm. When we arrived we ran into Peter in the yard who looked very shocked to see a little old woman on the back of a dirt bike. I ushered Mrs. Miller up to Ms. Elizabeth's bedroom where Charlotte and Cora had moved her. She was lying comfortably on top of the blankets and sheets propped up on pillows. She had since been changed into a light weight, dry night gown. Cora was diligently blotting her mother's head with a damp cloth, and Charlotte was working hard to fan her dear mother in law with a paper fan.

"Elizabeth Wilde, what seems to be the problem?" Mrs. Miller said as she leaned on her cane in the doorway of the bedroom.

"Oh, my dear Mrs. Miller, there was no need to bring yourself all the way down here. I am in good capable hands." Mrs. Elizabeth said patting the back of Cora's hand.

"Nonetheless, I am glad she is here." Cora said before handing the damp rag to Charlotte to take over.

"Mrs. Miller," Cora began, "I have dealt with heat stroke before, with my husband and father once, but my mother describes her head pain as very intense. We have no pain reliever and this is where I find myself at a loss." Cora explained.

"I see... tell me this, Elizabeth, when was the last time you drank a tall glass of water?" Mrs. Miller asked.

"I had tea this morning." Ms. Elizabeth answered.

"I do not mean tea, or a few sips of water, I mean a tall glass of nothing but pure clear water."

"I don't remember." Ms. Elizabeth replied.

"Cora, have your mother start sipping on some water. There isn't much we can do about the pain other than hope that steady even breathing, and a good drink of water will help it to naturally subside. As for you Elizabeth, I want bed rest for no less than two weeks."

"Two weeks!" Ms. Elizabeth exclaimed.

"Your eyes tell me that you have the weight of the world on your shoulders, one woman cannot handle it all you have succumbed to stress, worry, and the fact that you have not allowed yourself to rest doesn't help one bit."

"I have relaxed! I took a nap yesterday!" Ms. Elizabeth said.

"Naps are not the same. You have plenty of strong capable women and men here who will keep this farm going, two weeks, who knows maybe less, but those are my instructions. I don't want you doing any work, not even cooking." Mrs. Miller said.

"We will make sure she stays put, you can count on that." Cora said just as Poppy appeared in the doorway.

"Well, well, well, what do we have here!" Mrs. Miller said to Poppy.

"Oh... hello." Poppy said.

"I see that congratulations are in order, how far along with this little baby are you?"

"What? You can tell?" Poppy said all concerned looking down at her stomach, which, for the most part only had the teeniest of a little bump.

"I have seen dozens and dozens of expectant mothers in my life time, I know an expectant mother when I see one."

"Oh…" Poppy said.

"Well while I am here, and before sweet Mona takes me back home, let's give you a little examination." Mrs. Miller said taking Poppy's arm and guiding her to the next bedroom. While Poppy and Mrs. Miller were in the other room, I sat at the foot of Ms. Elizabeth's bed with a damp rag blotting the bottoms of her feet.

"So you're just going to relax for two weeks, no gardening, no cooking, no telling the boys to go hunt, no anything." Cora told her mother.

"Yes, Cora and I will handle everything, you don't need to worry." Charlotte affirmed.

"I don't know if I can sit still for two weeks!" Ms. Elizabeth sighed.

"You can and you will." Cora said; I stood up to go dampen my wash cloth some more, and as I did so the door to the room opened and both Poppy and Mrs. Miller emerged.

"I'd say you folks will have a healthy bundle of joy bouncing around here by late November or early December." Mrs. Miller said.

"We've been making sure Poppy stays out of things she ought not to be in." Ms. Elizabeth stated.

"Well I hope you don't have her under too many restrictions, she's the perfect image of health, restricting her too much would cause harm in my good opinion."

"Yes, yes! I'm not allowed to do anything anymore!" Poppy said.

"Well my dear, as long as it is safe and you feel comfortable without straining yourself, continue on doing what you were doing." Mrs. Miller assured Poppy. Poppy just grinned and left the room to go down stairs.

"Well Mona, I guess it's high time you take me home." Mrs Miller said. When we arrived back at Mrs. Miller's house, I was not surprised to see that Brady had found Amelia and they were sitting together on Mrs. Miller's front porch. They sat close together enthralled in conversation. They were so absorbed with one another that they hardly noticed that Mrs. Miller and I had arrived. Mrs

Miller just batted them with her cane so that she could get by. The couple just scooted to the side and continued talking.

"Should I just leave you here or…?" I said catching Amelia's attention.

"Oh… oh, I better go." She said turning to Brady.

"When will you be in town next?" he said standing up.

"Oh, I honestly don't know." She said sadly.

"Well, I'll just come to the farm then." Brady stated.

"If you want." Amelia said blushing. The two said goodbye to one another before Amelia got on the bike with me and we went back to the farm. I let Amelia off in front of the house so she could go see her grandmother and I went to take the bike down to the barn. Connor was stacking wood behind the barn so he caught me as I was putting the bike away. I hardly had time to see him coming before he grabbed me.

"How's my grandmother?" he asked as he played with my hair.

"She'll be fine, just heat stroke. She is ordered to strict bed rest." I replied.

"That's good."

"How has your day been?"

"It's been good, much better now that I know everything is alright and you're back. I don't like it when you leave." He said taking a strand of my hair and using it to make it into a mustache for himself.

"When am I ever gone? I'm always here." I laughed.

"Exactly and when you do go somewhere I miss you and I don't like it." he said.

"Well it must have been torture."

"It was." he said leaning down to kiss me, but I dodged him and darted a few feet away.

"Finish doing your chores." I ordered him before I turned to go to the house. I heard him chuckle as I walked back down to the house.

30.

Findings

Though there was much bickering and huffing and puffing, Ms. Elizabeth stayed in bed for the whole two weeks while Charlotte and Cora kept the house running. The month of July came and went faster than any month I had on memory, and soon August was at our door, as well as the thought that was in the back of all our minds that the season would be changing soon. One day, as if almost instantly, Poppy's belly popped and she had a full blown baby bump. She looked as though she stuffed a small ball under her blouse and was walking with a teeny waddle, her face filled out a bit and above all she looked absolutely adorable. There was no one who adored Poppy's newfound pregnancy glow more than William. He doted upon her and lit up whenever she was near, I had never seen such true love for another person as the way Poppy and William loved each other.

I made a new project for myself to start making baby clothes for our upcoming new member of the family. I spent the majority of my free time sitting by the window in the living room sewing little onesies and baby bloomers and teeny shirts. On many of these moments that I spent sewing, Connor would join me, cuddling up with me on a large wing chair just snoozing while I stitched. Although we spoke very little during those moments, I very much enjoyed them and looked forward to them every day. It was a peculiar feeling of contentment to just simply be either beside Connor or to be held by him, and he was perfectly content as well.

"Let's go hunting." He said during a moment when I thought he had been napping when really he was quietly watching me.

"We just went." I said putting the little yellow pants that I was sewing down on to the table beside the chair.

"No, like a three day trip. We could camp out for a weekend by the river and we will for sure catch a lot of stuff." He said taking a piece of ribbon that was tied around the waist of my dress and running it though his fingers.

"Three days?" I questioned.

"Yeah; it'll be nice." He smirked.

"I suppose it would be nice. Amelia should come too." I stated fully knowing that Connor had slight ulterior motives other than to hunt deer and other animals.

"My sister?" he mumbled.

"No, Amelia Earhart." I mused with the full intent to make sure that the statement dripped in sarcasm.

"Fine." He said in a low bellowing voice. The new way he fiddled with the ribbon on my dress and how he lounged on the chair signaled to me that by requesting that Amelia comes with us on the hunting excursion annoyed him.

"When will we go?" I asked in an effort to try and cheer him up.

"This Friday we could leave. There's a spot William and I had by the river." He said dropping the ribbon and running his hands over both his face and then through his hair.

"Then Friday it is then. I'll go tell Amelia." I added as I began to get up from the seat. Connor immediately leaned forward and wrapped his arms around my waist and pulled me back down to the chair. Fighting against Connor was useless, he was so much stronger than me, so I just sighed and made myself comfortable on his lap waiting for an opportunity to get up. The opportunity did not come for a while since Connor was perfectly content to keep me there forever, which I didn't at all mind. His new favorite thing to do was to cuddle; I wasn't safe from being grabbed at any moment. This new fascination of his was nice for the most part, unless I was trying to get something done, or if I had somewhere to go.

Connor finally let me go when Peter came into the living room to ask him to take a trip into town for some rope. I did have to admit that I was sad that he was now leaving, but I had things to do and so did he. I found Amelia in the kitchen, blissfully humming a tune of her own and washing some dishes in the sink. I told her about Connor's plan for the hunting trip and that we would leave on Friday. She seemed all excited and eager for Friday to come and completely forgot that she was doing the dishes and instead went out to the barn to start getting things together for the trip. I just laughed and finished off the last few plates that were in the sink before going out to the barn. While Amelia was packing things, I went over to William who was hammering and cutting wood to make some sort of piece of furniture.

"What are you making?" I asked.

"A crib." He said with a big smile on his face. William was going to be such a proud and loving father. I picked up a rod of wood that would most likely become a rod of some sort for the crib.

"What are you hoping for?" I asked.

"I honestly don't care," he began, "A boy would be great, but I would love a little girl too."

"Have you given any thoughts to what you would name it?"

"Not really, I guess I would want to meet the little thing first, ya know."

"Well you should have some favorite names."

"I like the name Asher, for a boy, and Helena for a girl."

"Those are beautiful names." I said as I put the wooden rod back onto its place. I left the barn with Amelia still tearing the place apart to get things packed and ready for the trip and William working on the crib.

***

On Friday morning, before the sun had even risen, Connor gently woke me up and told me it was time to get going. I got dressed in a pair of Amelia's jeans that she had and a t-shirt and boots. I was glad that Amelia, Charlotte, and I were relatively the same size, or else I would have had to go hunting in one of the many dresses I have had to make for myself. Everything was packed and ready to go, and so in the early morning, we threw the backpacks over our shoulders and began our hike out to the spot that Connor knew about. The sun had not even risen yet, but I was excited and wide awake. Connor held my hand as we marched through the forest. Connor wanted to reach the spot by noon, but until then, we had fifteen miles to hike.

"I would like to get at least a deer or two, it'll be a pain to lug back, but it'll last us. A couple birds won't hurt either." Connor said through the dim morning light for Amelia and I to hear.

"Are we going to that spot that's up stream but right on the bank of the river?" Amelia asked.

"Yes. I figured it would be great since all the animals will be going to the river to drink in the heat. It's a relatively calm place, like it." Connor said loud enough for Amelia to hear since she was a few yards behind us.

"It's a great spot," Connor began, but only speaking to me, "The bank of the river is very steep and exposes these huge boulders. Yet at the bottom there's this alcove where the sand and sediment from the river is really, really soft. It's always super quiet there and you can hear the water in the river flowing, and at night, you can see straight up into the sky and see the stars."

"It sounds beautiful." I said with a grin. The river was only about a 20 minute walk from the farm, but once we got to the river, we would have to follow it up stream until getting to Connor's spot. The walk upstream had a slight incline to it, and it was a tad physically exhausting, but I rather enjoyed the physical exertion. Connor didn't want to take many rest stops, but we did stop several times to drink water and cool down in the river. It hadn't gotten too hot yet, but by mid-morning we could feel the heat starting to creep up on us. Just when I began to start thinking that we would be walking at the hottest part of the day, we arrived at Connor's spot.

Connor's face went from being utterly excited about showing us the spot to being entirely disappointed. He had gone ahead of us during his excitement, and all I could do was watch his shoulders slump over and his head hang a little lower.

"What's wrong?" I said jogging up to meet him, I turned in the direction he was facing to see his alcove.

"Someone's been here." He said disappointed.

"It was probably Brady, he knows about this place too." Amelia said once catching up to us. I turned to examine the alcove and I saw that there were empty food cans piled up into a pyramid in one corner, an empty bottle of Budweiser beer, and charred, burnt wood from a fire that once burned for whomever used this spot.

"No, I don't think it was Brady." He said with his voice sounding a bit serious.

"What is it?" I said as he picked up one of the empty cans. I watched him lift it up to his nose and give a slight sniff.

"It's fresh, only maybe a day old." He said putting it back exactly the way it was. Once he said that Amelia went over to the fire pit and held her hand over the charred wood.

"It's still warm." She confirmed what I only thought that Connor already knew. He walked over to her and bent down to blow on the charred pile, we watched as a few areas of the wood glowed red a bit as the rush of air hit them.

"Come on, quick, let's get out of here." He said taking us both by the arms.

"Who do you think is using it?" Amelia asked.

"I don't know, but you can bet I will find out." Connor said harshly. We walked further up the river and then up the river bank and back into the forest. There was an area of land that dipped low between two small hills. It wasn't too far from the river that we wouldn't have to travel to far to hunt, but it was going to be an inconvenience. Connor remained silent for the remainder of the afternoon; I could tell he was angry. Once we got the tent set up and a small fire going, I placed my hands on his shoulders as he sat on a log staring into the flames.

"No need to be so upset, we will have a lovely weekend." I said softly to him

"I knew about the Campbell's using the spot, and I knew of one other family as well, and it can't be either of them." he said.

"How do you know?"

"Think about it, Mona, when was the last time you saw a bottle of beer, or canned food?" He said looking up at me. This new thought that he planted in my head made my stomach sink and I could feel my palms starting to get sweaty. He was right. We had not seen canned food or commercially made beer since during the quarantines of the cities. No one would have them, no one in town that is. It meant that it was someone else, someone from outside the town, an intruder. I took a step back from Connor as the seed that he had planted began to sprout and grow in my thoughts.

"A gang?" I breathlessly whispered low enough for only him to hear.

"That's what I'm afraid of." He said standing up and pulling me into an embrace. "I can feel your heart pounding." He said as we stood there.

"It has to be someone from town who had a nice food supply. Until we know otherwise, that is what I will decide that it is." I said, at that moment we both heard a twig snap. Both of our heads snapped to the direction of the noise, only it was just Amelia coming up from the river from refilling our water jars.

"You guys look like you have just seen a ghost!" She said with a laugh

"Amelia, I don't want you to go to the river alone, always tell one of us, or take one of us with you." Connor said.

"Oh alright." She said with a weird look on her face. I could tell that in her mind, the thought had not occurred to her as to what the findings in the hunting spot could potentially mean.

"So when do we start hunting?" Amelia cheerfully said.

"Not today, let's start tomorrow, for the rest of the day let's just chill." Connor said.

"Oh ok! Let's swim in the…"

"No!" Connor snapped at Amelia

"Wh…why?" she said with her feelings obviously a bit injured at the way he responded.

"Not until I know who is in my spot, I don't want it to be anyone dangerous, that's all. You are not to go to the river alone." He commanded.

"I see… Like I said before, it was probably just Brady." She said with a smile, I just looked at Connor, without having to say anything, he just nodded his head fully knowing that I was asking permission to tell her.

"Amelia, we don't think it's anyone from town. Since when is anyone nowadays eating food from a can and drinking Budweiser beer?" I saw at that very moment that the seed was planted in Amelia's thoughts, her eyes grew big and her mouth dropped open.

"No," She said.

"Yes, we don't know for sure, we will find out though. We could be wrong." Connor said taking his little sister's hand. Now that we all had this threatening thought implanted into our heads, it would be impossible for us to enjoy any part of that weekend. We spent the rest of that long afternoon just trying to finish setting up camp. As dusk approached Connor took us out to set some snares around the camp to hopefully capture a few small critters. The snares he set up were relatively harmless snares that would only trap an animal and not kill it; we mainly set them just to see what sort of little furry creatures liked this part of the woods.

When darkness came, we heated up some of the food that Ms. Elizabeth packed us over the fire and just listened to the night time noises of the summer. We barely spoke to one another; for the most part we just listened. What we were listening for, we did not know. It was going to be a long three days.

"We ought to get to bed early; we'll wake up at dawn again tomorrow and find a nice spot to make a stake out by the river to see if we get anything." Connor said getting up and going into the tent. I just continued to sit by the fire and I looked at Amelia who looked just as equally unhappy as Connor was. I let out a long sigh and went into the tent after Connor. In the dim orange light that played through the fabric of the tent from the fire outside, I could see him fumbling in the dark to get the sleeping bags arranged neatly on the ground.

"It won't be as good as the alcove; someone is bound to be sleeping on a stick all night." He said with a grumpy tone.

"Hey… hey," I said going over to him and cupping his face in my hands, 'There's no need to be such a grouch, I mean, yes we are all a little upset and concerned, but don't be so crabby about it." Connor relaxed his shoulders a bit and lifted his hands up to hold both of mine.

"I'm sorry." He said

"Let's just get to sleep and we will enjoy tomorrow." I said as I began to untie my boots and pull them off. Amelia too came into the tent and together in a matter of minutes we were all each comfortable in our own sleeping bags.

***

In the pale light of the morning we waited. From atop a hill we could see down on to an ideal strip of the river where Connor suspected a lot of animals went for a drink. We hid ourselves behind a large fallen tree and leaves and sticks we piled up to help hide us even more.

"Now what?" I asked once we were settled behind our little blind.

"We wait, keep your bow and arrow ready, and stay watching something could come at any moment." Connor said. The morning air was mild, and the birds sang high in the trees as the water in the river tinkled away. Seconds, minutes, and hours passed, and there wasn't any sign of any animals anywhere. Judging by how high the sun had gotten in the sky, it was nearing noon, yet still we waited. It was all about silence and waiting.

My eyes were beginning to grow heavy with drowsiness as the shadows that stretched across the land grew longer as the sun stretched across the sky. The sudden flapping of bird's wings and the screech of birds leaping into flight shook me awake and I gazed down at the river as a young buck made its way out of the forest and near to the river for a drink. Without making any noise, I tapped Connor. He had fallen into a slumber, but woke straight up upon seeing the deer.

"I got it." he whispered. Slowly and stealthily he moved into position, pulling the string of his bow back and taking aim with his arrow. Amelia and I became super attentive to his every move as he slowly prepared to let the arrow go to hit its target. Just as Connor was ready to let it go a loud bang echoed and split through the forest and the deer dropped dead. Connor didn't shoot the arrow, he carefully released the string so as not to fire and put the arrow on the ground.

It had been gun fire, gun fire from the other side of the river. Connor ducked back down and in silence the three of us watched and four people came out of the woods on the other side of the river. They were dressed mostly in black with burgundy colored arm bands or head bands. They carried with them assault rifles, not hunting rifles. I could not tell if the four people were men or women, but they were loud, cussing and hollering and cheering over the kill that they had just made. Soon a fifth member of the mysterious group appeared and began yelling at the others.

"Hurry up, get it back to camp!" he barked at them, the four soon scrambled and dragged the limp, lifeless body of the deer away, and just like that they were gone. I flopped back down on to the ground, Amelia was crying, and Connor's face was red with anger. Our worst fears had come true. A gang was treading dangerously close to our home, our family, and our town. For all we knew, an attack was almost imminent.

"Come on; let's get back to our camp." Connor instructed Amelia and I. Once back at camp we threw our bows down and sat down. We were angry, scared, and just in bewilderment. What were we going to do?

"We have to know how big this gang is." Connor said.

"And how are we going to do that?" Amelia asked.

"Tonight we will cross the river and see if we can see their camp."

"Connor, it's too dangerous." I cautioned.

"We need to know what we are dealing with before we go back home. It could be a large gang or a small group of nomadic people; we have to know for sure." He reasoned. Connor's reasoning was indeed sound. We did need to know what we would be up against if we were in fact facing a dangerous gang. It was decided upon. We would cross the river at night and go deep into the other side of the forest in search of this gang's camp. It was quite obvious that they wouldn't be too far with the river being the only water source.

We waited. We waited long after the sun set and the moon rose. We waited until the dead of night and when only the sounds of crickets could be heard in the darkness. Connor and I took nothing with us, yet Amelia carried her throwing knives with her. With the river being so low due to the drought it was easy to cross with only getting up to our ankles wet with water. We climbed the opposite river bank and made our way into the forest.

With the half-moon guiding our path with its dim light we went into the forest, but it didn't take long for us to hear the sounds and smell the smells that were coming from a nearby camp. They were about a quarter of a mile away from the river into the forest. Crouching down behind a bush and some trees we got a good look at the setup of their camp. Myself I counted 24 large tents in all as well as some make shift shelters. It was a large camp, large enough to overtake us and the town. As to how many gang members there actually were, I could not say. They moved about from tent to tent, from camp fire to camp fire, hollering, laughing, and talking. They had guns and knives, and quite a few of the gang members looked very intimidating. They all looked very well fed, and they looked like they didn't lack anything when it came to supplies.

“I tried counting, but there are so many.” Connor whispered.

“It’s close to the seventies.” Amelia said.

“We should go, we need to go home.” I said, we turned back and went back to the river and across. The three of us slept restlessly that night. The only thing we could think about was how badly we wanted to get back to the farm, and back to our family. Connor held me close that night while he slept, somehow we knew that our small period of peace might be at an end.

31.

Awareness

We packed up everything we could as soon as the first rays of sunshine made their way above the treetops that very next morning. We had gone out on this hunting excursion in vain, we would return with nothing except bad news that there was a gang a mere fifteen miles from the farm. When we emerged from the forest later that afternoon, we gazed down at our peaceful farm with great sorrow in our hearts. Amelia ran ahead a bit and then stopped to just look at the farm from the hill. Connor put his arm around me and we just stood there looking. We watched William carrying a load of wood into the kitchen, Poppy hanging laundry on the clothes line, Ms. Elizabeth bending down to weed in the garden, and Luke and Jonathan were on the roof of the house repairing loose shingles.

It took a moment for any of them to notice that we were standing atop the hill that looked down to the farm. It eventually was Peter, who after coming out of the house to bring his grandmother a glass of water, spotted the three of us standing there. He gave a shout and then waved to us. We did nothing, but start to slowly walk down to the farm. After hearing of our return from Peter, William came out and jogged up to meet us half way.

"What? You come back with nothing? We weren't expecting you home until tonight." He said with a chuckle.

"We couldn't get anything." Amelia said with a flat sorrowful tone in her voice.

"What do you mean?" he said asking her, but she just brushed him aside and continued down to the farm. "What happened?" he said looking at his younger brother, Connor took a step forward leaning close to his brother so that none other than the three of us could hear what had to be said.

"A gang, fifteen miles from here, not far from our hunting spot at the alcove." Connor gravely said.

"No… impossible." William said in disbelief.

"It is possible, we saw them with our own eyes, and we even went and saw their camp." I chimed in.

"How large are they? What are their numbers?" William demanded to know.

"Large enough to take down a home and a town." Connor replied, William looked down at his feet and then covered his face with both of his hands.

"What's the matter? You three look like you just heard news of something dreadful!" Poppy called out as she began to come close to us from the clothes line.

"Poppy…" William began; I could hear the silent yet ever present pain in his voice as he looked upon his wife and said her name, "Gather everyone in the house."

"Why?" She said

"Please… just tell everyone to go in the living room." He said to her before turning back to Connor and me.

"This cannot wait; we cannot sweep this under the carpet." William said turning back to Connor.

"Of course, what did you think I was going to do?" Connor said getting a bit angry at his brother. William just flared his nostrils and turned away from us to go to the house. Connor and I disposed of all the hunting equipment that we carried in the barn before going in the house. The entire family, with the exception of Amelia had gathered in the living room.

"What is the meaning of this?" Charlotte asked.

"Why are we all here?" Cora asked.

"I can't get Amelia to come down from her room." Poppy said.

"It's ok, she already knows what we are about to say." Connor said.

"Well what is it then?" Ms. Elizabeth said.

"While we were down by the river, we saw unusual activity," Connor began.

"What sort of unusual activity?" Johnathan asked.

"Well… there were people." Connor said.

"What people?"

"How many were there?"

"Did you know them?" The family just immediately began to spit questions at us not giving a second thought as to the seriousness of the situation.

"It's a gang!" I finally shouted out amongst the chaos of all the questions. The room fell silent.

"Are you positive?" Luke asked.

"Amelia, Mona, and I went and took a look for ourselves last night. After we saw them hunting on the opposite side of the river. They carried with them assault rifles, they have supplies, and there are a lot of them." Connor said.

"Amelia estimated that the gang is in its high seventies when it comes to members." I said, the silence soon ceased and the family broke out into shouts and questions and murmuring, but thorough all of the chaos of everyone talking I could hear one defined voice, one voice whom I knew would have more answers than any of us; Poppy.

"The colors, what colors did they wear?" She asked as she stood up from her seat. She had this look of aggression on her face, a look I had never seen before, nor did I ever care to see again.

"Black with maroon headbands or arm bands." Connor said, all eyes were then on Poppy as she crossed her arms, looked down at her feet, and cussed.

"Those were the colors of the gang I ran from. The second gang, the gang that I was sold to." She all but whispered.

"What do we do?" Peter asked.

"We do exactly as the CDC told us to do. We prepare as best we can, we need to tell everyone in town that there is a gang nearby. For all we know an attack could be only a matter of days away." Ms. Elizabeth said.

"I wouldn't count on days.... I would count on hours." Poppy said ominously.

"Poppy, please, if you know anything, you must tell us. You mustn't hold anything back." William said taking her hand.

"They have probably been at that camp for weeks if not months. They would have sent out scouts to see if there was anything around, they most likely know all about the town, and they probably know about us." She said.

"If all that is true, why haven't they attacked? Perhaps they are peaceful." Cora said.

"No... they are not peaceful, they are ruthless killers. The only reason they haven't attacked the town or us is because they are most likely waiting. They probably don't need to attack us yet, but they will." She explained.

"What do you mean by they might need to attack us?" Charlotte asked.

"Attacks mostly take place during the fall and winter, when food is scarce and supplies run thin. The gangs are mostly sedentary during the spring and summer." Poppy responded.

"So do you think they are planning?" Luke said.

"They aren't planning, they've already planned." Poppy said, everyone sunk down in their seats and the room grew silent.

"But Poppy, we don't know all of this for sure. We don't know if they know about us, and we don't know if they are just passing through peacefully." Peter tried to reason.

"You're right, Peter, there is a small chance that that might be true, but we cannot risk it. We must alert the town and we must prepare ourselves." Connor said. It was the truth, we couldn't wait another moment. We suggested that Peter go to town, but William insisted that it was he that should be the one to go.

William took the dirt bike and rode to town while the rest of us stayed on the farm. We knew that things had to be done, but we acted slowly in doing them. We had all those supplies that the CDC had given us, yet we had yet to use them in the way that they ought to be used. We had the stainless steel bins that were to hold emergency supplies, yet we had yet to fill them and bury them. The moment William disappeared from our sight at the end of the driveway; Ms. Elizabeth ordered Connor and Peter to find a place to bury the bin. It needed to be in a spot unnoticed, and unseen. If we were to bury something, it was going to be obvious for a while that the ground was dug up, so it would have to be easily hidden from sight. Poppy suggested that they burry it under the bus, after all, the grass that once grew under the bus was starting to die and fall away and the dirt already looked like it had been partially dug up during the original bus construction.

While Connor and Peter worked together to try and figure out how they were going to dig a big enough hole in a space that was already hard to work with, the rest of us worked on gathering supplies that would be put into the bin. We didn't have any nonperishable foods besides a few jarred and dried things that could be safely stored. If it was in a sealed jar, or stored in a tin and had a life span of a couple months, we put it into the bin. We also put in clothes, at least four sets of clothes for each person in the house; two sets of fall clothes, and two sets of winter clothes. Anything that would help us to survive a couple weeks after a potential attack, we put into the bin.

By the time we had the bin filled to maximum capacity for the family, Connor and Peter had finished digging a hole that was the exact size we needed. We sealed and locked the bin shut and then it took me, Amelia, Connor, Peter, Luke, and Jonathan to carry the bin over and maneuver it into the hole. Once it was snug in its new home, Luke covered it with a brown tarp and Connor and Peter got to work on covering it all again with dirt.

William arrived back on the farm around the time Peter and Connor were filling in the hole. He was impressed at what we had done, and was very proud of Poppy for thinking of such a smart hiding place for the bin. By dusk the bin was completely covered, and Peter and Connor used some hay to cover the freshly over turned soil.

"Tomorrow we'll let the chickens peck at the ground over here; they'll help it get all flat again." Jonathan said. The news that William brought back from the town wasn't good. The town was now in a panic as to what to do about the gang, some people wanted to go down and attack them during the night, while others just wanted to close the gates of the wall and never leave again. William told us that there would be a big town meeting the very next morning, which we would all attend.

"Alright, let's all just get inside for dinner; we'll worry about more things once we have full stomachs." Ms. Elizabeth said to all of us. The conversation that took place over dinner was all about what more we could possibly do to prepare for an attack. The first thing that the boys decided upon was to set up a night time watch rotation. Starting that very night they would take turns in shifts to watch for any activity. They also tossed around different ideas on how we would all evacuate the farm if need be.

"There's no use in even trying to put up a fight, our lives are much more precious than this farm, if we get enough warning to just flee, then that would be good enough." Connor said.

"This is our home, it's belonged to us for generations, and we can't just give up on it." Amelia said as she served herself another helping of green beans.

"But Connor is right, our lives are more important, and we don't have any chance against a well-equipped gang." I said.

"We need to consider both sides of the argument, we should come up with at least something that would both allow us time to escape, and even the possibility of saving the farm." William said.

"The possibility of saving the farm is pointless. They'll take everything and burn what's left, you know that." Poppy said to her husband.

"We shouldn't just give up though." He stated.

"I think for tonight that is enough talk about gangs and fleeing the farm. After everyone is finished, wash your plates as usual and we'll have a nice story in the living room; how about that?" Ms. Elizabeth said.

"Ma, we might not have until tomorrow. Please don't try and shove this aside, this is serious." Charlotte said to her mother.

"I am not shoving it aside. We all still have a life to live, and chores to do. If the gang comes tonight, then they come tonight, if they come months from now, then they come months from now. What I'm trying to say is that there is no use in trying to be as prepared as possible right at this very moment. No amount of preparation is going to fully prepare us to lose our homes and possibly our lives. We have no control over what happens tomorrow, all we can worry about is today and this moment." She said before standing up and taking her plate to the kitchen. Ms. Elizabeth's words were poignant. She was right; we had no control of what the future now held for us. We sat in silence while we finished our dinners, and one by one we all got up to take our plates to the kitchen to be washed and put away. I was rather exhausted from the day's activities, so instead of joining the family in the living room to read out loud, I said my goodnights and went up to bed.

***

The gates at the town wall were sealed shut when we arrived the very next morning. One of the townsmen who was now acting as a guard looked over the wall from a small little watch post and ordered the gates to be opened. Once we all walked inside, the gates were once again sealed. Everyone was in the town green ready for the town meeting. With each person that I passed I could read a look of concern and bewilderment on their faces. Everyone in town was frightened, as we all were.

The town meeting consisted mostly of the older men of the town bouncing ideas back and forth as to how to keep the town safe and what the action plans would be if there was to be an attack. William spoke up and pointed out that when the CDC visited the last time they had installed a radio communication link that would have us directed to the CDC in Amherst. William thought that if we informed the CDC that there was a gang nearby that they would send people to come help us with the situation before something bad happens. The majority of the people in town opposed that idea.

"They told us this would happen! They aren't going to help us now!" Someone yelled.

"We are on our own for survival! Sure they gave us supplies to give us a fighting chance, but they won't come now!" another yelled.

"We don't know that for sure! The CDC wants towns like ours to thrive, I feel like they would help us!" William interjected.

"They warned us, they knew this would happen, and they prepared us. By doing that, they might as well have just told us that we were on our own." An older man said.

"Inside the town walls is the safest place for anyone to be." A woman in the crowd yelled.

"But what about us who don't live in the walls?" a voice cried out at the back of the crowd. It was Brady, and he had brought his entire family with him, all seven of them. Ms. Elizabeth, Cora, and Charlotte moved over towards the Campbell's in order to greet the women and children that up until that very moment, I had no idea existed. The Campbell family, with the exception of Brady, mostly stayed on their own farm, it was a very special treat for all of them to come to town.

"Living outside the walls is a choice that the Wilde family and the Campbell family made. You can both come and live in town, or you can take your chances outside." Said one of the men whose name I soon learned to be Marshall Kent. Connor whispered to me that

Marshall Kent always managed to either be the devil's advocate or the instigator when it came to town issues, he resented anyone who chose to be different than him, and had a "me first" attitude.

"The Campbell farm has been the home to the Campbell's since 1892, my great, great, great, great, grandfather built the cabin we live in with his own bare hands. Every single Campbell that is standing here today was born in that cabin; we took our first steps on that land. The Wilde Family farm is older and their land is some of the most fertile around. Mr. Kent, how would you feel if we told you that you could either move from your home or take your chances?" Brady said in a commanding tone.

"I'm sorry young man, but I am not the one living outside the protection of these walls." Marshall said.

"Marshall! You're being hard hearted! Of course the Campbell's and the Wilde's know that they are taking a risk out on their own land, but we must put into place a way to accommodate their safety!" Someone shouted.

"We as a family have already taken steps to be prepared; we are working on a plan to evacuate the farm if the time comes. All we need is a safe place to run to, who will open the gate if we come running and who will help us fend off the people who took our homes from us?" Connor said.

"Of course we won't leave you out in the cold; but what if you come running and there is a gang hot on your trail, what if you bring them here to the town because they followed you?" Marshall said.

"That is a moot point. This whole topic of conversation is pointless. If a gang attacks the Campbell farm or if they attack the Wilde farm, we need to know that there is a situation happening, what we need is an alarm system, something that can be either heard of seen from both farms that way it also gives us warning." Another man from the town said.

"And how on earth are we supposed to manage that!?" Marshall said.

"Mr. Kent…" shouted a young boy from the crowd.

"What?" he spat back.

"I can see the barn of the Wide farm from the roof of the library and I can see the Campbell's chicken coop from there too." The boy said.

"And how did you manage that?" Marshall asked.

"Yesterday afternoon, I sat up there when it was my turn to keep watch, I noticed it." the boy said.

"The CDC gave us flares, perhaps we could store some at our homes and if something were to happen we could fire them and you all would know." William said, everyone in the crowd nodded and showed their agreement with William.

"Alright… we'll give you the flares." Marshall agreed.

"What is his problem? Why is he making this so difficult?" I asked Connor.

"I think it's his goal in life to make things difficult, you should have seen his protest he gave at a town meeting a couple years ago when they were voting on a project to repaint the school gymnasium." Connor whispered to me.

"I think that's enough for one day. We are all prepared, and you folks in town are well fortified and secure, my family and I will draw up a right and proper evacuation plan and once we have it down to a T we will let you all know." Jonathan said to both Marshall and the crowd. Everyone sensed that the meeting was at an end, and they started to disperse. Connor and I went back over to join the rest of our family, while we all stood there waiting to get ready to head back down to the farm, two older women in the town came over and took Poppy's hand and William's.

"I know you all don't want to leave your home and your family, but the safest place is here in the walls… think of the baby." Said one of the other women.

"You'll only get bigger as the weeks go on and running won't be easy." Said the other.

"Thank you very much, but my place and the baby's place is with the family, we will be alright." Poppy said, the two women nodded and turned to leave.

"What will you all do?" I overheard Amelia say to Brady.

"I don't know, I'll probably make Aunt Emma, my mom, and my baby sister stay here in town. Me, my dad, my uncle, cousin, and brother, we can handle the farm ourselves, it's no use putting the others in danger."

"I know the town is the safest place, but I need my family, and they need me." Amelia said.

"The thought of you even staying one night in town hasn't even popped into my head, Mel, you do what you think is best for your family." he said, Amelia nodded and hugged him before turning back to join us in our walk back to town. As both the Wilde family and the Campbell family left the gates of the wall, we received melancholy looks from the watchmen, and when the gates shut and locked behind us, we didn't bother to turn back and even look.

***

There was a small unused shed that was located about half a mile from the edge of the farm, yet at the same time a safe distance from the road so that it was unseen. This shed was very old and very dilapidated, so old in fact that Ms. Elizabeth didn't even know what it was once used for. The wood that the shed was made out of had blackened with time and its sagging roof was covered with moss and a layer of leaves. This shed would serve as a meeting spot for the entire family in the event that we would have to flee. From the shed it was a very easy walk up to the town. The boys spent a good day and a half marking out the path with inconspicuous markings on the trees that could be seen both during the day as well as night.

The plan would be, if it ever came down to it, to leave everything at the farm, meet at the shed, and flee as fast as we could to the town. The thought of leaving everything behind was very distressing to us, but it was the only option that we had. According to Poppy, if we kept a good look out on things we would have a decent amount of time to flee. She said that the gang would send scouts first, once the scouts find the farm they would go back to the gang so the gang could organize a proper attack, at most it would buy us 45 minutes at the most.

With everything all settled and plans well set into place both in town and at home on the farm, the only thing left to do was try and get back to normal with our lives. Chores had to be done, wood needed to be split for the coming months, and our garden was yielding its produce. During the day we carried on, but at night we slept with one eye open at all times.

There was a pile of wood that Connor, William, and Peter had worked hard to stack up against the house, yet it had attracted the unwanted guests of field mice. This was discovered by Cora one morning when she went down to the kitchen to start breakfast and she saw two little mice sitting on the counter as if greeting her. After that she demanded that the woodpile be moved to the edge of the forest just a bit northeast of William and Poppy's bus. With much frustration and grumbling, the boys got working to moving all the wood from the side of the house to the edge of the woods. It was a long way to carry all the wood, and especially in the heat, but they managed it. With the threat of a gang heavily on our minds, the everyday tasks that were still on our shoulders, and the unforgiving heat, we took every spare moment that we had to just be with each other as a family. Hardly anyone could sleep anymore, so we stuck together until the early hours of the morning, reading, talking, and just spending time together.

With a clear starry night above the farm one night, I woke up and soon found myself unable to fall back asleep. I rose out of bed and just went outside, from the kitchen door I could see Connor sitting up on a stool in the barn loft, just overlooking the farm. It was his shift to watch during the night. He was busy watching the edge of the forest just at the top of the hill; he didn't even notice me cross the yard from the house and into the barn. I quietly climbed the staircase to go join him. He finally noticed me when the top step of the staircase creaked.

"Hey." He said.

"How long has it been your turn to watch?" I asked.

"It's been nearly an hour."

"What time is it?" I said coming over to him and sitting down beside him.

"Nearly four in the morning; I'm always out here at this time."

"I should join you and keep you company from now on."

"I would like that, I hardly see you and I don't like it."

"I know, we are always so busy." I sadly confessed.

"I'm glad to get you alone though, I have something that I've been wanting to give you." He softly said as he dug into his pocket. He then pulled out a small heart shaped piece of wood that was attached to a piece of twine.

"I know it's not much, but I made It." he grinned ear to ear proudly. I took the heart shaped carving in my hand and examined it. It was carved and sanded smooth, and was just about a perfect heart except for a small indentation in the side.

"I love it, thank you." I said.

"Here, let me put it on you." he said taking it from me. I pulled my hair to the side while he tied it around my neck.

"I love it Connor, thank you."

"You're welcome." He said leaning down and planting a kiss on the top of my head. For the next hour or so we sat together in the darkness just watching the night pass by. I stayed with him until I began to doze off; I had been apparently nodding my head back and forth with sleepiness because that was when Connor told me to head on back to bed. He still had another hour to stay up on watch.

32.

Rain

On the first morning of October, I opened my eyes to an oddly darkened bedroom. Normally, my bedroom was bright and sunny, but that particular morning it was dull and gray. As my senses started to adjust to the new day I noticed the peculiar sound of light pattering on the roof. Tossing the sheets off my body I went to the window only to see the beaded droplets of water dripping down the glass and the joyous sight of rain. The morning was still early, and I quickly assumed that I was the first person awake in the house, with excitement I threw a shall around my shoulders and ran out of my room and down the hall to Connor and Peter's room. I eagerly jumped on Connor, causing him to cry out in a small fit of shock.

"Good Lord, what is wrong with you?" he said tossing me to the other side of his bed.

"It's raining." I said.

"Raining?" He questioned.

"What... oh my god, seriously, if you guys are going to do this, I think I want my own room." Peter said with the sound of sleep still in his voice as he looked at both me and Connor in the adjacent bed.

"No you idiot, look outside the window." Connor said throwing a pillow at his cousin. Peter laughed and got out of his bed and walked over to the window. Poor Peter, he was the youngest out of all of us and the least experienced in many things. I knew that Peter got on both Connor and William nerves when it came to things; things like his clumsiness, his lack of a sense of urgency, and his occasional selfishness, but deep down I knew that they loved him as if he were their other brother. With Peter's back turned Connor laid back down in bed and wrapped his arms around me and buried his face in my hair.

"Hey, it's raining!" Peter said turning around again. "Seriously, guys, you're gross."

"I'm leaving now." I said pushing Connor off of me as I got up.

"Who's on watch?" Connor asked Peter.

"I think it's my dad." Peter responded.

"Well, I'm going to wake up Amelia." I said as I left the room. Everyone in the house was delighted to see the rain falling. We could only hope that it would last the rest of the day if not more, and that it would quench the thirst of the earth. It wasn't a light rain that was coming down, it was a driving, steading stream of rain drops that came down and hit the ground.

The rain went from being the driving yet steady stream, to being torrential down pours, the ground turned into a muddy, soupy mess. This rain lasted with on and off steady rain, occasional downpours, and a few hours of light misting, for a solid week. Luke guessed that it was brought on by the change of the seasons, with the cooler air of the coming fall hitting the hot sweltering air, it caused the lingering rain.

When the sun reappeared, the land had been quenched ten times over, the grass was green again, birds were singing, and everything that had been lacking in water was bright, perky, and lush with life. The coolness that the rain had brought was a much deserved relief and we welcomed it. Days after the rain, beautiful baby blue wildflowers dotted the field behind the house. They were so beautiful and delicate.

Connor and I spread a blanket out in the field where the grass had grown knee high and the blue flowers were everywhere to be seen. It was amazing what water could do to the land. As we lounged in the grass, I slowly began to pick the flowers to weave them together in order to make a crown of flowers.

"All these little flowers needed was a little water, and look at them. I had no idea that they were even here in the field." Connor said taking them.

"Wildflowers are amazing."

"Really, how so?"

"Back in Baltimore, my mother used to love to take care of the window boxes on our house. She planted all sorts of flowers in the boxes and every day she would water them. One day, in one of the flower boxes outside of the living room window there was a bright little purple flower that had taken root in a small section of the soil. That year my mom had planted pink flowers, and I knew that this purple flower wasn't put there by my mother. I asked my father how the little purple flower got there, and he told me that it was a wildflower. He explained to me that wildflowers were flowers that grew by themselves, that they didn't need a planter or someone to look after them, and that despite hardship, they would always manage to flourish in their own time." I said.

"I guess you can say we are like wildflowers." He said.

"How are we like them?"

"No matter what life has thrown at us so far, we have managed to survive, and in fact flourish. We are like wildflowers." I smiled at what Connor had to say about that.

***

The air was cool and there wasn't a cloud in the sky to shield the night stars from our sight. Connor and I sat together under a light blanket as we kept watch over the farm. I could feel Connors fingers lightly twirling at the ends of my hair, and I could feel his cheek on top of my head. He liked it when I joined him for a while during his night time watches. My eyes scanned both the edge of the forest and the sky; I could hear the music of the late summer crickets in the grass. Colder air would be coming soon, and it would soon be the demise of this generation of crickets. I saw this movement of a figure, near the edge of the forest; it hopped around and ran through the grass. I pointed it out to Connor; he only chuckled and told me that it was a fox that often came out at this time of night. We watched the fox together, it was obviously hunting something. The fox stopped and gazed at the edge of the forest. It froze all together and then ran in the opposite direction, fleeing from the area. I felt it in my stomach, Connor felt it too, there was something, or someone in the forest that scared the fox off. We both stood up and fixed our eyes on that section of the forest. Out of the forest stepped a tall figure dressed all in black, they stood at the edge only for a few moments and then disappeared back behind a tree.

"Go wake up William and Poppy, I'll wake up the house, go immediately to the shed, we will all meet there." He said before pulling me into a hurried kiss and then parted ways. It was happening, the gang, they had found us, they knew, they were coming. I just ran as fast as my legs and feet would allow to Poppy and William's bus, I jammed my fingers between the bus doors and pried them open and ran up the stairs.

"Wake up! Wake up! It's happening!" I screamed, William jumped out of bed and hurried towards me as Poppy just started to get up.

"Are you sure?"

"We saw them… Connor and I." I said.

"Go, hurry, I'll help Connor." William ordered Poppy and I. As we left the bus, Poppy grabbed a small backpack that was by the door and we hurried towards the edge of the forest leading away from the farm and towards the shed. In the darkness we waited with nothing but silence surrounding us. We waited and we waited, yet no one arrived.

"Something's happened." Poppy said.

"They should be here by now." I added. The silence was broken by the sound of someone's feet running through the forest, their footsteps crunching against the leaves. As they came closer I could hear the soft sobs that came from the runner, it was Amelia. Amelia appeared, she carried with her four of the guns that we had stored in the barn, and she came to a stop and dropped everything to the ground.

"There were no scouts, they came all at once, I grabbed what I could, I think they saw me, I think they followed." She cried.

"Where is everyone else?" Poppy said kneeling down to comfort Amelia.

"They had no time. I only turned back once as I was leaving the barn, they were all running from the house as if trying to catch up with me; but the gang caught up, there were so many." She said, as she finished her sentence we could hear the sound of a single shot of gun fire in the distance, and then the flash of the orange flare streaming up into the sky.

"We can't leave them; we have to buy them time." Poppy said getting up.

"Amelia," I said as I bent down and handed her one of the guns, "you and I, we'll have to buy them time while Poppy runs to town." I said

"Me? I most certainly will not!" Poppy said.

"Poppy… you are in no condition," I was starting to try and tell Poppy that she was in no condition to put herself in any sort of harm's way, but the sound of strange voices and the crunching of leaves halted me.

"Amelia will run to town, she's faster than either of us anyway, and she saw the gang, she knows how many are out there." Poppy reasoned.

"We have to hurry, I knew they followed me." Amelia said standing up and taking the gun from my hands.

"Go Amelia, you can do this, you must, do this." Poppy said, Amelia nodded and pulled us both in to a hug before turning and running off into the darkness. The voices and the sound of leaves crunching was getting louder. I grabbed two of the guns that Amelia left and Poppy grabbed the other and we headed north through the woods.

"Do you have a plan?" She asked while we tried to make our way quietly in the darkness.

"What do you have in that bag you're carrying?" I asked.

"A blanket, matches, and some food." She said.

"The wood pile that the boys just moved to the edge of the forest, we could use the matches to light it on fire, it'll be a distraction and buy some time." I said.

"But the rain, it's probably soaked still." Poppy said.

"It's not too far from the chicken coop, there's an oil lantern in there with oil in it. I could grab it and we can use it."

"Sounds good to me." She said, we made it just to the edge of the forest again, and circled around until we were at the backside of the woodpile. Poppy began to set up a blind from behind two fallen trees that were laying on top of each other while I went down to see if I would make it to the chicken coop unnoticed. There were gang members going and coming through the field and up the hill, they had all but encircled the farm, and I could see some of them dragging Cora and Charlotte out of the house and throwing them where the others were being held by the well. I took deep breaths and counted to three before I ran down to the chicken coop, and with one fluid motion lifted the lantern off of its hook by the door of the coop and ran back to Poppy. Poppy had lined the guns up on a log so that we could safely aim from relative shelter as we lured gang members into our trap.

"What did you see?" She asked.

"They have everyone; they are holding them by the well." I said Poppy just nodded her head and took the lantern from me; she walked boldly over to the wood pile and poured the oil all over the top of it and took out a single match, stuck it and tossed it on to the pile. It went up in flames faster than the blink of an eye casting an orange glow down onto the farm and onto every member of our family and every gang member. They all stopped and looked up at the flames, I saw William stand up from where he had been ordered to sit and I knew that at that moment in his heart, he knew that Poppy was here beside me.

We squatted down the best we could in the dirt behind the logs with our guns ready. There were gang members making their way toward the fire and the edge of the forest, but we were in the ideal spot to catch them as they ran up.

"You aim for the feet; I'll aim for the head." Poppy said in a tone in her voice I had never heard before. This was a side of Poppy I had seen on the rarest of occasions, her angry side, her defensive side, this was her fighting side. Poppy took the first shot at the first gang member that came into our line of vision, and he fell flat on to the ground. After the first gunshot that came from our side, the rest of the gang members reached for their weapons and made haste to our direction. I made no hesitation as I pulled the trigger on my gun resulting in a gang member falling to the ground. I became sloppy when it came to aiming and hitting my targets, but I held back no anger. I looked over to Poppy once; she had a flat, emotionless look on her face as she fired shot after shot. It wasn't long before I ran out of bullets and I began to look for the third gun, but it was nowhere I could find.

"Do you remember that movie with Mel Gibson called The Patriot?" Poppy said without looking up from her gun.

"Yes."

"The third gun is behind that tree over there, run and start firing like mad, it'll confuse them. Just like that one scene in that movie" she said, I nodded, and after taking in three deep breaths, I ran like crazy to the tree she had pointed to, and sure enough it was there. I took it and began to prepare myself to start firing all over again. I was shooting at a whole different angle, I looked out to see where Poppy was so that I wouldn't obviously shoot over there, but I shot at anything that was making its way over there. I got sloppy again, missing my targets, one of the gang members fired at me and it hit the tree just above my head. I screamed and dropped the gun. When I reached down to grab it, someone grabbed me, dragging me through the dirt and the leaves by my hair. I fought back trying to get to my feet. I scratched at the hands that were holding onto my hair, but it was to no avail, from the way I was being dragged, I was defenseless. I heard a pop of gun fire and I was suddenly dropped, I leaned forward and saw Poppy standing up with her gun, facing my way, I crawled forward back to where I had been and found my gun, but when I had dropped it, it jammed. I ran back over to Poppy, we were together again. She continued to aim and fire as the gang members drew in closer. Time… all we needed was to buy time, the town would come, and everything would be alight. When Poppy ran out of bullets she threw the gun away from her and sat down next to me. We held each other as we waited to be discovered.

"Show yourselves! We have you surrounded!" One of the gang members yelled, I looked at Poppy and she nodded. Together we raised both our hands and slowly stood up from our hiding spot. We were surrounded by seven gang members, all with guns of their own. They drew in close to us, one grabbed my arm and one grabbed Poppy's arm and they forced us to our knees. I felt a circular metal object being pressed against the back of my head and through the corner of my eye I could see that the gang member that was holding Poppy had his gun pressed against her head. The other gang members stepped aside as one of them drew near. She was a woman, probably in her mid-twenties with dreadlocked red hair. She was dressed in black, with leather black boots and a leather black jacket, it was clear that she was some sort of high ranking leader to them.

"Wait…" she said with a pause, "I know your face." She said to Poppy. Poppy said nothing. "You are so familiar to me, as if I once knew you." The woman said pacing back and forth. "I know why I know you, and you know why you know me. You do know me though, right? You remember me, don't you?" She asked Poppy, but Poppy continued to remain silent. "I want an answer from you. Say something." She commanded.

"It's good to see you again Steph." Poppy responded, the woman, Steph, grinned and put her hands on her hips.

"Take them back down to the others; I am sure Andrew will want to see this." Steph said, we were practically lifted up and dragged down to where the rest of our family was. I was relieved to see that none of them had been severely harmed, bruised and a bit shocked maybe, but nothing severe. Connor pulled me immediately to him and William did the same with Poppy, it was their way of trying to be protective of us.

"What were you thinking?" Connor whispered to me.

"We were trying to buy you time. Amelia went to town, she's getting help." I said.

"Stop talking!" One of the gang members yelled at us. We waited for what felt like an eternity, I began to pray intensely for help from the town to come. What were these people waiting for, they had us, and they had the farm, why wait around? I saw that some of the gang members were growing restless, they too were wondering why they were standing around. There was a reason, and that reason was still unknown for us.

"Come on, Steph, he's just going to have us burn it, why don't we do it?" asked a gang member.

"Because this is different, there has been a plot twist to our arrangements." She said before looking at Poppy.

"Listen to me, all of you. Their leader, Andrew, he's coming; I need you to not do anything, let me talk. Especially you William, do nothing." Poppy commanded.

"I won't let them hurt you." he said.

"Do as I say, do nothing." She growled at him. Just then, more gang members appeared and this time they were led by a tall, menacing looking man with dark eyes, short think spiky hair, and a scruffy beard. He was their leader, and Poppy's former leader, Andrew. He began to pace around, looking at us, looking at the farm, and nodding his head in approval.

"Good work, good work indeed. We've known about this farm, that other farm, and that bloody town for months, it's about time we taste their spoils." He said causing everyone under his command to shout and cheer.

"Sir, there's been a slight, hiccup." Steph said stepping forward.

"Oh really?" Andrew said, Steph looked over at us and then pointed at Poppy. I could hear Poppy swallow hard before standing up and looking Andrew dead in the eye. Andrew's whole facial expression and demeanor changed once he looked upon Poppy. As quickly as Steph had recognized her, so did Andrew, and he did not look pleased to see her.

"Poppy." He lowly said.

"Andrew." Poppy replied.

"We spent weeks looking for you, we were so worried." He said with sarcasm in his voice.

"I'm sorry that you had worried." Poppy replied.

"You stand before me as if you were my equal, you are not my equal, Poppy, you never were and you never will be. For weeks I hoped that my scouts would find your cold, frozen, dead body in the woods, but they never did. They never did and it leads me to believe the only other logical explanation was that you deserted and you survived; and here you are, a vision of perfect health. Now how about that? I paid and traded a lot of goods in order to have you, and how did you show your gratitude? You showed it by abandoning me and this gang!" As Andrew spoke his anger rose and he turned into a mad man.

"Please…" Poppy began while raising her hand, Andrew took one step forward, grabbed her by the arm and dragged her away from us, we all gasped and shouted, but Poppy gave us all one look and it silenced us.

"You are property, you belong to me! I have had many dessert before you and I have had many after you; and I have hunted every single one of them down, one…by…one. Up until this very moment you were the only one that go away, you were the Holy Grail that could never find, the one thing I could never reach. But now look, have you, and do you want to know what I'm going to do with you?"

he said talking down to Poppy, causing her and all of us to quake with fear.

"Hey boss… don't go too hard, the traitor looks preggo." Said one of the gang members; this comment caused Andrew to stop and look for a moment, he grabbed Poppy by the hair at the nape of her neck and forced her to stand straight as he put his hand on her round belly.

"Andrew please, please, just leave us, we don't have much, let me go, let my family go." Poppy began to cry.

"I can't let you go Poppy, you see, it's not that simple. You see if I let you go then anyone can think that if they leave and start another life that I'll spare them as well." He said before throwing Poppy to the ground. It grew quiet for a few moments as Poppy knelt in the grass. I wanted to reach out and pull her back into our family circle, but we had to do as we were told, we had to do nothing.

"I have a new idea!" Andrew proclaimed loud enough for everyone to hear, "I will spare this farm and its residents, heck, I'll even spare the dang town. We have more than enough supplies and food to last us several winters." For a moment we all started to perk up, maybe this was it, maybe this was all that was going to happen. But then Andrew leaned down to Poppy and lifted her up straight off the ground by her hair.

"But I take her with me, and this part is nonnegotiable." He said sinisterly. Peter and Connor struggled to hold back William who wanted so desperately to get up and go after his wife, and yet we waited, we had no other choice.

"And Poppy, don't worry, I'm going to spare you… in a way, but you will still pay the price, and oh how much bigger your price is going to be. I'll get you fighting for this gang again, and I'll make sure you're in good fighting condition very shortly." He said. Tears were flowing down Poppy's face, she looked back at us and mouthed the words: "Do nothing" as Andrew dragged her away and the rest of the gang followed him. Silence then came back over the farm. Everything was still except for our hearts. William let out a cry of anguish and then stood up.

"We have to go after them. We have to get Poppy back. We can't let them do this!" He was crying, I had never seen him cry before. The strong, level headed young man I knew was gone and instead he was replaced with a broken down and sobbing one.

"The men in the town are coming; Amelia must have made it by now. When they come, we will go after them." Peter said.

"We will out gun them in every way, and we will get Poppy back safe and sound." Connor said.

"But why…" Charlotte began, "why has it taken so long, Amelia has run that path a dozen times, and it has only ever taken her a half hour." I stood up and looked towards that area of the forest where we had gone into find the safety of the shed. There had to be a reason why things were taking this long.

Through the quiet of the night, the crackling of the fire in the distance, and the soft sobs that came from my family behind me, I began to hear the rumblings of the engines of the ATVs from the town. They had finally come. The gang had been long gone and was probably already back at their camp by the time the town came, but at least they were here, and we would go get Poppy back.

33.

Bundles

One by one each ATV came up the drive way, and sitting on the back of each were at least two people who were ready to defend our farm and our town. They all slowed to a halt and every one stared at us as we all knelt in the grass with the exception of William who was off in the distance with his back to all of us. Amelia came forth from the crowd and ran into the arms of her mother, she was soon followed by Brady and then… Marshall.

"Well… we were told there was a gang attack, I don't see a gang." Marshall said.

"They came, and they left." Charlotte managed to say.

"Well.. I guess this was all for nothing then, we can go home." Marshall said turning back to the ATVs.

"No!" We all yelled at once.

"We have to go after them." I said.

"They took Poppy." Connor said.

"They took Poppy? Like they just came here, rounded you folks up and only took one of you?" Marshall said with disbelief.

"Marshall, it is a very long and complicated story, please we must go after them, we have to get her back." Ms. Elizabeth said.

"I can visually see that you folks are all unharmed and are well, risking all of our lives doesn't seem really…" before Marshall could finish his sentence William appeared out of nowhere and punched Marshall in the face. It was a good clean sucker punch to the jaw that threw Marshall to the ground and left him bewildered.

"I'm sick and tired of all you're excuses! You make things difficult for all of us. They took my wife and my child. I am going after them, and anyone who has the balls to come with me is more than welcome too." William yelled at Marshall, there were a few muffled "here, here's" from the crowd that had gathered with the ATVs and the weapons. William walked over to the ATV that Marshall had gotten off of and got on it, as soon as he did so, Brady pulled right up next to him.

"I got your back." He said.

"I'm coming too." Connor said.

"So am I." I chimed in. Many more people who were already on the ATVs agreed with William and the rest of us, the only one who had no nerve to want to go help was Marshall. Everyone in our family agreed to go, with the exception of Ms. Elizabeth, Charlotte, and Cora. We gathered our own weapons, said good bye to the three who would be staying behind, and we left.

There was no plan as to what had to be done; we would be going in blind. All that we knew for sure was that we had to get Poppy back, and because of Marshall's reluctance, we had lost so much time. Time was something that only a few hours before we wanted because we wanted to delay the attack, but now we wished it moved quicker. With every second that ticked by as our ATVs sped through the forest and toward the river, they were seconds that put Poppy in harm's way.

When we reached the river, William was at a loss as to where he should go from there. There was no sign of the gang; they were long gone, disappeared into the early morning and the darkness. Connor directed William to find a spot to cross the river, it was clear that the gang had already done so. Due to the rain the river was gushing and flowing rapidly, and it was much deeper than I had ever remembered, but William knew a spot where the silt built up and it was safe enough for the ATVs to cross. We crossed with no casualties or setbacks, and we continued on up the river towards what to me was the unknown.

Signs of the nearby gang began to appear. There was trash here and there, foot prints in the mud, and the nearby smell of burning wood. We crashed down onto their camp like a stampede of wild horses, only we were ready for an outright attack. Whether we took the gang by surprise or not, I did not know. With the light from all of the campfires lighting up the area, I hopped off the back of the ATV I was sharing with Connor and began to desperately search for Poppy.

With no regard for my own safety I pulled back the zippered doors of tents, startling the inhabitants, just hoping and praying that find Poppy swiftly. It turned into an outright firefight; there were gang members fleeing, and gang members fighting back. I had no weapon on me and as the shots of gunfire began to ring in my ears, I only then realized how vulnerable I was. I took shelter behind a large tree and was soon shielded by Connor who carried with him a gun; he had been following me from the moment I jumped off the ATV. I scanned the area hoping to see either William, Amelia, or Peter. I spotted William at the center, near another large tree, he had the woman Steph pinned against the tree with her feet lifted off the ground. She looked genuinely frightened as she pointed towards the direction of the river.

"Down by the river, Poppy is down by the river!" I shouted at Connor. I pushed him aside and just began to run towards the river. As I ran, I also caught sight of William who was only a bit farther ahead of me. I had only stopped paying attention for a brief moment before I was tripped up and a large gang member was standing over me, he raised the butt of his gun high, getting ready to strike me, but I saw this flash of silver pass between me and him and then he was on the ground with a very familiar throwing knife sticking out of his leg. Amelia soon appeared and pulled me to my feet before taking back the throwing knife from the man's leg.

"Sorry." She said to him as she yanked it out. Together we continued down towards the river. As the river came into sight we saw a group of five men, along with Andrew who was dragging Poppy along. I could not tell what state Poppy was in, if she was walking or if she was limp, but we saw them and we had to act. Amelia handed me a single handgun that she had managed to grab from the camp. Before we could both decide when to jump up and act, William busted through the trees, and with three swift punches, knocked out three of the men. As William went to strike down the fourth man, the fifth lunged forward, stabbing William in the upper thigh with a concealed knife.

The world at that point seemed to move in slow motion, William's head flung back as he let out a cry of pain, Poppy lifted her head and reached her arm out to William and she cried out his name. Andrew looked down at her, lifted up his fist and brought it down, striking her in the side of the head. Andrew lifted Poppy's now limp body and threw her to the side as if she were nothing more than a small rag doll, and the three men began their assault on William. Amelia and I sprang into action, we ran down towards them screaming. I just ran with the gun out in front of me and started to fire, hoping to hit one of the men. I was useless with a gun, I didn't hit a single target, but the distraction was enough to make them pause for a moment. I was soon out of bullets and all I could do was throw the actual gun at one of them, but all he had to do was raise his hand and bat it out of the way. The other man, thinking that Amelia too was about to throw a gun, reached up to bat what she threw at him, only he screamed and looked in horror to see a throwing knife in his hand. In his anger, he ran forward towards us, I ran slightly to the left, more towards Poppy, and the man whose hand was now all bloodied rammed himself into Amelia, knocking her against a tree, then onto the ground, from which she did not get up.

I was grabbed by the second man; he wrapped his one hand around my neck and forced me to the ground. He kicked me in the side, and slapped me across my face, I tried to crawl away, but I was only kicked again, sending a shooting pain through my back and chest. I involuntarily rolled on to my back and looked up to see the man coming down on me with a large stick. He held it against my throat, pinning me to the ground, and then he started to apply the pressure. I started to choke. I gaged. I gasped for air. I reached up to claw his eyes, but he pulled my hand away, bending my fingers, snapping them backwards, I cried out, but no sound escaped my mouth. I reached to push the stick from my throat, but he pressed down harder. He pressed and I felt the back of my head sink into the soft ground. I couldn't breathe; I could feel my legs starting to go limp, my arms not responding to the urgent thoughts that I had to fight back. My world was growing dark.

Then there was a sudden release. Air filled my lungs, my heart pounded in my chest. The man with the stick was gone, I rolled over and saw Andrew, dragging Poppy again, but this time he dragged her to the edge of the river, just over the edge of a boulder, and pushed her limp body into the rapid waters. I started to crawl, and then got to my feet. With every breath I took, shooting pains ran through my chest and back; but I moved forward. I looked back once to see that my savior from the man with the stick was Connor, and that Brady had subdued the second man as well. I broke into a jog as I headed for the river, and thus towards Andrew. He took no steps towards me, he just watched, as I got closer, Peter ran out and came between Andrew and me, giving me a clear path to the river. With one leap into the water, I was submerged over my head, being dragged down the river with the strong current.

I swam with the current, catching up to Poppy, lifting her head up out of the water. I held her tightly to me, determined to not let the current separate us. We floated down the river, I struggled to try and get us to the river bank. We were just tossed around in the waters. I tried my best to keep Poppy from hitting the rocks that stuck out in the river; I turned my body towards them taking the brunt of the impact. We were just thrown down river by the current, my mouth filled with water, my eyes stung from the cold, but I kept Poppy's head up, I did that much. At last the river slowed, the water quieted and I pulled us to a large rock mass that jutted out from the bank.

I came ashore, pulling Poppy up with me, resting her head on my lap. Light was just beginning to come into the sky, a start of a new day. I looked around and tried to catch my breath, but it was just not coming to me. My heart started to slow and the pounding that rang through my ears quieted. We were on that rock mass, the same boulder that we had come to only days before Poppy's wedding. It was here at this very location that we had had so much fun. I looked down at Poppy, both of her eyes were blackened and her bottom lip was split. Around her neck were the beginnings of bruises that took the forms of the hand of her attacker, and her wrists were rubbed almost raw, a sign that she had been tied up.

"Oh, Poppy, I'm so sorry." I whispered down to her, finding it hard and painful to even speak. She looked as though she were only sleeping; I wished that she were only just sleeping. I prayed that help would come, I prayed and I waited, and I cried. Out of the water I had grown cold. Poppy was still unresponsive, her chest would rise and fall with every breath she took, but I could not get her to wake up.

I wanted so badly to scream at the top of my lungs for help, I even tried, but shooting pains ran down my throat through my lungs and chest. I held Poppy's head close on my lap.

"Please Poppy, please wake up." I whispered, but it was to no avail. As the soft light of the dawn crept down into the river, I examined our surroundings once more. It was then that I started to notice that blood began to appear where Poppy lay. I watched with full knowledge as to the possibility as to what it meant as a large bead of blood dripped over the edge of the boulder and dropped into the river. In a panic I gently rolled Poppy onto her side and saw that the entire backside of her skirt was drenched with blood. I rolled her back over onto her back and cradled her head on my lap. I pressed my forehead against hers and just began to sob. I pulled away for a brief moment, and Poppy's eyes opened. I looked down at her, and her face coiled up to express the immense pain that she was feeling, she yelled out in pain and began to cry. Her breathing quickened, I tried to calm her, I tried to soothe her, but as quickly as she awoke, she fell unconscious again. I looked up and saw across the river, Peter and Connor appear on two ATVs, they crossed the river with no thought as to how deep it was, and made it to the other side.

"Poppy… take Poppy… the baby." I stammered, Connor came up and scooped Poppy away. I rose to my feet and climbed down the boulder, leaving the pool of blood behind.

***

Poppy drifted in and out of consciousness the entire ride back to the farm. She was in early labor. She would cry out in pain and grab at her hair and try and breathe before becoming unconscious again. Connor carried Poppy immediately upstairs into one of the bedrooms at the house where Ms. Elizabeth, Charlotte, and Cora had already readied rooms to take in the injured, but upon seeing Poppy, Charlotte dropped the water basin she carried and fell into hysterical shock, we had to remove her from the room.

It was left to me, Ms. Elizabeth and Cora now. Ms. Elizabeth worked by herself to try and work with Poppy. The baby was coming, there was no way to stop it. During a moment of stillness brought on by Poppy falling back into unconsciousness, Ms. Elizabeth pressed her ear against Poppy's stomach, and then looked beneath the sheets between Poppy's legs.

"Leave… both of you." Ms. Elizabeth ordered, we did not argue with her, and we vacated to the hallway. Ms. Elizabeth shut the door behind us. Down the hall I could hear William groaning and crying out in pain from his injuries.

"Poppy… where is Poppy!" he kept asking.

"She's down the hall, she is here." I heard someone say, it was the voice of Mrs. Miller. Minutes ticked by, it felt like hours. I heard nothing come from the other side of the door, I couldn't even hear Poppy. Was she awake, was she still out? I did not know. Then suddenly, the door flew open and Ms. Elizabeth stood there, her face pale as a ghost and her eyes wide. She carried with her one of the wash basins, only it was covered by a cloth.

"Please, clean her up, tend to her wounds, she will recover." Ms. Elizabeth said as her lips quivered, she turned from us and walked down the hall and then down the stairs. We paused before entering the room. Inside we found Poppy, drifting in a state between complete awareness and yet unawareness, she was delusional. She lay in bloodied sheets and reached out to us as we entered the room. Softly, gently, and quietly we removed all the bloodied sheets and the clothes from her, we washed her, cleaned her, and I combed her hair. After it was all said and done, Poppy lay sleeping soundly in the bed with a fresh night gown and fresh sheets.

"I'll take these down stairs, you stay with her." I told Cora as I gathered all the bloodied sheets to take down to the kitchen to be burned. As I stood quietly in the doorway of the kitchen, I saw Ms. Elizabeth standing over the sink, her shoulders moving as if she were crying. I put the sheets on the ground in front of the fireplace and silently moved towards her. I saw her crying as she wrapped crisp white cloth around more crisp white cloth into a bundle, when I moved forward I saw a little pink object sticking out of the side that Ms. Elizabeth was getting ready to cover with cloth. My heart stopped beating and I halted to a stop upon realizing what it was. My eyes were fixated on it, on the little, tiny, perfect hand that stuck out of the white cloth. It was probably no bigger than my thumb. Ms. Elizabeth continued to wrap the small bundle with the white cloth, wrapping and wrapping until it was just a rectangular little bundle no bigger than half the size of a loaf of bread. When she finished wrapping, she tied the bundle off with a blue ribbon. It had been a boy.

34.

Breaking

Ms. Elizabeth walked passed me with the bundle in her hands, where she went with it, I did not know. Silence enveloped the house, and as the madness and chaos subsided, I leaned my weight against the doorframe in the kitchen. Adrenaline had been pumping through me, dulling any small amount of pain that I had; but now my heart was slowing down to its normal rate. I could feel this flow of blood and this throbbing making its way to my neck, and my fingers on my left hand were pulsating, but most of all I could feel the shooting, stabbing, and agonizing pain throughout my torso. I slumped down onto the floor focusing on trying to shorten my breaths so that with each inhale the pain would not be so sharp.

On the floor I raised my hand to see that my pinky, ring, and middle fingers were swollen to the size of sausages and slowly turning the color purple, and around my neck it felt like I was bleeding, yet there was no blood.

Inhale.

Exhale.

Inhale.

Exhale.

With each breath was a shooting pain throughout my chest and ribs. I was panting like a dog in the summer, both trying to lessen the pain but to also try and breathe. I could hear the soft and muffled footsteps of people upstairs, walking, pacing, and moving about from room to room. I had not seen Amelia, I worried. Had she been forgotten about by the river? She dropped harder than a sack of potatoes. I tried to push myself back up to my feet, but the pain in my ribs and through my chest, it was too much.

Inhale.

Exhale.

Inhale.

Exhale.

I could hear someone coming down the stairs and towards the kitchen. A shadow was cast across me. I looked up and saw Connor. It was the first time I really looked at him. He had gotten us from the river and taken us back to the town, but I really didn't look at him.

His hair was disheveled, and he had a bruise forming on his left cheek, his shirt ripped around the collar, his jeans were torn around the knees, and one knee was scraped and bloodied.

"Mona... what's wrong?" He said kneeling down beside me. The pain had disillusioned me; the world seemed warped and contorted. Although I was looking at Connor, the surroundings around us seemed faded and unclear. There was this ringing in the back of my head that was progressively getting louder and louder.

"Amelia?" I asked.

"She's upstairs, she may have had a concussion, but other than that, she is well." Connor said taking my left hand in his, I immediately flinched and let out a soft cry of pain and pulled my hand away from him. A look of emotional hurt came over Connor's face as he realized that I was in pain.

"You're hurt. Tell me what hurts." Connor began to panic, but all I could do was just sit there taking in sharp breaths of air. The short breaths were not enough, I needed air, I could feel my head growing lighter. I gave in and took in one long deep breath, but it was not without a sob of pain and tears.

"Shh... Shh, it's ok." Connor said moving my hair aside, his fingers stopped right at my neck, and his eyes grew big, and then he had this look of panic on his face.

"Come on, we'll get you upstairs, I'm sorry." He said leaning forward and then scooping me up. Having him pick me up and hold me was not without pain. I pressed my face close into his chest as he carried me through the house and up the stairs. As we passed each bedroom I got to look inside at each of the room's occupants who were laid up in bed with their injuries. Charlotte sat beside Poppy's bed silently crying as Poppy slept; Brady stood guard over Amelia as she lay in her bed, and then William's room where Ms. Elizabeth, Cora, and Mrs. Miller were tending to William's wounds. As we passed William's room, Connor stopped and called out for his aunt. A spark of pain ran through my chest again as Connor shifted his weight as he stood in the hall, and I squeezed my eyes shut and gritted my teeth. I was put into my own bedroom on my own bed. Connor knelt down beside my bed and Cora started to tend to my fingers.

"Mona, Mona, can you hear me?" Cora asked, I must have not looked like I was there with them, the truth was, I wasn't; I was in too much pain. Each breath and each small amount of movement brought on a strong wave of pain. I did not respond to Cora or to Connor, I just laid there.

"Connor I think it's best if you leave now, I'm going to change Mona out of these clothes." I heard Cora say. Connor left the room and Cora closed the door behind him. She began to speak softly, almost like a whisper, instructing me what to do, telling me what she was going to do, and asking if I was alright. For the most part everything was ok, until it was time to lift my shirt off over my head. As Cora helped me I cried out in pain and just began to sob, making the pain even worse. She must have panicked because she left the room and returned with Ms. Elizabeth.

"This bruising, I don't like the look of it." I heard Ms. Elizabeth say.

"Look, around her neck too." Cora said.

"We sent for morphine, once we get William on it, we'll give her a dose too."

"Has the CDC been called?"

"Yes, Marshall did it, it's the only useful thing he's done." Ms. Elizabeth said. Cora silently dressed me from the waist down. Getting a shirt on me was not an option, instead she covered me with the sheet and held my right hand.

"Don't worry Mona, help is coming. Just rest, you'll be alright." Cora said, I nodded and just closed my eyes and tried to focus on my breathing again.

Inhale.

Exhale.

Inhale.

Exhale.

Inhale.

Ex.....

***

There was a bitter taste in my mouth, I must have slept with my mouth open for God knows how long. The room was dark when I awoke, with the exception of the oil lamp that burned on my nigh stand. I felt groggy, light, and slightly numb. Connor was sitting in a chair pulled close to my bed, he was slumped over with his face pressed into my sheets, with one hand holding my uninjured one and his other laying protectively on my stomach. I gave his hand a squeeze with mine, and then ran my fingers through his hair. As I moved around the sheet covering me slipped and I felt cool air on my shoulders. I looked down to see that I was still not entirely dressed, I had underwear and bloomers on, but from the top of my belly button up to just under my arm pits, I was tightly wrapped in bandages, with my breasts pressed almost completely flat by the wrappings. The bandages restrained my movement, but I hardly felt any pain, only slight discomfort. As for the fingers on my left hand, they had been placed straight on a splint and wrapped tightly.

Connor began to stir from his sleep, tossing and turning his head in the sheets until he finally woke up and looked at me. He gave me a soft smile and then sat straight up in his chair, no doubt his back and neck must have hurt him from the way he had been sleeping.

"I was so worried." He said as he caressed my face and hair.

"I'm fine. How is Poppy, William, and Amelia?" I asked.

"William is finally sleeping, we got him stitched up alright, his wound was deep but it was clean, it'll heal. Amelia is sleeping too, she had a nasty head ache once she finally came to. Brady hasn't left her side. And Poppy, well she hasn't woken up, she's just been sleeping, which I supposed is a good thing, it'll give her until later today to cope with things." Connor answered.

"Later today? How long have I been asleep?"

"Well, you conked out at around 7:30 yesterday morning. After Gran and Mrs. Miller examined you and wrapped you up they gave you a strong dose of morphine to keep you asleep. They gave everyone morphine just about. I don't suspect William to wake up until tonight that's how much they gave him." Connor replied moving his hand from my face and hair to my neck.

"I overheard that the CDC is coming?"

"Yes, we alerted them, they should be here by sunrise. Proper doctors will be with them."

"What's wrong with me?" I asked pointing to the bandages.

"Cracked ribs and bruising, pretty nasty stuff." He said putting his hand on my stomach again. I took a deep breath as the news of my injuries sunk in. It wasn't life threatening, but even so, I began to feel a twinge of pain that made me squish up my face.

"Is it hurting? I'll go get Gran." Connor said urgently, before I could stop him, he was out of his chair and out of the room. When he returned, Ms. Elizabeth was with him and she carried with her a syringe that came in its own little sanitary package and a vial of clear liquid. She said nothing as she took over Connor's seat, measured out the medicine in the syringe and then perfectly administered it into my arm.

"There, feel better." She said leaning down and kissing the top of my forehead. I began to feel rather doozy and floaty. As she left, Connor took up his seat again. He took my hand just as I began to feel the medicine starting to take over me.

"You look pretty sexy with that bruise on your cheek." I stammered out stupidly, he just laughed.

"Wow, the meds work quick on you." He said.

"Chair doesn't look comfy, share with me." I said patting the other side of the bed. He smiled, got up from the chair and came around to the other side of the bed and laid down on top of the sheets.

"Just rest." He said gently pulling me close to him. I don't know if I said anything after that, I just remember everything fading out.

***

I awoke much later to the other side of my bed being empty, yet still slightly warm. I pushed myself up and swung my legs off the side of the bed and stood up. I felt some slight discomfort, and my head was dizzy as soon as I stood up, but other than that, I was fine. I took a few steps toward the dresser in search of something to cover my shoulders with before I left the room, in doing so I caught a glimpse of myself in the mirror. I stood there for a moment, looking at the deep purple bruises that covered my neck. Bruises would fade, so I shrugged it off and found a shall to drape over myself. It was hard to move being wrapped up so tight with the bandages, but I managed.

I was probably still supposed to be in bed, and I probably shouldn't have been walking, but I needed to do two things. I needed to use the bathroom, and I needed to see Poppy. After I did the first, I went into Poppy's room to sit by her. I sat for a few moments just patting her hand before she stirred awake and her eyes fluttered open. She made no sound, she just turned her head back and forth, looking at me then looking at the ceiling.

"Hey." I said.

"Hey." She whispered back to me.

"How are you feeling?" I asked.

"I hurt."

"I do too." I began to wonder, did she know? Had she even realized everything that had happened? I didn't want to say anything, I just wanted to be there for her.

"Where's William?" She asked.

"In the other room."

"He's hurt isn't he? I saw what happened, it's the last thing I remember." She said.

"Yes, but he is doing well, he will be better just like you will be better." Poppy just nodded, she lifted her hand up and ran her fingers through her hair and then brought that hand down to rest on her stomach. In doing so that was when she had the realization. Her hand fell on a somewhat flat surface and her eyes grew wide.

"Pop…" I said softly, but I could not stop her. She kicked the blankets off of her body and knelt up in bed, revealing the towel that we had laid under her, on the towel were three small circles of blood. She pulled at the back of her nightgown and saw that the matching circles were also on the back of her nightgown. For a moment she began to panic, pulling at her hair and breathing quickly. She finally covered her face with her hands and slowed her breathing.

"The baby, did I lose the baby?" she said with her hands covering her face. I almost didn't want to answer, I paused and soon felt this hard ball beginning to well up in my throat.

"Ye…yes." I croaked out; for a moment Poppy stopped breathing all together, just sitting there in the center of the bed with her hands over her face. And then a wave came over her, this wave of sorrow unlike anything I had ever seen in a person before. She let out this deep, deep, sob, a sob that seemed to come out of her heart itself. It broke my heart and my stomach twisted into knots. I got up and sat on the edge of the bed and pulled Poppy to me, and we just cried. It only took a few moments before someone in the house heard us and came running. Cora appeared in the doorway and then called out for Ms. Elizabeth. By the time Ms. Elizabeth came, the rest of the family, with the exception of Amelia and William had gathered. We calmed Poppy, soothed her, and dried her tears. It was then that Peter and Connor went and got William. They helped him hobble down the hall and then helped him into the bed beside Poppy.

They held each other as the news was officially broken to them. They cried, we all cried. The feeling of loss was so immense. To see the suffering of William and Poppy, it destroyed us. I had never seen two people so devastated, so broken, and I hoped to never see it again. Ms. Elizabeth brought a little wooden box into the room, which we all knew had the little bundle inside. She placed it on Poppy's lap. Poppy looked at it, put her hands on it, and then bent over and pressed her head against it before bursting into sobs all over again; she was soon followed by William. Once William and Poppy had had enough Ms. Elizabeth took the box back.

"It was a boy." Ms. Elizabeth croaked out.

"A boy?" William asked.

"Yes." Ms. Elizabeth confirmed.

"We would have named him Asher." Poppy sobbed.

"Will you burry him next to Pop?" William asked.

"Of course. Do you want to be there?" Charlotte said through her own tears.

"No."

"No." with that Ms. Elizabeth left the room with the box, and we were left to soothe and comfort each other together. We circled around Poppy and William and just hugged them, we all did, together as a family.

The box was buried in a small plot next to the grave of Arnold Wilde at the edge of the property near a very large and very old elm tree. The spot was marked with a round stone and flowers were planted on top. Ms. Elizabeth and Jonathan were the only ones who did it, the rest of us were either too heartbroken or too unwell to attend.

35.
Safe

I knew not exactly when the CDC volunteers arrived to the farm or to town, all of that seemed to be a blur to me. The pain I had in my torso had increased significantly to the point that Ms. Elizabeth and Mrs. Miller thought it best to keep me sedated. When I woke again, I was in a very unfamiliar environment. I was neither in my room nor anywhere that I had any memory of. I was laying on a thin mat atop of a metal bed in a very narrow but long area. I could hear some buzzing coming from another area, and the light that filled the sterile, stainless steel looking environment looked very unnatural.

As I came to, I became aware of someone else in the space with me. A woman who looked only a few years older than I sat in a metal chair across from where I lay, she wore medical scrubs and had a badge clipped to her shirt. When she noticed I was waking up, she came over to me and spoke softly.

"It's quite alright, my name is Ashley, I'm a volunteer nurse, and we just had some X-rays done on you. Let's get you back to your house." She said helping me lean up. As I moved I noticed that the bandages I had on felt different, a kind of different I couldn't really describe. I peeked down the blouse I had been put in to see that the bandages were crisp white, different from the ones I remember myself being in before. The nurse helped me walk through the narrow space to a door that opened up to the farm. We were in a long RV that had been converted into some sort of mobile hospital. There were CDC people walking around the farm, many of which smiled as I passed and entered the house. Inside, Peter and Connor sat at the dining room table while they were being examined by other nurses who shined lights into their eyes and told them to follow their fingers as they moved them around. My nurse Ashley helped me climb the stairs, I instinctively flinched in preparation of the pain that would come, but instead of pain, I just felt numb.

As I passed the other rooms I saw other nurses inside examining the others, there were six people inside William and Poppy's room, quietly asking them questions and examining them. Once I was in my room and the nurse, Ashley, helped me back into my bed I had a flood of questions that I needed to ask.

"What has happened so far?" I asked her.

"We will know once your X-rays come back." She answered.

"No, I don't mean that. I want to know about the others, about William, Poppy, Amelia, and the gang."

"Well… Poppy will recover, no permanent damage done, William had a high fever when we arrived late yesterday, his wound had gotten infected, but we have him on an antibiotics drip, he will be fine. Amelia suffered a pretty bad concussion, but with some proper rest and observation, she too will recover. As for the gang… we won't know until the soldiers come back." She said reaching into a medical looking bag to pull a vial of medication out.

"Soldiers?" I asked.

"We came prepared with many soldiers. There have been many gang attacks, we want to bring their ruthless leaders to justice for what they have done to innocent people as well as free ones under their control." Ashely said as she injected the medicine into my arm.

"What is that?"

"Just some antibiotics, just to be sure." She said with a smile.

"Me, what about me?" I asked pointing to the bandages.

"You're lucky; you have fractures going up and down the left side of your rib cage, as well as severe bruising, and your three fingers are broken on your left hand. You'll be in pain for quite some time, they gave you some numbing medication for the area, but unfortunately it will wear off."

"Oh," I said looking down at my chest and then at my left hand.

"Just take it easy, no running, climbing, or anything that will make you want to breathe more, just rest." She smiled as she adjusted the blankets around me.

"Thank you." I said as she left the room. I waited alone in the room for a while, frankly, now that I was awake, it was rather boring. I wished I was in the next room with Poppy and William or downstairs with Connor. I just assumed I had to stay put. I was gazing out the window when I heard a soft knock on the door, when I turned I saw Amelia standing there.

"Can I come in?" she asked.

"Of course." I said, Amelia slowly entered the room and sat in the chair beside my bed.

"I heard about your brain." I said trying to make her smile.

"I heard about your ribs." She said.

"How are you feeling?"

"I have a nasty head ache that won't go away, they won't let me sleep and that's all I want to do, and Brady left an hour ago. How are you?"

"I guess I'm fine until whatever they gave me to numb my ribs wears off. Where did Brady go?"

"He hadn't been home since the attack, I told him to go."

"You mean he stayed with you this whole time?"

"It's been two days since the attack and he didn't go home, not even once."

"That boy loves you." I said.

"I know." She grinned.

"You do?"

"When he thought I was still unconscious I heard him praying at the edge of my bed, I could hear him saying how much he loved me and how much he needed me to be alright.

"That's beautiful, Amelia."

"I was glad I was able to hear it." she said, at that moment I could hear familiar footsteps coming down the hall, and soon Connor appeared in the doorway.

"I better go, they want me to stay awake as long as I can, so I'm going to go walk up and down the hallway aimlessly." Amelia said rolling her eyes, as she exited the room Connor entered and took her place on the chair.

"What did they examine you for?" I asked.

"Just routine stuff. I had to have like two stitches on my knuckles, but I'll live. How are you feeling?" He said taking my good hand in his.

"I'm on some numbing stuff so I don't have any pain right now, but it's going to wear off, but that's it." I said, Connor just nodded his head and his face got really serious for a few moments as he looked at my hand in his. Something was weighing on his mind, I could see the thought weighing him down, sinking him further and further. The temper of the room and the house changed in those few moments as he held my hand. Something grave was weighing on his mind. I took my hand from his and brought it up to his face, forcing his eyes to meet mine.

"What's wrong?" I softly spoke.

"I thought I lost you." I could hear his voice changing, I had yet to ever seen Connor cry, I had seen him upset, I had seen him frustrated, I had seen him overly happy, I had seen him mad, but I had never seen him like this. A single tear welled up from his eye and fell down his cheek and that was all it took for me too to have tears in my eyes.

"Peter and I, we looked and looked for you and Poppy, we scoured the river, and I really thought I had lost you. We thought we had lost both of you. That moment I felt exactly the same way William felt when they took Poppy. I felt so lost, like part of me was missing, like part of me had just suddenly disappeared and I didn't know what to do. I wanted to just be able to turn around and have you standing right there waving to me and calling out my name, but you weren't there, and I didn't like that, I didn't like you not being there."

"Oh Connor…" I began to say.

"And then I did find you, and for a moment just a small moment in my mind I thought it was going to be alright. But it wasn't. I can't even begin to describe what I thought and how I felt when I saw you how I still feel now when I look at you. I hadn't been there to help you; I couldn't save you from what they did to you." He said reaching his hand up to the bruises on my neck.

"Connor, everything is alright now. I'm here, you're here, we are all safe, I'm going to be ok." I said reaching both my hands out to him.

"I know that now, but I still feel that feeling, and it made me realize, it made me realize that there's so much I haven't said to you."

"Like what?"

"Well first off, I don't tell you that I love you very often, I should say it more, I know I should and I'm going to." he said.

"Oh Connor… I don't need you to say it; I know that you love me, showing it means so much more than saying it."

"You say that now as if it doesn't matter, but to me it does."

"Darling, I know, I know, and I love you for that, so very much so."

"I just don't ever want to have you not with me ever again. I don't think I could bare it." He softly said.

"Of course not, I promise, nothing like that will ever happen again, we're safe now. We won't ever be parted again." I said as I wiped the tears from Connor's face. He stayed with me for much of the remainder of the afternoon, leaving only once to go get a few books from the library. While the others milled about the house and the nurses came back and forth, we read to each other, until night time came and it was time for bed.

***

The CDC volunteers eventually left the farm, relocating to the town, finally leaving us with peace and quiet. I took the first opportunity I got to go to the room Poppy and William shared. The medicine to numb the pain had long since subsided and there was nothing to give me, all I could do was grit my teeth and suck it up and move slowly down the hall to their room. William sat in a chair with his leg propped up on a stool and Poppy sat in bed with her eyes lightly closed.

"May I come in?" I asked from the doorway, Poppy's eyes fluttered open and she smiled, she scooted over in the bed and made a spot for me to sit down.

"Any news about anything? Anything at all?" she asked.

"No, no news, how are you feeling? How are both of you feeling?" I asked.

"Ehh… I'm just fine, getting better." William said pointing to his leg.

"And you?" I asked Poppy.

"I am perfectly fine, health wise. I'm sore here, bruised there, it's just mostly my heart that hurts." She said gravely, I turned away from Poppy and looked over at William, his face had grown hard and he looked away from us and out the window.

"What did the nurses say?"

"They said that as soon as I am 100% better that we can try for another baby and that there would be absolutely no reason why I shouldn't be able to get pregnant again."

"Well that's good news, isn't it?" I said directing the question towards William.

"It is very good news, we are very happy that in due time we will be healthy and well again, as if nothing happened." William's tone of voice lingered on the last four words of his sentence, as if nothing happened. Something did happen though; they had lost their child, a child they had not yet gotten the chance to meet. It was cruelly unfair, but then again, the whole reason as to why life had brought us all together on the farm was cruelly unfair. For a few brief moments I began to wonder if Poppy and William were angry with each other over the loss of their baby. Did William blame Poppy? Did Poppy blame William? It was silly of me to even think that, of course they were not angry with each other, they were just very sad, and only time would make it better. If we weighed down everything, at the end of the day, the gang would have still come, the only difference was, if Poppy had not stood up to them, we all would have not survived and the farm wouldn't still be here.

I gave Poppy a hug and I gave William a hug too before going to leave; but before I got a chance to, William asked me to hand him this cane that he used to be able to move from the chair to the bed. Before I left the room William and Poppy were together sitting on the bed holding each other. As I walked down the hall back to my room I could hear a deep voice speaking softly, I peeked my head into Amelia's room to see Brady sitting over her bed with a small book in his hand, I listened to try and identify what exactly he was reading to her as she slept. It was poetry, John Keats to be exact. I smiled for a moment before shuffling back down the hall to my own room.

***

"You have a visitor." Charlotte said from the doorway to my room, I looked up from the cards that Connor and I were playing to see Mark Shaw walking through the door way. He had a smile on his face and a cheerful look in his eye, this could only mean that he was here to bring good news, good news from Amherst, and good news about my mother.

"Mark, it's so good to see you!" I said.

"It is, how are you feeling?" he asked.

"I hurt all the time, but Connor keeps me entertained and happy." I said grabbing Connors had, both out of nervousness and because I was scared.

"I have good news."

"About Mona's mother?" Connor asked.

"Yes. Mona, your mother has responded very well to being weaned off the drugs, so well in fact that we have decided that this week will be her very last week on the small dosage, and when I say it's a small dosage, I mean it, and it's so minuscule. She will be the first person to have ever been weaned off it and survive." I could feel a large ball well up in my throat, this fluttering sensation in my heart and this warmness. I was so very happy I could not contain it.

"I want to see her. I want my mother back with me." I said.

"Would that be possible? Could that ever be arranged?" Connor asked.

"I'm already working on it for you, but it will take time. Your mother now needs extensive rehabilitation if she is going to live outside of a medical facility, and we are both ready to provide her with that rehabilitation as well as provide it to all the patients we have. You would be so surprised to find out how many survivors there have been who want the release of their relatives from the Infirmaries."

"Actually that doesn't surprise me at all." I responded.

"I hope that this will be our first and only emergency visit up here to your family and to the town. We won't be coming back officially until the spring, we brought more supplies to the town to help you folks get through winter. I'm only saying this because by spring I hope to have your mother rehabilitated and ready to come here to the farm, so next time I am up here, if you are prepared, I would like to invite you and Connor, of course, to travel down to Amherst to collect your mother." Mark said

"That sounds wonderful; it sounds like an amazing idea!" I said as I clapped my hands in excitement, only to flinch in minor pain. I had forgotten for a brief moment my fingers were broken.

"Good. I'm glad to hear you're excited. Well, I have to head back into town; I doubt you'll be able to make the trip up to the town for the town meeting." Mark said.

"Oh, no I don't think so." I said looking at Connor.

"No, you won't, but I will go and I'll take notes, so it will be as if you didn't miss a thing." Connor said. Thomas smiled, said one more goodbye and left the room.

***

Connor was very detailed when it came down to the notes. The fool wrote everything, he wrote what all the speakers were wearing, he doodled in the corner of the paper in an attempt to describe what the inside of the library looked like, and he made a list of names of the people who asked how I was doing. His notes were quite funny, but they were also filled with important information.

The soldiers had caught up with the gang, arresting their leaders. The gang that had been a threat to us was now disbanded, and they had been given an option, they could either opt to assimilate back into society, or they would be forced to work at an infirmary. Logically, none of the gang members that were responsible in our attack would be assimilated into our town, they would be sent other places, but it was good to hear that innocents were being freed and evil was seeing justice.

There were dozens and dozens of gangs that were being disbanded. The much larger ones were given building supplies so that they might become settled communities. With the peaceful, genuine aided help from the CDC volunteers, many of the gangs were peacefully accepting the transition. As it turns out, the majority of gang members were not violent; rather they were just scared and longing for survival. The few that were violent were arrested and would be tried on the accounts of how many towns and innocent lives they destroyed.

Connor's notes went on to state that the statistics as to how many surviving towns had come back. Although most of all of the major cities were decimated, there were small concentrated pockets of surviving communities like ours. In fact, there were 12 communities like ours in Massachusetts, making the official population count for the state a little over 3,000. Sure 3,000 was a pathetic number compared what it once was, but it was still something. The number of people who had lost their lives from the plague was astronomical. The plague, although it had originated in the US, spilled over into

Canada, Mexico, and in to other modern countries, making the whole situation a bit more puzzling.

With these new statistics and numbers being analyzed, it led the researchers and the volunteers to come up with a new hypothesis as to what the plague could have possibly been, what it still is. The volunteers believe that the scientists and doctors were looking in all the wrong places, they believed that they needed to look for something that had previously not been thought of, something that normally one wouldn't think have much impact on lives. They believed that the plague was man made, that it stemmed from something that these modern societies that the plague affected had been doing for a few decades.

With this new hypothesis, it gave a new hope, a new possible answer as to why all of these things happened and what could possibly be done to stop it all. But it was only a hypothesis, a guess, a theory. It would take many, many more weeks, months, or years to find out what caused it all. I only prayed that it wouldn't take that long.

36.

Winter

Nothing worth noting or really reflecting upon happened during the first few weeks after the CDC volunteers left. Other than the weather changing, my mobility and pain improving, and Poppy and William becoming well enough to move back into the bus, life just went on. Connor, Peter, Luke, and Jonathan were able to harvest all of the potatoes out of the field before the first frost. We had baskets upon baskets full of different kinds of potatoes; I had never seen so many different varieties in my life. The harvest proving to be bountiful was a direct blessing; it was just what we needed. We had worried for so long about the crop being in danger due to the drought and the heat, but we had been saved and spared from a lean winter. It was a good thing too, because Ms. Elizabeth suspected that that winter would be the harshest winter ever experienced in quite a number of years.

Ms. Elizabeth was right. Not too long before the end of November we experienced our first snow storm. The first storm lasted for two straight days before blue skies appeared again and three feet of snow lay packed onto the ground. It seemed like by the time we finished shoveling out of the first three feet of snow, another storm hit us soon after, only that time it was rain and everything turned to ice. It was a struggle and it was very frustrating, but we made it through. All the hard work that the boys put in during the spring and summer paid off, we had more than enough meat stored away, and the firewood we had was plentiful. All the snow we had on the ground made the land look fresh and clean, and no doubt come spring time, the world would be fresh, lush, and green due to all the water.

"Snow is good; it traps nutrients from the atmosphere and brings it down to the earth. Snow is like a multivitamin for the ground." Ms. Elizabeth said one morning as she dusted away the snow that had managed to make its way through a small crack on the windowsill in the kitchen.

"That's all well and good Gran, but you're not the one who has to shovel the dang stuff." Connor said as he laced up his boots to get ready to help William and Peter remove some of the white powder to make a path out to the chickens.

“And I am very glad to have nice strong boys to do that for me.” Ms. Elizabeth said, Connor just rolled his eyes and kissed the top of my head before leaving to go outside. We tended to eat heavier foods in the winter now, foods that required a bit more work and more help than in the summer. I was, at the moment working on a sweet potato pie that was to be eaten for dessert that night. We were all working, Cora was preparing the shepherd’s pie that we would be eating, Ms. Elizabeth was making bread, Poppy was peeling potatoes, Amelia was chopping onions, and Charlotte was keeping up with washing all the dishes that we were dirtying.

It was a complete change of pace during the winter, a pace I was not completely used to. We spent the entirety of our time indoors, except for the boys who had to shovel, get wood, and occasionally hunt. There were times that I thought I was going to go stir crazy, but I just focused on mundane tasks. I read more, became more proficient with sewing and knitting, and I started to listen to Ms. Elizabeth more, learning more complicated recipes.

In late December, after a good long period of not having a single snowflake fall from the sky, we decided to take a small trip into town, just to check on the people there, and to get a few supplies. Amelia had accidentally broken six mason jars when she slipped on ice while bringing them in from the barn, and jarring was very important during the winter. I was the first to volunteer to go into town, I was longing for a brief change of scenery.

Right after the gang appeared on the farm, and everything was in chaos. When the CDC came to visit, they had brought with them more supplies, including a few more ATVs, one of which we had kept on the farm. Using this ATV and the dirt bike, Connor, Peter and I went into town. I thought it strange that Poppy and William didn’t want to go, but I soon learned that Poppy was not feeling well and that William wanted to stay behind to take care of her.

It took us much, much longer to get into town due to all the snow we had to maneuver through, but we did make it. The town was much the same as it had been the last time I saw it, except snow covered everything. I still saw all the same familiar faces, and everyone was still smiling despite the cold and snow. While Peter and Connor went to get the supplies we needed, I popped into to see Mrs.

Miller. She was very happy to see me, she gave me tea and a slice of warm bread before asking me how everything was at the farm. I gave her the good report that everyone was doing well, and she was pleased. Not wanting to keep Peter and Connor waiting after sitting with Mrs. Miller for a few hours, I went back to the dirt bike and ATV. I waited for a good fifteen minutes before getting too cold and going into the library to get warm.

"He's not back yet?" I heard a voice say, it was Peter who like me, had waited for Connor and gotten too cold to wait outside.

"I wonder where he went." I said looking out the front door.

"He said he had to go meet with someone about something. That's all I know."

"Someone about something? He didn't say who or what?"

"No those were his exact words, someone about something." Peter said. I found it very unusual for Connor to disappear like this. He had never been a secretive person, but when he appeared a half hour later he was just full of secrets, and I didn't appreciate it. He gave me no answer as to where he had been or what he had been doing, and he refused to give me any sort of answer really. It made me mad. Even long after we had gotten back to the farm, Connor still refused to tell me what he had been doing, so I just gave up trying to figure it out and I went to the living room to do some reading.

By the beginning of January Poppy still hadn't gotten completely better from what ever ailed her previously, and William had grown worried. We sent for Mrs. Miller, and although it was the dead of winter and there was still at least 5 feet of snow on the ground, the small old woman rode on the back of an ATV to get to the farm. Poppy and William had already suffered enough, they didn't need one more thing to plague them. But it turned out to be good news rather than bad. Poppy was pregnant again. Poppy and William were so happy, they hardly knew what to do with themselves, they didn't know whether they should laugh, cry, or celebrate.

We were all celebrating, although we would never forget what had previously happened, we were eager to have a new baby on the farm. While we all celebrated, there was one member of the family who although she had a smile on her face, was feeling very sad on the inside. It was Amelia. No one had noticed that she was feeling so sad she tried her very best to cover it up with false smiles, humming, and laughing. But she was feeling sad nonetheless. The reason for this, I soon found out, was linked to Brady. It hadn't really crossed my mind, and I felt foolish for not thinking of it sooner, but Brady and Amelia had not seen each other since before the first snowstorm way back in November, and it was now late January. Amelia worried, the Campbell farm, although similar to ours, didn't have as many accommodations, and the previous winter had proven to be extra hard for the Campbell family. So Amelia and I made a plan.

With the permission of the rest of the family, I would accompany Amelia to the Campbell farm. It would be quite the journey since the Campbell farm was twice the distance from the town than we were, but for Amelia's sake, and undoubtedly Brady's sake, we would go. Connor of course gave us a hard time about the whole thing, he didn't want me going, and he didn't want me to leave, but we would be perfectly fine and we would only be gone for one night. He still didn't like the idea, but it had to be done.

We each packed our own supply of food since we didn't want to be a burden on the Campbell family for one night, and we planned to leave early in the morning. Connor still gave me a big fight over leaving, but I just grabbed him, gave him a long kiss, and left before he said another word. We would be using the ATV to get to Brady's, it had a sufficient amount of gas in it, but Jonathan was worried, so he told us to top it off once we were in town.

The previous path that we had cleared when we went into town was still there so it was easy for the first leg of the journey. We did just as Amelia's father asked, and gave the ATV more gas before heading to the east gate that would lead us up the road towards the Campbell farm.

"Be careful, nobody has come down from the Campbell's in close to two months, and nobody here has gone up." Said the man who was working to open the gate for us.

"We'll be careful." I said.

"We should be back here around this time tomorrow, so keep a watch out, don't keep us locked out for too long." Amelia said. Once the gate was fully opened, we rode the ATV out and then the gate was shut immediately behind us. Hearing the gate lock behind us made me feel a bit scared for a few moments; we were completely on our own, out into a part of the world we had not previously ventured into. Amelia and I looked at each other for a moment before pushing onwards. We had nothing to fear, nothing to really worry about, we would stay on the road, we were well supplied, and plenty of people knew we were out here.

The snow on the road had become compacted on itself with a layer of ice over it. It would take us some hours to get to the Campbell's, but we would make it. Amelia and I took turns driving the ATV, sometimes one of us had to push, other times it would be smooth sailing. The sun was just starting to set when we began to drive up the driveway to the Campbell's. When we got up to the top, Austen, Brady's brother came running out at the sound of our motor.

"Hey!" He called out all excited.

"Hey!" Amelia said with a laugh.

"I'll go get Brady!" Austen said as he ran around towards the back of the house. The Campbell farm was much more rustic than ours. Their house was a log cabin, they did not have a barn, rather a dozen or so shabbily made sheds and shelters, and their chickens, goats, and sheep all roamed free in one very large enclosure. As we waited for Brady, Amelia mentioned to me that the cabin was relatively new compared to our over 100 year old farm house.

Brady came running up from behind the cabin and then down towards us. It was a heartwarming reunion between the two. Brady ordered Austen and his cousin Collin to put our ATV in a safe spot and to carry our things into the cabin. We were welcomed by the rest of the Campbell family with hugs and two big cups of hot apple cider. While we warmed up by their wood burning stove in their small homely living room, baby Daphne played on the floor. We gave Mrs. Campbell the food that we carried with us to help with dinner, and just relaxed by the fire while Brady worked hard to finish his chores so he could join Amelia. Everyone was so friendly and didn't even question the fact as to why Amelia and I were there. They knew that Amelia wanted to see Brady, and we were quite welcomed.

Dinner was served promptly when Brady returned to the house. Unlike our family, who made out good when it came to hunting during the summer, the Campbell family didn't do so well, so they relied on the enormous amounts of fish that Brady, his brother, his cousin, and his father caught. We ate well and enjoyed a good dessert of bread pudding before hunkering down by their wood burning stove again. They didn't have fireplaces like we did, rather, they had four wood burning stoves throughout the house to keep the place well heated, and boy, was it hot in the house.

Our family read during this time of night, but the Campbell family sang songs, they were all rather very musically gifted. Brady could play the guitar, his brother played the banjo, and his father played the fiddle, everyone else just had beautiful singing voices. When the hour grew late and everyone grew sleepy, it was time for bed. Amelia and I would sleep on the two couches right there in their living room by the stove. We didn't mind one bit. Brady kissed Amelia good night and all the lanterns in the house were blown out and we were snug under our blankets.

***

The next morning was rather sad, mostly because Amelia did not want to leave. She liked it with Brady's family, but mostly she just wanted to be with Brady. She didn't have to exactly say that she didn't want to leave, rather, the way she walked around, the way she spoke, and the way she just looked at Brady did all the talking for her. We would have to leave though, it had to be done. As breakfast was being made, we folded the blankets that we slept with, washed our faces, packed our bags, and for Amelia, she reluctantly let Brady load all of our belongings back on to the ATV. We would eat one more meal with the Campbell family before heading back home.

Watching Amelia and Brady say goodbye to each other was downright heartbreaking. I stood from a distance waiting by the ATV while they stood close together, whispering, and being gentle with one another. It was sad, judging by the crisp smell in the air and the look of the clouds that hung in the sky, we were due for another snow storm, and any more snow would make it impossible for us to ever make this trip again. With all the farewells said, hugs and kisses exchanged, we departed from the farm. I was eager to get home, but Amelia had left her heart at the Campbell's.

The journey back to the east gate was easier than when we originally went, and we got there just around the time when they would be expecting us. We refilled the ATV again just in case it ever needed to be used again this winter, and then headed home. On our way home, Amelia pointed out that there seemed to be more tracks in the snow from other vehicles than there were when we first went into town. I hadn't noticed at first, but after a while I knew she was right. The tracks were deeper and wider and there were more of them. They were more like truck tracks than ATV tracks. I couldn't make much sense of it, but when we got back home, the tracks just continued, right up the drive way and back down again.

Poppy and William were out in the yard when we got home. William shouted loudly just to let everyone know we had arrived. Poppy gave us both a hug and told us she was glad that we had gotten there and back again safely.

"Where's Connor?" I asked.

"Oh… Ummm…" Poppy began.

"He's coming." William said interrupting Poppy. Connor came running out of the barn and down to greet me. He pulled me into a big embrace and gave me a long kiss before letting me go.

"Remember how I said that I didn't like it when you weren't with me?" He asked.

"Yeah." I answered.

"Well… I still don't like it." he said with a frown.

"Oh, come on, I came back, you knew where I was." I said jokingly. He had some saw dust on his shoulder and I reached up to dust it off, but he lunged away from me.

"You have saw dust. Are you working on something?" I asked.

"Oh, yes… I mean no."

"Well which is it then?"

"It's a surprise." He said taking my hand.

"Oh… don't do this to me, it'll be torture!"

"You'll see when it's done."

"I'll find out, you know I will."

"No you won't, because you are no longer allowed in the barn. At all, and everyone here on the farm knows it." He said before backing away from me and heading back into the barn. I tried to protest, but it was no use, he was gone, and I just went back off into the house.

37.

Closure

Snow did come right after Amelia and I arrived back at the farm. It came and left another six inches, and then another storm came after that and left another foot. It would have to be spring before Amelia and Brady would see each other again. Or at least that's what we all thought. It was three weeks after our visit to the Campbell's that Brady actually showed up at our farm, and when he showed up, it was because he was on a mission. I was with Amelia when he arrived. He pulled up in his family's ATV, parked it in front of the barn, and went looking directly for William and then for Johnathan.

Amelia was beside herself with worry. It was two hours before Brady actually came into the house to see Amelia, and when he did, he asked to speak with her privately. I immediately knew what it would be about, that was for sure. Brady and Amelia went into the living room, and we all crammed into the doorway of the dining room across the entry way and strained to hear. They spoke softly for a while, too soft for any of us to hear, but when it came down to it, we all could make out the recognizable words of: "Amelia, will you marry me?" followed by the quick answer of "yes". After hearing Amelia's answer we all couldn't help ourselves from just running into the room and cheering. We were all so happy for them.

Brady had taken so long talking with William and Jonathan was because not only did Brady want to have the blessing of Amelia's father and cldest brother, but he wanted a rather quick wedding. Winter was not easing up one bit, and we all expected it to continue on its rough course. Brady wanted to be sure that it was alright, so long as Amelia agreed of course, if the wedding would be held in exactly three days from that very day. It took us all by a shock, but we would get it done that was for sure. Brady had it all well thought out, he already took measures in town and got Mr. Wilson, the town lawyer to draw up the same document used for William and Poppy's wedding, as well as to ask a few people to carefully and modestly decorate the library.

Amelia agreed to everything. She was on cloud nine with excitement. Brady knew about the Wilde family tradition of not seeing the bride and such, so although he had just proposed to his bride to be, he took his leave and informed us that he would be staying in town and would see us all the day of the wedding. After he left we just scrambled. Amelia needed a dress, and we were going to give her one.

Three days was nothing. We got that dress done, and we made sure that she had a proper bouquet to go with it at well. It was a delicately put together bouquet of pine branches, which we dusted lightly with flour to give the illusion of snow. We used much of the material that we had used for Poppy's dress. The dress was floor length and we bustled the back of it making it much puffier than Poppy's had been. It was a winter wedding dress after all. She had long sleeves and a big bow in the back. It looked absolutely splendid. To keep her warm Poppy and I worked hard to knit a white shawl for her. It all came together beautifully.

On the day of the wedding, we all dressed in whatever best attire we had for the cold weather, and precariously got Amelia onto an ATV to get her into town. Although Brady gave specific instructions to only a few people, the town indeed went above and beyond yet again. Just like the summer wedding, this winter one had the town decorated with banners, lanterns, and a cheering crowd.

Inside the library, it had been decorated all over with candles and cut out paper snowflakes, it was absolutely splendid. The ceremony went just the same as Poppy and William's had and within an hour, Brady and Amelia were married. It wasn't until after the wedding that it really started to sink in on us. There would be no reception, no celebration, no anything, just goodbye. Amelia wasn't staying on the farm, no, she was going with Brady back to the Campbell farm, and I hadn't quite realized this until she and Brady started heading for his ATV to head out the east gate. I began to cry. I stood in line to say goodbye to them, but when it was my turn, I really didn't know what to say, I just hugged both of them and stood there waving good bye as they left through the gate.

***

The weeks went by, the snow melted, Poppy's belly began to grow, birds began to sing, Connor spent hours working on his stupid secret project; life just went on. For the first few weeks after Amelia and Brady's wedding, it was odd not to have Amelia in the house, I had to take up extra chores that she had once done, and I often found myself going to look for her when I thought of something funny or saw something that she would like, but each time I would have to remind myself that she wasn't there. It wasn't until the season changed that we were able to see Amelia again.

When spring returned, we returned back to the town more frequently. Connor saw Amelia the most when he went to town since he was always going down there on secret business for his stupid secret project. I found myself growing very jealous of the thing, whatever it was. I really had nothing to complain about other than the fact that I didn't know what it was, Connor didn't neglect spending time with me, and he even took weekends off to not work on it just to spend it with me. It just bothered me that I didn't know what it was and everyone else did, and no one, no matter how hard I tried and asked, would tell me.

In April, once spring was in full bloom, when the air was crisp, clean, and warm, when we had new ducklings, lambs, and kittens on the farm, the CDC volunteers returned. They brought with them large construction equipment, including cranes, excavators, and tractors. They met with the entire town at a town meeting and asked our permission to build six new houses on a large empty lot of land just outside the town wall. They planned on extending the wall to include these six new homes, the reason for this was because tragedy had befallen another town a while away from ours. The winter had been too harsh on the other town, there had been severe food shortages, their water supply froze, and the cold killed a few. The CDC thought it best to relocate the families of the towns in small groups to other, more stable towns where the survival rate was higher. The news was very shocking, yet at the same time exciting, we would be welcoming six new families into our town. Work began right away in building the six new houses, everything would be built in a matter of three weeks, and by the end the new families would arrive.

During the time that they took to build the new houses, we also got word that the source of the plague was finally discovered. We all gathered onto the town green as each of the volunteers that we had become so acquainted with took the stage to talk about all the efforts that had been done, all the research, all the trials and errors. Thomas

Phillips, Mark Downs, Abigail Blake, and Mark Shaw all spoke. They talked about this and they talked about that, but it took them a while to get to the point, to get to the root cause of it all. I could tell by the way they spoke, by the way they stood at the podium, and by their mannerisms that they themselves knew that what they had to announce to us was very grave, and when they announced it, when they explained it all, for a brief moment, you could hear a pin drop in the audience. Yet, that moment faded, some cried, some yelled, they demanded to know more. Connor and I just held each other closer and looked at each other as we processed what we had just learned.

The plague was not only man made, but it was covered up for a very long time. It all stemmed back to a small company in the Midwest, a pesticide and fertilizer company called Farm Bio Chem Industries, or FBC Industries. Thirty years ago they had been a small company that was experimenting with innovative, cost efficient, low impact pesticides and fertilizers. Thirty years ago their chemists were striving to create an all-purpose pesticide that not only killed common pests that plagued many of the big cash crops of the world, but was also safe enough to be used in massive quantities by thousands of farmers around the world. They hit the jackpot when they created a pesticide that did everything that they wanted it to do, they named it FBC Clear. FBC Clear killed common pests, helped keep crops healthy, and washed off the crops with very small amounts of water. This new pesticide was named the safest and most effective pesticide in the world, it made FBC Industries a multibillion dollar company overnight, and FBC Clear started to be used on nearly every single big name farm in the modern world.

FBC Clear had no initial effect on humans or animals when the company tested it and when the FDA tested it. It passed every test that there was, but something was happening that no one anticipated and no one even thought possible. There was no way for the company to know what extreme prolonged exposure to the pesticide would do, back then they had no idea what would happen in thirty years, and they didn't know until now. For thirty years the chemical was sprayed onto plants and for thirty years it was washed off of plants, on the surface of the food there was no trace of the chemical, but it was still there, it was in the soil. The chemical would wash off of the plants and would dilute in the water. The chemical's molecules would break down into smaller units in the water and then be absorbed by the plant through its roots. Before anyone knew it, FDC Clear was in everything, it had become a part of everything. The molecules of the chemical would just break down into smaller molecules; it would never really go away. It wasn't until three years ago that FDC Industries realized what was happening, a small handful of the senior chemists who were on the original team for developing FDC Clear thirty years ago got unexplainably sick and died. FDC Industries launched a private investigation and discovered for themselves that FDC Clear was breaking down into smaller molecules, being absorbed by plants, being eaten by humans and animals, and then the chemical in turn being absorbed into our bodies. In small dosages FDC Clear was completely harmless, but after thirty years of it constantly being consumed, the chemical was building up in our systems until it reached a fatal toxicity level. That fatal toxicity level was reached two years ago by the first victims of the plague that made news headlines and it was just a domino effect from there.

FDC Industries had all the reports, paperwork, and documentation of what they had discovered locked away. Key investigators that the company used disappeared. High ranking FDC officials fled the country. Congressmen, senators, lawyers, scientists, and top doctors were all paid to be silent; they were paid to give the world the runaround as to what really was going on. But eventually all those congressmen, senators, lawyers, scientists, and doctors met their own demise at the hands of FDC Clear, and the information was all but lost. It took the unbiased, uncorrupted CDC Volunteers to make the rediscovery as to what had happened.

The majority of the people responsible for this heinous scandal were now all dead; victims of their own creation, there was now no one to currently hold responsible for the deaths of millions of people. We all wanted to know why we survived, why were we still living, what made us special? The answer was quite obvious. It was the way we had been living. All of us, all of the survivors, we all had one thing in common, and it was in how we ate and what we ate. Months and months ago when the CDC volunteers first arrived, when they first interviewed us, they asked us life style questions. The key reason as to why we had all survived was because we all either grew our own food, or we shopped smart and ate organically. Although all of us have trace amounts of FDC Clear in our bodies, it never reached the fatal toxicity level.

After learning this, we all had lots of questions. Would the chemical ever leave us? What would happen to future generations? What was going to happen to us now? Those questions would have to be answered in time. We knew what had caused the plague, but the volunteers still had a lot to work on. Now that there was an answer to the biggest question that had weighed on all our minds, we needed to know how we would overcome this. That would all come with time.

The volunteers assured us that the answers would come in a matter of weeks, but that for now there was nothing to worry about, we only had to focus on the recovery, and part of that recovery was to get ready to welcome the six new families into our town. The families arrived on a sunny May morning. They had children and animals with them, and they were eager to meet all of us. That was the day that Peter met Lucy. Connor told me that when Peter and Lucy locked eyes for the first time, it was like the lightning bolt of love hit both of them instantaneously. Of course I thought Connor's exact way of phrasing it was a bunch of soft sap, but it soon proved to be very true. Lucy was a very pretty girl with auburn colored hair, a heart shaped face, and hazel eyes, and Peter adored her.

After the families arrived, the presence of the volunteers left our little town and we were left alone again. Life continued as it had once before. Work was done on the farm, our garden grew, the boys went hunting, chores were done, and nothing was exciting or monumental. I wouldn't describe it as being boring, quite the contrary; rather life was perfect, almost. I accepted the fact that Connor spent hours a day working on his secret project, so long as I got to see him for a bit before I went up to bed, I was happy.

The volunteers did come back only five weeks after they had left. This time they brought an abundance of medical equipment with them. They had figured out a way in how to find out how much of the FDC Clear pesticide was in our bodies, and if we so chose to, we could get tested.

Half of me wanted to know how much of the chemical was inside of me, but the other half of me was very scared. I was worried that I was going to find out that the amount of the chemical in me was high and that I would be a ticking time bomb for me to get sick. Yet, the other half desperately wanted to know. The volunteers knew that having this new test available would make most of the survivors scared, I wasn't the only one. So they gave us time. They gave us time to think about if we wanted to get tested or not.

Everyone in the house decided that they wanted to get tested, but I still hadn't made up my mind. The dead line to get tested was rapidly approaching and I knew that I needed to just make a decision. The thought of it kept me up one night. I was up so late that it was nearing dawn and I knew that I would never even be able to get a wink of sleep. I decided that I wasn't just going to lay in bed in the warm hot air of the upstairs bedroom, so I got up and went down to the kitchen for a drink of water. I gazed out into the yard from the kitchen window and saw that there was still a lantern burning up in the barn loft. Connor was up there working. He would be mad if I went in there to bother him, but I needed him to help me make up my mind.

The cool dew of the grass wet my toes and the hem of my nightgown as I crossed the yard to the barn. As I neared I could hear Connor hammering and sawing away at his surprise. I stopped at the entry way of the barn and just leaned against the door frame.

"Connor?" I called out in the direction of the staircase. The noise from above stopped and I heard his heavy footsteps cross from one side to the other and then eventually to the staircase. He was covered in head to toe in some sort of white powder.

"What are you doing up? Is everything alright?" He asked me as he came closer.

"I'm fine. I just don't know what to do." I said while looking down at my feet.

"To do about what?"

"About the testing thing, I don't know if I should get tested or if I shouldn't. What are you going to do?" I said looking up at him.

"I thought I'd get tested."

"I'm just a big chicken."

"Are you scared? What is there to be scared about?"

"I don't know. I want to get tested but I'm afraid that the results might not be good."

"The results aren't going to be good for anybody. Practically everyone in the world was exposed to this stuff. We all have it; it's just a matter of knowing how much we currently have in us." Connor tried to reason with me.

"I know all that."

"Then why be scared? You're not going to get sick."

"How do you know?"

"You heard what they said. The reason we are all alive to begin with is because of our lifestyles, we're living because of how we're living. I personally can't think of a better way to live than off the land and working hard for what you get." He said, I just let out a long sigh and slumped my shoulders.

"We'll go in the afternoon and get tested together, how does that sounds?" he said lifting up my head with his dusty finger under my chin.

"Alright." I said.

"Good." He then took my hand and kissed the back of it like gentlemen used to do in old movies, and it made me laugh.

"How about you let me take a peek at what you're working on?" I whispered.

"No way José." He said.

"Aww please?" I begged.

"Nope."

"When will it be done?"

"It'll be done, when it's done." He said taking a step forwarc pressing me even closer to the doorframe.

"You're impossible." I said rolling my eyes and pushing hin away.

"Where are you going?" he said as I began to walk back to the house.

"Back to bed, I'm quite tired all of a sudden." I said only briefly turning my head for a moment. As I walked I felt a round object hit the back of my thigh and I jolted around to see Conno where I had just left him, standing there with a stupid look on his face.

“It was a wood chip. I meant to aim just a little higher.” He said with a chuckle.

38.

Homecoming

The volunteers set up some screens to partition a section of the library for a private area for the test to be done. Inside the partitioned area were two chairs, the chairs similar to the ones that you would sit in when you get blood drawn at a hospital. My hands were sweaty and I had butterflies in my stomach.

"It'll be fine." Connor said putting his hand on my shoulder, I nodded and went over and sat down in one of the chairs while Connor sat in the one beside mine. Before even getting into the partition we had to fill out this small stack of paperwork with odd questions. Some of them were like: "how often did you eat ground beef from a grocery store?" or "did you always wash your fruits and vegetables after purchasing them?" I thought the questions were odd, but I guess they were important to an extent.

As I sat in the chair I just let my eyes wander around the screened off area. With the exception of the two chairs there was nothing else, until I noticed an orange power cord running in through a window and laying in the corner. The nurse came into the area and smiled.

"Let's get you two prepped." She said. I thought they were just going to take a few blood samples and look at them under a microscope, but it was quickly becoming clear that that was not to be the case. The nurse rubbed iodine all over the insides of our left elbows where our veins run, and then, using some numbing solution, she injected us in the area until our whole left arms were numb from about three inches above the inside of our elbows down to our finger tips. When she first injected the numbing solution, it burned like fire, but quickly dissipated until I felt nothing. It was a very strange sensation. I would try and tell my fingers to move, but nothing would happen.

The nurse then strapped our arms in two places to the arm rest of the chair and draped our laps with this blue medical material that was a cross between a paper and a cloth. As she was finishing the prep work I could hear some voices of other people in the distance as well as them moving something. Soon enough four people came into the partitioned area pushing with them these two machines. The machines were on wheels and were about just as tall as I was with this computer monitor on them and lights and buttons. The machines looked quite scary.

"What is that!?" Connor said with a hint of panic in his voice.

"These... well they are... what are we calling them?" asked one of the nurses.

"Well I call the white one Sally, and I call the gray one Betty." another said.

"But what are they really called?" said the first nurse.

"Wait... You're hooking us up to those and you don't even know what they are!?" I said.

"No... no... it's not like that. Let me explain. When we made the discovery of FBC Clear being in the human body, a special machine had to be developed to find the chemical and measure it. These machines are hybrid machines. They are part dialysis machines, part cell savers, and part new technology. They aren't going to hurt you, you won't lose an ounce of your blood, and it's perfectly safe and ethical. The engineers and doctors that worked on this machine did an amazing job, basically what these babies are going to do is filter through every little drop of your blood, and they can pin point the FBC Clear chemical, at the end it'll add up every molecule it counted and give us a percentage of what's in you." She said.

"We can't just take a sample of blood from you and test to see if you have the chemical or not. We need to know very precise numbers. The chemical is extremely complex, and the molecule very small. Each and every molecule needs to be counted." The other nurse said.

"I once knew someone on dialysis, it always made them tired." I said as one of the nurses started to put on a fresh set of gloves.

"This isn't like that. You might feel light headed while hooked up to the machine, but once it's all over you'll be normal. When we attach the tubes to you with the needles the machine and the tubes will act like an extension of your veins, and the machine doesn't turn off or stop until every last drop of your blood is back in your body." She said as she took a pack of sterile tubes and needles out of one of the machines.

"So who wants to go first?" She asked, I turned to Connor who just had a look of horror on his face.

"I'll go first." I said. I was given a stress ball to squeeze in my right hand while everything was hooked up to my left arm. The machine was wheeled behind me and plugged into the power cord. One of the other nurses turned the machine on so it would boot up. It made all this chiming noises and humming but then it just purred silently. The nurse did a few more checks on my left arm to make sure it was complexly numb before taking the first needle and tube. The needle was rather large, about the thickness of a piece of spaghetti. I squeezed my eyes shut as she inserted it. I didn't feel a thing, but it was seeing it that made me feel queasy. She then went to my right arm and did the whole process on that arm too. I now had these two medical tubes with little stoppers at the ends of them holding my blood at bay. I didn't see much of what she was doing behind me with the machine, but I guessed that it was running new sterile tubing in the machine which she then connected to the two tubes in my arms. In one tube blood would flow out, and in the other the blood would flow back in.

I watched with amazement as my blood flowed down through the tube, back to the machine, and then after two or three minutes back into my other arm through the second tube. It was fascinating.

"Alright, Mona, this takes two hours. So feel free to take a nap." She said after pressing one more button on my machine. I wasn't quite ready to nap yet, not until I saw Connor get his needles. He was just a big baby, I couldn't help but laugh. He bit his lip, squeezed his eyes shut, and held his breath as the nurse inserted the needles. Once we were all hooked up and the machines purring softly behind us, the nurse left and said she would be back in two hours.

"This is so weird." Connor said looking at his arms.

"I'm beginning to feel the light headedness… is it because half of all my blood is in the machine?" I said.

"I believe so." Connor said without taking his eyes off of his arms.

"Here I was, just yesterday all scared, and then today you were the scared one!" I said to him.

"Needles, Mona, needles, I hate them."

"Oh boohoo!" I laughed, as I laughed I could feel a buzzing, and woozy sensation in my head.

"Let's not laugh anymore, I'm getting dizzy." I said.

"I'm going to take a nap. My head is bubbly." Connor said. I turned my head away from him and made myself as comfortable as possible on the chair before dozing off.

***

I woke up to the machine beeping and my head beginning to feel better. I looked over at the tubes and saw that the tube that had the blood flowing out of me was clear and clean, like it hadn't even been used, and the one that flowed into me was still pumping away, pushing my blood back into my body.

"Connor," I said trying to wake him up, "Connor!" I said a bit louder. He stirred a bit and eventually his eyes fluttered open.

"Has it been two hours?" he groaned.

"I think so. Mine is beeping and look! All the blood is pumping back in." I said pointing to my arm. A few moments went by before Connor's machine started beeping too. With all the beeping the nurse came back, waited for the last drops of our blood to be pumped back into our bodies, and then started unhooking us. After being freed from the tubes and needles, we were left with two little band aids on our numb arms. Until the numbing wore off we would have to wear slings so our arms wouldn't flop around. The nurse was kind and gentle and made sure our arms were snug before having us go to the other side of the library to hear our results.

It was Abigail Blake who was going to talk to us about our results. She greeted us with a warm smile, asked if our arms were alright, and then excused herself to go grab our paperwork which the machines printed out.

"Alright… alright… these look good, very good." She said cheerfully which made me feel secure and good.

"So, what's the verdict?" Connor asked.

"Well it's all very complicated as to how these numbers are counted and what not." She said.

"They told us the machine counts each and every molecule." I said.

"Yes that is true, and the machine does the entire math. So what the machine did was it not only counted the FBC Clear molecules, but also protein levels, vitamins, minerals, fats, acids, and the such. Basically the machine counted everything your blood is made out of. So with all those numbers, which were in the trillions, it did some math and gave us back this final number as to how much of the chemical is in your bodies. So FBC Clear at a 75% toxicity level is fatal. At 65% toxicity is when the symptoms and the shutdown of the body occurs, when the shutdown starts to occur is hinders the body's ability to ward off different things, making it easier for the body to absorb more of the chemical quicker which was why people died so rapidly. With those little dreary facts out of the way, are you ready to hear your results?" Abigail asked.

"Yes." Connor and I both said together.

"Alright then… Connor, you have an FBC Clear level of 21% and Mona, you have 23%. Those are very low levels, which is very good."

"Wow… that's amazing." Connor said.

"Now… you two are a couple, am I correct?" Abigail asked.

"Yes we are." I said.

"Do you plan on having a family? Children maybe?". she asked.

"Maybe one day." Connor said turning to me.

"Yes, maybe one day." I affirmed.

"Well, if you want I can give you the estimates as to what your children's percentages will be."

"Yes, of course." Connor said.

"Now these numbers are only estimates," she said taking out a calculator, "We don't estimate for the chemical to totally be eradicated from plants, animals, and soil for another 10 to 20 years. We do know that the chemical can be passed on from mother to child by about 50 percent."

"So when I have a baby, I lose 50 percent of the chemical I have now?" I asked.

"No, it doesn't work exactly like that. You will always have a percentage of 23 for your entire life, it will never leave you, but the percentage your children are born with is roughly half of that. It's all very complicated and confusing, believe me, I know. So any children you two do have will be born with a percentage of 11.5 percent, and if you have daughters and they grow up and have children, their children, your grandchildren, will have a percentage of 5.75 percent."

"So from here on out our children, everyone's children, will be born with less and less of the chemical?" Connor asked.

"Precisely, we estimate that by the time your generation has great-great-grandchildren, the chemical will be completely gone."

"That is wild." I said leaning over to look at the actual paperwork that Abigail held in her hand.

"Here, you can keep all of this, we already have copies." She said handing us our own paperwork. Connor and I looked at each other's as we left the library to head back home. There were all sorts of numbers printed out on the papers but the one that was important, our percentages, were clearly printed in red ink. Connor and I walked slowly through the town green towards the direction of the gate. I heard my name being called out in the distance before we made it. We both turned around to see Mark Shaw running towards us.

"Mona, Connor, I am glad to catch you." He said a bit out of breath .

"What's the matter?" Connor asked.

"Oh, nothing is wrong, I just have good news, news about your mother, Mona." He said with a big smile.

"Really?!"

"Yes, she is ready to leave the facility. She is free to go home with you."

"Oh, that is great news!" I said jumping up and down.

"When will she be here?" Connor asked.

"As soon as you are ready for her; unfortunately due to some protocol, I simply cannot just bring her up here myself, you will have to go down to get her." He said to me.

"I see. And we'll need to prepare to have her home." I said

"Yes, of course, I have the final medical report on your mother, I think you'll be able to assess for yourself what sort of things she may need." Mark said pulling a piece of paper out of his breast pocket. I briefly scanned the paper while Connor and Mark chatted about a few things. Most of my mother's conditions had improved.

She was mobile to an extent. The paper said she walked and climbed stairs with the assistance of a cane. Her left arm was still useless and she still could not speak, but according to the paper, there was nothing else wrong with her.

"Thank you Mr. Shaw." I heard Connor say as I lifted my eyes from the paper.

"What was that about?" I asked as we walked away back to the gate.

"Made arrangements to get your mother home. We have three weeks to get the house ready, the family ready, and you ready to bring her home. Mark said he would drive up himself and bring us to go get her."

"That is so very generous of him." I said.

"Three weeks, we have a lot of work to do."

***

The idea of adding another person to the home wasn't and had never been an unusual idea, but the idea of adding a person who would not be able to pull their own weight in the home was something of a different story. I understood that my mother would be another person to feed, clothe, bathe, and keep warm in the winter, all of which we would have to provide for her without her being able to provide anything in return. It would mean that there would be extra added chores to everyone's plates. The amount of laundry would slightly go up, the availability of the bathroom, the portion sizes of meals, and so on. Although they were minor things that would be changing to having an additional helpless individual to the house, it all made me feel a bit uneasy.

"Suppose she is very unwell, supposed she needs twenty four hour care, what are we to do then?" Ms. Elizabeth asked when I brought up the topic once Connor and I returned from the town.

"Then I supposed we must, to the best of our ability, provide that care." I said.

"Suppose she falls ill and our normal course of treatments do her harm? There are no formal doctors in the town." Cora said.

"They would not be releasing her if that were the case." I said.

"Mona, what if she isn't the same person as before? What if all those experiments changed her personality, what if for some reason she doesn't remember you?" Charlotte asked.

"This is all why we will be going to get her ourselves. Once we are at the infirmary we will assess the situation before making any decisions. If we feel it wouldn't be a good idea for her to live here with us, then we will not bring her back." Connor chimed in.

"Well I am glad to hear of that. We just don't want something that could potentially bring disaster and heartache. The world isn't as it once was. There are no doctors or nearby hospitals, we don't even have the luxury of transportation aside from the ATVs and dirt bike. We just all want you two to be sure that you are making the right choice." Ms. Elizabeth said.

"No matter what we choose, it will be because we came to the decision together." I said before turning to Connor. The whole matter was nerve racking yet exciting at the same time. Half of me wanted to urgently prepare the house and a room for her, yet the other half of me was like a child excited to be reunited with their mother, I had to keep reminding myself that there was a strong possibility that the person that would be coming back to the farm might not exactly be the same person I was torn away from in Baltimore.

In the days and weeks that followed, Poppy and I worked on getting clothes ready for my mom. We estimated based on the paperwork that the Mark Shaw had given to me as to what her size may be when it came to the clothing. Amelia even came over twice, with Brady of course, to drop off some clothes that were no longer needed at the Campbell farm as a gift to my mother and the rest of us.

We also rearranged one of the spare bedrooms so that it would be accommodating for my mother. It would be near to the bathroom, and near to my own room. It would have a twin bed, a sitting chair, writing table, and a dresser. It was all rather very simple, but I had to be sure that it was perfect and that everything was in just the right position so that there would be no difficulty with her roaming about the room.

I had grown rather hysterical over the whole thing, Connor even said that I was becoming rather paranoid, which I resented him saying, yet it was nonetheless true. I began thinking about what if's and hypothetical scenarios in my head. I was rearranging the oil lamp in my mother's room when Poppy came in in an attempt to try and get me to be normal again. I felt that I couldn't put the lamp on her night stand because what if my mother were to roll over in bed and knock it over? But I couldn't put the lamp on the dresser because then it would be too far in case she needed to get up at night. Poppy just calmly took the lamp from my hand, moved the night stand over three more inches away from the bed and then placed it on top.

"Let's go for a walk." Poppy said. For the initial first part of our walk we said nothing to each other. We walked down the drive way and then down the road. The weather was very fine that day. The birds were singing in the trees, the sky was sapphire blue and the clouds as fluffy as cotton balls. As we walked the breeze toyed with the hems of our skirts and it tangled up our hair.

"Do you remember this spot?" Poppy asked, I took a moment to look around, and soon the memory came back, it was the same spot Poppy and I had come to when we snuck out of the house the previous spring and went for a joy ride on the dirt bike.

"That was a fun night." I said with a laugh.

"It sure was. Haven't had too many of those with you since then."

"Connor told me that farm down there is abandoned. We should go check it out." I said.

"What? No, that's crazy." Poppy said putting her hand protectively on her belly. She probably didn't even realize she did it, but it did remind me that I wasn't in the presence of a one hundred percent carefree individual.

"Fine." I said with a sigh, we both just stood there for a while, while the breeze danced around us.

"Alright let's go. It's probably still abandoned." She said shrugging her shoulders before heading off down the hill. I stood there in minor disbelief before going after her. It was about a half a mile walk until we reached the driveway of the farm, or what once was the driveway. The house was fairly small, a good old fashioned farmhouse probably built in the early 1930s. The house probably at one time was painted white, but weather and sun had dried and chipped it away until it was a dingy grey. The barn that stood towards the side of the property was just of unpainted, weathered, and slightly rotting wood. The middles of the roofs of both the house and the barn sagged, and the shingles had moss growing on them. Everything on the property was overgrown and slowly being reclaimed by the earth.

We aimlessly walked around the property looking at different objects that we covered in a fine layer of dirt and had grass growing up all around them. There was a tractor, a car, and children's toys that seemed to have now become one with the earth.

"Mona!" I heard Poppy call from the other side of the yard. I rushed over to where she was standing looking out at a space between two trees. At first I didn't really notice what she was looking at, but when I finally reached her, I could see clearly what she was gazing at. Between the trees were five little posts clearly marking out the graves of the five family members that once lived on the farm. There were two large posts and three small ones. Poppy and I gazed at them for a while and it made us sad.

"I wonder how old the children were." Poppy said after a while.

"I wonder how long the husband and wife had been married?" I asked. We just stood there looking at the posts before Poppy turned away and walked towards the backdoor of the house. I watched as she pulled open the screen door, it creaked slowly, and then she stepped inside the porch.

"Poppy." I said just before she appeared in the doorway again.

"The door is unlocked." She said, this peaked my curiosity. I followed her up through the porch and into the house. As we walked the floor creaked with each of our footsteps. The interior of the house had been sealed like a time capsule. We had entered in through the kitchen; light beamed though the plastic shades that covered the two little windows. A coffee pot, blender, and toaster sat on the counter by the sink. A pile of dishes that had probably been washed by their previous users sat in the drying rack. The old stove and oven sat unused, and a clock that hung above the stove permanently now read 3:04, the last minute it ever ticked on.

I walked over to one of the kitchen cabinets and opened it, inside, stacked in neat rows was canned food, green beans, corn, and cranberry sauce. I closed the cabinet. It felt like we were in a time warp, thrown back in time to what would have been only a few years ago. I watched Poppy continue through the house. I followed though the dining room, where six chairs sat around a large dining room table that was covered in a white table cloth. A china cabinet stood against the wall displaying white and blue porcelain. We continued into the front living room. Against one wall sat a large flat screen TV that now had a layer of dust on it, there was a couch and a love seat, and a side table that had picture frames sitting on top of it. All of the pictures had a layer of dust on them. I walked over to grab the picture nearest to me, and as I did so, my foot landed on something metal. I looked down to see that it was a little toy car. I smiled for a moment and then picked up the picture frame.

After dusting it off I gazed down at what probably was the very last family portrait of the family that lived in this house. A mother, father, a daughter, and two little twin boys. They looked like the most average family there was. As I gazed down at them Poppy came over too and began looking.

"I feel so sad." She said.

"Me too." I said placing the picture back to the exact spot I had found it in. We decided it was best not to further investigate the house. We went back out the back door and shut it tightly just as we had found it and went back home.

39.

Amherst

I paced back and forth in the front entryway. I had barely eaten breakfast and with each passing minute it felt like an eternity. We had received word from Mark Shaw about him coming to take Connor and I to go get my mother. He specified what day he would be here, but he didn't specify exactly what time to expect him. So Connor and I packed the day before and now I was just pacing back and forth, occasionally pausing to try and hear if there was a vehicle driving up the driveway.

It was only midmorning and he probably wouldn't arrive until the afternoon, but I just felt the need to wait. I wanted to be ready the exact moment that he came. It was half past twelve when an SUV made its way up the driveway.

"Connor!" I called out. Before Mark even got out of his vehicle, Connor was there with me on our way out the front door to meet him.

"Hope I haven't been keeping you waiting long." Mark said with a chuckle.

"Oh no, we're fine." Connor said.

"Are you ready for the trip?" he asked.

"More than ready." I said throwing my backpack over my shoulder.

"Excuse me! Aren't you going to say goodbye to us!" Connor and I turned around to see Ms. Elizabeth and Charlotte standing in the front door. Both of us turned away and went to hug them goodbye before loading up into the SUV. We would be gone for, at most, two days and two nights. It was an odd feeling getting into the large SUV. The last time I was in a vehicle I had been with Connor and William and we were trying to get to the farm. Now, Connor and I were doing the exact opposite, we were leaving the farm.

I looked out the back window as the farm faded away and until we turned on the road. While in a car, it felt strange to reach the abandoned farm in such a short amount of time. We zipped by it and kept going, driving down the road at a high speed. A mere 45 minutes of driving at nearly 60 miles per hour had passed before Mark slowed down the SUV in order to safely pass an abandoned, leaf and dirt covered CDC truck that was precariously left off the side of the road.

"That darn truck has always been a mystery to me, what the heck was a CDC security truck doing out here?" Mark said with a chuckle.

"I could tell you." Connor said.

"Really?"

"My brother, Mona, and I, we stole it back in Jersey City, it was how we got the majority of the way back home." Connor said, the memory of the three of us in that truck both made me smile and made me sad.

The drive continued, and as we worked our way south east we also worked our way down the Berkshire Mountains, causing my ears to pop due to the change in elevation. While we drove, Mark had his old iPod Shuffle hooked up to the car radio and he played old songs by Bon Jovi, Queen, and Michael Jackson. Songs that I hadn't heard in a very long time. We were the only vehicle for miles and miles that was on the road. It was sad to me when we drove, no longer on narrow, winding country roads, but rather, wide two lane highways that passed through once populated areas. We passed old department stores, restaurants, and gas stations, all of them empty of people and overrun by grass sprouting up through the cracks in the pavement.

All together it was about a two hour drive from the farm until we saw another vehicle on the road. We were only minutes from the Umass Amherst campus, and I could feel fluttering in my stomach. The closer we got to the campus, the more our surroundings seemed to change. There were buildings, that judging by their tidiness, were in use, and occasionally I would see a person walking on the sidewalk down the road.

As with everything the CDC did, a massive wall of fences, cement dividers, and barbed wire separated the world from the actual campus. We passed through a gate where a CDC officer, dressed in the usual black CDC officer's uniform, checked Mark Shaw's badges and paperwork, before letting us through. Inside the gates it was like nothing on the outside ever happened. There were men and women walking around with ID badges around their necks, they dressed in normal clothes, I say normal because compared to Connor and I, they were normal. I was in a handmade sundress of my own making, and Connor was in well-worn jeans and a button down with a grass stain near the bottom.

Mark navigated the SUV down the streets, passing various buildings, and people walking around. It was amazing to see exactly how many people there were. Were they all volunteers or were they still here from being rounded up by the CDC? As I thought about this, it was Connor who actually asked the question.

"It's a strong mix of both. About four months ago they allowed the majority of doctors and scientists to go looking for their families that they had left behind. Most came back without anything or anyone to go back to. A few brought their families back with them, and a very small amount just never came back at all. Then there are the volunteers like me, we make up about 65 percent of the population here." Mark answered.

"How many people are here?" I asked.

"Well… counting all the patients, and everyone carrying a CDC identification badge, or they happen to have the privilege to live inside the gates, I'd say about 2,000 altogether. We're the largest concentration of people on the east coast right now. This infirmary location was meant to handle all the doctors and scientists from Florida, Michigan, Maine, and all the states in-between." All I could think about what how exactly that many people could fit on this campus. This was a massive campus, but it to me it still wouldn't have been large enough to hold that many people; and I was right. The further we drove the more Mark would add his own bit of commentary to the drive. Occasionally we would pass a building that required a short story behind it about what it was used for. Eventually we passed a very large field, a field that I guessed at one time was a soccer field, but it was dotted with little white posts, too numerous to number just by driving by.

"That's the graveyard. There are a lot of people living here now on the campus, but when the program was first set in place; this place was bursting at the seams with 60,000 plus people. That graveyard and one other on the other side of the campus hold the final resting places of nearly 57,000 people, give or take a few hundred."

"Was it because of FBC Clear?" I asked.

"That, and all of the medical testing." He said gravely. The road we were on soon led us away from the large buildings that was the main heart of the campus and brought us to a very old section of houses and buildings that looked very similar to a little New England town. Mark informed us that not only did the gates and walls encompass the Umass campus, but a fair majority of the town, which was where we now were. The old town hall was what now served as the rehabilitation center for people like my mother. Mark parked the car and the three of us got out and made our way up the front steps of a church like brick building that had a large clock tower on it.

We made our way through the halls, passing patients that sat in the hallways in their wheelchairs. The interior of the building looked like an old town hall, but with all the beeping medical equipment and the patients, it felt more like a nursing home. We entered an office where a woman in a red sweater and dark wash blue jeans sat behind a desk clicking away at a computer.

"Excuse me." Mark said, getting her attention.

"Oh… Mark, how are you!" The woman said getting up to give him an awkward hug across the desk.

"I am well. I hope I caught you at good time."

"Oh, every time is a good time. I'm just emailing some release papers over to the Westfield State College campus. It's so thrilling to be reuniting so many people with their families." She said with a smile.

"Well I'm glad to hear it, because I have someone here who would really like to be reunited with their mother." Mark said turning to me.

"Yes, I said stepping forward. My mom."

"Oh goodie," She said with enthusiasm. "Let's get started. Please, all of you have a seat. You might have to pull some over." We all sat in chairs in front of her desk that we had to pull from different rooms as she began to click away at the computer and papers started to print from a nearby printer. Soon I was faced with a half inch thick stack of paperwork. The amount of paperwork seemed to me to be just about the same amount one would have to read when signing a complex contract.

“I know, all the papers are scary, but we just want to make sure you’re informed with what has happened here. We want everyone to know what the CDC has done, what they are now continuing to do, and what they plan on doing to help restore society.” She said. Paper by paper she summarized every detail, details that were interesting, and details I wished I hadn’t learned. The CDC had begun to do much good to help restore society, but in the beginning, there was much corruption and mismanagement. Before the volunteers were involved, the CDC had been doing inhumane and unjust things to the doctors, scientists, officers, and anyone they came across. I learned that the reason I almost starved to death back in Baltimore was because the CDC made up the lie about there being a food shortage in order to feed higher ranking individuals. The information that Connor and I learned was both sickening and eye opening.

“Why are you telling us all of this? Usually this stuff is kept confidential and secret by the government.” Connor said.

“Well… there is no more government. There is nothing left really. Now that we know what caused the plague, we want to make sure that the world knows that there was a high chance that it could have been stopped earlier had there been honest individuals taking the lead. A large percentage of the world has suffered, millions of people have died, not only because FBC Industries covered up their blunders, but because there were greedy men and women who only cared for themselves. You’ll be happy to know that the CDC is now run, not by former US government officials, but by a team of doctors, scientists, and volunteers who had been involved in the process of finding FBC Clear. We want the world to know what happened so that it is never repeated again.” She said as she took the stack of papers and stabled them together before having me sign at the very bottom of the last page.

“Now, your mother, can I have her name?” She said turning back to the computer.

“Yes, Christine Lancaster.” I waited patiently while the woman searched her computer to pull up my mother’s file.

“Oh dear…” she said.

“What? What happened?” I said panicking a bit.

"Oh, it's nothing terrible, it seems like we no longer are housing Dr. Lancaster here at this facility, her health condition improved so much that she was transferred a few days ago to the Westfield State College campus. That campus is where we've sent our older doctors and scientists as well as our patients who are no longer undergoing treatments and are healthy to live a more normal lifestyle."

"This is my fault, I should have made sure she was here before I brought you guys all the way down here. I called last week and she was here, but I should have called yesterday." Mark said.

"Well where is this Westfield campus?" I asked.

"It's about a 45 minute drive from here. Not too far." She said with a smile.

"Oh well that's good news." Connor said.

"I'll tell you what, lets pull all the appropriate paperwork for your mom to be released, I'll send it over tonight, and tomorrow you can just go and you won't have to worry about any lengthy office visits." The woman said with a smile. Soon all the paperwork regarding my mother, and not the CDC, was printed and we got to work. I learned about all the treatments and trials that my mother had endured, at the very end of all of it, I learned about her state of heath presently. Presently she was doing very well. Walking, interacting with others, smiling. Although she could not talk and her left arm was paralyzed, she was in great health. There was just one thing, one thing that I did not like at all. One of the medical trials that she endured had something to do with the heart.

"Mona," the woman began, "There is a very high probability of heart complications with your mother. That trial weakened her heart significantly raising her chances of having a severe heart attack or suffering from sudden heart failure. When your mother gets sent home with you, they will send you home with a stethoscope and a blood pressure cuff, and they will teach you how to use them. Your mother risks suffering from low blood pressure, which could lead to death, also you can't let her strain too much and get her blood pressure up because it could induce a heart attack. They will go over this more with you when you see her."

"I understand." I said, with the last few documents signed and placed in a pink folder on the woman's desk, we were free to go. When we left the building the sun had just started to go down and with all the thinking and listening that I had to do in that office, I was exhausted.

"Come on, we'll get some nice dinner and have a nice sleep back at my place." Mark said as we loaded back into the SUV.

***

I poked at the mac n' cheese that was in the bowl in front of me; I was hungry, yet at the same time, I couldn't eat because I was too worried about what tomorrow would bring. Mark lived in a very large old house with three other Volunteers, two of which had their spouses and children now living with them. Judging by the Greek letters over the fireplace and on the front door knocker, the house was probably the house for a fraternity or sorority or something. There were plenty of rooms to house every one that lived there, but there was only one extra room for guests. Connor gave me the room and opted to sleep out on the very plush and large couch in the living room. Frankly I think he got the better end of that deal since the bed in the room I stayed in was squeaky and slightly lumpy.

The next morning, I got to take a hot shower, the first time since Baltimore. Here in Amherst they had modern amenities like heat, air conditioning, electricity, and on demand hot water. After well over a year of taking a bath by lugging boiling water up from the kitchen into the bathtub and mixing it with cold water that came from the tap, it was nice to have a quicker and less strenuous shower. But I would still prefer the bath over anything, it was much more relaxing.

I was the first one to be completely ready to head out. Connor was thrilled about the shower; he couldn't stop talking about it. Eventually the three of us loaded up into the SUV and made our way towards the town of Westfield. It was a beautiful little town with large Victorian houses, a lovely main street, and large old trees that stood guard over the roads. We just about got to see the entire town before making our way up a long straight and wide road that was lined with regal Victorian houses. As we made our way, the left side of the road emptied to reveal what was once a large park, now turned into a mass cemetery for the former residents of the town. It was sad seeing the dug up earth with patchy grass growing behind the stone wall that marked out the park.

Westfield State College wasn't as large as Umass; in fact it was much, much, much smaller. There weren't as many people as there had been at the Umass campus, and it was much quieter and much more peaceful. I stopped paying attention to exactly where we were going, but eventually the car was parked and we entered a building to go into an office. My paperwork had made it just like the woman in Amherst said it would, it was at the top of the pile on the front desk of this particular office. With a big red stamp, the man attending us stamped the papers, and handed me some copies before calling for a nurse to show me to my mother's room.

When the nurse finally came, Connor tried to walk with me, but the nurse stopped him, stating that only the signing guardian, who would be me, could accompany her to my mother's room. I immediately started to panic inside, and Connor knew it because he pulled me in for a hug and a kiss before I followed the nurse out of the office, down the hall, out the door, around the corner and to a waiting golf cart. The nurse drove the golf cart down and around some little roads and sidewalks before coming to a former dormitory. She led me to the fifth floor and down a hall where there were open doorways that led off into little living spaces, some were occupied, and some were not. My mother's was all the way at the end.

"Stay right here. With her heart, we just want to make sure she won't get overly excited." She whispered to me before entering the room. I had to stay for those agonizing moments while I overheard the nurse look over my mother. Finally, the nurse came out of the room.

"She's doing very well today, she does well every day. I mentioned to her that she has a visitor, she probably expects the doctor, but no worries, and I'll be right out in the hall if you need me." I just nodded and made my way over to the door. The room was filled with sunlight. I squinted as my eyes adjusted to the brightness and took one step into the room. It was a very simple room. A twin sized bed against one wall with a night stand beside it, and a dresser on the other wall. Sitting in a rocking chair, with her back to the door, my mother sat looking out the window, she gave no indication that she knew I had entered the room. She just rocked back and forth, back and forth. Her dark hair, with light curls similar to mine, had been cut very short, and she wore hospital like scrubs and a blanket over her lap, as for anything else, I couldn't say, I needed her to turn around.

"Mom?" I said softly, she stopped rocking and sat motionless for a moment before turning around. She looked at me with this blank expression, her eyes wide and her mouth slightly opened, and then she stood. It was then that I noticed that she kept a cane beside her. I took three strides toward her as she staggered towards me. Although her left arm was useless, she used it to hold the cane. I guessed when they said paralyzed, they must have gotten it wrong, it seemed slightly useable to me. We met each other at the center of the room, she reached out with her right hand and placed it on my cheek. I looked her up and down. It was my mom, my beautiful mother. With the exception of the limp, her left arm, and short hair, it was all still her. I examined her face, and my eyes drifted upwards towards a thick, perfectly straight scar that was visible through her hair on her scalp. I guessed that was where the procedure was done that caused her to lose her speech and her left arm.

We pulled each other into an embrace. I was, by this time, crying. I could hear her making an "mm mm" sound in her throat, most likely trying to say my name. She was crying too. For so long I thought this day wouldn't come. We had been separated. We bother thought the other was dead, yet here we were, together again. We sat down on the edge of the bed, Mom wiped her tears away and I wiped mine. She motioned with her hand to wait for just one moment, and she turned to her nightstand and pulled out a pencil and a very beat up notepad and began writing.

"I've missed you so much. You have no idea what it was like to be without you." she wrote.

"I've missed you too, mommy, I've needed you, and now here you are." I said before she began writing again.

"I heard about Baltimore burning. They gave a detailed report at the Amherst campus, it was that day that I thought my whole world had ceased. First I lost your father, and then I thought I lost you. I didn't want to live anymore." She scratched out.

"I know, I know, they said you signed up for the medical trials."

"But they put me on suicide watch, they were so strict, during that time there wasn't a moment when I was alone. They treated us like slaves. It seemed like I had no choice but to sign up, I hoped to die quickly."

"No… I'm glad you are here, I'm glad I found you." I said.

"They started to take me off that horrid medicine. That junk made me like a vegetable, it was worse than death. Eventually though, I knew why they were doing it, just when I hoped to go to sleep and die, they told me about you, about how alive you were. I knew I needed to live."

"Mom, I can't tell you how happy I am." I said.

"My heart is beating with so much joy, I feel like I could float to the ceiling. Now tell me, where have you been? How did you survive?" She wrote out. It was then that I began to tell her the whole story, I told her about Molly and Collin, about the fences being torn down. I told her about the trek to Jersey City, and about how we stole the truck. I told her all about everything Connor did. She remembered Connor of course and was thrilled nothing bad had become of him. I told her all about the farm and I tried to describe it as best as I could. I told her about Poppy and William, and eventually the gangs. I told her everything, and she just intently listened, only occasionally raising her finger to ask me to stop while she scribbled out a question for me on her note pad.

"So what happens now? Must you leave me?" She wrote.

"No, you're coming home with me." I said. She started to make this blubbering noise that I could only make out to be the beginnings of the word: Baltimore.

"No. Back to the farm, the farm is safe and beautiful, and you will love it there." I said, she got all excited and went to her drawers to start to pack her things, but I stopped her.

"No, I have everything for you back home. You don't need a thing." I said.

***

Eventually we were reunited with Connor and Mark. My mother greeted Connor with the biggest of hugs. After that lesson with the blood pressure cuff and the stethoscope, we were ready to go. We would spend one more night at Mark Shaw's place before heading back to the farm in the morning. The whole ride back to Amherst my mother was grinning ear to ear, and so was I. I gave her the extra room in Mark's place, and since the couch was massive in the living room, it easily fit both me and Connor for one night.

The drive back home seemed to go by much quicker than when we had come down. We made our way back up the mountains, past our abandoned truck, past the abandoned farm, and slowly up the driveway to the farm.

"Here it is Mamma. The farm." I said rolling down the window for her to see. The farm was always beautiful, but it was even more beautiful on that particular day. The grass was lush and green, all the flowers were blooming. There was a mother duck walking her little ducklings through the yard, and as soon as we pulled up the front door of the house flew open, and the whole family, even Amelia and Brady, filed out to greet us. I introduced mom to them one by one. And with each introduction she gave everyone a hug. When I came to Poppy and William, I could tell that she was thinking about what I had told her the day before, about the gangs. She stopped and put her hand on Poppy's belly and then gave Poppy a kiss. At the very end was Ms. Elizabeth. I had spent the majority of our trip back to the farm talking about Ms. Elizabeth and about how she and her would be very close. My mom pointed to herself, then to Ms. Elizabeth, and then crossed her fingers, telling Ms. Elizabeth that they were going to be very close.

I couldn't thank Mark Shaw enough for everything that he did. Eventually he did bid us farewell and left us. I got mom inside and showed her around the main floor of the house before showing her to her room. Judging by the smile on her face she loved her room. I even couldn't help but smile, someone had picked flowers and put them in a vase beside her bed. A full day of travel had been enough to tire her out. I left her to take a nap.

Everything was perfect, I couldn't have asked for anything more. I descended the staircase to see Connor waiting at the bottom. I stopped at the first step, which was enough added height for me to almost be eye level with him.

"I love you very much." I said to him.

"I love you more." He responded.

40.

Ever after

I had worried for no reason as to how mom would adapt to being on the farm. After a few weeks of learning where things were and a few basic tasks that she could handle herself, she was pretty much self-sufficient. She was helping out with small, simple tasks, such as washing eggs, setting the table for dinner, kneading bread dough, and folding linens. Ms. Elizabeth believed that with enough exercise and by constantly trying to use her arm, that my mother could regain the use of her disabled arm. This was a thrilling thought for sure.

As spring turned into summer, this new season was proving to be far better than the summer previously. With regular showers and the occasional thunderstorm, not only was the season not as exceptionally hot as the previous one, but we had no fear of drought. Everything we planted grew like it was on steroids. We grew cucumbers the size of my head, and tomatoes the size of both my fists put together. Ms. Elizabeth credited the large produce to the snow that we got during the winter.

"Snow, it brings minerals down from the atmosphere, makes the greatest plant food." She said. It seemed like there was this new found peace everywhere. There was no news about any new dangers that would or could be fall us, and there was nothing that we currently had to worry about. I couldn't have been more grateful with how things were going having my mother live with us. Connor was always so helpful and attentive to her, making sure she had everything that she needed. He would occasionally stop whatever he was doing in the middle of the day to sit with her, and then come sit with me. I had given up almost entirely as to what Connor was working on up in the barn. It had been an awfully long time to wait around for some sort of surprise, and I just grew tired of waiting.

I was lying in bed one morning, just lying there staring up at the ceiling. I was having one of those days where I just didn't want to do anything except lay in bed, when there was a knock at the door. I rolled over to see Connor standing in the door way.

"Can I come in?" He asked.

"Yeah." I said sitting up in the bed and straightening out the sheets and the pillows. He just came over and sat on the edge of the bed and leaned down to kiss my forehead. I half wanted him to get in bed with me, but I knew he was here for a purpose.

"What's up?" I asked.

"Nothin, I just wanted to know if you wanted to go for a walk later today." He said.

"Yes, I would love to." I replied. Connor smiled and kissed me before leaving the room. I decided then to get up, get a clean sun dress and take a bath before going down stairs to find something to eat. On our lazier days, Ms. Elizabeth would just boil a dozen or so eggs and place them in a bowl for us to grab and go. I supposed that this day was a lazy day since there was a high pile of boiled eggs sitting in a basket at the center of the counter in the kitchen.

I peeled the shell off the egg and just let the little pieces fall onto the grass as I walked about the yard towards the garden. My mother and Ms. Elizabeth were standing in the garden with watering cans giving the vegetables a light drink of water. When my mother caught sight of me she flashed me a big smile and waved. She looked so pretty with her skin starting to get a healthy tan from being outside, and her hair starting to grow.

From where I stood in the yard I could see clear down to where Poppy and William's bus was. From that distance I could see Poppy wringing out clothes from her metal laundry tub and pinning them to her clothes line that William had recently installed on the side of the bus. Poppy's stomach was popping out of her dress like she had stuffed a small melon under there. She wasn't due until the fall, but we almost wondered if there were twins in there. I walked on down and began helping her wring out the clothes from her washtub and hang them.

"William finished the little crib." She said.

"He did, when did he do that?" I asked.

"Yesterday, he put the rest together and painted it. I didn't think he would ever want to finish that particular one." She said with a hint of sadness in her voice.

"Did you think of names for this one yet?" I asked as I wrung out a sopping wet dress from the laundry.

"Well, if it's a girl, we are going with Emery Jane, if it's a boy, William thought the idea of having a William Junior running around was a good idea."

"I think they are both very good names." I said with a smile. We continued to work on hanging the laundry for a while, usually Poppy and I are talking about things, but today she was being unusually silent, only humming a soft tune. Soon Connor came over to steal me away for our walk. When he appeared he carried with him two bows and quite a few arrows.

"I thought we might as well be a little useful while on our walk." He said with a coy smile.

We departed from the farm and from everyone else and headed off into the woods and towards the direction of the river. Along the way we listened for any birds or animals we could try and hunt, but there were none, not even a quail. As the sun reached its highest point in the sky, so did the temperature, and it was at that point that Connor and I had broken out into a sweat and I was longing for the luxury of a hair elastic to tie my hair up. The sound of the water tinkling downstream from the river sounded like heaven as we neared it. I was panting and my forehead was dripping with sweat when we finally reached the river bank. Connor's hair was plastered to his forehead and his shirt was just about soaked. It definitely had to be the hottest day we had had all summer; then again it was just only the beginning of August.

"I give up. No hunting for today." Connor said as he placed his bow and arrow down against a tree stump. A breeze came down through the river clearing and made all the leaves on the trees dance and the skirt of my dress flutter along. I watched, half with embarrassment, and half with utter amusement, as Connor made his way up towards the top of the boulder, leaving his shirt, shoes, and pants as a trail before jumping into the water in his underwear. When he returned to the surface of the water, it was then that it occurred to me that we were at the boulder. The same boulder that Poppy, Amelia, and I had gone to for swimming before Poppy's wedding, and the same boulder that I crawled up onto with Poppy, the night the gang attacked. This thought made my heart sink into my stomach, and them my stomach to tie up in knots.

"Mona, come in, the water is so refreshing." Connor called out. I couldn't let the thought of the memories of this place get to me. They were memories, things that I had to remember, but not things that I had to let define my life. I made my way up to the boulder, grabbing Connor's discarded clothes as I went along, and tediously folding them and placing them in a neat pile. I did this frankly because I knew it would slightly annoy Connor in a certain way that he liked to be annoyed, before I kicked off my shoes and jumped off the boulder and into the water with my dress on. I plunged down towards the river bottom, with the water a good three feet above my head. I opened my eyes to see the bubbles swirling around me and then with one push, I pushed myself back to the surface where Connor was waiting.

In movies when a girl comes out of the water, her hair is all sleek, perfect, and out of her eyes. That was a lie, because I always came up out of the water with my hair all over my face, covering my eyes and mouth, I just end up looking like a recently baptized cat. As I was rearranging my hair so that it was no longer sticking to my eyes, face, and mouth, Connor swam over and pulled me close so that we could float near each other.

"You're right, the water is perfect." I said. The temperature of the water was just the right kind of cool; I kicked and spread my toes out so that the water could cool down my feet. We floated around together, staying near the boulder, neither of us speaking, just floating, listening to the water flow and the song birds sing from the trees. When our legs grew tired, we climbed up onto the boulder, and laid in the sun to dry. We rested together, me with my head resting on his chest and him with his arm around my waist. I was inexplicably comfortable, I could just fall asleep. I thought for a moment how funny it would be if we were to fall asleep and then wake up with Connor having a tan line where I was laying. I chuckled at this thought, and it startled Connor.

"What's so funny?" He asked.

"I was just thinking. If I lay here, with my head on your chest, eventually you would get a tan line of my face." This too made Connor laugh, before he started to try and get up, removing me from my comfortable position. The afternoon had drawn on, and judging by the look of the sun, it was nearing 4 o'clock in the afternoon. Connor got up and started getting dressed, signaling that it was our time to head back to the farm. I stood and wrung out the skirt of my dress. At least with a damp dress, I would be cool as we walked back to the farm.

We made it back to the farm, empty handed. I'm sure we could have tried better when it came to trying to hunt, but it didn't matter at that point. I followed Connor into the barn and we put away the arrows and the bows. I thought we were heading back to the house, but Connor stopped at the bottom of the barn loft steps and pointed upwards.

"Wanna see what I've been working on, it's finally done." He said. I paused for a moment, was he serious? He had been working on that project for months and months and months, and now it was ready.

"Well it's about damn time." I said pushing him aside and heading up the stairs. At the top there were newly installed walls and a door separating the stairs from the rest of the loft. This peaked my curiosity. Before Connor started this project, the barn loft was nothing more than just a loft with old brownish, grey barn wood, slanted walls and creaky floors. Here I now faced a brand new door that looked like it was just purchased from a Home Depot. I grasped the doorknob and pushed it open, revealing, to my shock, a totally different space.

Connor had hung drywall and painted it a powdery blue, the wood floors had been cleaned, and a pretty white railing with a window box was put up where the large barn door sat open to the summer air. He had hung sheer curtains around that door, and had a chest of drawers, a large iron bed, a couch, and a wood burning stove all in the space. It was all a lot to take in, nothing really clicked for a few moments. He had done what William had done with the bus. He had made a space, a home, and it was perfect. When I turned around, Connor was down on one knee, and I lost it.

"Mona?" he said taking my hand.

"Yes?"

"I know it's been a long time coming, but will you marry me?" He asked.

"Yes." I whispered. The answer was always yes, he didn't really need to ask because he already knew I would say yes and would say yes a thousand times. Connor stood up and pulled me in for a kiss and before we had finished we could hear the sound of applause coming from the bottom of the stairs. Everyone had gathered, even Amelia and Brady were there.

"We were due for another wedding!" Amelia said. Everyone had been in on it, everyone except me. It explained the reason why Poppy had been so silent, she would have given it away had she spoke. Everything was blurry for the rest of the day. I was asked a zillion questions about what I wanted for a wedding, if I liked this color or that. Frankly I didn't care, if Connor and I could just sign the papers Mr. Wilson had in town, I would be completely content with that. Of course it wouldn't be an option, we would have a real wedding, and the preparations would start the very next day.

"We could get everything together in a week." Ms. Elizabeth said.

"A week!?" I exclaimed

"Oh don't worry, we've known about Connor planning on proposing to you for months, even your mother knew, we've just about finished your wedding dress." Ms. Elizabeth said as we, we being me, Amelia, Poppy, Charlotte, Cora, and my mom, stood in the kitchen on the following morning of the proposal.

"Yes, all we need to do is give Mr. Wilson the heads up, tell everyone in town, and finish our bridesmaid dresses." Amelia said.

"You guys can finish, I have to make mine, and I didn't want to make a dress I wasn't going to fit into." Poppy laughed.

"Well hurry up and go measure the circumference of your torso so you can fit into a dress!" I said with a laugh. Poppy just stuck her tongue out at me and left to go do just that. I had been a part of planning two weddings in this house, but the thought as to how it would feel to be planning my own never occurred to me, in fact it was quite a boring process. Everyone had already planned exactly what was going to happen and when. They all knew me so well that there wasn't a single doubt in anyone's minds that I would dislike anything. Everyday passed extremely quick, I would see Connor in the mornings when we first wake up, and then for a few moments before bed. He and William were busy going into town every single day to get ready. By the end of the week it annoyed me that I saw so little of the one person I wanted to see most, but I had to keep reminding myself that with each passing day, it was one day closer to being able to spend every waking minute and moment with him.

I had this brief thought that there was a high probability that our wedding was going to be an even bigger affair than Poppy and William's. I don't remember there being such a big fuss when they were getting married, there wasn't this much pomp and circumstance, but then again I hadn't been on the receiving end of the attention before.

When the day arrived, I hardly believed it had finally come. I half expected me to not be able to sleep or eat, but with all the ruckus, it felt like another day of wedding planning, only this time everyone was dressed in their finest with their hair all done up with flower petals scattered everywhere, and Connor no longer anywhere to be found on the farm. Everyone fussed and poked and pinched at me. I had everyone around while I tried to take a bath, everyone was there while Cora braided my hair, and everyone was there while Charlotte did my makeup. But when those two things were finally completed Ms. Elizabeth came into the room, clapped her hands and ordered everyone out.

Once everyone was gone, my mom entered the room, carrying with her my dress that she had draped over one arm. Ms. Elizabeth closed the door leaving the two of us in the room. My mom smiled and placed the dress on the bed. It was the first time I was seeing it. I ran the white fabric through my fingers. Chiffon and lace. I stepped into the dress and waited for my mom to button it up. Before looking in the mirror I looked down at myself. Aside from the sweetheart neckline, spaghetti straps, and flowing skirt, I couldn't tell much, it was only when I looked in the mirror that I realized the full extent of the dress.

I had never felt more beautiful in my entire life. The bodice was fitted with a sweetheart neckline, thin spaghetti straps that crisscrossed at the back. The fitted lace bodice, held me snugly until it reached my waist where the soft, delicate chiffon fabric began. When I turned around I saw the little crystal buttons that went down the back to my waist where a big floppy bow sat at the top of my butt before the river of silky chiffon took over, pooling down into a regal train. I began to cry. My mom took my face in her hand and wiped the tears away.

"No." I heard her say, this caused me to stop and look at her. With all the progress she had made, speaking was the most difficult, for her to say a simple word such as no, was a big deal, and what happened next I would never forget. Although she spoke with little ability to fully pronounce the words correctly, and some were harder than others, she managed and she formed the first full sentence I had heard her speak since arriving.

"You look beautiful, your father would love." She said. I began to cry when I heard her say this, and then she started to cry, so we cried together, before Ms. Elizabeth came into the room.

"You'll ruin your makeup!" Ms. Elizabeth said, at that we all laughed.

"Girls, the van is here to take us to town." Cora said as she peeked through the doorway. The time had come.

***

It wasn't real yet, it hadn't sunk in. As the car drove through the gates of the wall into the town, I couldn't help but smile. All the flowers, all the decorations, were they really for us? There were white streamers blowing in the wind and everyone in the town had lined up on each side of the street to wave as we passed by. The car pulled in front of the library and everyone got out, except for me and my mom, we lingered for a few moments. I suddenly wished I had gotten a chance to take a look at everything before now, I was for sure going to be shocked as to how they decorated the inside, and I was afraid that I was going to be distracted from what really was important. When my mom and I got out of the car we were greeted by everyone in town. I stood still as my mom took the skirt of my dress and fluffed it a bit. As I stood there Lucy ran up to me. She ran up to me and gave me a hug and handed me a bouquet of flowers.

"Peter told me they forgot to get you a bouquet. So I made one." She said.

"Oh! This might sound funny, but I didn't notice that I didn't have one!" I said with a laugh. Lucy smiled, hugged me again and then went back to where her family was standing off to the side of the library. My mom, although she wanted to be the one leading me along, needed some help to get up the front steps before we stood at the doorway of the building. The sun was shining so brightly that everything inside the building just looked dark. It wasn't until we stepped inside that I got to see all the streamers and flowers everywhere. It looked like a fairy land inside the library and my eyes were darting everywhere until they found where they belonged, on Connor. We walked up the aisle where Connor and Mr. Wilson waited. Connor took my hand and together we faced Mr. Wilson.

"I cannot express how honored I am that I have so far been able to be the one conducting three weddings so far for this family. Shall we begin?" Mr. Wilson said. To my memory, I didn't listen to what Mr. Wilson had to say at Poppy and William's wedding or at Amelia and Brady's, but this time, since he was speaking to the two of us, I held on to every word. Mr. Wilson spoke words of wisdom, advice, and poetry. Each word he spoke had so much meaning to me now, and I am sure Connor as well. Mr. Wilson then asked us to turn towards each other, and it was then that everything felt so real, so very overwhelmingly real.

"Connor, do you take Mona to be your lawfully wedded wife?" Mr. Wilson asked.

"I do." Connor said without hesitation.

"And do you Mona; take Connor to be your lawfully wedded husband?"

"I do." I said without really thinking, I didn't need to. Mr. Wilson pronounced us man and wife and I was now Mona Wilde. My hand shook as we signed the contract that Mr. Wilson drew up, and I needed to lean on Connor for balance as we left the Library and into the waiting crowd outside. I paid no attention to my surroundings. I found myself just dumbly looking at Connor the entire time. We received every single person in town. They all wished us well and their congrats, but I hardly remember what they all exactly said to me. Everything was so blurry and it didn't really calm down until I heard the crowd of people chanting for Connor and me to dance. My world slowed down when my shoes felt the smooth flat surface of the dance floor that had been built at the center of the town green.

"I picked the song. I hope you don't mind." Connor whispered down to me as he held me close.

"I don't mind one bit." I said. The makeshift town band, which was, in my opinion, the best band around, began to play a soft tune. Since the addition of new families to the town, we also had had some additions to the band, including Lucy, who had a beautiful singing voice. Her voice was smooth like velvet, and she crooned and left all her listeners hanging and reaching for more at the end of each note. She did a fantastic job covering the song "Hold Me, Thrill Me, Kiss Me" and her voice, the music, and everything else transported Connor and I into our own little universe. I saw no one else but him. It was a relatively short song, and I wished it lasted longer, but when the music ceased, we halted in our steps and just smiled. The night flew on with food, dancing, and laughter, there was not a dull moment or any moment that I wished to forget. Poppy and I spun around the dance floor to a wild song and we tried to keep in step with the banjo, but it left us panting for air and laughing at our stupidity.

"Ya know…" Poppy began as she put one arm around my shoulder and pulled me tight, "After tonight, there's a high probability that you'll end up just like this." She said pointing to her stomach.

"Oh hush!" I said with embarrassment. We walked over to where Connor and William were sitting, leaning suavely to the side. Poppy went and sat on William's lap. Connor looked up at me. It was getting late. He stood up and took my hand and brought me in close. We swayed back and forth to the music for a moment before we separated and he held my hand. Connor gave me a crooked smile, and we began to make our way towards the direction of the gate, away from the party, to make our get away. We weren't going to tell anyone we were leaving, except Poppy and William who followed us all the way to the gate.

"Hey… behave and be good." William said as he handed Connor the keys to a waiting ATV.

"No scratch that. Don't listen to him. Be bad." Poppy said swatting William's arm before pointing at me and then pointing at her stomach. I just laughed. Connor and I got on the ATV and we carelessly sped off back down to the farm. Connor and I had both liked William and Poppy's idea of disappearing into the woods for a few days, so that was what we were going to do. I left to go change out of my dress while Connor loaded up the ATV with the things we would need. By the time I had changed into some hiking clothes, Connor had already loaded up the ATV with our stuff and was waiting, ready to go.

"Are we going to that alcove by the river?" I asked as I slowly walked towards him.

"Why do you foil my plans" he chuckled, I just smirked and reached out for his hand.

"You ready?" He asked.

"I'm ready."

Epilogue

The cry of a seagull caused my eyes to flutter open. Everything was just as it was. Sybil and Alice were splashing in their little metal tub just like I left them. They turned and looked over at me just to make sure I was still there. I leaned forward and smiled as they turned back towards each other to continue splashing around. I stood up and walked to the other end of the porch where I could see down towards the beach. I squinted and saw my eldest two, Georgiana and Riley splashing in the waves with little Will, Hawkin, and Ace, three of Poppy and William's five children. As I watched them I stretched my arms and then brought them back to rest on my tummy, my soon to be growing tummy again. With only three girls and one boy, I was desperately hoping that my fourth little baby would be a boy, but we would only know with time.

We were no longer living on the farm. The farm was very far away from us now, and although it made me sad to not be there, we knew that we could go and visit any time we chose. Shortly after my eldest, Georgiana was born, my mother passed away. I had found her sleeping peacefully in her bed, it had been her heart that gave out. I cried and wailed and mourned during that time, but with Connor and little new born Georgiana's constant need for attention, I made it through.

Some months later, the CDC came and asked Poppy, William, Connor and I if we would consider relocating our young families. There was a new program the CDC started that would help the new generation of children to grow up with other children their age. Naturally, being new parents, we wanted what was best, and the thought of our kids being able to have friends other than their own relatives was a good idea. So me moved to a new town about two hours from the farm, right on the ocean, and into a beautiful little white cottage that overlooked the sea. Now, Connor and I had Georgiana, Riley, Sybil, and Lucy, and we were only a short walking distance away from Poppy and William.

After Poppy and William had Little Will, they couldn't help but to have four more after that. After Little Will came Hawkin, then Ace, then Brody, and then finally a girl, little Emery Jane. But Emery Jane proved to be the difficult child. All of Poppy's previous pregnancies had been without worry or concern, but with baby Emery Jane, things were a bit tougher. Poppy had no choice but to go to a CDC clinic to give birth to Emery Jane, and then have a procedure so she and William wouldn't have to worry about having any more kids. It all didn't bother them one bit though, they were perfectly happy.

Brady and Amelia stayed up in town on the Campbell farm. For reasons Amelia never wished to discover, she and Brady were never able to have children. Instead they focused on their own farm, and the town. Plus they had a zillion nieces and nephews to love.

Peter had to go on and be the troublemaker. Not even three weeks after Connor and I were married, Peter and Lucy announced that they were expecting a baby. No one was too happy on the farm that Peter and Lucy had been so careless, but they loved each other and were soon married weeks before their own baby was born.

Everything on the farm has pretty much stayed the same. Ms. Elizabeth still runs everything and knows everything. Cora and Charlotte are still there, as well as their loving husbands Luke and Johnathan. Aside from the long road we had to take to get where were stood today, I am very glad to have taken it.

The End

I would like to take the time to dedicate this work to my mom and dad, my brother, and every last one of my family and friends.

With love,

Victoria
waves